Praise for #1 *New York Times* bestselling author

NORA
ROBERTS

"America's favorite writer."

—*The New Yorker*

"When Roberts puts her expert fingers on the pulse of romance, legions of fans feel the heartbeat."

—*Publishers Weekly*

"Nora Roberts is among the best."

—*The Washington Post*

"Roberts' bestselling novels are some of the best in the romance genre."

—*USA TODAY*

"Roberts' style has a fresh, contemporary snap."

—*Kirkus Reviews*

"You can't bottle wish fulfillment, but Nora Roberts certainly knows how to put it on the page."

—*New York Times*

NORA ROBERTS

HIDDEN HEART

Silhouette Books

Published by Silhouette Books

America's Publisher of Contemporary Romance

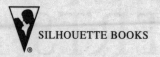

SILHOUETTE BOOKS

Hidden Heart

ISBN-13: 978-0-373-28246-3

Copyright © 2017 by Harlequin Books S.A.

The publisher acknowledges the copyright holder of the individual works as follows:

This Magic Moment
Copyright © 1983 by Nora Roberts

Storm Warning
Copyright © 1984 by Nora Roberts

Recycling programs for this product may not exist in your area.

CONTENTS

THIS MAGIC MOMENT

Chapter 1

He'd chosen it for the atmosphere. Ryan was certain of it the moment she saw the house on the cliff. It was stone gray and solitary. It turned its back on the Pacific. It wasn't a symmetrical structure, but rambling, with sections of varying heights rising up here and there, giving it a wild sort of grace. High at the top of a winding cliff road, with the backdrop of an angry sky, the house was both magnificent and eerie.

Like something out of an old movie, Ryan decided as she shifted into first to take the climb. She had heard Pierce Atkins was eccentric. The house seemed to testify to that.

All it needs, she mused, is a thunderclap, a little fog and the howl of a wolf; just some minor special effects. Amused at the thought, she drew the car to a stop and looked the house over again. You wouldn't see many like it only a hundred and fifty miles north of L.A. You wouldn't, she corrected silently, see many like it anywhere.

The moment she slid from the car, the wind pulled at her, whipping her hair around her face and tugging at her skirt. She was tempted to go to the seawall and take a look at the ocean but hurried up the steps instead. She hadn't come to admire the view.

The knocker was old and heavy. It gave a very impressive thud when she pounded it against the door. Ryan told herself she wasn't the least bit nervous but switched her briefcase from hand to hand as she waited. Her father would be furious if she walked away without Pierce Atkins's signature on the contracts she carried. No, not furious, she amended. Silent. No one could use silence more effectively than Bennett Swan.

I'm not going to walk away empty-handed, she assured herself. I know how to handle temperamental entertainers. I've spent years watching how it's done and—

Her thoughts were cut off as the door opened. Ryan stared. Staring back at her was the largest man she had ever seen. He was at least six foot five, with shoulders that all but filled the doorway. And his face. Ryan decided he was, indisputably, the ugliest human being she had ever seen. His broad face was pale. His nose had obviously been broken and had reknit at an odd angle. His eyes were small, a washed-out brown that matched his thick mat of hair. Atmosphere, Ryan thought again. Atkins must have chosen him for atmosphere.

"Good afternoon," she managed. "Ryan Swan. Mr. Atkins is expecting me."

"Miss Swan." The slow, barrel-deep voice suited him

perfectly. When the man stepped back, Ryan found herself fighting a reluctance to enter. Storm clouds, a hulking butler and a brooding house on a cliff. Oh, yes, she decided. Atkins knows how to set the stage.

She walked in. As the door closed behind her, Ryan took a quick glimpse around.

"Wait here," the laconic butler instructed and walked, lightly for a big man, down the hall.

"Of course, thank you very much," she muttered to his back.

The walls were white and draped with tapestries. The one nearest her was a faded medieval scene depicting the young Arthur drawing the sword from the stone, with Merlin the Enchanter highlighted in the background. Ryan nodded. It was an exquisite piece of work and suited to a man like Atkins. Turning, she found herself staring at her own reflection in an ornate cheval glass.

It annoyed her to see that her hair was mussed. She represented Swan Productions. Ryan pushed at the stray misty blond wisps. The green of her eyes had darkened with a mixture of anxiety and excitement. Her cheeks were flushed with it. Taking a deep breath, she ordered herself to calm down. She straightened her jacket.

Hearing footsteps, she quickly turned away from the mirror. She didn't want to be caught studying herself or attempting last-minute repairs. It was the butler again, alone. Ryan repressed a surge of annoyance.

"He'll see you downstairs."

"Oh." Ryan opened her mouth to say something else, but he was already retreating. She had to scramble to keep up.

The hall wound to the right. Ryan's heels clicked

quickly as she trotted to match the butler's pace. Then he stopped so abruptly, she nearly collided with his back.

"Down there." He had opened a door and was already walking away.

"But…" Ryan scowled after him, then made her way down the dimly lighted steps. Really, this was ridiculous, she thought. A business meeting should be conducted in an office, or at least in a suitable restaurant. Show business, she mused scornfully.

The sound of her own footfalls echoed back at her. There was no sound at all from the room below. Oh, yes, she concluded, Atkins knows how to set the stage. She was beginning to dislike him intensely. Her heart was hammering uncomfortably as she rounded the last curve in the winding staircase.

The lower floor was huge, a sprawling room with crates and trunks and paraphernalia stacked all around. The walls were paneled and the floor was tiled, but no one had bothered with any further decoration. Ryan looked around, frowning, as she walked down the last of the steps.

He watched her. He had the talent for absolute stillness, absolute concentration. It was essential to his craft. He also had the ability to sum up a person quickly. That, too, was part of his profession. She was younger than he had expected, a fragile-looking woman, small in stature, slight in build, with clouds of pale hair and a delicately molded face. A strong chin.

She was annoyed, he noted, and not a little apprehensive. A smile tugged at his mouth. Even after she began to wander around the room, he made no move to go to her. Very businesslike, he thought, with her trim, tailored suit, sensible shoes, expensive briefcase and very feminine hands. Interesting.

"Miss Swan."

Ryan jolted, then swore at herself. Turning in the direction of the voice, she saw only shadows.

"You're very prompt."

He moved then, and Ryan saw that he stood on a small stage. He wore black and blended with the shadows. With an effort, she kept the annoyance from her voice. "Mr. Atkins." Ryan went toward him then, fixing on a trained smile. "You have quite a house."

"Thank you."

He didn't come down to her but stood on the stage. Ryan was forced to look up at him. It surprised her that he was more dramatic in person than on tape. Normally, she had found the reverse to be true. She had seen his performances. Indeed, since her father had taken ill and reluctantly turned Atkins over to her, Ryan had spent two entire evenings watching every available tape on Pierce Atkins.

Dramatic, she decided, noting a raw-boned face with a thick, waving mane of black hair. There was a small scar along his jawline, and his mouth was long and thin. His brows were arched with a slight upsweep at the tips. But it was the eyes under them which held her. She had never seen eyes so dark, so deep. Were they gray? Were they black? Yet it wasn't their color that disconcerted her, it was the absolute concentration in them. She felt her throat go dry and swallowed in defense. She could almost believe he was reading her mind.

He had been called the greatest magician of the decade, some said the greatest of the last half of the century. His illusions and escapes were daring, flashy and unexplainable. It was a common thing to hear of him referred to as a wizard. Staring into his eyes, Ryan began to understand why.

She shook herself free of the trance and started again. She didn't believe in magic. "Mr. Atkins, my father apologizes for not being able to come himself. I hope—"

"He's feeling better."

Confused, she stopped. "Yes. Yes, he is." She found herself staring again.

Pierce smiled as he stepped down to her. "He phoned an hour ago, Miss Swan. Long-distance dialing, no telepathy." Ryan glared before she could stop herself, but his smile only widened. "Did you have a nice drive?"

"Yes, thank you."

"But a long one," he said. "Sit." Pierce gestured to a table, then took a chair behind it. Ryan sat opposite him.

"Mr. Atkins," she began, feeling more at ease now that business was about to begin. "I know my father has discussed Swan Productions' offer with you and your representative at length, but perhaps you'd like to go over the details again." She set her briefcase on the table. "I could clarify any questions you might have."

"Have you worked for Swan Productions long, Miss Swan?"

The question interrupted the flow of her presentation, but Ryan shifted her thoughts. Entertainers often had to be humored. "Five years, Mr. Atkins. I assure you, I'm qualified to answer your questions and negotiate terms if necessary."

Her voice was very smooth, but she was nervous. Pierce saw it in the careful way she folded her hands on the table. "I'm sure you're qualified, Miss Swan," he agreed. "Your father isn't an easy man to please."

Surprise and a trace of apprehension flickered into her eyes. "No," she said calmly, "which is why you can be sure of receiving the best promotion, the best production staff, the best contract available. Three one-hour television specials over three years, guaranteed prime time, with a budget that ensures quality." She paused only for a moment. "An advantageous arrangement for you and for Swan Productions."

"Perhaps."

He was looking at her too closely. Ryan forced herself not to fidget. Gray, she saw. His eyes were gray—as dark as was possible without being black.

"Of course," she continued, "your career has been aimed primarily at live audiences in clubs and theaters. Vegas, Tahoe, the London Palladium and so forth."

"An illusion means nothing on film, Miss Swan. Film can be altered."

"Yes, I realize that. To have any impact, a trick has to be performed live."

"Illusion," Pierce corrected. "I don't do tricks."

Ryan stopped. His eyes were steady on hers. "Illusion," she amended with a nod. "The specials would be broadcasted live, with a studio audience as well. The publicity—"

"You don't believe in magic, do you, Miss Swan?" There was the slightest of smiles on his mouth, the barest trace of amusement in his voice.

"Mr. Atkins, you're a very talented man," she said carefully. "I admire your work."

"A diplomat," he concluded, leaning back. "And a cynic. I like that."

Ryan didn't feel complimented. He was laughing at her without making the smallest attempt to conceal it.

Your job, she reminded herself as her teeth clenched. Do your job. "Mr. Atkins, if we could discuss the terms of the contract—"

"I don't do business with anyone until I know who they are."

Ryan let out a quick breath. "My father—"

"I'm not talking to your father," Pierce interrupted smoothly.

"I didn't think to type up a bio," she snapped, then bit her tongue. Damn! She couldn't afford to lose her temper. But Pierce grinned, pleased.

"I don't think that will be necessary." He had her hand in his before she realized what he was doing.

"Nevermore."

The voice from behind had Ryan jolting in her chair.

"That's just Merlin," Pierce said mildly as she twisted her head.

There was a large black myna bird in a cage to her right. Ryan took a deep breath and tried to steady her nerves. The bird was staring at her.

"Very clever," she managed, eyeing the bird with some reservation. "Did you teach him to talk?"

"Mmm."

"Buy you a drink, sweetie?"

Wide-eyed, Ryan gave a muffled laugh as she turned back to Pierce. He merely gave the bird a careless glance. "I haven't taught him manners."

She struggled not to be amused. "Mr. Atkins, if we could—"

"Your father wanted a son." Ryan forgot what she had been about to say and stared at him. "That made it difficult for you." Pierce was looking into her eyes again, her hand held loosely in his. "You're not married, you live alone. You're a realist who considers herself very practical. You find it difficult to control your temper, but you work at it. You're a very cautious woman, Miss Swan, slow to trust, careful in relationships. You're impatient because you have something to prove—to yourself and to your father."

His eyes lost their intense directness when he smiled at her. "A parlor game, Miss Swan, or telepathy?" When Pierce released her hand, Ryan pulled it from the table into her lap. She hadn't cared for his accuracy.

"A little amateur psychology," he said comfortably, enjoying her stunned expression. "A basic knowledge of Bennett Swan and an understanding of body language." He shrugged his shoulders. "No trick, Miss Swan, just educated guesswork. How close was I?"

Ryan gripped her hands together in her lap. Her right palm was still warm from his. "I didn't come here to play games, Mr. Atkins."

"No." He smiled again, charmingly. "You came to close a deal, but I do things in my own time, in my own way. My profession encourages eccentricity, Miss Swan. Humor me."

"I'm doing my best," Ryan returned, then took a deep breath and sat back. "I think it's safe to say that we're both very serious about our professions."

"Agreed."

"Then you understand that it's my job to sign you with Swan, Mr. Atkins." Perhaps a bit of flattery would work, she decided. "We want you because you're the best in your field."

"I'm aware of that," he answered without batting an eye.

"Aware that we want you or that you're the best?" she found herself demanding.

He flashed her a very appealing grin. "Of both."

Ryan took a deep breath and reminded herself that entertainers were often impossible. "Mr. Atkins," she began.

With a flutter of wings, Merlin swooped out of his cage and landed on her shoulder. Ryan gasped and froze.

"Oh, God," she murmured. This was too much, she thought numbly. Entirely too much.

Pierce frowned at the bird as it settled its wings. "Odd, he's never done that with anyone before."

"Aren't I lucky," Ryan muttered, sitting perfectly still. Did birds bite? she wondered. She decided she didn't care to wait to find out. "Do you think you could—ah, persuade him to perch somewhere else?"

A slight gesture of Pierce's hand had Merlin leaving Ryan's shoulder to land on his own.

"Mr. Atkins, please, I realize a man in your profession would have a taste for—atmosphere." Ryan took a breath to steady herself, but it didn't work. "It's very difficult to discuss business in—in a dungeon," she said with a sweep of her arm. "With a crazed raven swooping down on me and…"

Pierce's shout of laughter cut her off. On his shoulder the bird settled his wings and stared, steely-eyed, at Ryan. "Ryan Swan, I'm going to like you. I work in this dungeon," he explained good-naturedly. "It's private and quiet. Illusions take more than skill; they take a great deal of planning and preparation."

"I understand that, Mr. Atkins, but—"

"We'll discuss business more conventionally over dinner," he interrupted.

Ryan rose as he did. She hadn't planned to stay more than an hour or two. It was a good thirty-minute drive down the cliff road to her hotel.

"You'll stay the night," Pierce added, as if he had indeed read her thoughts.

"I appreciate your hospitality, Mr. Atkins," she began, following as he walked back to the stairs, the bird remaining placidly on his shoulder. "But I have a reservation at a hotel in town. Tomorrow—"

"Do you have your bags?" Pierce stopped to take her arm before he mounted the steps.

"Yes, in the car, but—"

"Link will cancel your reservation, Miss Swan. We're in for a storm." He turned his head to glance at her. "I wouldn't like to think of you driving these roads tonight."

As if to accentuate his words, a blast of thunder greeted them as they came to the top of the stairs. Ryan murmured something. She wasn't certain she wanted to think of spending the night in this house.

"Nothing up my sleeve," Merlin announced.

She shot him a dubious look.

Chapter 2

Dinner did much to put Ryan's mind at rest. The dining room was huge, with a roaring fire at one end and a collection of antique pewter at the other. The long refectory table was set with Sèvres china and Georgian silver.

"Link's an excellent cook," Pierce told her as the big man set a Cornish hen in front of her. Ryan caught a glimpse of his huge hands before Link left the room. Cautiously, she picked up her fork.

"He's certainly quiet."

Pierce smiled and poured a pale gold wine into her glass. "Link only talks when he has something to say. Tell me, Miss Swan, do you enjoy living in Los Angeles?"

Ryan looked over at him. His eyes were friendly now, not intense and intrusive, as they had been before. She allowed herself to relax. "Yes, I suppose I do. It's convenient for my work."

"Crowded?" Pierce cut into the poultry.

"Yes, of course, but I'm used to it."

"You've always lived in L.A.?"

"Except when I was in school."

Pierce noted the slight change in tone, the faintest hint of resentment no one else might have caught. He went on eating. "Where did you go to school?"

"Switzerland."

"A beautiful country." He reached for his wine. *And she didn't care to be shipped off,* he thought. "Then you began to work for Swan Productions?"

Frowning, Ryan stared into the fire. "When my father realized I was determined, he agreed."

"And you're a very determined woman," Pierce commented.

"Yes," she admitted. "For the first year, I shuffled papers, went for coffee, and was kept away from the talent." The frown vanished. A gleam of humor lit her eyes. "One day some papers came across my desk, quite by mistake. My father was trying to sign Mildred Chase for a miniseries. She wasn't cooperating. I did a little research and went to see her." Laughing with the memory, she sent Pierce a grin. "*That* was quite an experience. She lives in this fabulous place in the hills—guards, a dozen dogs. She's very 'old Hollywood.' I think she let me in out of curiosity."

"What did you think of her?" he asked, mainly to keep her talking, to keep her smiling.

"I thought she was wonderful. A genuine *grande dame.* If my knees hadn't been shaking, I'm sure I would have curtsied." A light of triumph covered her face. "And when I left two hours later, her signature was on the contract."

"How did your father react?"

"He was furious." Ryan picked up her wine. The fire sent a play of shadow and light over her skin. She was to think of the conversation later and wonder at her own expansiveness. "He raged at me for the better part of an hour." She drank, then set down the glass. "The next day, I had a promotion and a new office. Bennett Swan appreciates people who get things done."

"And do you," Pierce murmured, "get things done, Miss Swan?"

"Usually," she returned evenly. "I'm good at handling details."

"And people?"

Ryan hesitated. His eyes were direct again. "Most people."

He smiled, but his look remained direct. "How's your dinner?"

"My…" Ryan shook her head to break the gaze, then glanced down at her plate. She was surprised to see she had eaten a healthy portion of the hen. "It's very good. Your…" She looked back at him again, not certain what to call Link. *Servant? Slave?*

"Friend," Pierce put in mildly and sipped his wine.

Ryan struggled against the uncomfortable feeling that he saw inside her brain. "Your friend is a marvelous cook."

"Appearances are often deceiving," Pierce pointed out, amused. "We're both in professions that show an audience something that isn't real. Swan Productions deals in illusions. So do I." He reached toward her, and Ryan sat back quickly. In his hand was a long-stemmed red rose.

"Oh!" Surprised and pleased, Ryan took it from him.

Its scent was strong and sweet. "I suppose that's the sort of thing you have to expect when you have dinner with a magician," she commented and smiled at him over the tip of the bud.

"Beautiful women and flowers belong together." The wariness that came into her eyes intrigued him. A very cautious woman, he thought again. He liked caution, respected it. He also enjoyed watching people react. "You're a beautiful woman, Ryan Swan."

"Thank you."

Her answer was close to prim and had his mouth twitching. "More wine?"

"No. No, thank you, I'm fine." But her pulse was throbbing lightly. Setting the flower beside her plate, she went back to her meal. "I've rarely been this far up the coast," she said conversationally. "Have you lived here long, Mr. Atkins?"

"A few years." He swirled the wine in his glass, but she noted he drank very little. "I don't like crowds," he told her.

"Except at a performance," she said with a smile.

"Naturally."

It occurred to Ryan, when Pierce rose and suggested they sit in the parlor, that they hadn't discussed the contract. She was going to have to steer him back to the subject.

"Mr. Atkins…" she began as they entered. "Oh! What a beautiful room!"

It was like stepping back to the eighteenth century. But there were no cobwebs, no signs of age. The furniture shone, and the flowers were fresh. A small upright piano stood in a corner with sheet music open. There were small, blown-glass figurines on the mantel. A menagerie, she noted on close study—unicorns, winged horses, centaurs, a three-headed hound. No conventional animals in Pierce Atkins's collection. Yet the fire in the grate was sedate, and the lamp standing on a piecrust table was certainly a Tiffany. It was a room Ryan would have expected to find in a cozy English country house.

"I'm glad you like it," Pierce said, standing beside her. "You seemed surprised."

"Yes. The outside looks like a prop from a 1945 horror movie, but…" Ryan stopped herself, horrified. "Oh, I'm sorry, I didn't mean…" But he was grinning, obviously delighted with her observation.

"It was used for just that more than once. That's why I bought it."

Ryan relaxed again as she wandered around the room. "It did occur to me that you might have chosen it for the atmosphere."

Pierce lifted a brow. "I have an—affection for things others take at face value." He stepped to a table where cups were already laid out. "I can't offer you coffee, I'm afraid. I don't use caffeine. The tea is herbal and very good." He was already pouring as Ryan stepped up to the piano.

"Tea's fine," she said absently. It wasn't printed sheet music on the piano, she noted, but staff paper. Automatically, she began to pick out the handwritten notes. The melody was hauntingly romantic. "This is beautiful." Ryan turned back to him. "Just beautiful. I didn't know you wrote music."

"I don't." Pierce set down the teapot. "Link does." He watched Ryan's eyes widen in astonishment. "Face value, Miss Swan?"

She lowered her eyes to her hands. "You make me quite ashamed."

"I've no intention of doing that." Crossing to her, Pierce took her hand again. "Most of us are drawn to beauty."

"But you're not?"

"I find surface beauty appealing, Miss Swan." Quickly, thoroughly, he scanned her face. "Then I look for more."

Something in the contact made her feel odd. Her voice wasn't as strong as it should have been. "And if you don't find it?"

"Then I discard it," he said simply. "Come, your tea will get cold."

"Mr. Atkins." Ryan allowed him to lead her to a chair. "I don't want to offend you. I can't afford to offend you, but…" She let out a frustrated breath as she sat. "I think you're a very strange man."

He smiled. She found it compelling, the way his eyes smiled a split second before his mouth. "You'd offend me, Miss Swan, if you didn't think so. I have no wish to be ordinary."

He was beginning to fascinate her. Ryan had always been careful to keep her professional objectivity when dealing with talent. It was important not to be awed. If you were awed, you'd find yourself adding clauses to contracts and making rash promises.

"Mr. Atkins, about our proposition."

"I've given it a great deal of thought." A crash of thunder shook the windows. Ryan glanced over as he lifted his cup. "The roads will be treacherous tonight." His eyes came back to Ryan's. Her hands had balled into fists at the blast. "Do storms upset you, Miss Swan?"

"No, not really." Carefully, she relaxed her fingers. "But I'm grateful for your hospitality. I don't like to drive in them." Lifting her cup, she tried to ignore the slashes of lightning. "If you have any questions about the terms, I'd be glad to go over them with you."

"I think it's clear enough." He sipped his tea. "My agent is anxious for me to accept the contract."

"Oh?" Ryan had to struggle to keep the triumph from her voice. It would be a mistake to push too soon.

"I never commit myself to anything until I'm certain it suits me. I'll tell you what I've decided tomorrow."

She nodded, accepting. He wasn't playing games, and she sensed that no agent, or anyone, would influence him beyond a certain point. He was his own man, first and last.

"Do you play chess, Miss Swan?"

"What?" Distracted, she looked up again. "I beg your pardon?"

"Do you play chess?" he repeated.

"Why, yes, I do."

"I thought so. You know when to move and when to wait. Would you like to play?"

"Yes," she agreed without hesitation. "I would."

Rising, he offered his hand and led her to a table by the windows. Outside, the rain hurled itself against the glass. But when she saw the chessboard already set up, she forgot the storm.

"They're exquisite!" Ryan lifted the white king. It was oversized and carved in marble. "Arthur," she said, then picked up the queen. "And Guinevere." She studied the other pieces. "Lancelot the knight, Merlin the bishop, and, of course, Camelot." She turned the castle over in her palm. "I've never seen anything like these."

"Take the white," he invited, seating himself behind the black. "Do you play to win, Miss Swan?"

She took the chair opposite him. "Yes, doesn't everyone?"

He gave her a long, unfathomable look. "No. Some play for the game."

After ten minutes Ryan no longer heard the rain on the windows. Pierce was a shrewd player and a silent one. She found herself watching his hands as they slid pieces over the board. They were long, narrow hands with nimble fingers. He wore a gold ring on his pinky with a scrolled symbol she didn't recognize. Ryan had heard it said those fingers could pick any lock, untie any knot. Watching them, she thought they were more suited for tuning a violin. When she glanced up, she found him watching her with his amused, knowing smile. She channeled her concentration on her strategy.

Ryan attacked, he defended. He advanced, she countered. Pierce was pleased to have a well-matched partner. She was a cautious player, given to occasional bursts of impulse. He felt her game-playing reflected who she was. She wouldn't be easily duped or easily beaten. He admired both the quick wits and the strength he sensed in her. It made her beauty all the more appealing.

Her hands were soft. As he captured her bishop, he wondered idly if her mouth would be, too, and how soon he would find out. He had already decided he would; now it was a matter of timing. Pierce understood the invaluable importance of timing.

"Checkmate," he said quietly and heard Ryan's gasp of surprise.

She studied the board a moment, then smiled over at

him. "Damn, I didn't see that coming. Are you sure you don't have a few extra pieces tucked up your sleeve?"

"Nothing up my sleeve," Merlin cackled from across the room. Ryan shot him a glance and wondered when he had joined them.

"I don't use magic when skill will do," Pierce told her, ignoring his pet. "You play well, Miss Swan."

"You play better, Mr. Atkins."

"This time," he agreed. "You interest me."

"Oh?" She met his look levelly. "How?"

"In several ways." Sitting back, he ran a finger down the black queen. "You play to win, but you lose well. Is that always true?"

"No." She laughed but rose from the table. He was making her nervous again. "Do you lose well, Mr. Atkins?"

"I don't often lose."

When she looked back, he was standing at another table handling a pack of cards. Ryan hadn't heard him move. It made her uneasy.

"Do you know Tarot cards?"

"No. That is," she corrected, "I know they're for telling fortunes or something, aren't they?"

"Or something." He gave a small laugh and shuffled the cards gently. "Mumbo jumbo, Miss Swan. A device to keep someone's attention focused and to add mystery to quick thinking and observation. Most people prefer to be fooled. Explanations leave them disappointed. Even most realists."

"You don't believe in those cards." Ryan walked over to join him. "You know you can't tell the future with pasteboard and pretty colors."

"A tool, a diversion." Pierce lifted his shoulders. "A

game, if you like. Games relax me." Pierce fanned the oversized cards in a quick, effective gesture, then spread them on the table.

"You do that very well," Ryan murmured. Her nerves were tight again, but she wasn't sure why.

"A basic skill," he said easily. "I could teach you quickly enough. You have competent hands." He lifted one, but it was her face he examined, not her palm. "Shall I pick a card?"

Ryan removed her hand. Her pulse was beginning to race. "It's your game."

With a fingertip, Pierce drew out a card and flipped it faceup. It was the Magician. "Confidence, creativity," Pierce murmured.

"You?" Ryan said flippantly to conceal the growing tension.

"So it might seem." Pierce laid a finger on another card and drew it out. The High Priestess. "Serenity," he said quietly. "Strength. You?"

Ryan shrugged. "Simple enough for you to draw whatever card you like after you've stacked the deck."

Pierce grinned, unoffended. "The cynic should choose the next to see where these two people will end. Pick a card, Miss Swan," he invited. "Any card."

Annoyed, Ryan plucked one and tossed it faceup on the table. After a strangled gasp, she stared at it in absolute silence. The Lovers. Her heart hammered lightly at her throat.

"Fascinating," Pierce murmured. He wasn't smiling now, but he studied the card as if he'd never seen it before.

Ryan took a step back. "I don't like your game, Mr. Atkins."

"Hmmm?" He glanced up distractedly, then focused on her. "No? Well then…" He carelessly flipped the cards together and stacked them. "I'll show you to your room."

Pierce had been as surprised by the card as Ryan had been. But he knew reality was often stranger than any illusion he could devise. He had work to do, a great deal of final planning for his engagement in Las Vegas in two weeks' time. Yet as he sat in his room, he was thinking of Ryan, not of the mechanics of his craft.

There was something about her when she laughed, something brilliant and vital. It appealed to him the same way her low-key, practical voice had appealed to him when she spoke of contracts and clauses.

He already knew the contract backward and forward. He wasn't a man to brush aside the business end of his profession. Pierce signed his name to nothing unless he understood every nuance. If the public saw him as mysterious, flashy and odd, that was all to the good. The image was part illusion, part reality. That was the way he preferred it. He had spent the second half of his life arranging things as he preferred them.

Ryan Swan. Pierce stripped off his shirt and tossed it aside. He wasn't certain about her just yet. He had fully intended to sign the contracts until he had seen her coming down the stairs. Instinct had made him hesitate. Pierce relied heavily on his instincts. Now he had some thinking to do.

The cards didn't influence him. He could make cards stand up and dance if that's what he wanted. But coincidence influenced him. It was odd that Ryan had turned over the card symbolizing lovers when he had been thinking what she would feel like in his arms.

With a laugh, he sat down and began to doodle on a pad of paper. The plans he was forming for a new escape would have to be torn up or revised, but it relaxed him to turn it over in his mind, just as he turned Ryan over in his mind.

It might be wise to sign her papers in the morning and send her on her way. He didn't care to have a woman intrude on his thoughts. But Pierce didn't always do what was wise. If he did, he would still be playing the club field, pulling rabbits out of his hat and colored scarves out of his pocket at union scale. Now he turned a woman into a panther and walked through a brick wall.

Poof! he thought. Instant magic. And no one remembered the years of frustration and struggle and failure. That, too, was exactly as he wanted it. There were few who knew where he had come from or who he had been before he was twenty-five.

Pierce tossed aside the pencil. Ryan Swan was making him uneasy. He would go downstairs and work until his mind was clear. It was then he heard her scream.

Ryan undressed carelessly. Temper always made her careless. Parlor tricks, she thought furiously and pulled down the zipper of her skirt. Show people. She should be used to their orchestrations by now.

She remembered a meeting with a well-known comedian the month before. He had tried out a twenty-minute routine on her before he had settled down to discuss plans for a guest appearance on a Swan Production presentation. All the business with the Tarot cards had been just a show, designed to impress her, she decided and kicked off her shoes. Just another ego trip for an insecure performer.

Ryan frowned as she unbuttoned her blouse. She couldn't agree with her own conclusions. Pierce Atkins didn't strike her as an insecure man—on stage or off. And she would have sworn he had been as surprised as she when she had turned over that card. Ryan shrugged out of her blouse and tossed it over a chair. Well, he was an actor, she reminded herself. What else was a magician but a clever actor with clever hands?

She remembered the look of his hands on the black marble chess pieces, their leanness, their grace. She shook off the memory. Tomorrow she would get his name on that contract and drive away. He had made her uneasy; even before the little production with the cards, he had made her uneasy. Those eyes, Ryan thought and shivered. There's something about his eyes.

It was simply that he had a very strong personality, she decided. He was magnetic and yes, very attractive. He'd cultivated that, just as he had no doubt cultivated the mysterious air and enigmatic smile.

Lightning flashed, and Ryan jolted. She hadn't been completely honest with Pierce: storms played havoc with her nerves. Intellectually, she could brush it aside, but lightning and thunder always had her stomach tightening. She hated the weakness, a primarily feminine weakness. Pierce had been right; Bennett Swan had wanted a son. Ryan had gone through her life working hard to make up for being born female.

Go to bed, she ordered herself. Go to bed, pull the covers over your head and shut your eyes. Purposefully, she walked over to draw the drapes. She stared at the window. Something stared back. She screamed.

Ryan was across the room like a shot. Her damp palms skidded off the knob. When Pierce opened the door, she fell into his arms and held on.

"Ryan, what the hell's going on?" He would have drawn her away, but the arms around his neck were locked tight. She was very small without her heels. He could feel the shape of her body as she pressed desperately against him. Through concern and curiosity, Pierce experienced a swift and powerful wave of desire. Annoyed, he pulled her firmly away and held her arms.

"What is it?" he demanded.

"The window," she managed, and would have been back in his arms again if he hadn't held her off. "At the window by the bed."

Setting her aside, he walked to it. Ryan put both hands to her mouth and backed into the door, slamming it.

She heard Pierce's low oath as he drew up the glass and reached outside. He pulled in a very large, very wet black cat. On a moan, Ryan slumped against the door.

"Oh, God, what next?" she wondered aloud.

"Circe." Pierce set the cat on the floor. She shook herself once, then leaped onto the bed. "I didn't realize she was outside in this." He turned to look at Ryan. If he had laughed at her, she would never have forgiven him. But there was apology in his eyes, not amusement. "I'm sorry. She must have given you quite a scare. Can I get you a brandy?"

"No." Ryan let out a long breath. "Brandy doesn't do anything for acute embarrassment."

"Being frightened is nothing to be embarrassed about."

Her legs were still shaking, so she stayed propped against the door. "You might warn me if you have any more pets." Making the effort, she managed a smile. "That way, if I wake up with a wolf in bed with me, I can shrug it off and go back to sleep."

He didn't answer. As she watched, his eyes drifted slowly down her body. Ryan became aware she wore only a thin silk teddy. She straightened bolt upright against the door. But when his eyes came back to hers, she couldn't move, couldn't speak. Her breath had started to tremble before he took the first step toward her.

Tell him to go! her mind shouted, but her lips wouldn't form the words. She couldn't look away from his eyes. When he stopped in front of her, her head tilted back so that the look continued to hold. She could feel her pulse hammer at her wrists, at her throat, at her breast. Her whole body vibrated with it.

I want him. The knowledge stunned her. I've never wanted a man the way I want him. Her breath was audible now. His was calm and even. Slowly, Pierce took his finger to her shoulder and pushed aside the strap. It fell loosely on her arm. Ryan didn't move. He watched her intensely as he brushed aside the second strap. The bodice of the teddy fluttered to the points of her breasts and clung tenuously. A careless movement of his hand would have it falling to her feet. She stood transfixed.

Pierce lifted both hands, pushing the hair back from her face. He let his fingers dive deep into it. He leaned closer, then hesitated. Ryan's lips trembled apart. He watched her eyes shut before his mouth touched hers.

His lips were firm and gentle. At first they barely touched hers, just tasted. Then he lingered for a moment, keeping the kiss soft. A promise or a threat; Ryan wasn't certain. Her legs were about to buckle. In defense, she curled her hands around his arms. There were muscles, hard, firm muscles that she wouldn't think of until much later. Now she thought only of his mouth. He was barely kissing her at all, yet the shock of the impact winded her.

Degree by aching degree he deepened the kiss. Ryan's fingers tightened desperately on his arms. His mouth brushed over hers, then came back with more pressure. His tongue feathered lightly over hers. He only touched her hair, though her body tempted him. He drew out every ounce of pleasure with his mouth alone.

He knew what it was to be hungry—for food, for love, for a woman—but he hadn't experienced this raw, painful need in years. He wanted the taste of her, only the taste of her. It was at once sweet and pungent. As he drew it inside him, he knew there would come a time when he would take more. But for now her lips were enough.

When he knew he had reached the border between backing away and taking her Pierce lifted his head. He waited for Ryan to open her eyes.

Her green eyes were darkened, cloudy. He saw that she was as stunned as she was aroused. He knew he could take her there, where they stood. He had only to kiss her again, had only to brush aside the brief swatch of silk she wore. But he did neither. Ryan's fingers loosened, then her hands dropped away from his arms. Saying nothing, Pierce moved around her and opened the door. The cat leaped off the bed to slip through the crack before Pierce shut it behind him.

Chapter 3

By morning the only sign of the storm was the steady drip of water from the balcony outside Ryan's bedroom window. She dressed carefully. It was important that she be perfectly poised and collected when she went downstairs. It would have been easier if she could have convinced herself that she had been dreaming—that Pierce had never come to her room, that he had never given her that strange, draining kiss. But it had been no dream.

Ryan was too much a realist to pretend otherwise or to make excuses. A great deal of what had happened had been her fault, she admitted as she folded yesterday's suit. She had acted like a fool, screaming because a cat had wanted in out of the rain. She had thrown herself into Pierce's arms wearing little more than shattered nerves. And lastly and most disturbing she had made no protest. Ryan was forced to concede that Pierce had given her ample time to object. But she had done nothing, made no struggle, voiced no indignant protest.

Maybe he had hypnotized her, she thought grimly as she brushed her hair into order. The way he had looked at her, the way her mind had gone blank… With a sound of frustration, Ryan tossed the brush into her suitcase. You couldn't be hypnotized with a look.

If she was to deal with it, she first had to admit it. She had wanted him to kiss her. And when he had, her senses had ruled her. Ryan clicked the locks on the suitcase, then set it next to the door. She would have gone to bed with him. It was a cold, hard fact, and there was no getting around it. Had he stayed, she would have made love with him—a man she had known for a matter of hours.

Ryan drew a deep breath and gave herself a moment before opening the door. It was a difficult truth to face for a woman who prided herself on acting with common sense and practicality. She had come to get Pierce Atkins's name on a contract, not to sleep with him.

You haven't done either yet, she reminded herself with a grimace. And it was morning. Time to concentrate on the first and forget the second. Ryan opened the door and started downstairs.

The house was quiet. After peeking into the parlor and finding it empty, she continued down the hall. Though her mind was set on finding Pierce and completing the business she had come for, an open door to her right tempted her to stop. The first glance drew a sound of pleasure from her.

There were walls—literally walls—of books. Ryan had never seen so many in a private collection, not even her father's. Somehow she knew these books were more than an investment, they were read. Pierce would know each one of them. She walked into the room for a closer look. There was a scent of leather and of candles.

The Unmasking of Robert-Houdin, by Houdini; *The Edge of the Unknown,* by Arthur Conan Doyle; *Les Illusionnistes et Leurs Secrets.* These and dozens of other books on magic and magicians Ryan expected. But there was also T. H. White, Shakespeare, Chaucer, the poems of Byron and Shelley. Scattered among them were works by Fitzgerald, Mailer and Bradbury. Not all were leather bound or aged and valuable. Ryan thought of her father, who would know what each of his books cost, down to the last dollar and who had read no more than a dozen in his collection.

He has very eclectic taste, she mused as she wandered the room. On the mantelpiece were carved, painted figures she recognized as inhabitants of Tolkien's Middle Earth. There was a very modern metal sculpture on the desk.

Who is this man? Ryan wondered. Who is he really? Lyrical, fanciful, with hints of a firm realist beneath. It annoyed her to realize just how badly she wanted to discover the full man.

"Miss Swan?"

Ryan swung around to see Link filling the doorway. "Oh, good morning." She wasn't certain if his expression was disapproving or if it was simply her impression of his unfortunate face. "I'm sorry," she added. "Shouldn't I have come in here?"

Link lifted his massive shoulders in a shrug. "He would have locked it if he wanted you to stay out."

"Yes, of course," Ryan murmured, not certain if she should feel insulted or amused.

"Pierce said you can wait for him downstairs after you've had breakfast."

"Has he gone out?"

"Running," Link said shortly. "He runs five miles every day."

"Five miles?" But Link was already turning away. Ryan dashed across the room to keep up.

"I'll make your breakfast," he told her.

"Just coffee—tea," she corrected, remembering. She didn't know what to call him but realized that she would soon be too breathless from trying to keep pace with him to call him anything. "Link." Ryan touched his arm, and he stopped. "I saw your work on the piano last night." He was looking at her steadily, without any change of expression. "I hope you don't mind." He shrugged again. Ryan concluded he used the gesture often in place of words. "It's a beautiful melody," she continued. "Really lovely."

To her astonishment, he blushed. Ryan hadn't thought it possible for a man of his size to be embarrassed. "It's not finished," he mumbled, with his wide, ugly face growing pinker.

Ryan smiled at him, touched. "What is finished is beautiful. You have a wonderful gift."

He shuffled his feet, then mumbled something about getting her tea and lumbered off. Ryan smiled at his retreating back before she walked to the dining room.

Link brought her toast, with a grumble about her having to eat something. Ryan finished it off dutifully, thinking of Pierce's remark about face value. If nothing else came of her odd visit, she had learned something. Ryan didn't believe she would ever again make snap decisions about someone based on appearance.

Though she deliberately loitered over the meal, there was still no sign of Pierce when Ryan had finished. Reluctance to brave the lower floor again had her sipping at cold tea and waiting. At length, with a sigh, she rose, picked up her briefcase and headed down the stairs.

Someone had switched on the lights, and Ryan was grateful. The room wasn't brilliantly illuminated; it was too large for the light to reach all the corners. But the feeling of apprehension Ryan had experienced the day before didn't materialize. This time she knew what to expect.

Spotting Merlin standing in his cage, she walked over to him. The door of the cage was open, so she stood cautiously to the side as she studied him. She didn't want to encourage him to perch on her shoulder again, particularly since Pierce wasn't there to lure him away.

"Good morning," she said, curious as to whether he'd talk to her when she was alone.

Merlin eyed her a moment. "Buy you a drink, sweetie?"

Ryan laughed and decided Merlin's trainer had an odd sense of humor. "I don't fall for that line," she told him and bent down until they were eye to eye. "What else can you say?" she wondered out loud. "I bet he's taught you quite a bit. He'd have the patience for it." She grinned, amused that the bird seemed to be listening attentively to her conversation. "Are you a smart bird, Merlin?" she demanded.

"Alas, poor Yorick!" he said obligingly.

"Good grief, the bird quotes *Hamlet*." Shaking her head, Ryan turned toward the stage. There were two large trunks, a wicker hamper and a long, waist-high table. Curious, Ryan set down her briefcase and mounted the stairs. On the table was a deck of playing cards, a pair of empty cylinders, wine bottles and glasses and a pair of handcuffs.

Ryan picked up the playing cards and wondered fleetingly how he marked them. She could see nothing, even when she held them up to the light. Setting them aside, she examined the handcuffs. They appeared to be regulation police issue. Cold, steel, unsympathetic. She searched the table for a key and found none.

Ryan had done her research on Pierce thoroughly. She knew there wasn't supposed to be a lock made that could hold him. He had been shackled hand and foot and stuffed into a triple-locked steamer trunk. In less than three minutes he had been out, unmanacled. Impressive, she admitted, still studying the cuffs. Where was the trick?

"Miss Swan."

Ryan dropped the handcuffs with a clatter as she spun around. Pierce stood directly behind her. But he couldn't have come down the stairs, she thought. She would have heard, or certainly seen. Obviously, there was another entrance to his workroom. And how long, she wondered, had he been standing and watching? He was doing no more than that now while the cat busied herself by winding around his ankles.

"Mr. Atkins," she managed in a calm enough voice.

"I hope you slept well." He crossed to the table to join her. "The storm didn't keep you awake?"

"No."

For a man who had just run five miles, he looked remarkably fresh. Ryan remembered the muscles in his arms. There was strength in him, and obviously stamina. His eyes were very steady, almost measuring, on hers.

There was no hint of the restrained passion she had felt from him the night before.

Abruptly, Pierce smiled at her, then gestured with his hand. "What do you see here?"

Ryan glanced at the table again. "Some of your tools."

"Ah, Miss Swan, your feet are always on the ground."

"I like to think so," she returned, annoyed. "What should I see?"

He seemed pleased with her response and poured a small amount of wine into a glass. "The imagination, Miss Swan, is an incredible gift. Do you agree?"

"Yes, of course." She watched his hands carefully. "To a point."

"To a point." He laughed a little and showed her the empty cylinders. "Can there be restrictions on the imagination?" He slipped one cylinder inside the other. "Don't you find the possibilities of the power of the mind over the laws of nature interesting?" Pierce placed the cylinders over the wine bottle, watching her.

Ryan was frowning at his hands now. "As a theory," she replied.

"But only a theory." Pierce slipped one cylinder out and set it over the wineglass. Lifting the first cylinder, he showed her that the bottle remained under it. "Not in practice."

"No." Ryan kept her eyes on his hands. He could hardly pull anything off right under her nose.

"Where's the glass, Miss Swan?"

"It's there." She pointed to the second cylinder.

"Is it?" Pierce lifted the tube. The bottle stood under it. With a sound of frustration, Ryan looked at the other tube. Pierce lifted it, revealing the partially filled glass.

"They seem to have found the theory more viable," he stated and dropped the cylinders back in place.

"That's very clever," she said, irritated that she had stood inches away and not seen the trick.

"Would you care for some wine, Miss Swan?"

"No, I…"

Even as she spoke, Pierce lifted the cylinder. There, where she had just seen the bottle, stood the glass. Charmed despite herself, Ryan laughed. "You're very good, Mr. Atkins."

"Thank you."

He said it so soberly, Ryan looked back at him. His eyes were calm and thoughtful. Intrigued, she tilted her head. "I don't suppose you'd tell me how you did it."

"No."

"I didn't think so." She lifted the handcuffs. The briefcase at the foot of the stage was, for the moment, forgotten. "Are these part of your act, too? They look real."

"They're quite real," he told her. He was smiling again, pleased that she had laughed. He knew it was a sound he would be able to hear clearly whenever he thought of her.

"There's no key," Ryan pointed out.

"I don't need one."

She passed the cuffs from hand to hand as she studied him. "You're very sure of yourself."

"Yes." The hint of amusement in the word made her wonder what twist his thoughts had taken. He held out his hands, wrists close. "Go ahead," he invited. "Put them on."

Ryan hesitated only a moment. She wanted to see him do it—right there in front of her eyes. "If you can't get them off," she said as she snapped the cuffs into place, "we'll just sit down and talk about those contracts." She glanced up at him, eyes dancing. "When you've signed them, we can send for a locksmith."

"I don't think we'll need one." Pierce held up the cuffs, dangling and open.

"Oh, but how…" She trailed off and shook her head. "No, that was too quick," she insisted, taking them back from him. Pierce appreciated the way her expression changed from astonishment to doubt. It was precisely what he had expected from her. "You had them made." She was turning them over, searching closely. "There must be a button or something."

"Why don't you try it?" he suggested and had the cuffs snapped on her wrists before she could decline. Pierce waited to see if she'd be angry. She laughed.

"I talked myself right into that one." Ryan gave him a good-humored grimace, then concentrated on the cuffs. She juggled her wrists. "They certainly feel real enough." Though she tried several different angles, the steel held firmly shut. "If there's a button," she muttered, "you'd have to dislocate your wrist to get to it." She tugged another moment, then tried to slip her hands through the opening. "All right, you win," she announced, giving up. "They're real." Ryan grinned up at him. "Can you get me out of these?"

"Maybe," he murmured, taking her wrists in his hands.

"That's a comforting answer," she returned dryly, but they both felt her pulse leap as his thumb brushed over it. He continued to stare down at her until she felt the same draining weakness she had experienced the night before. "I think," she began, her voice husky as she struggled to clear it. "I think you'd better..." The sentence trailed off as his fingers traced the vein in her wrist. "Don't," she said, not even certain what she was trying to refuse.

Silently, Pierce lifted her hands, slipping them over his head so that she was pressed against him.

She wouldn't allow it to happen twice. This time she would protest. "No." Ryan tugged once, uselessly, but his mouth was already on hers.

This time his mouth wasn't so patient or his hands so still. Pierce held her hips as his tongue urged her lips apart. Ryan fought against the helplessness—a helplessness that had more to do with her own needs than the restraints on her wrists. She was responding totally. Under the pressure of his, her lips were hungry. His were cool and firm while hers heated and softened. She heard him murmur something as he dragged her closer. An incantation, she thought dizzily. He was bewitching her; there was no other explanation.

But it was a moan of pleasure, not of protest, that slipped from her when his hands trailed up to the sides of her breasts. He drew slow, aching circles before his thumbs slipped between their bodies to stroke over her nipples. Ryan pressed closer, nipping at his bottom lip as she craved more. His hands were in her hair, pulling her head back so that his lips had complete command of hers.

Perhaps he was magic. His mouth was. No one else had ever made her ache and burn with only a kiss.

Ryan wanted to touch him, to make him hunger as desperately as she. She fretted against the restraints on her wrists, only to find her hands were free. Her fingers could caress his neck, run through his hair.

Then, as quickly as she had been captured, she was released. Pierce had his hands on her shoulders, holding her away.

Confused, still aching, Ryan stared up at him. "Why?"

Pierce didn't answer for a moment. Absently, he caressed her shoulders. "I wanted to kiss Miss Swan. Last night I kissed Ryan."

"You're being ridiculous." She started to jerk away, but his hands were suddenly firm.

"No. Miss Swan wears conservative suits and worries about contracts. Ryan wears silk and lace underneath and is frightened of storms. The combination fascinates me."

His words troubled her enough to make her voice cool and sharp. "I'm not here to fascinate you, Mr. Atkins."

"A side benefit, Miss Swan." He grinned, then kissed her fingers. Ryan jerked her hand away.

"It's time we settled our business one way or the other."

"You're right, Miss Swan." She didn't like the hint of amusement or the way he emphasized her name. Ryan found she no longer cared whether or not he signed the papers she carried. She simply wanted to shake loose of him.

"Well, then," she began and stooped to pick up her briefcase.

Pierce laid his hand over hers on the handle. His fingers closed gently. "I'm willing to sign your contracts with a few adjustments."

Ryan schooled herself to relax. Adjustments normally meant money. She'd negotiate with him and be done with it. "I'll be glad to discuss any changes you might want."

"That's fine. I'll want to work with you directly. I want you to handle Swan's end of the production."

"Me?" Ryan's fingers tightened on the handle again. "I don't get involved with the production end. My father—"

"I'm not going to work with your father, Miss Swan, or any other producer." His hand was still gently closed over hers, with the contracts between them. "I'm going to work with you."

"Mr. Atkins, I appreciate—"

"I'll need you in Vegas in two weeks."

"In Vegas? Why?"

"I want you to watch my performances—closely. There's nothing more valuable to an illusionist than a cynic. You'll keep me sharp." He smiled. "You're very critical. I like that."

Ryan heaved a sigh. She would have thought criticism would annoy, not attract. "Mr. Atkins, I'm a business-woman, not a producer."

"You told me you were good at details," he reminded her amiably. "If I'm going to break my own rule and per-form on television, I want someone like you handling the details. More to the point," he continued, "I want *you* handling the details."

"You're not being practical, Mr. Atkins. I'm sure your agent would agree. There are any number of people at Swan Productions who are better qualified to produce your special. I don't have any experience in that end of the business."

"Miss Swan, do you want me to sign your contracts?"

"Yes, of course, but—"

"Then make the changes," he said simply. "And be at Caesar's Palace in two weeks. I have a week's run." Stooping, he lifted the cat into his arms. "I'll look forward to working with you."

Chapter 4

When she stalked into her office at Swan Productions four hours later, Ryan was still fuming. He had nerve, she decided. She would give him top of the list for nerve. He thought he had her boxed into a corner. Did he really imagine he was the only name talent she could sign for Swan Productions? What outrageous conceit! Ryan slammed her briefcase down on her desk and flopped into the chair behind it. Pierce Atkins was in for a surprise.

Leaning back in her chair, Ryan folded her hands and waited until she was calm enough to think. Pierce didn't know Bennett Swan. Swan liked to run things his own way. Advice could be considered, discussed, but he would never be swayed on a major decision. As a matter of fact, she mused, he would more than likely go in the opposite direction he was pushed. He wouldn't appreciate being told who to put in charge of a production. Particularly, Ryan thought ruefully, when that person was his daughter.

There was going to be an explosion when she told her father of Pierce's conditions. Her only regret was that the magician wouldn't be there to feel the blast. Swan would find another hot property to sign, and Pierce could go back to making wine bottles disappear.

Ryan brooded into space. The last thing she wanted to do was worry about rehearsal calls and shooting schedules—and all the thousands of other niggling details involved in producing an hour show—not to mention the outright paranoia of it being a live telecast. What did she know about dealing with technical breakdowns and union rules and set designing? Producing was a complicated job. She had never had any desire to try her hand at that end of the business. She was perfectly content with the paperwork and preproduction details.

She leaned forward again, elbows on the desk, and cupped her chin in her hands. How foolish it is, she mused, to lie to yourself. And how fulfilling it would be to follow through on a project from beginning to end. She had ideas—so many ideas that were constantly being restricted by legal niceties.

Whenever she had tried to convince her father to give her a chance on the creative side, she had met the same unyielding wall. She didn't have the experience; she was too young. He conveniently forgot that she had been around the business all of her life and that she would be twenty-seven the following month.

One of the most talented directors in the business had done a film for Swan that had netted five Oscars. And he'd been twenty-six, Ryan remembered indignantly.

How could Swan know if her ideas were gold or trash if he wouldn't listen to them? All she needed was one opportunity.

No, she had to admit that nothing would suit her better than to follow a project from signing to wrap party. But not this one. This time she would cheerfully admit failure and toss the contracts and Pierce Atkins right back in her father's lap. There was enough Swan in her to get her back up when given an ultimatum.

Change the contracts. With a snort of derision, Ryan flipped open her briefcase. He overplayed his hand, she thought, and now he'll... She stopped, staring down at the neatly stacked papers inside the case. On top of them was another long-stemmed rose.

"Now how did he..." Ryan's own laughter cut her off. Leaning back, she twirled the flower under her nose. He was clever, she mused, drawing in the scent. Very clever. But who the devil was he? What made him tick? Sitting there in her tailored, organized office, Ryan decided she very much wanted to know. Perhaps it would be worth an explosion and a bit of conniving to find out.

There were depths to a man who spoke quietly and could command with his eyes alone. Layers, she thought. How many layers would she have to peel off to get to the core of him? It would be risky, she decided, but... Shaking her head, Ryan reminded herself that she wasn't going to be given the opportunity to find out, in any case. Swan would either sign him on his own terms or forget him. She drew out the contracts, then snapped the briefcase shut. Pierce Atkins was her father's problem now. Still, she kept the rose in her hand.

The buzzer on her phone reminded her she didn't have time for daydreaming. "Yes, Barbara."

"The boss wants to see you."

Ryan grimaced at the intercom. Swan would have known she was back the moment she passed the guard at the gate. "Right away," she agreed. Leaving the rose on her desk, Ryan took the contracts with her.

Bennett Swan smoked an expensive Cuban cigar. He liked expensive things. More, he liked knowing his money could buy them. If there were two suits of equal cut and value, Swan would choose the one with the biggest price tag. It was a matter of pride.

The awards in his office were also a matter of pride. Swan Productions was Bennett Swan. Oscars and Emmys proved he was a success. The paintings and sculptures his art broker had advised him to purchase showed the world that he knew the value of success.

He loved his daughter, would have been shocked if anyone had said otherwise. There was no doubt in his mind that he was an excellent father. He had always given Ryan everything his money could buy: the best clothes, an Irish nanny when her mother had died, an expensive education, then a comfortable job when she had insisted on working.

He had been forced to admit that the girl had more on the ball than he had expected. Ryan had a sharp brain and a way of cutting through the nonsense and getting to the heart of a matter. It proved to him that the money spent on the Swiss school had been well spent. Not that he would begrudge his daughter the finest education. Swan expected results.

He watched the smoke curl from the tip of his cigar. Ryan had paid off for him. He was very fond of his daughter.

She knocked, then entered when he called out. He

watched her cross the wide space of thick carpet to his desk. A pretty girl, he thought. Looks like her mother.

"You wanted to see me?" She waited for the signal to sit. Swan wasn't a big man but had always made up for his lack of size with expansiveness. The wide sweep of his arm told her to sit. His face was still handsome in the rugged, outdoorsy manner women found appealing. He had put on a bit of flesh in the last five years and had lost a bit of hair. Essentially, however, he looked the same as Ryan's earliest memory of him. Looking at him, she felt the familiar surge of love and frustration. Ryan knew too well the limitations of her father's affection for her.

"You're feeling better?" she asked, noting that his bout with the flu hadn't left any mark of sickness on him. His face was healthily ruddy, his eyes clear. With another sweeping gesture, he brushed the question aside. Swan was impatient with illness, particularly his own. He didn't have time for it.

"What did you think of Atkins?" he demanded the moment Ryan was settled. It was one of the small concessions Swan made to her, the asking of her opinion on another. As always, Ryan thought carefully before answering.

"He's a unique man," she began in a tone that would have made Pierce smile. "He has extraordinary talent and a very strong personality. I'm not sure that one isn't the cause for the other."

"Eccentric?"

"No, not in the sense that he does things to promote an eccentric image." Ryan frowned as she thought of his house, his lifestyle. *Face value.* "I think he's a very deep man and one who lives precisely as he chooses.

His profession is more than a career. He's dedicated to it the way an artist is to painting."

Swan nodded and blew out a cloud of expensive smoke. "He's hot box office."

Ryan smiled and shifted the contracts. "Yes, because he's probably the best at what he does; plus he's dynamic on stage and a bit mysterious off it. He seems to have locked up the beginnings of his life and tossed away the key. The public loves a puzzle. He gives them one."

"And the contracts?"

Here it comes, Ryan thought, bracing herself. "He's willing to sign, but with certain conditions. That is, he—"

"He told me about his conditions," Swan interrupted.

Ryan's carefully thought out dissertation was thrown to the winds. "He told you?"

"Phoned a couple of hours ago." Swan plucked the cigar from his mouth. The diamond on his finger shot light as he eyed his daughter. "He says you're cynical and dedicated to details. That's what he claims he wants."

"I simply don't believe his tricks were anything but clever staging," Ryan countered, annoyed that Pierce had spoken to Swan before she had. She felt, uncomfortably, as if she were playing chess again. He'd already outmatched her once. "He has a habit of incorporating his magic into the everyday. It's effective, but distracting at a business meeting."

"Insulting him seems to have turned the trick," Swan commented.

"I didn't insult him!" At that Ryan rose with the contracts in her hand. "I spent twenty-four hours in that house with talking birds and black cats, and I didn't insult him. I did everything I could to get his name on these except letting him saw me in half." She dropped the papers on her father's desk. "There are limits to what I'll do to humor the talent, no matter how hot they are at the box office."

Swan steepled his fingers and watched her. "He also said he didn't mind your temper. He doesn't like to be bored."

Ryan bit off the next words that sprang to mind. Carefully, she sat back down. "All right, you told me what he said to you. What did you say to him?"

Swan took his time answering. It was the first time anyone connected with the business had referred to Ryan's temper. Swan knew she had one and knew, too, that she kept it scrupulously controlled on the job. He decided to let it pass. "I told him we'd be glad to oblige him."

"You…" Ryan choked on the word and tried again. "You agreed? Why?"

"We want him. He wants you."

No explosion, she thought, not a little confused. What spell had Pierce used to manage this one? Whatever it was, she told herself grimly, she wasn't under it. She rose again. "Do I have any say in this?"

"Not as long as you work for me." Swan gave the contracts an idle glance. "You've been itching to do something along these lines for a couple of years," he reminded her. "I'm giving you your chance. And," he looked up then and met her eyes, "I'll be watching you closely. If you mess it up, I'll pull you."

"I'm not going to mess it up," she retorted, barely controlling a new wave of fury. "It'll be the best damn special Swan's ever produced."

"Just see that it is," he warned. "And that you don't go over budget. Take care of the changes and send the new contracts to his agent. I want him signed before the end of the week."

"He will be." Ryan scooped up the papers before she headed for the door.

"Atkins said you two would work well together," Swan added as she yanked the door open. "He said it was in the cards."

Ryan shot an infuriated glance over her shoulder before she marched out, slamming the door behind her.

Swan grinned a little. She certainly did favor her mother, he thought, then pushed a button to summon his secretary. He had another appointment.

If there was one thing Ryan detested, it was being manipulated. By the time her temper had cooled and she was back in her office, it dawned on her how smoothly both Pierce and her father had maneuvered her. She didn't mind it as much from Swan—he had had years to learn that to suggest she might not be able to handle something was the certain way to see that she did. Pierce was a different matter. He didn't know her at all, or shouldn't have. Yet he had handled her, subtly, expertly, in the same the-hand-is-quicker-than-the-eye fashion he had handled the empty cylinders. He had what he wanted. Ryan drafted out the new contracts and brooded.

She had gotten past that one little point, and she had what she wanted as well. She decided to look at the entire matter from a new angle. Swan Productions would have Pierce sewed up for three prime-time specials, and she would have her chance to produce.

Ryan Swan, Executive Producer. She smiled. Yes, she liked the sound of it. She said it again to herself and felt the first stirring of excitement. Pulling out her date book, Ryan began to calculate how quickly she could tie up loose ends and devote herself to the production.

Ryan had plowed through an hour's paperwork when the phone interrupted her. "Ryan Swan," she answered briskly, balancing the receiver on her shoulder as she continued to scribble.

"Miss Swan, I've interrupted you."

No one else called her *Miss Swan* in just that way. Ryan broke off the sentence she had been composing and forgot it. "That's all right, Mr. Atkins. What can I do for you?"

He laughed, annoying her instantly.

"What's so funny?"

"You've a lovely business voice, Miss Swan," he said with the trace of humor still lingering. "I thought, with your penchant for detail, you'd like to have the dates I'll need you in Vegas."

"The contracts aren't signed yet, Mr. Atkins," Ryan began primly.

"I open on the fifteenth," he told her as if she hadn't spoken. "But rehearsals begin on the twelfth. I'd like you there for them as well." Ryan frowned, marking down the dates. She could almost see him sitting in his library, holding the cat in his lap. "I close on the twenty-first." She noted idly that the twenty-first was her birthday.

"All right. We could begin outlining the production of the special the following week."

"Good." Pierce paused a moment. "I wonder if I could ask you for something, Miss Swan."

"You could ask," Ryan said cautiously.

Pierce grinned and scratched Circe's ears. "I have an engagement in L.A. on the eleventh. Would you come with me?"

"The eleventh?" Ryan shifted the phone and turned back the pages of her desk calendar. "What time?"

"Two o'clock."

"Yes, all right." She marked it down. "Where should I meet you?"

"I'll pick you up—one-thirty."

"One-thirty. Mr. Atkins…" She hesitated, then picked up the rose on her desk. "Thank you for the flower."

"You're welcome, Ryan."

Pierce hung up, then sat for a moment, lost in thought. He imagined Ryan was holding the rose even now. Did she know that her skin was as soft as its petals? Her face, just at the jawline—he could still clearly feel its texture on his fingertips. He ran them down the cat's back. "What did you think of her, Link?"

The big man continued to push books back into place and didn't turn. "She has a nice laugh."

"Yes, I thought so, too." Pierce could remember the tone of it perfectly; it had been unexpected, a stark contrast to her serious expression of a moment before. Both her laugh and her passion had surprised him. He remembered the way her mouth had heated under his. He hadn't been able to work at all that night, thinking of her upstairs in bed with only that swatch of silk covering her.

He didn't like having his concentration disturbed, yet he was pulling her back. Instinct, he reminded himself. He was still following his instinct.

"She said she liked my music," Link murmured, still shuffling books.

Pierce glanced up, bringing his thoughts back. He knew how sensitive Link was about his music. "She did like it, very much. She thought the melody you'd left on the piano was beautiful."

Link nodded, knowing Pierce would tell him nothing but the truth. "You like her, don't you?"

"Yes." Pierce answered absently as he stroked the cat. "Yes, I believe I do."

"I guess you must want to do this TV thing."

"It's a challenge," Pierce replied.

Link turned then. "Pierce?"

"Hmmm?"

He hesitated to ask, afraid he already knew the answer. "Are you going to do the new escape in Las Vegas?"

"No." Pierce frowned, and Link felt a flood of relief. Pierce remembered that he'd been trying to work on that particular escape the night Ryan had stayed in his house in the room just down the hall from his own. "No, I haven't worked it all out yet." Link's relief was short-lived. "I'll use it for the special instead."

"I don't like it." It came out quickly, causing Pierce to look up again. "Too many things can go wrong."

"Nothing's going to go wrong, Link. It just needs some more work before I use it in the act."

"The timing's too close," Link insisted, taking an uncharacteristic step by arguing. "You could make some changes or just postpone it. I don't like it, Pierce," he said again, knowing it was useless.

"You worry too much," Pierce assured him. "It's going to be fine. I just have a few more things to work out."

But he wasn't thinking of the mechanics of his escape. He was thinking of Ryan.

Chapter 5

Ryan caught herself watching the clock. *One-fifteen.* The days before the eleventh had gone quickly. She had been up to her ears in paperwork, often working ten hours a day trying to clear her desk before the trip to Las Vegas. She wanted a clear road and no lingering contractual problems hanging over her head once she began work on the special. She would make up for lack of experience by giving the project all of her time and attention.

She still had something to prove—to herself, to her father, and now, to Pierce. There was more to Ryan Swan than contracts and clauses.

Yes, the days had gone quickly, she mused, but this last hour...*one-seventeen.* With a sound of annoyance, Ryan pulled out a file folder and opened it. She was watching the clock as if she were waiting for a date rather than a business appointment. That was ridiculous. Still, when the knock came, her head shot up and she forgot the neatly typed pages in the folder. Pushing away a surge of anticipation, Ryan answered calmly.

"Yes, come in."

"Hi, Ryan."

She struggled with disappointment as Ned Ross strolled into the room. He gave her a polished smile.

"Hello, Ned."

Ned Ross—thirty-two, blond and personable with casual California chic. He let his hair curl freely and wore expensive designer slacks with quiet silk shirts. No tie, Ryan noted. It went against his image, just as the subtle whiff of breezy cologne suited it. Ned knew the effects of his charm, which he used purposefully.

Ryan chided herself halfheartedly for being critical and returned his smile, though hers was a great deal cooler.

Ned was her father's second assistant. For several months, up to a few weeks ago, he had also been Ryan's constant escort. He had wined and dined her, given her a few thrilling lessons in surfing, showed her the beauty of the beach at sunset and made her believe she was the most attractive, desirable woman he had ever met. It had been a painful disillusionment when she had discovered he was more interested in cultivating Bennett Swan's daughter than Ryan herself.

"The boss wanted me to check in with you, see how things were shaping up before you take off for Vegas." He sat on the corner of her desk, then leaned over to give her a light kiss. He still had plans for his boss's daughter. "And I wanted to say goodbye."

"All my work's cleared up," Ryan told him, casually

shifting the file folder between them. It was still difficult to believe that the attractive, tanned face and amiable smile masked an ambitious liar. "I intended to bring my father up to date myself."

"He's tied up," Ned told her easily and picked up the folder to flip through it. "Just took off for New York. Something on a location shoot he wants to see to personally. He won't be back until the end of the week."

"Oh." Ryan looked down at her hands. He might have taken a moment to call her, she thought, then sighed. When had he ever? And when would she ever stop expecting him to? "Well, you can tell him everything's taken care of." She took the folder back from him and set it down again. "I've a report written out."

"Always efficient." Ned smiled at her again but made no move to leave. He knew too well he had made a misstep with Ryan and had some lost ground to cover. "So, how do you feel about moving up to producer?"

"I'm looking forward to it."

"This Atkins," Ned continued, overlooking the coolness, "he's kind of a strange guy, isn't he?"

"I don't know him well enough to say," Ryan said evasively. She found she didn't want to discuss Pierce with Ned. The day she had spent with him was hers, personally. "I have an appointment in a few minutes, Ned," she continued, rising. "So if you'd—"

"Ryan." Ned took her hands in his as he had habitually done when they had dated. The gesture had always made her smile. "I've really missed you these past weeks."

"We've seen each other several times, Ned." Ryan allowed her hands to lie limply in his.

"Ryan, you know what I mean." He massaged her

wrists gently but felt no increase in her pulse. His voice softened persuasively. "You're still angry with me for making that stupid suggestion."

"About using my influence with my father to have you head the O'Mara production?" Ryan lifted a brow. "No, Ned," she said evenly, "I'm not angry with you. I heard Bishop was given the job," she added, unable to resist the small jibe. "I hope you're not too disappointed."

"That's not important," he replied, masking his annoyance with a shrug. "Let me take you to dinner tonight." Ned drew her a fraction closer, and Ryan didn't resist. Just how far, she wondered, would he go? "That little French place you like so much. We could go for a drive up the coast and talk."

"Doesn't it occur to you that I might have a date?"

The question stopped him from lowering his mouth to hers. It hadn't occurred to him that she would be seeing anyone else. He was certain that she was still crazy about him. He had spent a lot of time and effort leading her to that end. He concluded she wanted to be persuaded.

"Break it," he murmured and kissed her softly, never noticing that her eyes stayed open and cold.

"No."

Ned hadn't expected a flat, unemotional refusal. He knew from experience that Ryan's emotions were easily tapped. He'd been prepared to disappoint a very friendly assistant director to be with Ryan again. Off guard, he raised his head to stare at her. "Come on, Ryan, don't be—"

"Excuse me." Ryan whipped her hands from Ned's and looked to the doorway. "Miss Swan," Pierce said with a nod.

"Mr. Atkins." She was flushed and furious to have

been caught in a compromising situation in her own office. Why hadn't she told Ned to shut the door when he had come in? "Ned, this is Pierce Atkins. Ned Ross is my father's assistant."

"Mr. Ross." Pierce moved into the room but didn't extend his hand.

"A pleasure to meet you, Mr. Atkins." Ned flashed a smile. "I'm a big fan."

"Are you?" Pierce gave him a polite smile that made Ned feel as though he had been thrust into a very cold, very dark room.

His eyes faltered, then he turned back to Ryan. "Have a good time in Vegas, Ryan." He was already heading to the door. "Nice to have met you, Mr. Atkins."

Ryan watched Ned's hurried retreat with a frown. He had certainly lost his characteristic laid-back style. "What did you do to him?" she demanded when the door shut.

Pierce lifted a brow as he crossed to her. "What do you think I did?"

"I don't know," Ryan muttered. "But whatever you did to him don't ever do it to me."

"Your hands are cold, Ryan." He took them in his. "Why didn't you just tell him to go?"

He unnerved her when he called her Ryan. He unnerved her when he called her Miss Swan in the lightly mocking tone he used. Ryan looked down at their joined hands. "I did—that is, I was…" She caught herself, amazed that she was stammering out an explanation. "We'd better go if you're going to make your engagement, Mr. Atkins."

"Miss Swan." Pierce's eyes were full of humor as he lifted her hands to his lips. They were no longer cold.

"I've missed that serious face and professional tone." Leaving her with nothing to say, Pierce took her arm and led her from the room.

Once they had settled in his car and joined the streaming traffic, Ryan tried for casual conversation. If they were going to be working closely together, she had to establish the correct relationship and quickly. *Queen's pawn to bishop two,* she thought, remembering the chess game. "What sort of engagement do you have this afternoon?"

Pierce stopped at a red light and glanced at her. His eyes met hers with brief but potent intensity. "A gig's a gig," he said enigmatically. "You're not fond of your father's assistant."

Ryan stiffened. He attacked, she defended. "He's good at his job."

"Why did you lie to him?" Pierce asked mildly when the light turned. "You could have told him you didn't want to have dinner with him instead of pretending you had a date."

"What makes you think I was pretending?" Ryan countered impulsively, hurt pride in her voice.

Pierce downshifted into second to take a corner and maneuvered his way around the point. "I simply wondered why you felt you had to."

Ryan didn't care for his calmness. "That's my affair, Mr. Atkins."

"Do you think we could drop the 'Mr. Atkins' for the afternoon?" Pierce pulled off into a lot and guided the car into a parking space. Then, turning his head, he smiled at her. He was, Ryan decided, entirely too charming when he smiled in just that way.

"Maybe," she agreed when her lips curved in response. "For the afternoon. Is Pierce your real name?"

"As far as I know." With this, he slid from the car. When Ryan climbed out her side, she noted they were in the parking lot of Los Angeles General Hospital.

"What are we doing here?"

"I have a show to do." Pierce took a black bag, not unlike one a doctor might use, from the trunk. "Tools of the trade," he told Ryan as she gave it a curious study. "No hypos or scalpels," he promised and held out a hand to her. His eyes were on hers, patient as she hesitated. Ryan accepted his hand, and together they walked through the side door.

Wherever Ryan had expected to spend the afternoon, it hadn't been in the pediatric ward of L.A. General. Whatever she had expected of Pierce Atkins, it hadn't been a communion with children. After the first five minutes, Ryan saw that he gave them much more than a show and a bagful of tricks. He gave himself.

Why, he's a beautiful man, she realized with something of a jolt. He plays in Vegas for thirty-five dollars a head, crams Covent Garden, but he comes here just to give a bunch of kids a good time. There were no reporters to note his humanitarianism and write it up in tomorrow's columns. He was giving his time and his talent for nothing more than bringing happiness. Or perhaps more accurately, she thought, relieving unhappiness.

That was the moment, though she didn't realize it, when Ryan fell in love.

She watched as he slipped a ball in and out of his fingers with continual motion. Ryan was as fascinated as the children. With a quick movement of his hand, the ball vanished, only to be plucked from the ear of a boy who squealed in delight.

His illusions were unsophisticated, flashy little bits of business an amateur could have performed. The ward was noisy with gasps and giggles and applause. It obviously meant more to Pierce than the thundering approval he heard on stage after a complicated feat of magic. His roots were there, among children. He had never forgotten it. He remembered too well the antiseptic and floral smell of a sick room and the confinement of a hospital bed. Boredom, he thought, could be the most debilitating disease there.

"You'll notice I brought along a beautiful assistant," Pierce pointed out. It took Ryan a moment to realize he meant her. Her eyes widened in astonishment, but he only smiled. "No magician travels without one. Ryan." He held out a hand, palm up. Amid giggles and applauses, she had no choice but to join him.

"What are you doing?" she demanded in a quick whisper.

"Making you a star," he said easily before turning back to the audience of children in beds and wheelchairs. "Ryan will tell you she keeps her lovely smile by drinking three glasses of milk every day. Isn't that so, Ryan?"

"Ah—yes." She glanced around at the expectant faces. "Yes, that's right." *What is he doing?* She'd never had so many large, curious eyes on her at one time.

"I'm sure everyone here knows how important it is to drink milk."

This was answered by some unenthusiastic agreements and a few muffled moans. Pierce looked surprised as he reached in his black bag and pulled out a glass already half-filled with white liquid. No one questioned why it hadn't spilled. "You do all drink milk, don't you?" He got laughter this time, along with more moans. Shaking his head, Pierce pulled out a newspaper and began to fashion it into a funnel. "This is a very tricky business. I don't know if I can make it work unless everyone promises to drink his milk tonight."

Immediately a chorus of promises sprang out. Ryan saw that he was as much Pied Piper as magician, as much psychologist as entertainer. Perhaps it was all the same. She noticed that Pierce was watching her with a lifted brow.

"Oh, I promise," she said agreeably and smiled. She was as entranced as the children.

"Let's see what happens," he suggested. "Do you suppose you could pour the milk from that glass into here?" he asked Ryan, handing her the glass. "Slowly," he warned, winking at the audience. "We wouldn't want to spill it. It's magic milk, you know. The only kind magicians drink." Pierce took her hand and guided it, holding the top of the funnel just above her eye level.

His palm was warm and firm. There hung about him some scent she couldn't place. It was of the outdoors, of the forest. Not pine, she decided, but something darker, deeper, closer to the earth. Her response to it was unexpected and unwanted. She tried to concentrate on holding the glass directly above the opening of the funnel. A few drops of milk dripped out of the bottom.

"Where do you buy magic milk?" one of the children wanted to know.

"Oh, you can't buy it," Pierce said gravely. "I have to get up very early and put a spell on a cow. There, now, that's good." Smoothly, Pierce dropped the empty glass back into his bag. "Now, if all's gone well..." He stopped, then frowned into the funnel. "This was my milk, Ryan," he said with a hint of censure. "You could have had yours later."

As she opened her mouth to speak, he whipped the funnel open. Automatically, she gasped and stepped back to keep from being splashed. But the funnel was empty.

The children shrieked in delight as she gasped at him. "She's still beautiful," he told the audience as he kissed Ryan's hand. "Even if she is greedy."

"I poured that milk myself," she stated later as they walked down the hospital corridor to the elevator. "It was dripping through the paper. I *saw* it."

Pierce nudged her into the elevator. "The way things seem and the way things are. Fascinating, isn't it, Ryan?"

She felt the elevator begin its descent and stood in silence for a moment. "You're not entirely what you seem, either, are you?"

"No. Who is?"

"You did more for those kids in an hour than a dozen doctors could have done." He looked down at her as she continued. "And I don't think it's the first time you've done this sort of thing."

"No."

"Why?"

"Hospitals are a hell of a place to be when you're a child," he said simply. It was all the answer he would give her.

"They didn't think so today."

Pierce took her hand in his again when they reached the first level. "There's no tougher audience than children. They're very literal-minded."

Ryan had to laugh. "I suppose you're right. What

adult would have thought to ask you where you buy your magic milk?" She shot Pierce a look. "I thought you handled that one rather smoothly."

"I've had a bit of practice," he told her. "Kids keep you on your toes. Adults are more easily distracted by some clever patter and flash." He smiled down at her. "Even you. Though you watch me with very intriguing green eyes."

Ryan looked across the parking lot as they stepped outside. When he looked at her, it wasn't easy to focus on anything but him when he spoke. "Pierce, why did you ask me to come with you today?"

"I wanted your company."

Ryan turned back to him. "I don't think I understand."

"Do you have to?" he asked. In the sunlight her hair was the color of early wheat. Pierce ran his fingers through it, then framed her face with his hands as he had done that first night. "Always?"

Ryan's heart pounded in her throat. "Yes, I think…"

But his mouth was already on hers, and she could think no longer. It was just as it had been the first time. The gentle kiss drew everything from her. She felt a warm, fluttering ache pass through her as his fingers brushed her temple and then traveled to just under her heart. People walked by them, but she never knew. They were shadows, ghosts. The only things of substance were Pierce's mouth and hands.

Was it the wind she felt, or his fingers gliding over her skin? Did he murmur something, or had she?

Pierce drew her away. Ryan's eyes were clouded. They began to clear and focus as if she were coming out of a dream. He wasn't ready for the dream to end.

Bringing her back, he took her lips again and tasted the dark, mysterious flavor of her.

He had to fight with the need to crush her against him, to savage her warm, willing mouth. She was a woman made for a gentle touch. Desire tore at him, and he suppressed it. There were times when he was locked in a dark, airless box that he had to push back the need to rush, the urge to claw his way out. Now he almost felt the same hint of panic. *What was she doing to him?* The question ran through his mind even as he brought her closer. Pierce knew only that he wanted her with a desperation he hadn't thought himself capable of.

Was there silk next to her skin again? Thin, fragile silk lightly scented with the fragrance she wore? He wanted to make love to her by candlelight or in a field with the sun pouring over her. Dear God, how he wanted her.

"Ryan, I want to be with you." The words were whispered inside her mouth and made her tremble. "I need to be with you. Come with me now." With his hands he tilted her head to another angle and kissed her again. "Now, Ryan. Let me love you."

"Pierce." She was sinking and struggling to find solid ground. She leaned against him even as she shook her head. "I don't know you."

Pierce controlled a sudden wild desire to drag her to his car, to take her back to his home. To his bed. "No." He said it as much to himself as to Ryan. Drawing her away, he held her by the shoulders and studied her. "No, you don't. And Miss Swan would need to." He didn't like the erratic beating of his heart. Calm and control were intimate parts of his work, and therefore, of him. "When you know me," he told her quietly, "we'll be lovers."

"No." Ryan's objection sprang from his matter-of-fact tone, not from the statement. "No, Pierce, we won't be lovers unless it's what I want. I make deals on contracts, not in my personal life."

Pierce smiled, more relaxed with her annoyance than he would have been with malleability. Anything that came too easily he suspected. "Miss Swan," he murmured as he took her arm. "We've already seen the cards."

Chapter 6

Ryan arrived in Las Vegas alone. She had insisted on it. Once her nerves had settled and she had been able to think practically, she had decided it would be unwise to have too much personal contact with Pierce. When a man was able to make you forget the world around you with a kiss, you kept your distance. That was Ryan Swan's new rule.

Through most of her life she had been totally dominated by her father. She had been able to do nothing without his approval. He might not have given her his time, but he had always given her his opinion. And his opinion had been law.

It was only upon reaching her early twenties that Ryan had begun to explore her own talents, her own independence. The taste of freedom had been very sweet. She wasn't about to allow herself to be dominated again, certainly not by physical needs. She knew from experience that men weren't particularly trustworthy. Why should Pierce Atkins be any different?

After paying off the cab, Ryan took a moment to look around. It was her first trip to Vegas. Even at ten in the morning it was an eye-opener. The Strip stretched long in both directions, and lining it were names like The Dunes, The Sahara, The MGM. The hotels vied for attention with gushing fountains, elaborate neon and fabulous flowers.

Billboards announced famous names in huge letters. Stars, stars, stars! The most beautiful women in the world, the most talented performers, the most colorful, the most exotic—they were all here. Everything was packed together; an adult amusement park circled by desert and ringed by mountains. The morning sun baked the streets; at night the neon would light them.

Ryan turned and looked at Caesar's Palace. It was huge and white and opulent. Above her head in enormous letters was Pierce's name and the dates of his engagements. What sort of feeling did it give a man like him, she wondered, to see his name advertised so boldly?

She lifted her bags and took the moving walkway that would transport her past the glittering fountain and Italian statues. In the morning quiet she could hear the water spurt up and splash down. She imagined that at night the streets would be noisy, filled with cars and people.

The moment she entered the hotel lobby, Ryan heard the whirl and chink of the slot machines. She had to curb a desire to walk into the casino for a look instead of going to the front desk.

"Ryan Swan." She set down her suitcases at the foot of the long counter. "I have a reservation."

"Yes, Miss Swan." The desk clerk beamed at her without checking his files. "The bellboy will take your bags." He signaled, then handed a key to the answering bellboy. "Enjoy your stay, Miss Swan. Please let us know if there's anything we can do for you."

"Thank you." Ryan accepted the clerk's deference without a thought. When people knew she was Bennett Swan's daughter, they treated her like a visiting dignitary. It was nothing new and only mildly annoying.

The elevator took her all the way to the top floor with the bellboy keeping a respectful silence. He led the way down the corridor, unlocked the door, then stepped back to let her enter.

Ryan's first surprise was that it wasn't a room but a suite. Her second was that it was already occupied. Pierce sat on the sofa working with papers he had spread out on the table in front of him.

"Ryan." He rose, then, going to the bellboy, handed him a bill. "Thank you."

"Thank *you*, Mr. Atkins."

Ryan waited until the door shut behind him. "What are you doing here?" she demanded.

"I have a rehearsal scheduled this afternoon," he reminded her. "How was your flight?"

"It was fine," she told him, annoyed with his answer and with the suspicions that were creeping into her mind.

"Can I get you a drink?"

"No, thank you." She glanced around the well-appointed room, took a brief glimpse out the window, then gestured broadly. "What the hell is this?"

Pierce lifted a brow at her tone but answered mildly. "Our suite."

"Oh, no," she said with a definite shake of her head. "*Your* suite." Picking up her bags, she headed for the door.

"Ryan." It was the calm quality of his voice that stopped her—and that snapped her temper.

"What a very small, very dirty trick!" Ryan dropped her bags with a thud and turned on him. "Did you really think you could change my reservation and—and—"

"And what?" he prompted.

She gestured around the room again. "Set me up here with you without me making a murmur? Did you really think I'd pop cozily into your bed because you arranged it so nicely? How *dare* you! How dare you lie to me about needing me to watch you perform when all you wanted was for me to keep your bed warm!"

Her voice had changed from low accusation to high fury before Pierce grabbed her wrist. The strength in his fingers had her gasping in surprise and alarm. "I don't lie," Pierce said softly, but his eyes were darker than she had ever seen them. "And I don't need tricks to find a woman for my bed."

She didn't try to free herself. Instinct warned her against it, but she couldn't control her temper. "Then what do you call this?" she tossed back.

"A convenient arrangement." He felt her pulse racing under his fingers. Anger made his voice dangerously cool.

"For whom?" she demanded.

"We'll need to talk over a number of things in the next few days." He spoke with quiet deliberation, but his grip never slackened. "I don't intend to run down to your room every time I have something to say to you. I'm here to work," he reminded her. "And so are you."

"You should have consulted me."

"I didn't," he countered icily. "And I don't sleep with a woman unless she wants me to, Miss Swan."

"I don't appreciate you taking it upon yourself to change arrangements without discussing it with me first." Ryan stood firm on this, though her knees were threatening to tremble. His fury was all the more frightening in its restraint.

"I warned you before, I do things in my own way. If you're nervous, lock your door."

The jibe made her voice sharp. "A lot of good that would do with you. A lock would hardly keep you out."

His fingers tightened on her wrist quickly, painfully, before he tossed it aside. "Perhaps not." Pierce opened the door. "But a simple *no* would."

He was gone before Ryan could say any more. She leaned back against the door as the shudders ran through her. Until that moment she hadn't realized how badly she had been frightened. She was accustomed to dealing with histrionic bursts of temper or sulky silences from her father. But this…

There had been ice-cold violence in Pierce's eyes. Ryan would rather have faced the raging, shouting fury of any man than the look that could freeze her.

Without knowing she did so, Ryan rubbed her wrist. It throbbed lightly in each separate spot that Pierce's fingers had gripped. She had been right when she had said she didn't know him. There was more to him than she had ever guessed. Having uncovered one layer, she wasn't entirely certain she could deal with what she had discovered. For another moment she leaned against the door, waiting for the shaking to stop.

She looked around the room. Perhaps she had been wrong to have reacted so strongly to a harmless business arrangement, she finally decided. Sharing a suite was essentially the same thing as having adjoining rooms. If that had been the case, she would have thought nothing of it.

But he had been wrong, too, she reminded herself. They might have come to an easy agreement about the suite if he had only discussed it with her first. She had promised herself when she had left Switzerland that she would no longer be directed.

And Pierce's phrasing had worried her. *He didn't sleep with a woman unless she wanted him to.* Ryan was too aware that they both knew she wanted him.

A simple *no* would keep him out. Yes, she mused as she picked up her bags. That she could depend on. He would never force himself on any woman—very simply, he would have no need to. She wondered how long it would be before she forgot to say no.

Ryan shook her head. The project was as important to Pierce as it was to her. It wasn't smart to start off by bickering over sleeping arrangements or worrying about remote possibilities. She knew her own mind. She went to unpack.

When Ryan went down to the theatre, the rehearsal was already underway. Pierce held center stage. There was a woman with him. Even though she was dressed plainly in jeans and a bulky sweatshirt, Ryan recognized the statuesque redhead who was Pierce's assistant. On the tapes, Ryan recalled, she had worn brief, sparkling costumes or floaty dresses. *No magician travels without a beautiful assistant.*

Hold on, Ryan, she warned herself. No business of yours. Quietly, she walked down and took a seat in the center of the audience. Pierce never glanced in her direction. Hardly aware of what she did, Ryan began to think of camera angles and sets.

Five cameras, she thought, and nothing too showy in the background. Nothing glittery to pull attention away from him. Something dark, she decided. Something to enhance the image of wizard or warlock rather than showman.

It came as a complete surprise to her when Pierce's assistant drifted slowly backward until she was lying horizontally in thin air. Ryan stopped planning and watched. He used no patter now but only gestures—wide, sweeping gestures that brought black capes and candlelight to mind. The woman began revolving, slowly at first and then with greater speed.

Ryan had seen the illusion on tape, but seeing it in the flesh was a totally different experience. There were no props to distract from the two at stage center, no costumes, music or flashing lights to enhance the mood. Ryan discovered she was holding her breath and forced herself to let it out. The woman's cap of red curls fluttered as she spun. Her eyes were closed, her face utterly peaceful while her hands were folded neatly at her waist. Ryan watched closely, looking for wires, for gimmicks. Frustrated, she leaned forward.

She couldn't prevent a small gasp of appreciation as the woman began to roll over and over as she continued to spin. The calm expression on her face remained unchanged, as if she slept rather than whirled and circled three feet above the stage floor. With a gesture, Pierce stopped the motion, bringing her vertical again, slowly, until her feet touched the stage. When he passed his hand in front of her face, she opened her eyes and grinned.

"How was it?"

Ryan almost jolted at the commonplace words that bounced cheerfully off the theater walls.

"Good," Pierce said simply. "It'll be better with the music. I want red lights, something hot. Start soft and then build with the speed." He gave these orders to the lighting director before turning back to his assistant. "We'll work on the transportation."

For an hour Ryan watched, fascinated, frustrated and undeniably entertained. What seemed to her flawless, Pierce repeated again and again. With each illusion, he had his own ideas of the technical effects he wanted. Ryan could see that his creativity didn't stop at magic. He knew how to use lighting and sound to enhance, accent, underline.

A perfectionist, Ryan noted. He worked quietly, without the dynamics he exuded in a performance. Nor was there the careless ease about him she had seen when he had entertained the children. He was working. It was a plain and simple fact. A wizard, perhaps, she mused with a smile, but one who pays his dues with long hours and repetition. The longer she watched, the more respect she felt.

Ryan had wondered what it would be like to work with him. Now she saw. He was relentless, tireless and as fanatical about details as she was herself. They were going to argue, she predicted and began to look forward to it. It was going to be one hell of a show.

"Ryan, would you come up, please?"

She was startled when he called her. Ryan would have sworn he hadn't known she was in the theater. Fatalistically, she rose. It was beginning to appear that there was nothing he didn't know. As Ryan came forward, Pierce said something to his assistant. She gave a quick, lusty laugh and kissed him on the cheek.

"At least I get to stay all in one piece on this run," she told him, then turned to grin at Ryan as she mounted the stage.

"Ryan Swan," Pierce said, "Bess Frye."

On closer study Ryan saw the woman wasn't a beauty. Her features were too large for classic beauty. Her hair was brilliantly red and cropped into curls around a large-boned face. Her eyes were almost round and shades darker than Ryan's green. Her make-up was as exotic as her clothes were casual, and she was nearly as tall as Pierce.

"Hi!" There was a burst of friendliness in the one word. Bess extended her hand to give Ryan's an enthusiastic shake. It was hard to believe that the woman, as solid as a redwood, had been spinning three feet above the stage. "Pierce has told me all about you."

"Oh?" Ryan glanced over at him.

"Oh, yeah." She rested an elbow on his shoulder as she spoke to Ryan. "Pierce thinks you're real smart. He likes the brainy type, but he didn't say you were so pretty. How come you didn't tell me she was so pretty, sweetie?" It didn't take Ryan long to discover that Bess habitually spoke in long, explosive bursts.

"And have you accuse me of seeing a woman only as a stage prop?" He dipped his hands into his pockets.

Bess gave another burst of lusty laughter. "He's smart,

too," she confided to Ryan, giving Pierce a squeeze. "You're going to be the producer on this special?"

"Yes." A little dazed by the overflowing friendliness, Ryan smiled. "Yes, I am."

"Good. About time we had a woman running things. I'm surrounded by men in this job, sweetie. Only one woman in the road crew. We'll have a drink sometime soon and get acquainted."

Buy you a drink, sweetie? Ryan remembered. Her smile became a grin. "I'd like that."

"Well, I'm going to see what Link's up to before the boss decides to put me back to work. See you later." Bess strode off stage—six feet of towering enthusiasm. Ryan watched her all the way.

"She's wonderful," Ryan murmured.

"I've always thought so."

"She seems so cool and reserved on stage." Ryan smiled up at Pierce. "Has she been with you long?"

"Yes."

The warmth Bess had brought was rapidly fading. Clearing her throat, Ryan began again. "The rehearsal went very well. We'll have to discuss which illusions you plan to incorporate into the special and whatever new ones you intend to develop."

"All right."

"There'll have to be some adjustments, naturally, for television," she continued, trying to overlook his mono-syllabic responses. "But basically I imagine you want a condensed version of your club act."

"That's right."

In the short time Ryan had known Pierce, she had come to learn he possessed a natural friendliness and humor. Now he was looking at her with his eyes guarded, obviously impatient for her to leave. The apology she had planned couldn't be made to this man.

"I'm sure you're busy," she said stiffly and turned away. It hurt, she discovered, to be shut out. He had no right to hurt her. Ryan left the stage without looking back.

Pierce watched her until the doors at the back of the theatre swung shut behind her. With his eyes still on the door, he crushed the ball he held in his hand until it was flat. He had very strong fingers, strong enough to have snapped the bones of her wrist instead of merely bruising it.

He hadn't liked seeing those bruises. He didn't like remembering how she had accused him of trying to take her by deceit. He had never had to take any woman by deceit. Ryan Swan would be no different.

He could have had her that first night with the storm raging outside and her body pressed close to his.

And why didn't I? he demanded of himself and tossed the mangled ball aside. Why hadn't he taken her to bed and done all the things he had so desperately wanted to do? Because she had looked up at him with her eyes full of panic and acceptance. She had been vulnerable. He had realized, with something like fear, that he had been vulnerable, too. And still she haunted his mind.

When she had walked into the suite that morning, Pierce had forgotten the careful notes he had been making on a new illusion. He had seen her, walking in wearing one of those damn tailored suits, and he had forgotten everything. Her hair had been windblown from the drive, like the first time he had seen her. And all he had wanted to do was hold her—to feel the small, soft body yield against his.

Perhaps his anger had started to grow even then, to fire up with her words and accusing eyes.

He shouldn't have hurt her. Pierce stared down at his empty hands and swore. He had no right to mark her skin—the ugliest thing a man could do to a woman. She was weaker than he, and he had used that—used his temper and his strength, two things he had promised himself long, long ago he would never use on a woman. In his mind no provocation could justify it. He could blame no one but himself for the lapse.

He couldn't dwell on it or on Ryan any longer and continue to work. He needed his concentration. The only thing to do was to put their relationship back where Ryan had wanted it from the beginning. They would work together successfully, and that would be all. He had learned to control his body through his mind. He could control his needs, his emotions, the same way.

With a final oath Pierce walked back to talk with his road crew about props.

Chapter 7

Las Vegas was difficult to resist. Inside the casinos it was neither day nor night. Without clocks and with the continual clinking of slots, there was a perpetual time-lessness, an intriguing disorientation. Ryan saw people in evening dress continuing a night's gambling into late morning. She watched thousands of dollars change hands at the blackjack and baccarat tables. More than once she held her breath while the roulette wheel spun with a small fortune resting on the caprices of the silver ball.

She learned that the fever came in many forms—cool, dispassionate, desperate, intense. There was the woman feeding the nickel slot machine and the dedicated player tossing the dice. Smoke hung in the air over the sounds of winning and of losing. The faces would change, but the mood remained. Just one more roll of the dice, one more pull of the lever.

The years in the prim Swiss school had cooled the gambling blood Ryan had inherited from her father. Now, for the first time, Ryan felt the excitement of the urge to test Lady Luck. She refused it, telling herself she was content to watch. There was little else for her to do.

She saw Pierce onstage at rehearsals and hardly at all otherwise. It was amazing to her that two people could share a suite and so rarely come into contact with each other. No matter how early she rose, he was already gone. Once or twice after she was long in bed, Ryan heard the quick click of the lock on the front door. When they spoke, it was only to discuss ideas on how to alter his club act for television. Their conversations were calm and technical.

He's trying to avoid me, she thought the night of his opening performance, and doing a damn good job of it. If he had wanted to prove that sharing a suite meant nothing personal, he had succeeded beautifully. That, of course, was what she wanted, but she missed the easy camaraderie. She missed seeing him smile at her.

Ryan decided to watch the show from the wings. There she would have a perfect view and be in a position to note Pierce's timing and style while getting a backstage perspective. Rehearsals had given her an insight into his work habits, and now she would watch him perform from as close to his point of view as she could manage. She wanted to see more than the audience or a camera would see.

Careful to stay out of the way of the stagehands and grips, Ryan settled herself into a corner and watched. From the first wave of applause as he was introduced, Pierce had his audience in the palm of his hand. *My God, he's beautiful!* she thought as she studied his style and flare. Dynamic, dramatic, his personality alone would have held the audience. The charisma he possessed was no illusion but as integral a part of him as the color of his hair. He dressed in black, as was his habit, needing no brilliant colors to keep eyes glued to him.

He spoke as he performed. Patter, he would have called it, but it was much more. He tuned the mood with words and cadence. He could string them along, then dazzle them completely—a shot of flame from his naked palm, a glittering silver pendulum that swung, unsupported, in thin air. He was no longer pragmatic, as he had been in rehearsals, but dark and mysterious.

Ryan watched as he was padlocked into a duffel bag, slipped into a chest and chained inside. Standing on it, Bess pulled up a curtain and counted to twenty. When the curtain dropped, Pierce himself stood on the chest in a complete costume change. And, of course, when he unlocked the chest and bag, Bess was inside. He called it transportation. Ryan called it incredible.

His escapes made her uneasy. Watching volunteers from the audience nail him into a sturdy packing crate she herself had examined had her palms dampening. She could imagine him in the dark, airless box and feel her own breath clogging in her lungs. But his freedom was accomplished in less than two minutes.

For the finale, he locked Bess in a cage, curtaining it and levitating it to the ceiling. When he brought it down moments later, there was a sleek young panther in her place. Watching him, seeing the intensity of his eyes, the mysterious hollows and shadows on his face, Ryan almost believed he had transcended the laws of nature. For that moment before the curtain came down, the panther was Bess and he was more enchanter than showman.

Ryan wanted to ask him, convince him to explain just this one illusion in terms she could understand. When he came offstage and their eyes held, she swallowed the words.

His face was damp from the lights and his own concentration. She wanted to touch him, finding, to her own astonishment, that watching him perform had aroused her. The drive was more basic and more powerful than anything she had ever experienced. She could imagine him taking her with his strong, clever hands. Then his mouth, his impossibly sensual mouth, would be on hers, taking her to that strange, weightless world he knew. If she went to him now—offered, demanded—would she find him as hungry as herself? Would he say nothing, only lead her away to show her his magic?

Pierce stopped in front of her, and Ryan stepped back, shaken by her own thoughts. Her blood was heated, churning under her skin, demanding that she make the move toward him. Aware, aroused but unwilling, she kept her distance.

"You were marvelous," she said but heard the stiffness in the compliment.

"Thank you." Pierce said nothing more as he moved past her.

Ryan felt pain in her palms and discovered she was digging her nails into her flesh. This has got to stop, she told herself and turned to go after him.

"Hey, Ryan!" She stopped as Bess poked her head out of her dressing room. "What did you think of the show?"

"It was wonderful." She glanced down the corridor; Pierce was already out of reach. Perhaps it was for the best. "I don't suppose you'd let me in on the secret of the finale?" she asked.

Bess laughed. "Not if I value my life, sweetie. Come on in; talk to me while I change."

Ryan obliged, closing the door behind her. The air tingled with the scents of greasepaint and powder. "It must be quite an experience, being turned into a panther."

"Oh, Lord, Pierce has turned me into everything imaginable that walks, crawls or flies; he's sawed me to pieces and balanced me on swords. In one gag he had me sleeping on a bed of nails ten feet above the stage." As she spoke, she stripped out of her costume with no more modesty than a five-year-old.

"You must trust him," Ryan commented as she looked around for an empty chair. Bess had a habit of strewing her things over all available space.

"Just toss something out of your way," she suggested as she plucked a peacock blue robe from the arm of a chair. "Trust Pierce?" she continued as she belted the robe. "He's the best." Sitting at the vanity, she began to cream off her stage make-up. "You saw how he is at rehearsals."

"Yes." Ryan folded a crumpled blouse and set it aside. "Exacting."

"That's not the half of it. He works out his illusions on paper, then goes over them again and again in that dungeon of his before he even thinks about showing anything to me or Link." She looked at Ryan with one eye heavily mascaraed and the other naked. "Most people don't know how hard he works because he makes it look so easy. That's the way he wants it."

"His escapes," Ryan began as she straightened Bess's clothes. "Are they dangerous?"

"I don't like some of them." Bess tissued off the last of the cream. Her exotic face was unexpectedly young and fresh. "Getting out of manacles and a straightjacket is one thing." She shrugged as she rose. "But I've never liked it when he does his version of Houdini's Water Torture or his own A Thousand Locks."

"Why does he do it, Bess?" Ryan set a pair of jeans aside but continued to roam the room restlessly. "His illusions would be enough."

"Not for Pierce." Bess dropped the robe, then snapped on a bra. "The escapes and the danger are important to him. They always have been."

"Why?"

"Because he wants to test himself all the time. He's never satisfied with what he did yesterday."

"Test himself," Ryan murmured. She had sensed this herself but was a long way from understanding it. "Bess, how long have you been with him?"

"Since the beginning," Bess told her as she tugged on jeans. "Right from the beginning."

"Who is he?" Ryan demanded before she could stop herself. "Who is he really?"

With a shirt hanging from her fingertips, Bess gave Ryan a sudden, penetrating glance. "Why do you want to know?"

"He…" Ryan stopped, not knowing what to say. "I don't know."

"Do you care about him?"

Ryan didn't answer at once. She wanted to say no and shrug it off. She had no reason to care. "Yes, I do," she heard herself say. "I care about him."

"Let's go have a drink," Bess suggested and pulled on her shirt. "We'll talk."

"Champagne cocktails," Bess ordered when they slipped into a booth in the lounge. "I'm buying." She pulled out a cigarette and lit it. "Don't tell Pierce," she added with a wink. "He frowns on the use of tobacco. He's a fanatic about body care."

"Link told me he runs five miles every day."

"An old habit. Pierce rarely breaks old habits." Bess drew in smoke with a sigh. "He's always been really determined, you know? You could see it, even when he was a kid."

"You knew Pierce when he was a boy?"

"We grew up together—Pierce, Link and me." Bess glanced up at the waitress when their cocktails were served. "Run a tab," she directed and looked back at Ryan. "Pierce doesn't talk about back then, not even to Link or me. He's shut it off—or tried to."

"I thought he was trying to promote an image," Ryan murmured.

"He doesn't need to."

"No." Ryan met her eyes again. "I suppose he doesn't. Did he have a difficult childhood?"

"Oh, boy." Bess took a long drink. "And then some. He was a real puny kid."

"Pierce?" Ryan thought of the hard, muscled body and stared.

"Yeah." Bess gave a muffled version of her full-throated laugh. "Hard to believe, but true. He was small for his age, skinny as a rail. The bigger kids tormented him. They needed someone to pick on, I guess. Nobody likes growing up in an orphanage."

"Orphanage?" Ryan pounced on the last word. Studying Bess's open, friendly face, she felt a flood of sympathy. "All of you?"

"Oh, hell." Bess shrugged. Ryan's eyes were full of eloquent distress. "It wasn't so bad, really. Food, a roof over your head, plenty of company. It's not like you read about in that book, that *Oliver Twist*."

"Did you lose your parents, Bess?" Ryan asked with interest rather than the sympathy she saw was unwanted.

"When I was eight. There wasn't anybody else to take me. It was the same with Link." She continued with no trace of self-pity or regret. "People want to adopt babies, mostly. Older kids aren't placed so easily."

Lifting her drink, Ryan sipped thoughtfully. It would have been twenty years ago, before the current surge of interest in adoptable children. "What about Pierce?"

"Things were different with him. He had parents. They wouldn't sign, so he was unadoptable."

Ryan's brows creased with confusion. "But if he had parents, what was he doing in an orphanage?"

"Courts took him away from them. His father…" Bess let out a long stream of smoke. She was taking a chance, talking like this. Pierce wasn't going to like it if he found out. She could only hope it paid off. "His father used to beat his mother."

"Oh, my God!" Ryan's horrified eyes clung to Bess's. "And—and Pierce?"

"Now and again," Bess answered calmly. "But mostly his mother. First he'd hit the booze, then he'd hit his wife."

A surge of raw pain spread in the pit of her stomach. Ryan lifted her drink again. Of course she knew such things happened, but her world had always been so shielded. Her own parents might have ignored her a great deal of her life, but neither had ever lifted a hand to her. True, her father's shouting had been frightening at times, but it had never gone beyond a raised voice and impatient words. She had never dealt with physical violence of any sort firsthand. Though she tried to conceive the kind of ugliness Bess was calmly relating, it was too distant.

"Tell me," she asked finally. "I want to understand him."

It was what Bess wanted to hear. She gave Ryan a silent vote of approval and continued. "Pierce was five. This time his father beat his mother badly enough to put her in the hospital. Usually, he locked Pierce in a closet before he started on one of his rages, but this time he knocked him around a little first."

Ryan controlled the need to protest what she was hearing but kept silent. Bess watched her steadily as she spoke. "That's when the social workers took over. After the usual paperwork and court hearings, his parents were judged unfit, and he was placed in the orphanage."

"Bess, his mother." Ryan shook her head, trying to think it through. "Why didn't she leave his father and take Pierce with her? What kind of woman would—"

"I'm not a psychiatrist," Bess interrupted. "As far as Pierce ever knew, she stayed with his father."

"And gave up her child," Ryan murmured. "He must have felt so completely rejected, so frightened and alone."

What sort of damage does that do to a small mind? she wondered. What sort of compensations does a child like that make? Did he escape from chains and trunks and safes because he had once been a small boy locked in a dark closet? Did he continually seek to do the impossible because he had once been so helpless?

"He was a loner," Bess continued as she ordered another round. "Maybe that's one of the reasons the other kids tormented him. At least until Link came." Bess grinned, enjoying this part of her memories. "Nobody ever touched Pierce when Link was in sight. He's always been twice as big as anyone else. And that face!"

She laughed again, but there was nothing callous in the sound. "When Link first came, none of the other kids would go near him. Except Pierce. They were both outcasts. So was I. Link's been attached to Pierce ever since. I really don't know what might have happened to him without Pierce. Or to me."

"You really love him, don't you?" Ryan asked, drawn close in spirit to the large, exuberant redhead.

"He's my best friend," Bess answered simply. "They let me into their little club when I was ten." She smiled over the rim of her glass. "I saw Link coming and climbed up a tree. He scared me to death. We called him the Missing Link."

"Children can be cruel."

"You betcha. Anyway, just as he was passing underneath, the branch broke and I fell out. He caught me." She leaned forward, cupping her chin on her hands. "I'll never forget that. One minute I'm falling a mile a minute, and the next he's holding me. I looked up at that face and got ready to scream blue blazes. Then he laughed. I fell in love on the spot."

Ryan swallowed champagne quickly. There was no mistaking the dreamy look in Bess's eyes. "You—you and Link?"

"Well, me, anyway," Bess said ruefully. "I've been nuts about the big lug for twenty years. He still thinks I'm Little Bess. All six feet of me." She grinned and winked. "But I'm working on him."

"I thought you and Pierce…" Ryan began, then trailed off.

"Me and Pierce?" Bess let loose with one of her lusty

laughs, causing heads to turn. "Are you kidding? You know enough about show business to cast better than that, sweetie. Do I look like Pierce's type?"

"Well, I..." Embarrassed by Bess's outspoken humor, Ryan shrugged. "I wouldn't have any idea what his type would be."

Bess laughed into her fresh drink. "You look smarter than that," she commented. "Anyway, he was always a quiet kid, always—what's the word?" Her forehead furrowed in thought. "Intense, you know? He had a temper." Grinning again, she rolled her eyes. "He gave a black eye for every one he got in the early days. But as he got older, he'd hold back. It was pretty clear he'd made up his mind not to follow in his old man's footsteps. When Pierce makes up his mind, that's it."

Ryan remembered the cold fury, the iced-over violence, and began to understand.

"When he was about nine, I guess, he had this accident." Bess drank, then scowled. "At least that's what he called it. He went head first down a flight of stairs. Everybody knew he'd been pushed, but he'd never say who. I think he didn't want Link to do something he could have gotten in trouble for. The fall hurt his back. They didn't think he'd walk again."

"Oh, no!"

"Yeah." Bess took another long drink. "But Pierce said he was going to walk. He was going to run five miles every day of his life."

"Five miles," Ryan murmured.

"He was determined. He worked at therapy like his life depended on it. Maybe it did," she added thoughtfully. "Maybe it did. He spent six months in the hospital."

"I see." She was seeing Pierce in the pediatric ward,

giving himself to children, talking to them, making them laugh. Bringing them magic.

"While he was in, one of the nurses gave him a magic set. That was it." Bess toasted with her glass. "A five-dollar magic set. It was like he'd been waiting for it, or it was waiting for him. By the time he got out, he could do things a lot of guys in the club field have trouble with." Love and pride mingled in her voice. "He was a natural."

Ryan could see him, a dark, intense boy in a white hospital bed, perfecting, practicing, discovering.

"Listen," Bess laughed again and leaned forward. Ryan's eyes were speaking volumes. "Once when I visited him in the hospital, he set the sheet on fire." She paused as Ryan's expression became one of horror. "I swear, I *saw* it burning. Then he patted it with his hand." She demonstrated with her palm on the table. "Smoothed it out, and there was nothing. No burn, no hole, not even a singe. The little creep scared me to death."

Ryan found herself laughing despite the ordeal he must have experienced. He'd beaten it. He'd won. "To Pierce," she said and lifted her glass.

"Damn right." Bess touched rims before she tossed off the champagne. "He took off when he was sixteen. I missed him like crazy. I never thought I'd see him or Link again. I guess it was the loneliest two years of my life. Then, one day I was working in this diner in Denver, and he walks in. I don't know how he found me, he never said, but he walks in and tells me to quit. I was going to go work for him."

"Just like that?" Ryan demanded.

"Just like that."

"What did you say?"

"I didn't say anything. It was Pierce." With a smile, Bess signaled the waitress again. "I quit. We went on the road. Drink up, sweetie, you're one behind."

Ryan studied her a moment, then obliged by finishing off her drink. It wasn't every man who could command that sort of unquestioning loyalty from a strong woman. "I usually stop at two," Ryan told her, indicating the cocktail.

"Not tonight," Bess announced. "I always drink champagne when I get sentimental. You wouldn't believe some of the places we played those first years," she went on. "Kids' parties, stag parties, the works. Nobody handles a rowdy crowd like Pierce. When he looks at a guy, then whips a fireball out of his pocket, the guy quiets down."

"I imagine so," Ryan agreed and laughed at the image. "I'm not even sure he'd need the fireball."

"You got it," Bess said, pleased. "Anyway, he always knew he was going to make it, and he took Link and me along. He didn't have to. That's just the kind of man he is. He doesn't let many people in close, but the ones he does, it's forever." She stirred the champagne quietly a moment. "I know Link and me could never keep up with him up here, you know?" Bess tapped her temple. "But it doesn't matter to Pierce. We're his friends."

"I think," Ryan said slowly, "he chooses his friends very well."

Bess sent her a brilliant smile. "You're a nice lady, Ryan. A real lady, too. Pierce is the kind of man who needs a lady."

Ryan became very interested in the color of her drink. "Why do you say that?"

"Because he has class, always has. He needs a classy woman and one who's warm like he is."

"Is he warm, Bess?" Ryan's eyes came back up, searching. "Sometimes he seems so...distant."

"You know where he got that stupid cat?" Ryan shook her head at the question. "Somebody'd hit it and left it on the side of the road. Pierce was driving back after a week's run in San Francisco. He stopped and took it to the vet. Two o'clock in the morning, and he's waking up the vet and making him operate on some stray cat. Cost him three hundred dollars. Link told me." She pulled out another cigarette. "How many people you know who'd do that?"

Ryan looked at her steadily. "Pierce wouldn't like it if he knew you'd told me all this, would he?"

"No."

"Why have you?"

Bess flashed her a smile again. "It's a trick I learned from him over the years. You look dead in somebody's eyes and you know if you can trust them."

Ryan met the look and spoke seriously. "Thank you."

"And," Bess added casually as she downed more champagne, "you're in love with him."

The words Ryan had begun to say jammed in her throat. She began coughing fitfully.

"Drink up, sweetie. Nothing like love to make you choke. Here's to it." She clinked her glass against Ryan's. "And good luck to both of us."

"Luck?" Ryan said weakly.

"With men like those two, we need it."

This time Ryan signaled for another round.

Chapter 8

When Ryan walked through the casino with Bess, she was laughing. The wine had lifted her mood, but more, Bess's company had cheered her. Since she had returned from school, Ryan had given herself little time to develop friendships. Finding one so quickly took her higher than the champagne.

"Celebrating?"

Both of them looked up and spotted Pierce. In unison, their faces registered the abashed guilt of children caught with one hand in the cookie jar. Pierce's brow lifted. With a laugh, Bess leaned over and kissed him enthusiastically.

"Just a little girl talk, sweetie. Ryan and I found out we have a lot in common."

"Is that so?" He watched as Ryan pressed her fingers to her mouth to stifle a giggle. It was apparent they'd had more than talk.

"Isn't he terrific when he's all serious and dry?" Bess asked Ryan. "Nobody does it better than Pierce." She kissed him again. "I didn't get your lady drunk, just maybe a little looser than she's used to. Besides, she's a big girl." Still resting her hand on his shoulder, Bess looked around. "Where's Link?"

"Watching the keno board."

"See you later." She gave Ryan a wink and was off.

"She's crazy about him, you know," Ryan said confidentially.

"Yes, I know."

She took a step closer. "Is there anything you don't know, Mr. Atkins?" She watched his lips curve at her emphasis on his surname. "I wondered if you'd ever do that for me again."

"Do what?"

"Smile. You haven't smiled at me in days."

"Haven't I?" He couldn't stop the surge of tenderness but contented himself with brushing the hair back from her face.

"No. Not once. Are you sorry?"

"Yes." Pierce steadied her with a hand on her shoulder and wished she wouldn't look at him in quite that way. He had managed to back down on needs while sharing the same set of rooms with her. Now, surrounded by noise and people and lights, he felt the force of desire building. He removed his hand. "Would you like me to take you upstairs?"

"I'm going to play blackjack," she informed him grandly. "I've wanted to for days, but I kept remembering gambling was foolish. I've just forgotten that."

Pierce held her arm as she started to walk to the table. "How much money do you have on you?"

"Oh, I don't know." Ryan rummaged in her purse. "About seventy-five dollars."

"All right." If she lost, Pierce decided, seventy-five would put no great hole in her bank account. He went with her.

"I've been watching this for days," she whispered as she took a seat at a ten-dollar table. "I've got it all figured out."

"Doesn't everyone?" he muttered and stood beside her. "Give the lady twenty dollars worth of chips," he told the dealer.

"Fifty," Ryan corrected, counting out bills.

With a nod from Pierce, the dealer exchanged the bills for colored chips.

"Are you going to play?" Ryan asked him.

"I don't gamble."

She lifted her brows. "What do you call being nailed inside a packing crate?"

He gave her one of his slow smiles. "My profession."

She laughed and sent him a teasing grin. "Do you disapprove of gambling and other vices, Mr. Atkins?"

"No." He felt another leap of desire and controlled it. "But I like to figure my own odds." He nodded as the cards were dealt. "It's never easy to beat the house at its own game."

"I feel lucky tonight," she told him.

The man beside Ryan swirled a bourbon and signed his name on a sheet of paper. He had just dropped over two thousand dollars. Philosophically, he bought another five thousand dollars worth of chips. Ryan watched a diamond glitter on his pinky as the cards were dealt. A triple deck, she remembered and lifted the tips of her own cards carefully. She saw an eight and a five. A young blonde in a black Halston took a hit and busted on twenty-three. The man with the diamond held on eighteen. Ryan took a hit and was pleased with another five. She held, then waited patiently as two more players took cards.

The dealer turned over fourteen, flipped over his next card and hit twenty. The man with the diamond swore softly as he lost another five hundred dollars.

Ryan counted her next cards, watched the hits and lost again. Undaunted, she waited for her third deal. She drew seventeen. Before she could signal the dealer she would hold, Pierce nodded for the hit.

"Wait a minute," Ryan began.

"Take it," he said simply.

With a huff and a shrug, she did. She hit twenty. Eyes wide, she swiveled in her chair to stare at him, but he was watching the cards. The dealer held on nineteen and paid her off.

"I won!" she exclaimed, pleased with the stack of chips pushed at her. "How did you know?"

He only smiled at her and continued to watch the cards.

On the next hand she drew a ten and a six. She would have taken the hit, but Pierce touched her shoulder and shook his head. Swallowing her protest, Ryan stayed pat. The dealer broke on twenty-two.

She laughed, delighted, but looked over at him again. "How do you do that?" she demanded. "It's a triple deck. You can't possibly remember all the cards dealt or figure what's left." He said nothing, and her brow creased. "Can you?"

Pierce smiled again and shook his head simply. Then he steered Ryan to another win.

"Want to take a look at mine?" the man with the diamond demanded, pushing aside his cards in disgust.

Ryan leaned toward him. "He's a sorcerer, you know. I take him everywhere."

The young blonde tucked her hair behind her ear. "I could use a spell or two myself." She sent Pierce a slow invitation. Ryan caught her eye as the cards were dealt.

"Mine," she said coolly and didn't see Pierce's brow go up. The blonde went back to her cards.

For the next hour Ryan's luck—or Pierce's—held. When the pile of chips in front of her had grown considerably, he opened her purse and swept them inside.

"Oh, but wait. I'm just getting started!"

"The secret of winning is knowing when to stop," Pierce told her and helped her off the stool. "Cash them in, Ryan, before you take it into your head to lose them at baccarat."

"But I did want to play," she began, casting a glance behind her.

"Not tonight."

With a heavy sigh she dumped the contents of her purse at the cashier's booth. Along with the chips was a comb, a lipstick and a penny that had been flattened by the wheel of a train.

"That's for luck," she said when Pierce picked it up to examine it.

"Superstition, Miss Swan," he murmured. "You surprise me."

"It's not superstition," she insisted, stuffing bills in her purse as the cashier counted them out. "It's for luck."

"I stand corrected."

"I like you, Pierce." Ryan linked her arm with his. "I thought I should tell you."

"Do you?"

"Yes," she said definitely. She could tell him that, she thought as they moved to the elevators. That was safe and certainly true. She wouldn't tell him what Bess had said so casually. *Love him?* No, that was far from safe, and it wasn't necessarily true. Even though...even though she was becoming more and more afraid it was.

"Do you like me?" Ryan turned to him and smiled as the elevator doors clicked shut.

"Yes, Ryan." He ran his knuckles over her cheek. "I like you."

"I wasn't sure." She stepped closer to him, and he felt a tingle race along his skin. "You've been angry with me."

"No, I haven't been angry with you."

She was staring up at him. Pierce could feel the air grow thick, as it did when the lid closed on him in a box or a trunk. His heart rate speeded up, and with sheer mental determination, he leveled it. He wasn't going to touch her again.

Ryan saw something flicker in his eyes. A hunger. Hers grew as well, but more, she felt a need to touch, to soothe. To love. She knew him now, though he was unaware of it. She wanted to give him something. She reached up to touch his cheek, but Pierce caught her fingers in his as the door opened.

"You must be tired," he said roughly and drew her into the corridor.

"No." Ryan laughed with the new sense of power. He was just a little afraid of her. She sensed it. Something shot into her—a combination of wine and winning and knowledge. And she wanted him.

"Are you tired, Pierce?" she asked when he unlocked the door to the suite.

"It's late."

"No. No, it's never late in Las Vegas." She tossed her purse aside and stretched. "There's no time here, don't you know? No clocks." Lifting her hair, she let it fall slowly through her fingers. "How can it be late when you don't know what time it is?" She spotted his papers on the table and crossed to them, kicking off her shoes as she went. "You work too much, Mr. Atkins." Laughing, she turned back to him. "Miss Swan's like that, isn't she?"

Her hair had tumbled over her shoulders, and her cheeks were flushed. Her eyes were alive, dancing, alluring. In them he saw that his thoughts were no secret to her. Desire was a hammer thrust in his stomach. Pierce said nothing.

"But you like Miss Swan," she murmured. "I don't always. Come sit down. Explain this to me." Ryan dropped to the couch and picked up one of his papers. It was covered with drawings and notes that made absolutely no sense to her.

Pierce moved then, telling himself it was only to keep her from disturbing his work. "It's too complicated." He took the sheet from her hand and set it back down.

"I've a very quick mind." Ryan pulled his arm until he sat beside her. She looked at him and smiled. "Do you know, the first time I looked into your eyes I thought my heart stopped." She put her hand to his cheek. "The first time you kissed me I knew it did."

Pierce caught her hand again, knowing he was close to the edge. Her free one ran up his shirtfront to his throat. "Ryan, you should go to bed."

She could hear the desire in his voice. Under her fingertip the pulse in his throat throbbed quickly. Her own heart began to match the rhythm. "No one's ever kissed me like that before," she murmured and slipped her fingers to the first button of his shirt. She freed it, watching his eyes. "No one's ever made me feel like that before. Was it magic, Pierce?" She loosened the second and third buttons.

"No." He reached up to stop the questing fingers that were driving him mad.

"I think it was." Ryan shifted and caught his earlobe lightly between her teeth. "I know it was." The whispering breath went straight to the pit of his stomach to stoke the flames. They flared high and threatened to explode. Catching her by the shoulders, Pierce started to draw her away, but her hands were on his naked chest. Her mouth brushed his throat. His fingers tightened as the tug of war went on inside him.

"Ryan." Though he concentrated, he couldn't steady his pulse. "What are you trying to do?"

"I'm trying to seduce you," she murmured, trailing her lips down to follow her fingers. "Is it working?"

Her hands ran down his rib cage to play lightly over his stomach. She felt the quiver of response and grew bolder.

"Yes, it's working very well."

Ryan laughed, a throaty, almost mocking sound that made his blood pound. Though he didn't touch her, he was no longer able to stop her from touching him. Her hands were soft and teasing while her tongue flicked lightly at his ear.

"Are you sure?" she whispered as she slipped his shirt from his shoulders. "Maybe I'm doing something wrong." She trailed her mouth to his chin, then let her tongue run briefly over his lips. "Maybe you don't want me to touch you like this." She ran a fingertip down the center of his chest to the waist of his jeans. "Or like this." She nipped his bottom lip, still watching his eyes.

No, she'd been wrong. They were black—black, not gray. Needs drove her until she thought she would be swallowed by them. Could it be possible to want so much? So much that your whole body ached and pounded and threatened to shatter?

"I wanted you when you walked offstage tonight," she said huskily. "Right then, while I still half-believed you were a wizard and not a man. And now." She ran her hands up his chest to link them behind his neck. "Now, knowing you're a man, I want you more." She let her eyes lower to his mouth, then lifted them back to his. "But maybe you don't want me. Maybe I don't… arouse you."

"Ryan." He'd lost the ability to control his pulse, his thoughts, his concentration. He'd lost the will to try to find it again. "There won't be any turning back in a moment."

She laughed, giddy with excitement, driven by desire. She let her lips hover a breath from his. "Promise?"

Ryan exulted in the power of the kiss. His mouth was on hers fiercely, painfully. She was under him with such speed, she never felt the movement, only his hard body on hers. He was pulling at her blouse, impatient with buttons. Two flew off to land somewhere on the carpet before his hand took her breast. Ryan moaned and arched against him, desperate to be touched. His tongue went deep to tangle with hers.

Desire was white-hot—flashes of heat, splashes of

color. Her skin was searing wherever he touched. She
was naked without knowing how she had become so,
and his bare flesh was melded to hers. His teeth were
on her breast, lightly at the edge of control, then his
tongue swept across her nipple until she moaned and
pressed closer.

Pierce could feel the hammer beat of her pulse, almost taste it as his mouth hurried to her other breast. Her
moans and her urging hands were driving him beyond
reason. He was trapped in a furnace, but there would
be no escape this time. He knew his flesh would melt
into hers until there was nothing left to keep him separate. The heat, her scent, her taste all whirled inside his
head. Excitement? No, this was more than excitement.
It was obsession.

He slipped his fingers inside her. She was so soft, so
warm and moist, he had no more will left.

He entered her with a wildness that stunned them
both. Then she was moving with him, frantic and strong.
He felt the pain of impossible pleasure, knowing he had
been the enchanted, not the enchanter. He was utterly
hers.

Ryan felt his ragged breath against her neck. His heart
was still racing. For me, she thought dreamily as she
floated on the aftermath of passion. *Mine,* she thought
again and sighed. How had Bess known before she had?
Ryan closed her eyes and let herself drift.

It must show on her face like a neon sign. Is it too
soon to tell him? she wondered. Wait, she decided,
touching his hair. She would let herself have time to
get used to love before she proclaimed it. At that moment she felt she had all the time in the world.

She gave a murmured protest when Pierce took his

weight from her. Slowly, she opened her eyes. He stared down at his hands. He was cursing himself steadily.

"Did I hurt you?" he demanded in a quick, rough burst.

"No," she said, surprised, then remembered Bess's story. "No, you didn't hurt me, Pierce. You couldn't. You're a very gentle man."

His eyes whipped back to hers, dark, anguished. There had been no gentleness in him when he had loved her. Only needs and desperation. "Not always," he said sharply and reached for his jeans.

"What are you doing?"

"I'll go down and get another room." He was dressing swiftly as she looked on. "I'm sorry this happened. I won't..." He stopped when he looked and saw tears welling in her eyes. Something ripped inside his stomach. "Ryan, I am sorry." Sitting beside her again, he brushed a tear away with his thumb. "I swore I wasn't going to touch you. I shouldn't have. You'd had too much to drink. I knew that and should've—"

"Damn you!" She slapped his hand away. "I was wrong. You *can* hurt me. Well, you don't have to get another room." She reached down for her blouse. "I'll get one myself. I won't stay here after you've turned something wonderful into a mistake."

She was up and tugging on her blouse, which was inside out.

"Ryan, I—"

"Oh, shut up!" Seeing the two middle buttons were missing, she tore the blouse off again and stood facing him, haughtily naked, eyes blazing. He nearly pulled her to the floor and took her again. "I knew exactly what I was doing, do you hear? Exactly! If you think it only takes a few drinks to make me throw myself at a man, then you're wrong. I wanted you, I thought you wanted me. So if it was a mistake, it was yours."

"It wasn't a mistake for me, Ryan." His voice had softened, but when he reached out to touch her, she jerked back. He let his hand drop to his side and chose his words carefully. "I wanted you; perhaps, I thought, too much. And I wasn't as gentle with you as I wanted to be. It's difficult for me to deal with knowing I couldn't stop myself from having you."

For a moment she studied him, then brushed tears away with the back of her hand. "Did you want to stop yourself?"

"The point is, I tried and couldn't. And I've never taken a woman with less..." He hesitated. "Care," he murmured. "You're very small, very fragile."

Fragile? she thought and lifted a brow. No one had ever called her that before. At another time she might have enjoyed it, but now she felt there was only one way to handle a man like Pierce. "Okay," she told him and took a deep breath. "You've got two choices."

Surprised, Pierce drew his brows together. "What are they?"

"You can get yourself another room or you can take me to bed and make love to me again." She took a step toward him. "Right now."

He met the challenge in her eyes and smiled. "Those are my only choices?"

"I suppose I could seduce you again if you want to be stubborn," she said with a shrug. "It's up to you."

He let his fingers dive into her hair as he drew her closer. "What if we combined two of those choices?"

She gave him a look of consideration. "Which two?"

He lowered his mouth to hers for a soft, lingering kiss. "How about I take you to bed and you seduce me?"

Ryan allowed him to lift her into his arms. "I'm a reasonable person," she agreed as he walked to the bedroom. "I'm willing to discuss a compromise as long as I get my own way."

"Miss Swan," Pierce murmured as he laid her gently on the bed, "I like your style."

Chapter 9

Ryan's body ached. Sighing, she snuggled deeper into the pillow. It was a pleasant discomfort. It reminded her of the night—the night that had lasted until dawn.

She hadn't known she had so much passion to give or so many needs to fill. Each time she had thought herself drained, body and mind, she had only to touch him again, or he her. Strength would flood back into her, and with it the unrelenting demands of desire.

Then they had slept, holding each other as the rosy tones of sunrise had slipped into the room. Drifting awake, clinging to sleep, Ryan shifted toward Pierce, wanting to hold him again.

She was alone.

Confusion had her eyes slowly opening. Sliding her hand over the sheets beside her, Ryan found them cold. *Gone?* she thought hazily. How long had she been sleeping alone? All of her dreamy pleasure died. Ryan touched the sheets again. No, she told herself and stretched, he's just in the other room. He wouldn't have left me alone.

The phone shrilled and jolted her completely awake.

"Yes, hello." She answered it on the first ring and pushed her hair from her face with her free hand. *Why was the suite so quiet?*

"Miss Swan?"

"Yes, this is Ryan Swan."

"Bennett Swan calling, please hold."

Ryan sat up, automatically pulling the sheets to her breast. Disoriented, she wondered what time it was. And where, she thought again, was Pierce?

"Ryan, give me an update."

An update? she repeated silently, hearing her father's voice. She struggled to put her thoughts into order.

"Ryan!"

"Yes, I'm sorry."

"I haven't got all day."

"I've watched Pierce's rehearsals daily," she began, wishing for a cup of coffee and a few moments to pull herself together. "I think you'll find he has the technical areas and his own crew well in hand." She glanced around the bedroom, looking for some sign of him. "He opened last night, flawlessly. We've already discussed some alterations for the special, but nothing's firmed up as yet. At this point whatever new routines he's worked out he's keeping to himself."

"I want some firm estimates on the set within two weeks," he told her. "We might have a change in the scheduling. You work it out with Atkins. I want a list of his proposed routines and the time allowance for each one."

"I've already discussed it with him," Ryan said coolly, annoyed that her father was infringing on her territory. "I am the producer, aren't I?"

"You are," he agreed. "I'll see you in my office when you get back."

Hearing the click, Ryan hung up with a sigh of exasperation. It had been a typical Bennett Swan conversation. She pushed the phone call from her mind and scrambled from the bed. Pierce's robe lay draped over a chair, and picking it up, Ryan slipped it on.

"Pierce?" Ryan hurried out into the living area of the suite but found it empty. "Pierce?" she called again, stepping on one of the lost buttons from her blouse. Absently, Ryan picked it up and dropped it in the pocket of the robe before she walked through the suite.

Empty. The pain started in her stomach and spread. He had left her alone. Shaking her head, Ryan searched the rooms again. He must have left her a note telling her why and where he'd gone. He wouldn't just wake up and leave her, not after last night.

But there was nothing. Ryan shivered, suddenly cold.

It was the pattern of her life, she decided. Moving to the window, she stared out at unlit neon. Whoever she cared for, whoever she gave love to, always went their own way. Yet somehow, she still expected it to be different.

When she had been small, it had been her mother, a young, glamour-loving woman jetting off to follow Bennett Swan all over the world. *You're a big girl, Ryan, and so self-sufficient. I'll be back in a few days.* Or a few weeks, Ryan remembered. There had always been a housekeeper and other servants to see that she was tended to. No, she had never been neglected or abused. Just forgotten.

Later it had been her father, dashing here and there at a moment's notice. But of course, he'd seen that she had had a solid, dependable nanny whom he had paid a very substantial salary. Then she'd been shipped off to Switzerland, the best boarding school available. *That daughter of mine has a head on her shoulders. Top ten percent of her class.*

There'd always been an expensive present on her birthday with a card from thousands of miles away telling her to keep up the good work. Of course, she had. She would never have risked disappointing him.

Nothing ever changes, Ryan thought as she turned to stare at herself in the mirror. Ryan's strong. Ryan's practical. Ryan doesn't need all the things other women do—hugs, gentleness, romance.

They're right, of course, she told herself. It's foolish to be hurt. We wanted each other. We spent the night together. Why romanticize it? I don't have any claim on Pierce. And he has none on me. She fingered the lapel of his robe, then quickly dropped her hand. Moving swiftly, Ryan stripped and went to shower.

Ryan kept the water almost unbearably hot, allowing it to beat full force against her skin. She wasn't going to think. She knew herself well. If she kept her mind a blank, when she opened it again, she'd know what she had to do.

The air in the bath was steamy and moist when she stepped out to towel herself. Her moves were brisk again. There was work to be done—notes to write on ideas and plans. Ryan Swan, Executive Producer. That's what she had to concentrate on. It was time to stop worrying about the people who couldn't—or wouldn't—give her what she wanted. She had a name to make for herself in the industry. That was all that really mattered.

As she dressed, she was perfectly calm. Dreams were for sleeping, and she was wide awake. There were dozens of details to be seen to. She had meetings to set up, department heads to deal with. Decisions had to be made. She had been in Las Vegas long enough. She knew Pierce's style as well as she ever would. And, more important to her at the moment, she knew precisely what she wanted in the finished product. Back in Los Angeles, Ryan could start putting her ideas into motion.

It was going to be her first production, but she'd be damned if it was going to be her last. This time she had places of her own to go to.

Ryan picked up her comb and ran it through her damp hair. The door opened behind her.

"So, you're awake." Pierce smiled and started to cross to her. The look in her eyes stopped him. Angry hurt—he could feel waves of it.

"Yes, I'm awake," she said easily and continued to comb her hair. "I've been up for some time. My father called earlier. He wanted a progress report."

"Oh?" Her emotions weren't directed toward her father, Pierce decided, watching her steadily. "Have you ordered anything from room service?"

"No."

"You'll want some breakfast," he said, taking another step toward her. He went no farther, feeling the wall she had thrown up between them.

"No, actually, I don't." Ryan took out her mascara and began to apply it with great care. "I'll get some coffee at the airport. I'm going back to L.A. this morning."

The cool, matter-of-fact tone had his stomach muscles tightening. Could he have been so wrong? Had the night they had shared meant so little to her? "This morning?" he repeated, matching her tone. "Why?"

"I think I have a fairly good handle on how you work and what you'll want for the special." She kept her eyes focused only on her own in the mirror. "I should start on the preliminary stages, then we can set up a meeting when you're back in California. I'll call your agent."

Pierce bit off the words he wanted to say. He never put chains on anyone but himself. "If that's what you want."

Ryan's fingers tightened on the tube of mascara before she set it down. "We both have our jobs to do. Mine's in L.A.; yours, for the moment, is here." She turned to go to the closet, but he laid a hand on her shoulder. Pierce dropped it immediately when she stiffened.

"Ryan, have I hurt you?"

"Hurt me?" she repeated and continued on to the closet. Her tone was like a shrug, but he couldn't see her eyes. "How could you have possibly hurt me?"

"I don't know." He spoke from directly behind her. Ryan pulled out an armful of clothes. "But I have." He turned her to face him. "I can see it in your eyes."

"Forget it," she told him. "I will." She started to walk away, but this time he kept his hands firm.

"I can't forget something unless I know what it is." Though he kept his hands light, annoyance had crept into his tone. "Ryan, tell me what's wrong."

"Drop it, Pierce."

"No."

Ryan tried to jerk away again, and again he held her still. She told herself to be calm. "You *left* me!" she exploded and tossed the clothes aside. The passion erupted from her so swiftly, it left him staring and speechless. "I woke up and you were gone, without a word. I'm not used to one-night stands."

His eyes kindled at that. "Ryan—"

"No, I don't want to hear it." She shook her head vigorously. "I expected something different from you. I was wrong. But that's all right. A woman like me doesn't need all the niceties. I'm an expert on surviving." She twisted but found herself held against him. "Don't! Let me go, I have to pack."

"Ryan." Even as she resisted, he held her closer. The hurt went deep, he thought, and hadn't started with him. "I'm sorry."

"I want you to let me go, Pierce."

"You won't listen to me if I do." He stroked a hand down her wet hair. "I need you to listen."

"There's nothing to say."

Her voice had thickened, and he felt a wicked stab of self-blame. How could he have been so stupid? How could he not have seen what would be important to her?

"Ryan, I know a lot about one-night stands." Pierce drew her away, just far enough so that he could see her eyes. "That isn't what last night was for me."

She shook her head fiercely, struggling for composure. "There's no need for you to say that."

"I told you once, I don't lie, Ryan." He slipped his hands up to her shoulders. "What we had together last night is very important to me."

"You were gone when I woke up." She swallowed and shut her eyes. "The bed was cold."

"I'm sorry. I went down to smooth out a few things before tonight's show."

"If you'd woke me—"

"I never thought to wake you, Ryan," he said quietly. "Just as I never thought how you might feel waking up alone. The sun was coming in when you fell asleep."

"You were up as long as I was." She tried to turn away again. "Pierce, *please!*" Hearing the desperation in the word, she bit her lip. "Let me go."

He lowered his hands, then watched as she gathered her clothes again. "Ryan, I never sleep more than five or six hours. It's all I need." Was this panic he was feeling watching her fold a blouse into a suitcase? "I thought you'd still be sleeping when I got back."

"I reached for you," she said simply. "And you were gone."

"Ryan—"

"No, it doesn't matter." She pressed her hands to her temples a moment and let out a deep breath. "I'm sorry. I'm acting like a fool. You haven't done anything, Pierce. It's me. I always expect too much. I'm always floored when I don't get it." Quickly, she began to pack again. "I didn't mean to make a scene. Please forget it."

"It isn't something I want to forget," he murmured.

"I'd feel less foolish if I knew you would," she said, trying to make her voice light. "Just put it down to a lack of sleep and a bad disposition. I should be going back, though. I've a lot of work to do."

He had seen her needs from the first—her response to gentleness, her pleasure in the gift of a flower. She was an emotional, romantic woman who tried very hard not to be. Pierce cursed himself, thinking how she must have felt to find the bed empty after the night they had spent together.

"Ryan, don't go." That was difficult for him. It was something he never asked of anyone.

Her fingers hesitated at the locks of her suitcase. Clicking them shut, Ryan set it on the floor, then turned. "Pierce, I'm not angry, honestly. A little embarrassed, maybe." She managed a smile. "I really should go back and start things moving. There might be a change in the scheduling, and—"

"Stay," he interrupted, unable to stop himself. "Please."

Ryan remained silent a moment. Something she saw in his eyes had a block lodging in her throat. It was costing him something to ask. Just as it was going to cost her something to ask. "Why?"

"I need you." He took a breath after what was for him a staggering admission. "I don't want to lose you."

Ryan took a step toward him. "Does it matter?"

"Yes. Yes, it matters."

She waited for a moment but was unable to convince herself to walk out the door. "Show me," she told him.

Going to her, he gathered her close. Ryan shut her eyes. It was exactly what she had needed—to be held, just to be held. His chest was firm against her cheek, his arms strong around her. Yet she knew she was being held as if she were something precious. Fragile, he had called her. For the first time in her life, Ryan wanted to be.

"Oh, Pierce, I'm an idiot."

"No." He lifted her chin with a finger and kissed her. "You're very sweet." He smiled then and laid his forehead on hers. "Are you going to complain when I wake you up after five hours sleep?"

"Never." Laughing, she threw her arms around his neck. "Or maybe just a little."

She smiled at him, but his eyes were suddenly serious. Pierce slid a hand up to cup the back of her neck before his mouth lowered to hers.

It was like the first time—the gentleness, the feather-light pressure that turned her blood to flame. She was utterly helpless when he kissed her like this, unable to pull him closer, unable to demand. She could only let him take in his own time.

Pierce knew that this time the power was his alone. It made his hands move tenderly as they undressed her. He let her blouse slip slowly off her shoulders, down her back, to flutter to the floor. Her skin quivered as his hands passed over it.

Unhooking her trousers, he drew them down her hips, letting his fingers toy with the tiny swatch of silk and lace that rose high at her thighs. All the while his mouth nibbled at hers. Her breath caught, then she moaned as he trailed a finger inside the silk. But he didn't remove it. Instead, he slid his hand to her breast to stroke and tease until she began to tremble.

"I want you," she said shakily. "Do you know how much I want you?"

"Yes." He brushed soft, butterfly kisses over her face. "Yes."

"Make love to me," Ryan whispered. "Pierce, make love to me."

"I am," he murmured and pressed his mouth to the frantic pulse in her neck.

"Now," she demanded, too weak to pull him to her.

He laughed, deep in his throat, and lowered her to the bed. "You drove me mad last night, Miss Swan, touching me like this." Pierce trailed a finger down the center of her body, stopping to linger at the soft mound between her legs. Slowly, lazily, he took his mouth to follow the trail.

In the night a madness had been on him. He had

known impatience, desperation. He had taken her again and again, passionately, but had been unable to savor. It was as though he had been starved, and greed had driven him. Now, though he wanted her no less, he could restrain the need. He could taste and sample and enjoy.

Ryan's limbs were heavy. She couldn't move them, could only let him touch and caress and kiss wherever he wished. The strength that had driven her the night before had been replaced by a honeyed weakness. She lay steeped in it.

His mouth loitered at her waist, his tongue circling lower while he ran his hands lightly over her, tracing the shape of her breasts, stroking her neck and shoulders. He teased rather than possessed, aroused rather than fulfilled.

He caught the waistband of the silk in his teeth and took it inches lower. Ryan arched and moaned. But it was the skin of her thigh he tasted, savoring until she knew madness was only a breath away. She heard herself sighing his name, a soft, urgent sound, but he made no answer. His mouth was busy doing wonderful things to the back of her knee.

Ryan felt the heated skin of his chest brush over her leg, though she had no idea how or when he had rid himself of his shirt. She had never been more aware of her own body. She learned of the drugging, heavenly pleasure that could come from the touch of a fingertip on the skin.

He was lifting her, Ryan thought mistily, though her back was pressed into the bed. He was levitating her, making her float. He was showing her magic, but this trance was no illusion.

They were both naked now, wrapped together as his

mouth journeyed back to hers. He kissed her slowly, deeply, until she was limp. His nimble fingers aroused. She hadn't known passion could pull two ways at once— into searing fire and into the clouds.

Her breath was heaving, but still he waited. He would give her everything first, every dram of pleasure, every dark delight he knew. Her skin was like water in his hands, flowing, rippling. He nibbled and sucked gently on her swollen lips and waited for her final moan of surrender.

"Now, love?" he asked, spreading light, whispering kisses over her face. "Now?"

She couldn't answer. She was beyond words and reason. That was where he wanted her. Exhilarated, he laughed and pressed his mouth to her throat. "You're mine, Ryan. Tell me. Mine."

"Yes." It came out on a husky breath, barely audible. "Yours." But his mouth swallowed the words even as she said them. "Take me." She didn't hear herself say it. She thought the demand was only in her brain, but then he was inside her. Ryan gasped and arched to meet him. And still he moved with painful slowness.

The blood was roaring in her ears as he drew the ultimate pleasure to its fullest. His lips rubbed over hers, capturing each trembling breath.

Abruptly, he crushed his mouth on hers—no more gentleness, no more teasing. She cried out as he took her with a sudden, wild fury. The fire consumed them both, fusing skin and lips until Ryan thought they both had died.

Pierce lay on her, resting his head between her breasts. Under his ear he heard the thunder of her heartbeat. She had yet to stop trembling. Her arms were twined around him, with one hand still tangled in his hair. He didn't want to move. He wanted to keep her like this—alone, naked, his. The fierce desire for possession shook him. It wasn't his way. Had never been his way before Ryan. The drive was too strong to resist.

"Tell me again," he demanded, lifting his face to watch hers.

Ryan's eyes opened slowly. She was drugged with love, sated with pleasure. "Tell you what?"

His mouth came to hers again, seeking, then lingered to draw the last taste. When he lifted it, his eyes were dark and demanding. "Tell me that you're mine, Ryan."

"Yours," she murmured as her eyes closed again. She sighed into sleep. "For as long as you want me."

Pierce frowned at her answer and started to speak, but her breathing was slow and even. Shifting, he lay beside her and pulled her close.

This time he would wait until she woke.

Chapter 10

Ryan had never known time to pass so quickly. She should have been glad of it. When Pierce's Las Vegas engagement was over, they could begin work on the special. It was something she was eager to do, for herself and for him. She knew it could be the turning point of her career.

Yet she found herself wishing the hours wouldn't fly by. There was something fanciful about Vegas, with its lack of time synchronization, its honky-tonk streets and glittery casinos. There, with the touch of magic all around, it seemed natural to love him, to share the life he lived. Ryan wasn't certain it would be so simple once they returned to the practical world.

They were both taking each day one at a time. There was no talk of the future. Pierce's burst of possessiveness had never reoccurred, and Ryan wondered at it. She nearly believed she had dreamed those deep, insistent words—*You're mine. Tell me.*

He had never demanded again, nor had he given her any words of love. He was gentle, at times achingly so, with words or looks or gestures. But he was never completely free with her. Nor was Ryan ever completely free with him. Trusting came easily to neither of them.

On closing night Ryan dressed carefully. She wanted a special evening. Champagne, she decided as she slipped into a frothy dress in a rainbow of hues. She would order champagne to be sent up to the suite after the performance. They had one long, last night to spend together before the idyll ended.

Ryan studied herself critically in the mirror. The dress was sheer and much more daring, she noted, than her usual style. Pierce would say it was more Ryan than Miss Swan, she thought and laughed. He would be right, as always. At the moment she didn't feel at all like Miss Swan. Tomorrow would be soon enough for business suits.

She dabbed perfume on her wrists, then at the hollow between her breasts.

"Ryan, if you want dinner before the show, you'll have to hurry along. It's nearly…" Pierce broke off as he came into the room. He stopped to stare at her. The dress floated here, clung there, wisping enticingly over her breasts in colors that melded and ran like a painting left in the rain.

"You're so lovely," he murmured, feeling the familiar thrill along his skin. "Like something I might have dreamed."

When he spoke like that, he had her heart melting and her pulse racing at the same time. "A dream?" Ryan walked to him and slid her arms around his neck. "What sort of a dream would you like me to be?" She kissed one cheek, then the other. "Will you conjure a dream for me, Pierce?"

"You smell of jasmine." He buried his face in her neck. He thought he had never wanted anything—anyone—so much in his life. "It drives me mad."

"A woman's spell." Ryan tilted her head to give his mouth more freedom. "To enchant the enchanter."

"It works."

She gave a throaty laugh and pressed closer. "Wasn't it a woman's spell that was Merlin's undoing in the end?"

"Have you been researching?" he asked in her ear. "Careful, I've been in the business longer than you." Lifting his face, he touched his lips to hers. "It isn't wise to tangle with a magician, you know."

"I'm not in the least wise." She let her fingers run up the back of his neck, then through the thick mane of his hair. "Not in the least."

He felt a wave of power—and a wave of weakness. It was always the same when she was in his arms. Pierce pulled her close again just to hold her. Sensing some struggle, Ryan remained passive. He had so much to give, she thought, so much emotion he would offer or hold back. She could never be sure which he would choose to do. Yet wasn't it the same with her? she asked herself. She loved him but hadn't been able to say the words aloud. Even as the love grew, she still wasn't able to say them.

"Will you be in the wings tonight?" he asked her. "I like knowing you're there."

"Yes." Ryan tilted back her head and smiled. It was so rare for him to ask anything of her. "One of these days I'm going to spot something. Even *your* hand isn't always quicker than the eye."

"No?" He grinned, amused at her continued determination to catch him. "About dinner," he began and toyed with the zipper at the back of her dress. He was beginning to wonder what she wore under it. If he chose, he could have the dress on the floor at her feet before she could draw a breath.

"What about it?" she asked with a gleam of mischief in her eyes.

The knock at the door had him swearing.

"Why don't you turn whoever it is into a toad?" Ryan suggested. Then, sighing, she rested her head on his shoulder. "No, that would be rude, I suppose."

"I rather like the idea."

She laughed and drew back. "I'll answer it. I can't have that on my conscience." Toying with his top button, she lifted a brow. "You won't forget what you were thinking about while I'm sending them away?"

He smiled. "I have a very good memory." Pierce let her go and watched her walk away. Miss Swan hadn't picked out that dress, he decided, echoing Ryan's earlier thoughts.

"Package for you, Miss Swan."

Ryan accepted the small plainly wrapped box and the card from the messenger. "Thank you." After closing the door, she set down the package and opened the envelope. The note was brief and typewritten.

Ryan,
Your report in good order. Expect a thorough briefing on Atkins project on your return. First full meeting scheduled one week from today. Happy birthday.
Your Father

Ryan read it over twice, then glanced briefly at the package. He wouldn't miss my birthday, she thought as she scanned the typed words a third time. Bennett Swan always did his duty. Ryan felt a surge of disappointment, of anger, of futility. All the familiar emotions of Swan's only child.

Why? she demanded of herself. Why hadn't he waited and given her something in person? Why had he sent an impersonal note that read like a telegram and a proper token his secretary no doubt selected? Why couldn't he have just sent his love?

"Ryan?" Pierce watched her from the doorway of the bedroom. He had seen her read the note. He had seen the look of emptiness in her eyes. "Bad news?"

"No." Quickly, Ryan shook her head and slipped the note into her purse. "No, it's nothing. Let's go to dinner, Pierce. I'm starving."

She was smiling, reaching out her hand for his, but the hurt in her eyes was unmistakable. Saying nothing, Pierce took her hand. As they left the suite, he glanced at the package she had never opened.

As Pierce had requested, Ryan watched the show from the wings. She had blocked all thoughts of her father from her mind. It was her last night of complete freedom, and Ryan was determined to let nothing spoil it.

It's my birthday, she reminded herself. I'm going to have my own private celebration. She had said nothing to Pierce, initially because she had forgotten her birthday entirely until her father's note had arrived. Now, she decided, it would be foolish to mention it. She was twenty-seven, after all, too old to be sentimental about the passing of a year.

* * *

"You were wonderful, as always," she told Pierce as he walked offstage, applause thundering after him. "When are you going to tell me how you do that last illusion?"

"Magic, Miss Swan, has no explanation."

She narrowed her eyes at him. "I happen to know that Bess is in her dressing room right now, and that the panther—"

"Explanations disappoint," he interrupted. He took her hand to lead her into his own dressing room. "The mind's a paradox, Miss Swan."

"Do tell," she said dryly, knowing full well he was going to explain nothing.

He managed to keep his face seriously composed as he stripped off his shirt. "The mind wants to believe the impossible," he continued as he went into the bath to wash. "Yet it doesn't. Therein lies the fascination. If the impossible is *not* possible, then how was it done before your eyes and under your nose?"

"That's what I want to know," Ryan complained over the sound of running water. When he came back in, a towel slung over his shoulder, she shot him a straight, uncompromising look. "As your producer in this special, I should—"

"Produce," he finished and pulled on a fresh shirt. "I'll do the impossible."

"It's maddening not to know," she said darkly but did up the buttons of his shirt herself.

"Yes." Pierce only smiled when she glared at him.

"It's just a trick," Ryan said with a shrug, hoping to annoy him.

"Is it?" His smile remained infuriatingly amiable.

Knowing defeat when faced with it, Ryan sighed. "I suppose you'd suffer all sorts of torture and never breathe a word."

"Did you have some in mind?"

She laughed then and pressed her mouth to his. "That's just the beginning," she promised dangerously. "I'm going to take you upstairs and drive you crazy until you talk."

"Interesting." Pierce slipped an arm around her shoulders and led her into the corridor. "It could take quite a bit of time."

"I'm in no hurry," she said blithely.

They rode to the top floor, but when Pierce started to slip the key into the lock of the suite, Ryan laid her hand on his. "This is your last chance before I get tough," she warned. "I'm going to make you talk."

He only smiled at her and pushed the door open.

"Happy birthday!"

Ryan's eyes widened in surprise. Bess, still in costume, opened a bottle of champagne while Link did his best to catch the spurt of wine in a glass. Speechless, Ryan stared at them.

"Happy birthday, Ryan." Pierce kissed her lightly.

"But how…" She broke off to look up at him. "How did you know?"

"Here you go." Bess stuck a glass of champagne in Ryan's hand, then gave her a quick squeeze. "Drink up, sweetie. You only get one birthday a year. Thank God. The champagne's from me—a bottle for now and one for later." She winked at Pierce.

"Thank you." Ryan looked helplessly into her glass. "I don't know what to say."

"Link's got something for you, too," Bess told her.

The big man shifted uncomfortably as all eyes turned to him. "I got you a cake," he mumbled, then cleared his throat. "You have to have a birthday cake."

Ryan walked over to see a sheet cake decorated in delicate pinks and yellows. "Oh, Link! It's lovely."

"You have to cut the first piece," he instructed.

"Yes, I will in a minute." Reaching up, Ryan drew his head down until she could reach it on tiptoe. She pressed a kiss on his mouth. "Thank you, Link."

He turned pink, grinned, then sent Bess an agonized look. "Welcome."

"I have something for you." Still smiling, Ryan turned to Pierce. "Will you kiss me, too?" he demanded.

"After I get my present."

"Greedy," he decided and handed her a small wooden box.

It was old and carved. Ryan ran her finger over it to feel the places that had worn smooth with age and handling. "It's beautiful," she murmured. She opened it and saw a tiny silver symbol on a chain. "Oh!"

"An ankh," Pierce told her, slipping it out to fasten it around her neck. "An Egyptian symbol of life. Not a superstition," he said gravely. "It's for luck."

"Pierce." Remembering her flattened penny, Ryan laughed and threw her arms around him. "Don't you ever forget anything?"

"No. Now you owe me a kiss."

Ryan complied, then forgot there were eyes on them.

"Hey, look, we want some of this cake. Don't we, Link?" Bess slipped an arm around his thick waist and grinned as Ryan surfaced.

"Will it taste as good as it looks?" Ryan wondered aloud as she picked up the knife and sliced through it. "I don't know how long it's been since I've eaten birthday cake. Here, Link, you have the first piece." Ryan licked icing from her finger as he took it. "Terrific," she judged, then began to cut another slice. "I don't know how you found out. I'd forgotten myself until…" Ryan stopped cutting and straightened. "You read my note!" she accused Pierce. He looked convincingly blank.

"What note?"

She let out an impatient breath, not noticing that Bess had taken the knife and was slicing the cake herself. "You went in my purse and read that note."

"Went in your purse?" Pierce repeated, lifting a brow. "Really, Ryan, would I do something so crude?"

She thought about that for a moment. "Yes, you would."

Bess snickered, but he only sent her a mild glance. He accepted a piece of cake. "A magician doesn't need to stoop to picking pockets to gather information."

Link laughed, a deep rumbling sound that caught Ryan by surprise. "Like the time you lifted that guy's keys in Detroit?" he reminded Pierce.

"Or the earrings from the lady in Flatbush," Bess put in. "Nobody's got a smoother touch than you, Pierce."

"Really?" Ryan drew out the word as she looked back at him. Pierce bit into a piece of cake and said nothing.

"He always gives them back at the end of the show," Bess went on. "Good thing Pierce didn't decide on a life of crime. Think of what would happen if he started cracking safes from the outside instead of the inside."

"Fascinating," Ryan agreed, narrowing her eyes at him. "I'd love to hear more about it."

"How about the time you broke out of that little jail

in Wichita, Pierce?" Bess continued obligingly. "You know when they locked you up for—"

"Have some more champagne, Bess," Pierce suggested, lifting the bottle and tilting it into her glass.

Link let out another rumbling laugh. "Sure would liked to've seen that sheriff's face when he looked in and saw an empty cell, all locked up and tidy."

"Jail-breaking," Ryan mused, fascinated.

"Houdini did it routinely." Pierce handed her a glass of champagne.

"Yeah, but he worked it out with the cops first." Bess chuckled at the look Pierce sent her and cut Link another piece of cake.

"Picking pockets, breaking jail." Ryan enjoyed the faint discomfort she saw in Pierce's eyes. It wasn't often she had him at a disadvantage. "Are there any other things I should know about?"

"It would seem you know too much already," he commented.

"Yes." She kissed him soundly. "And it's the best birthday present I've ever had."

"Come on, Link." Bess lifted the half-empty bottle of champagne. "Let's go finish this and your cake. We'll leave Pierce to work his way out of this one. You ought to tell her the one about that salesman in Salt Lake City."

"Good night, Bess," Pierce said blandly and earned another chuckle.

"Happy birthday, Ryan." Bess gave Pierce a flashing grin as she pulled Link out of the room.

"Thank you, Bess. Thank you, Link." Ryan waited until the door shut before she looked back at Pierce. "Before we discuss the salesman in Salt Lake City, why were you in a little cell in Wichita?" Her eyes laughed at him over the rim of her glass.

"A misunderstanding."

"That's what they all say." Her brow arched. "A jealous husband, perhaps?"

"No, an annoyed deputy who found himself locked to a bar stool with his own handcuffs." Pierce shrugged. "He wasn't appreciative when I let him go."

Ryan smothered a laugh. "No, I imagine he wasn't."

"A small wager," Pierce added. "He lost."

"Then instead of paying off," Ryan concluded, "he tossed you in jail."

"Something like that."

"A desperate criminal." Ryan heaved a sigh. "I suppose I'm at your mercy." Setting down her glass, she went to him. "It was very sweet of you to do this for me. Thank you."

Pierce brushed back her hair. "Such a serious face," he murmured and kissed her eyes shut. He thought of the hurt he had seen in them when she had read her father's letter. "Aren't you going to open the present from your father, Ryan?"

She shook her head, then laid her cheek on his shoulder. "No, not tonight. Tomorrow. I've been given the presents that matter already."

"He didn't forget you, Ryan."

"No, he wouldn't forget. It would be marked on his calendar. Oh, I'm sorry." She shook her head again, drawing away. "That was petty. I've always wanted too much. He does love me— in his own way."

Pierce took her hands in his. "He only knows his own way."

Ryan looked back up at him. Her frown cleared into

an expression of understanding. "Yes, you're right. I've never thought about it that way. I keep struggling to please him so he'll turn to me one day and say, 'Ryan, I love you. I'm proud to be your father.' It's silly." She sighed. "I'm a grown woman, but I keep waiting."

"We don't ever stop wanting that from our parents." Pierce drew her close again.

Ryan thought of his childhood while he wondered about hers.

"We'd be different people, wouldn't we, if our parents had acted differently?"

"Yes," he answered. "We would."

Ryan tilted her head back. "I wouldn't want you to be any different, Pierce. You're exactly what I want." Hungrily, she pressed her mouth to his. "Take me to bed," she whispered. "Tell me what you were thinking all those hours ago before we were interrupted."

Pierce swept her up, and she clung, delighting in the strength of his arms. "Actually," he began, crossing to the bedroom, "I was wondering what you had on under that dress."

Ryan laughed and pressed her mouth to his throat. "Well, there's hardly anything there to wonder about at all."

The bedroom was dark and quiet as Ryan lay curled up at Pierce's side. His fingers played absently with her hair. He thought she was sleeping; she was very still. He didn't mind his own wakefulness. It allowed him to enjoy the feel of her skin against his, the silken texture of her hair. While she slept, he could touch her without arousing her, only to comfort himself that she was there.

He didn't like knowing she wouldn't be in his bed the following night.

"What are you thinking about?" she murmured and startled him.

"About you." He drew her closer. "I thought you were sleeping."

"No." He felt the brush of her lashes on his shoulder as she opened her eyes. "I was thinking about you." Lifting her finger, she traced it along his jawline. "Where did you get this scar?"

He didn't answer immediately. Ryan realized she'd unwittingly probed into his past. "I suppose it was in a battle with a sorceress," she said lightly, wishing she could take the question back.

"Not quite so romantic. I fell down some stairs when I was a kid."

She held her breath a moment. She hadn't expected him to volunteer anything on his past, even so small a detail. Shifting, she rested her head on his chest. "I tripped over a stool once and loosened a tooth. My father was furious when he found out. I was terrified it would fall out and he'd disown me."

"Did he frighten you so much?"

"His disapproval, yes. I suppose it was foolish."

"No." Staring up at the dark ceiling, Pierce continued to stroke her hair. "We're all afraid of something."

"Even you?" she asked with a half-laugh. "I don't believe you're afraid of anything."

"Of not being able to get out once I'm in," he murmured.

Surprised, Ryan looked up and caught the gleam of his eyes in the darkness. "Do you mean in one of your escapes?"

"What?" He brought his thoughts back to her. He hadn't realized he had spoken aloud.

"Why do you do the escapes if you feel that way?"

"Do you think that if you ignore a fear it goes away?" he asked her. "When I was small," he said calmly, "it was a closet, and I couldn't get out. Now it's a steamer trunk or a vault, and I can escape."

"Oh, Pierce." Ryan turned her face into his chest. "I'm sorry. You don't have to talk about it."

But he was compelled to. For the first time since his childhood, Pierce heard himself speak of it. "Do you know, I think that the memory of scent stays with you longer than anything else. I could always remember the scent of my father so clearly. It wasn't until ten years after I last saw him that I learned what it was. He smelled of gin. I couldn't have told you what he looked like, but I remembered that smell."

He continued to stare up at the ceiling as he spoke. Ryan knew he had forgotten her as he went back into his own past. "One night when I was about fifteen, I was down in the cellar. I used to like to explore down there when everyone was in bed. I came across the janitor passed out in a corner with a bottle of gin. That smell—I remember being terrified for a moment without having any idea why. But I went over and picked up the bottle, and then I knew. I stopped being afraid."

Pierce was silent for a long time, and Ryan said nothing. She waited, wanting him to continue yet knowing she couldn't ask him to. The room was quiet but for the sound of his heart beating under her ear.

"He was a very cruel, very sick man," Pierce murmured, and she knew he spoke again of his father. "For years I was certain that meant I had the same sickness."

Gripping him tighter, Ryan shook her head. "There's nothing cruel in you," she whispered. "Nothing."

"Would you think so if I told you where I came from?" he wondered. "Would you be willing to let me touch you then?"

Ryan lifted her head and swallowed tears. "Bess told me a week ago," she said steadily. "And I'm here." He said nothing, but she felt his hand fall away from her hair. "You have no right to be angry with her. She's the most loyal, the most loving woman I've ever met. She told me because she knew I cared, knew I needed to understand you."

He was very still. "When?"

"The night..." Ryan hesitated and took a breath. "Opening night." She wished she could see his expression, but the darkness cloaked it. "You said we'd be lovers when I knew you," she reminded him. "You were right." Because her voice trembled, she swallowed. "Are you sorry?"

It seemed to her an eternity before he answered. "No." Pierce drew her down to him again. "No." He kissed her temple. "How could I be sorry to be your lover?"

"Then don't be sorry that I know you. You're the most magnificent man I've ever met."

He laughed at that, half amused, half moved. And relieved, he discovered. The relief was tremendous. It made him laugh again. "Ryan, what an incredible thing to say."

She tilted up her chin. There would be no tears for him. "It's very true, but I won't tell you again. You'll get conceited." She lifted her palm to his cheek. "But just for tonight I'll let you enjoy it. And besides," she added, pulling his ear, "I like the way your eyebrows sweep up at the ends." She kissed his mouth, then let her lips roam his face. "And the way you write your name."

"The way I what?" he asked.

"On the contracts," Ryan elaborated, still planting light kisses all over his face. "It's very dashing." She felt the smile move his cheeks. "What do you like about me?" she demanded.

"Your taste," he said instantly. "It's impeccable."

Ryan bit his bottom lip, but he only rolled her over and turned the punishment into a very satisfying kiss. "I knew it would make you conceited," she said disgustedly. "I'm going to sleep."

"I don't think so," Pierce corrected, then lowered his mouth.

He was right again.

Chapter 11

Saying goodbye to Pierce was one of the most difficult things Ryan had ever done. She had been tempted to forget every obligation, all of her ambitions, and ask him to take her with him. What were ambitions but empty goals if she was without him? She would tell him that she loved him, that nothing mattered but that they be together.

But when they had parted at the airport, she made herself smile, kiss him goodbye, and let go. She had to drive into Los Angeles, and he had to drive up the coast. The work that had brought them together would also keep them apart.

There had still been no talk of the future. Ryan had come to learn that Pierce didn't speak of tomorrows. That he had spoken to her of his past, however briefly, reassured her. It was a step, perhaps a bigger one than either of them realized.

Time, Ryan thought, would tell if what had been between them in Las Vegas would strengthen or fade. This was the period of waiting. She knew that if he had regrets they would surface now while they were apart. Absence didn't always make the heart grow fonder. It also allowed the blood and the brain to cool. Doubts had a habit of forming when there was time to think. When he came to L.A. for the first meetings, she would have her answer.

When Ryan entered her office, she glanced at her watch and ruefully realized that time and schedules were part of her world again. She had left Pierce only an hour before and missed him unbearably already. Was he thinking of her—right now, at this moment? If she concentrated hard enough, would he know that she thought of him? With a sigh Ryan sat behind her desk. Since she had become involved with Pierce, she'd become freer with her imagination. There were times, she had to admit, that she believed in magic.

What's happened to you, Miss Swan? she asked herself. Your feet aren't on the ground, where they belong. Love, she mused and cupped her chin on her hands. When you're in love, nothing's impossible.

Who could say why her father had taken ill and sent her to Pierce? What force had guided her hand to choose that fateful card from the Tarot deck? Why had the cat picked her window in the storm? Certainly there were logical explanations for each step that had taken her closer to where she was at that moment. But a woman in love doesn't want logic.

It *had* been magic, Ryan thought with a smile. From the first moment their eyes had met, she had felt it. It had simply taken her time to accept it. Now that she did, her only choice was to wait and see if it lasted. No, she corrected, this wasn't a time for choices. She was going to make it last. If it took patience, then she'd be patient. If it took action, then she would act. But she was going to make it work, even if it meant trying her own hand at enchantment.

Shaking her head, she sat back in her chair. Nothing could be done until he was back in her life again. That would take a week. For now, there was still work to do. She couldn't wave a wand and brush the days away until he came back. She had to fill them. Flipping open her notes on Pierce Atkins, Ryan began to transcribe them. Less than thirty minutes later her buzzer sounded.

"Yes, Barbara."

"The boss wants you."

Ryan frowned at the litter of papers on her desk. "Now?"

"Now."

"All right, thanks." Swearing under her breath, Ryan stacked her papers, then separated what was in order to take with her. He might have given her a few hours to get organized, she thought. But the fact remained that he was going to be looking over her shoulder on this project. She was a long way from proving her worth to Bennett Swan. Knowing this, Ryan slipped papers into a folder and went to see her father.

"Good morning, Miss Swan." Bennett Swan's secretary glanced up as Ryan entered. "How was your trip?"

"It went very well, thank you." Ryan watched the woman's eyes shift briefly to the discreet, expensive pearl clusters at her ears. Ryan had worn her father's birthday gift knowing he would want to see them to assure himself they were correct and appreciated.

"Mr. Swan had to step out for a moment, but he'll be right with you. He'd like you to wait in his office. Mr. Ross is already inside."

"Welcome back, Ryan." Ned rose as she shut the door behind her. The coffee he held in his hand was steaming.

"Hello, Ned. Are you in on this meeting?"

"Mr. Swan wants me to work with you on this." He gave her a charming, half-apologetic smile. "Hope you don't mind."

"Of course not," she said flatly. Setting down the folder, she accepted the coffee Ned offered her. "In what capacity?"

"I'll be production coordinator," he told her. "It's still your baby, Ryan."

"Yes." With you as my proctor, she thought bitterly. Swan would still be calling the shots.

"How was Vegas?"

"Unique," Ryan told him as she wandered to the window.

"I hope you found some time to try your luck. You work too hard, Ryan."

She fingered the ankh at her neck and smiled. "I played some blackjack. I won."

"No kidding! Good for you."

After sipping at the coffee, she set the cup aside. "I think I have a firm basis for what will suit Pierce, Swan Productions and the network," she went on. "He doesn't need names to draw ratings. I think more than one guest star would crowd him. As for the set, I'll need to talk to the designers, but I have something fairly definite in mind already. As to the sponsors—"

"We can talk shop later," Ned interrupted. He moved to her and twined the ends of her hair around his fingers. Ryan stayed still and stared out of the window. "I've missed you, Ryan," Ned said softly. "It seemed as though you were gone for months."

"Strange," she murmured watching a plane cruise across the sky. "I've never known a week to pass so quickly."

"Darling, how long are you going to punish me?" He kissed the top of her head. Ryan felt no resentment. She felt nothing at all. Oddly, Ned had found himself more attracted to her since she had rejected him. There was something different about her now, which he couldn't quite put his finger on. "If you'd just give me a chance, I could make it up to you."

"I'm not punishing you, Ned." Ryan turned to face him. "I'm sorry if it seems that way."

"You're still angry with me."

"No, I told you before that I wasn't." She sighed, deciding it would be better to clear the air between them. "I was angry and hurt, but it didn't last. I was never in love with you, Ned."

He didn't like the faint apology in her voice. It put him on the defensive. "We were just getting to know each other." When he started to take her hands, she shook her head.

"No, I don't think you know me at all. And," she added without rancor, "if we're going to be honest, that wasn't what you were after."

"Ryan, how many times do I have to apologize for that stupid suggestion?" There was a combination of hurt and regret in his voice.

"I'm not asking for an apology, Ned, I'm trying to make myself clear. You made a mistake assuming I could influence my father. You have more influence with him than I have."

"Ryan—"

"No, hear me out," she insisted. "You thought because I'm Bennett Swan's daughter I have his ear. That's just not true and never has been. His business associates have more input with him than I do. You wasted your time cultivating me to get to him. And, leaving that aside," she continued, "I'm not interested in a man who wants to use me as a springboard. I'm sure we'll work together very well, but I have no desire to see you outside of the office."

They both jolted when they heard the office door shut.

"Ryan... Ross." Bennett Swan walked over to his desk and sat down.

"Good morning." Ryan fumbled a bit over the greeting before she took a chair. How much had he heard? she wondered. His face revealed nothing, so Ryan reached for the folder. "I've outlined my thoughts and ideas on Atkins," she began, "though I haven't had time to complete a full report."

"Give me what you have." He waved Ned to a chair, then lit a cigar.

"He has a very tight club act." Ryan laced her fingers together to keep them still. "You've seen the tapes yourself, so you know that his act ranges from sleight of hand to large, complicated illusions to escapes that take two or three minutes. The escapes will keep him off camera for that amount of time, but the public expects that." She paused to cross her legs. "Of course, we know there'll have to be modifications for television, but I see no problem. He's an extraordinarily creative man."

Swan gave a grunt that might have been agreement

and held out his hand for Ryan's report. Rising, she handed it to him, then took her seat again. He wasn't in one of his better moods, she noted. Someone had displeased him. She could only be grateful she hadn't been that someone.

"This is pretty slim," he commented, scowling at the folder.

"It won't be by the end of the day."

"I'll talk to Atkins myself next week," Swan stated as he skimmed through the papers. "Coogar's going to direct."

"Good, I'd like to work with him. I want Bloomfield on the set design," she said casually, then held her breath.

Swan glanced up and stared at her. Bloomfield had been his own choice. He'd decided on him less than an hour before. Ryan met the hard look unwaveringly. Swan wasn't altogether certain if he was pleased or annoyed that his daughter was one step ahead of him. "I'll consider it," he said and went back to her report. Quietly, Ryan let out her breath.

"He'll bring his own music director," she went on, thinking of Link. "And his own crew and gimmicks. If we have a problem, I'd say it'll be getting him to cooperate with our people in preproduction and on the set. He has his own way of doing things."

"That can be dealt with," Swan muttered. "Ross will be your production coordinator." Lifting his eyes, he met Ryan's.

"So I understand." Ryan met the look equally. "I can't argue with your choice, but I do feel that if I'm the producer on this project, I should pick my own team."

"You don't want to work with Ross?" Swan demanded as if Ned hadn't been sitting beside her.

"I think Ned and I will deal very well together," she said mildly. "And I'm sure Coogar knows the camera people he wants. It would be ridiculous to interfere with him. However," she added with a hint of steel in her voice, "I also know who *I* want working on this project."

Swan sat back and puffed for a moment on his cigar. The flush of color in his cheeks warned of temper. "What the hell do you know about producing?" he demanded.

"Enough to produce this special and make it a success," she replied. "Just as you told me to do a few weeks ago."

Swan had had time to regret the impulse that had made him agree to Pierce's terms. "You're the producer on record," he told her shortly. "Your name will be on the credits. Just do as you're told."

Ryan felt the tremor in her stomach but kept her eyes level. "If you feel that way, pull me now." She rose slowly. "But if I stay, I'm going to do more than watch my name roll on the credits. I know how this man works, and I know television. If that isn't enough for you, get someone else."

"Sit down!" he shouted at her. Ned sank a bit deeper in his own chair, but Ryan remained standing. "Don't give me ultimatums. I've been in this business for forty years." He banged his palm on the desk. "*Forty years!* So you know television," he said scornfully. "Pulling off a live show isn't like changing a damn contract. I can't have some hysterical little girl come running to me five minutes before air time telling me there's an equipment failure."

Ryan swallowed raw rage and answered coldly. "I'm not an hysterical little girl, and I've never come running to you for anything."

Completely stunned, he stared at her. The twinge of guilt made his anger all the more explosive. "You're just getting your feet wet," he snapped as he flipped the folder shut. "And you're getting them wet because I say so. You're going to take my advice when I give it to you."

"Your advice?" Ryan countered. Her eyes glistened with conflicting emotions, but her voice was very firm. "I've always respected your advice, but I haven't heard any here today. Just orders. I don't want any favors from you." She turned and headed for the door.

"Ryan!" There was absolute fury in the word. No one but no one walked out on Bennett Swan. "Come back here and sit down. *Young lady!*" he bellowed when she ignored the command.

"I'm not your young lady," she returned, spinning back. "I'm your employee."

Taken aback, he stared at her. What answer could he make to that? He waved his hand at a chair impatiently. "Sit down," he said again, but she stayed at the door. "Sit, sit," he repeated with more exasperation than temper.

Ryan came back and calmly took her place.

"Take Ryan's notes and start working on a budget," he told Ned.

"Yes, sir." Grateful for the dismissal, Ned took the folder and retreated. Swan waited for the door to close before he looked back at his daughter.

"What do you want?" he asked her for the first time in his life. The fact occurred to them both at the same moment.

Ryan took time to separate her personal and professional feelings. "The same respect you'd show any other producer."

"You haven't got any track record," he pointed out.

"No," she agreed. "And I never will if you tie my hands."

Swan let out a sigh, saw his cigar was dead and dropped it into an ashtray. "The network has a tentative slot, the third Sunday in May, nine to ten east coast time."

"That only gives us two months."

He nodded. "They want it before the summer season. How fast can you work?"

Ryan lifted a brow and smiled. "Fast enough. I want Elaine Fisher to guest star."

Swan narrowed his eyes at her. "Is that all?" he asked dryly.

"No, but it's a start. She's talented, beautiful and as popular with women as she is with men. Plus, she's had experience at working clubs and live theater," she pointed out as Swan frowned and said nothing. "That guileless, wide-eyed look of hers is the perfect contrast for Pierce."

"She's shooting in Chicago."

"That film wraps next week." Ryan sent him a calm smile. "And she's under contract with Swan. If the film goes a week or two over schedule, it won't matter," she added as he remained silent. "We won't need her in California for more than a few days. Pierce carries the show."

"She has other commitments," Swan pointed out.

"She'll fit it in."

"Call her agent."

"I will." Ryan rose again. "I'll set up a meeting with Coogar and get back to you." She paused a moment, then on impulse walked around his desk to stand beside his chair. "I've watched you work for years," she began. "I don't expect you to have the confidence in me you have in yourself or someone with experience. And if I make mistakes, I wouldn't want them to be overlooked. But if I do a good job, and I'm going to, I want to be sure *I* did it, not that I just got the credit for it."

"Your show," he said simply.

"Yes." Ryan nodded. "Exactly. There are a lot of reasons why this project is particularly important to me. I can't promise not to make mistakes, but I can promise you there's no one else who'll work harder on it."

"Don't let Coogar push you around," he muttered after a moment. "He likes to drive producers crazy."

Ryan smiled. "I've heard the stories, don't worry." She started to leave again, then remembered. After a brief hesitation, she leaned down to brush his cheek with her lips. "Thank you for the earrings. They're lovely."

Swan glanced at them. The jeweler had assured his secretary they were an appropriate gift and a good investment. What had he said in the note he had sent with them? he wondered. Chagrined that he couldn't remember, he decided to ask his secretary for a copy of it.

"Ryan." Swan took her hand. Seeing her blink in surprise at the gesture, he stared down at his own fingers. He had heard all of her conversation with Ned before he had come into the office. It had angered him, disturbed him, and now, when he saw his daughter stunned that he took her hand, it left him frustrated.

"Did you have a good time in Vegas?" he asked, not knowing what else to say.

"Yes." Uncertain what to do next, Ryan went back to business. "I think it was a smart move. Watching Pierce work up close gave me a good perspective. It's a much more overall view than a tape. And I got to know the people who work with him. That won't hurt when they have to work with me." She gave their joined hands another confused look. Could he be ill? she wondered and glanced quickly at his face. "I'll—I'll have a much more concise report for you by tomorrow."

Swan waited until she was finished. "Ryan, how old were you yesterday?" He watched her closely. Her eyes went from bewildered to bleak.

"Twenty-seven," she told him flatly.

Twenty-seven! On a long breath, Swan released her hand. "I've lost some years somewhere," he mumbled. "Go set up with Coogar," he told her and shuffled through the papers on his desk. "Send me a memo after you contact Fisher's agent."

"All right."

Over the top of the papers, Swan watched her walk to the door. When she had left him, he sat back in his chair. He found it staggering to realize he was getting old.

Chapter 12

Producing, Ryan found, kept her as effectively buried in paperwork as contracts had. She spent her days behind her desk, on the phone or in someone else's office. It was hard, grueling work with little glamour. The hours were long, the problems endless. Yet she found she had a taste for it. She was, after all, her father's daughter.

Swan hadn't given her a free hand, but their confrontation on the morning of her return to L.A. had had its benefits. He was listening to her. For the most part she found him surprisingly agreeable to her proposals. He didn't veto arbitrarily as she had feared he would but altered from time to time. Swan knew the business from every angle. Ryan listened and learned.

Her days were full and chaotic. Her nights were empty. Ryan had known Pierce wouldn't phone her. It wasn't his way. He would be down in his workroom, planning, practicing, perfecting. She doubted he would even notice the passing of time.

Of course, she could phone him, Ryan thought as she wandered around her empty apartment. She could invent any number of viable excuses for calling him. There was the change in the taping schedule. That was a valid reason, though she knew he'd already been informed through his agent. And there were at least a dozen minor points they could go over before the meeting the following week.

Ryan glanced thoughtfully at the phone, then shook her head. It wasn't business that she wanted to discuss with him, and she wouldn't use it as a smoke screen. Going into the kitchen, she began to prepare herself a light supper.

Pierce ran through the water illusion for a third time. It was nearly perfect. But nearly was never good enough. He thought, not for the first time, that the camera's eye would be infinitely sharper than the human eye. Every time he had watched himself on tape, he had found flaws. It didn't matter to Pierce that only he knew where to look for them. It only mattered that they were there. He ran through the illusion again.

His workroom was quiet. Though he knew Link was upstairs at the piano, the sound didn't carry down to him. But he wouldn't have heard it if they had been in the same room. Critically, he watched himself in a long mirror as water seemed to shimmer in an unsupported tube. The mirror showed him holding it, top and bottom, while it flowed from palm to palm. Water. It was only one of the four elements he intended to command for Ryan's special.

He thought of the special as hers more than his own. He thought of her when he should have been thinking of his work. With a graceful movement of his hands, Pierce had the water pouring back into a glass pitcher.

He had almost phoned her a dozen times. Once, at three o'clock in the morning, his hand had been on the dial. Just her voice—he had only wanted to hear her voice. He hadn't completed the call, reminding himself of his vow never to put obligations on anyone. If he phoned, it meant he expected her to be there to answer. Ryan was free to do as she pleased; he had no claim on her. Or on anyone. Even the bird he kept had its cage door open at all times.

There had been no one in his life whom he had belonged to. Social workers had brought rules and compassion, but ultimately he had been just one more name in the file. The law had seen to it that he was properly placed and properly cared for. And the law had kept him bound to two people who didn't want him but wouldn't set him free.

Even when he loved—as with Link and Bess—he accepted but demanded no bonds. Perhaps that was why he continued to devise more complicated escapes. Each time he succeeded, it proved no one could be held forever.

Yet he thought of Ryan when he should have been working.

Picking up the handcuffs, Pierce studied them. They had fit cleanly over her wrist. He had held her then. Idly, he snapped one half over his right wrist and toyed with the other, imagining Ryan's hand locked to his.

Was that what he wanted? he wondered. To lock her to him? He remembered how warm she was, how steeped in her he would become after one touch. Who would be locked to whom? Annoyed, Pierce released himself as swiftly as he had snapped on the cuff.

"Double, double, toil and trouble," Merlin croaked from his perch.

Amused, Pierce glanced over. "I think you're quite right," he murmured, jiggling the cuffs in his hand a moment. "But then, you couldn't resist her either, could you?"

"Abracadabra."

"Abracadabra indeed," Pierce agreed absently. "But who's bewitched whom?"

Ryan was just about to step into the tub when she heard the knock on the door. "Damn!" Irritated by the interruption, she slipped back into her robe and went to answer. Even as she pulled the door open, she was calculating how to get rid of the visitor before her bath water chilled.

"Pierce!"

He saw her eyes widen in surprise. Then, with a mixture of relief and pleasure, he saw the joy. Ryan launched herself into his arms.

"Are you real?" she demanded before her mouth fastened on his. Her hunger shot through him, matching his own. "Five days," Ryan murmured and clung to him. "Do you know how many hours there are in five days?"

"A hundred and twenty." Pierce drew her away to smile at her. "We'd better go inside. Your neighbors are finding this very entertaining."

Ryan pulled him in and shut the door by pressing him back against it. "Kiss me," she demanded. "Hard. Hard enough for a hundred and twenty hours."

His mouth came down on hers. She felt the scrape of his teeth against her lips as he groaned and crushed her to him. Pierce struggled to remember his strength and her fragility, but her tongue was probing, her hands were seeking. She was laughing that husky, aroused laugh that drove him wild.

"Oh, you're real." Ryan sighed and rested her head on his shoulder. "You're real."

But are you? he wondered, a little dazed by the kiss.

After one last hug she pulled out of his arms. "What are you doing here, Pierce? I didn't expect you until Monday or Tuesday."

"I wanted to see you," he said simply and lifted his palm to her cheek. "To touch you."

Ryan caught his hand and pressed the palm to her lips. A fire kindled in the pit of his stomach. "I've missed you," she murmured as her eyes clung to his. "So much. If I had known wishing you here would bring you, I'd have wished harder."

"I wasn't certain you'd be free."

"Pierce," she said softly and laid her hands on his chest. "Do you really think I want to be with anyone else?"

He stared down at her without speaking, but she felt the increased rate of his heartbeat under her hand. "You interfere with my work," he said at length.

Puzzled, Ryan tilted her head. "I do? How?"

"You're in my mind when you shouldn't be."

"I'm sorry." But she smiled, clearly showing she wasn't. "I've been breaking your concentration?"

"Yes."

She slid her hands up to his neck. "That's too bad."

Her voice was mocking and seductive. "What are you going to do about it?"

For an answer, Pierce dragged her to the floor. The movement was so swift, so unexpected, Ryan gasped but the sound was swallowed by his mouth. The robe was whipped from her before she could draw a breath. Pierce took her to the summit so quickly, she was powerless to do anything but answer the desperate mutual need.

His clothes were gone with more speed than was reasonable, but he gave her no time to explore him. In one move Pierce rolled her on top of him, then, lifting her as though she were weightless, he set her down to plunge fully inside her.

Ryan cried out, stunned, exhilarated. The speed had her mind spinning. The heat had her skin drenched. Her eyes grew wide as pleasure went beyond all possibilities. She could see Pierce's face, damp with passion, eyes closed. She could hear each tearing breath as he dug his long fingers into her hips to keep her moving with him. Then a film was over her eyes—a white, misty film that hazed her vision. She pressed her hands to his chest to keep from falling. But she was falling, slowly, slowly, drained of everything.

When the mist cleared, Ryan found she was in his arms with his face buried in her hair. Their damp bodies were fused together.

"Now I know you're real, too," Pierce murmured and helped himself to her mouth. "How do you feel?"

"Dazed," Ryan answered breathlessly. "Wonderful."

Pierce laughed. Rising, he lifted her into his arms. "I'm going to take you to bed and love you again before you recover."

"*Mmm,* yes." Ryan nuzzled his neck. "I should let the water out of the tub first."

Pierce lifted a brow, then smiled. With Ryan half-dozing in his arms, he wandered the apartment until he found the bath. "Were you in the tub when I knocked?"

"Almost." Ryan sighed and snuggled against him. "I was going to get rid of whoever had interrupted me. I was very annoyed."

With a flick of his wrist, Pierce turned the hot water on full. "I didn't notice."

"Couldn't you see how I was trying to get rid of you?"

"I have very thick skin at times," he confessed. "I suppose the water's cooled off a bit by now."

"Probably," she agreed.

"You use a free hand with the bubbles."

"*Mmm-hmm.* Oh!" Ryan's eyes shot open as she found herself lowered into the tub.

"Cold?" He grinned at her.

"No." Ryan reached up and turned off the water that steamed hot into the tub. For a moment she allowed her eyes to feast on him—the long, lean body, the wiry muscles and narrow hips. She tilted her head and twirled a finger in the bubbles. "Would you like to join me?" she invited politely.

"The thought had crossed my mind."

"Please." She gestured with her hand. "Be my guest. I've been very rude. I didn't even offer you a drink." She gave him a sassy grin.

The water rose when Pierce lowered himself into it. He sat at the foot of the tub, facing her. "I don't often drink," he reminded her.

"Yes, I know." She gave him a sober nod. "You don't

smoke, rarely drink, hardly ever swear. You're a paragon of virtue, Mr. Atkins."

He threw a handful of bubbles at her.

"In any case," Ryan continued, brushing them from her cheek, "I did want to discuss the sketches for the set design with you. Would you like the soap?"

"Thank you, Miss Swan." He took it from her. "You were going to tell me about the set?"

"Oh, yes, I think you'll approve the sketches, though you might want some minor changes." She shifted, sighing a little as her legs brushed against his. "I told Bloomfield I wanted something a little fanciful, medieval, but not too cluttered."

"No suits of armor?"

"No, just atmosphere. Something moody, like…" She broke off when he took her foot in his hand and began to soap it.

"Yes?" he prompted.

"A tone," she said as gentle pulses of pleasure ran up her leg. "Muted colors. The sort you have in your parlor."

Pierce began to massage her calf. "Only one set?"

Ryan trembled in the steamy water as he slid soapy fingers up her leg. "Yes, I thought—*mmm*—I thought the basic mood…" He moved his hands slowly up and down her legs as he watched her face.

"What mood?" He lifted a hand to soap her breast in circles while using his other to massage the top of her thigh.

"Sex," Ryan breathed. "You're very sexy onstage."

"Am I?" Through drugging ripples of sensation, she heard the amusement in the question.

"Yes, dramatic and rather coolly sexy. When I watch you perform…" She trailed off, struggling for breath.

The heady scent of the bath salts rose around her. She felt the water lap under her breasts, just below Pierce's clever hand. "Your hands," she managed, steeped in hot, tortured pleasure.

"What about them?" he asked as he slipped a finger inside her.

"Magic." The word trembled out. "Pierce, I can't talk when you're doing things to me."

"Shall I stop?" She was no longer looking at him. Her eyes were closed, but he watched her face, using fingertips only to arouse her.

"No." Ryan found his hand under the water and pressed it against herself.

"You're so beautiful, Ryan." The water swayed as he moved to nibble at her breast, then at her mouth. "So soft. I could see you when I was alone in the middle of the night. I could imagine touching you like this. I couldn't stay away."

"Don't." Her hands were in his hair, pulling his mouth more firmly to hers. "Don't stay away. I've waited so long already."

"Five days," he murmured as he urged her legs apart.

"All my life."

At her words something coursed through him which passion wouldn't permit him to explore. He had to have her, that was all.

"Pierce," Ryan murmured hazily. "We're going to sink."

"Hold your breath," he suggested and took her.

"I'm sure my father will want to see you," Ryan told Pierce the next morning as he pulled into her space in the parking complex of Swan Productions. "And I imagine you'd like to see Coogar."

"Since I'm here," Pierce agreed and shut off the ignition. "But I came to see you."

With a smile Ryan leaned over and kissed him. "I'm so glad you did. Can you stay over the weekend, or do you have to get back?"

He tucked a lock of hair behind her ear. "We'll see."

She slid from the car. She could hope for no better answer. "Of course, the first full meeting isn't scheduled until next week, but I imagine they'll accommodate you." They walked into the building. "I can make the calls from my office."

Ryan led him down the corridors briskly, nodding or answering now and again when someone greeted her. She was all business, he noted, the moment she stepped through the front doors.

"I don't know where Bloomfield is today," she continued as she pushed the button in the elevator for her floor. "But if he's unavailable, I can get the sketches and go over them with you myself." They stepped inside as she began to outline her day's schedule, balancing and altering to allow for Pierce's presence. "You and I might go over the timing, too," she continued. "We have fifty-two minutes to fill. And…"

"Will you have dinner with me tonight, Miss Swan?"

Ryan broke off what she was saying and found him smiling at her. The look in his eyes made it difficult for her to recall her plans for the day. She could only remember what had passed in the night. "I think I might fit that into my schedule, Mr. Atkins," she murmured as the elevator doors opened.

"You'll check your calendar?" he asked and kissed her hand.

"Yes." Ryan had to stop the doors from closing again. "And don't look at me like that today," she said breathlessly. "I'll never be able to function."

"Is that so?" Pierce let her pull him into the corridor. "I might consider it suitable revenge for all the times you've made it impossible for me to do my work."

Unnerved, Ryan led him into her office. "If we're going to manage to pull off this show..." she began.

"Oh, I have complete faith in the very organized, very dependable Miss Swan," Pierce said easily. He took a chair and waited for her to sit behind her desk.

"You're going to be difficult to work with, aren't you?" she asked.

"Most likely."

Wrinkling her nose at him, Ryan picked up the phone and pushed a series of buttons. "Ryan Swan," she announced, deliberately keeping her eyes away from Pierce. "Is he free?"

"Please hold, Miss Swan."

In a moment she heard her father's voice answer impatiently. "Make it fast, I'm busy."

"I'm sorry to disturb you," she said automatically. "I have Pierce Atkins in my office. I thought you might like to see him."

"What's he doing here?" Swan demanded, then continued before Ryan could answer. "Bring him up." He hung up without waiting for her agreement.

"He'd like to see you now," Ryan said as she replaced the receiver.

Pierce nodded, rising as she did. The brevity of the phone conversation had told him a great deal. Minutes later, after entering Swan's office, he learned a great deal more.

"Mr. Atkins." Swan rose to come around his massive desk with his hand extended. "What a pleasant surprise. I didn't expect to meet you personally until next week."

"Mr. Swan." Pierce accepted the offered hand and noted Swan had no greeting for his daughter.

"Please sit down," he suggested with a wide sweep of his hand. "What can I get for you? Coffee?"

"No, nothing."

"Swan Productions is very pleased to have your talents, Mr. Atkins." Swan settled behind his desk again. "We're going to put a lot of energy into this special. Promotion and press have already been set into motion."

"So I understand. Ryan keeps me informed."

"Of course." Swan sent her a quick nod. "We'll shoot in studio twenty-five. Ryan can arrange for you to see it today if you'd like. And anything else you'd like to see while you're here." He sent her another look.

"Yes, of course," she answered. "I thought Mr. Atkins might like to see Coogar and Bloomfield if they're available."

"Set it up," he ordered, dismissing her. "Now, Mr. Atkins, I have a letter from your representative. There are a few points we might go over before you meet the more artistic members of the company."

Pierce waited until Ryan had shut the door behind her. "I intend to work with Ryan, Mr. Swan. I contracted with you with that stipulation."

"Naturally," Swan answered, thrown off balance. As a rule talent was flattered to receive his personal attention. "I can assure you she's been hard at work on your behalf."

"I don't doubt it."

Swan met the measuring gray eyes levelly. "Ryan is producing your special at your request."

"Your daughter is a very interesting woman, Mr. Swan." Pierce waited a moment, watching Swan's eyes narrow. "On a professional level," he continued smoothly. "I have complete faith in her abilities. She's sharp and observant and very serious about her business."

"I'm delighted you're satisfied with her," Swan replied, not certain what lay beyond Pierce's words.

"It would be a remarkably stupid man who wasn't satisfied with her," Pierce countered, then continued before Swan could react. "Don't you find talent and professionalism pleasing, Mr. Swan?"

Swan studied Pierce a moment, then leaned back in his chair. "I wouldn't be the head of Swan Productions if I didn't," he said wryly.

"Then we understand each other," Pierce said mildly. "Just what are the points you would like to clear up?"

It was five-fifteen before Ryan was able to wind up the meeting with Bloomfield and Pierce. She'd been on the run all day, arranging spur-of-the-moment conferences and covering her scheduled work. There had been no moment to spare for a *tête-à-tête* with Pierce. Now, as they walked down the corridor together from Bloomfield's office, she let out a long breath.

"Well, that seems to be about it. Nothing like the unexpected appearance of a magician to throw everybody into a dither. As seasoned as Bloomfield is, I think he was just waiting for you to pull a rabbit out of your hat."

"I didn't have a hat," Pierce pointed out.

"Would that stop you?" Ryan laughed and checked her watch. "I'll have to stop by my office and clear up a couple of things, touch base with my father and let him know the talent was properly fussed over, then…"

"No."

"No?" Ryan looked up in surprise. "Is there something else you wanted to see? Was there something wrong with the sketches?"

"No," Pierce said again. "You're not going back to your office to clear up a couple of things or to touch base with your father."

Ryan laughed again and continued to walk. "It won't take long, twenty minutes."

"You agreed to have dinner with me, Miss Swan," he reminded her.

"As soon as I clear my desk."

"You can clear your desk Monday morning. Is there something urgent?"

"Well, no, but…" She trailed off when she felt something on her wrist, then stared down at the handcuff. "Pierce, what are you doing?" Ryan tugged her arm but found it firmly chained to his.

"Taking you to dinner."

"Pierce, take this thing off," she ordered with amused exasperation. "It's ridiculous."

"Later," he promised before he pulled her to the elevator. He waited calmly for it to reach their floor as two secretaries eyed him, the cuffs and Ryan.

"Pierce," she said in undertones. "Take these off right now. They're staring at us."

"Who?"

"Pierce, I mean it!" She let out a frustrated moan as the doors opened and revealed several other members of Swan Productions' staff. Pierce stepped inside the car, leaving her no choice but to follow. "You're going to pay for this," she muttered, trying to ignore speculative stares.

"Tell me, Miss Swan," Pierce said in a friendly, carrying voice, "is it always so difficult to persuade you to keep a dinner engagement?"

After an unintelligible mutter, Ryan stared straight ahead.

Still handcuffed to Pierce, Ryan walked across the parking lot. "All right, joke's over," she insisted. "Take these off. I've never been so embarrassed in my life! Do you have any idea how—"

But her heated lecture was cut off by his mouth. "I've wanted to do that all day," Pierce told her, then kissed her again before she could retort.

Ryan tried her best to hang on to her annoyance. His mouth was so soft. His hand, as it pressed into the small of her back, was so gentle. She drew closer to him, but when she started to lift her arms around his neck, the handcuff prevented her. "No," she said firmly, remembering. "You're not going to sneak out of this one." Ryan pulled away, ready to rage at him. He smiled at her. "Damn you, Pierce," she said on a sigh. "Kiss me again."

He kissed her softly. "You're very exciting when you're angry, Miss Swan," he whispered.

"I *was* angry," she muttered, kissing him back. "I *am* angry."

"And exciting." He drew her over to the car.

"Well?" Holding their joined wrists aloft, she sent him an inquiring glance. Pierce opened the car door and gestured her inside. "Pierce!" Exasperated, Ryan jiggled her arm. "Take these off. You can't drive this way."

"Of course I can. You'll have to climb over," he instructed, nudging her into the car.

Ryan sat in the driver's seat a moment and glared at him. "This is absurd."

"Yes," he agreed. "And I'm enjoying it. Move over."

Ryan considered refusing but decided he would simply lift her into the passenger seat bodily. With little trouble and less grace, she managed it. Pierce gave her another smile as he switched on the ignition.

"Put your hand on the gearshift and we'll do very well."

Ryan obeyed. His palm rested on the back of her hand as he put the car in reverse. "Just how long are you going to leave these on?"

"Interesting question. I haven't decided." He pulled out of the parking lot and headed north.

Ryan shook her head, then laughed in spite of herself. "If you'd told me you were this hungry, I'd have come along peacefully."

"I'm not hungry," he said easily. "I thought we'd stop and eat on the way."

"On the way?" Ryan repeated. "On the way where?"

"Home."

"Home?" A glance out the window showed her he was heading out of L.A. in the opposite direction of her apartment. "*Your* home?" she asked incredulously. "Pierce, that's a hundred and fifty miles from here."

"More or less," he agreed. "You're not needed in L.A. until Monday."

"Monday! Do you mean we're going there for the weekend? But I can't." She hadn't thought she could be any more exasperated than she already was. "I can't just pop in the car and go off for a weekend."

"Why not?"

"Well, I…" He made it sound so reasonable, she had to search for the flaw. "Because I can't. I don't have any clothes, for one thing, and—"

"You won't need them."

That stopped her. Ryan stared at him while a strange mixture of excitement and panic ran through her. "I think you're kidnapping me."

"Exactly."

"Oh."

"Any objections?" he asked, giving her a brief glance.

"I'll let you know Monday," she told him and settled back in the seat, prepared to enjoy her abduction.

Chapter 13

Ryan awoke in Pierce's bed. She opened her eyes to streaming sunlight. It had barely been dawn when Pierce had awakened her to murmur that he was going down to work. Ryan reached for his pillow, drew it closer and lingered a few minutes longer in bed.

What a surprising man he was, she mused. She would never have thought he would do anything as outrageous as handcuffing her to him and bundling her off for a weekend with nothing more than the clothes on her back. She should have been angry, indignant.

Ryan buried her face in his pillow. How could she be? Could you be angry with a man for showing you—with a look, with a touch—that you were needed and desired? Could you be indignant when a man wanted you enough to spirit you off to make love to you as though you were the most precious creature on earth?

Ryan stretched luxuriously, then picked up her watch from the nightstand. Nine-thirty! she thought with a jolt. How could it be so late? It seemed only moments ago that Pierce had left her. Jumping from the bed, she raced to the shower. They only had two days together; she wasn't going to waste them sleeping.

When she came back into the bedroom with a towel wrapped around her, Ryan studied her clothes dubiously. There was something to be said for being kidnapped by a dashing magician, she admitted, but it was really too bad he hadn't let her pack something first. Philosophically, she began to dress in the suit she had worn the day before. He'd simply have to find her something else to wear, she decided, but for now she'd make do.

With some consternation Ryan realized she didn't even have her purse with her. It was still in the bottom drawer of her desk. She wrinkled her nose at the reflection in the mirror. Her hair was tumbled, her face naked of cosmetics. Not even a comb and a lipstick, she thought and sighed. Pierce was going to have to conjure up something. With this in mind she went downstairs to look for him.

When she came to the foot of the stairs, she saw Link getting ready to leave. "Good morning." Ryan hesitated, unsure what to say to him. He'd been nowhere to be seen when they had arrived the night before.

"Hi." He grinned at her. "Pierce said you were here."

"Yes, I—he invited me for the weekend." It seemed the simplest way to put it.

"I'm glad you came. He missed you."

Her eyes lit up at that. "I missed him, too. Is he here?"

"In the library. He's on the phone." He hesitated, and Ryan saw the faint pink flush in his cheeks.

Smiling, she came down the last step. "What is it, Link?"

"I—uh—I finished writing that song you liked."

"That's wonderful. I'd love to hear it."

"It's on the piano." Excruciatingly embarrassed, he lowered his eyes to his shoes. "You can play it later if you want to."

"Won't you be here?" She wanted to take his hand as she would a little boy's but felt it would only embarrass him more. "I've never heard you play."

"No, I'm…" His color deepened, and he sent her a quick look. "Bess and I…well, she wanted to drive to San Francisco." He cleared his throat. "She likes to ride the streetcars."

"That's nice, Link." On impulse, Ryan decided to see if she could give Bess a hand. "She's a very special lady, isn't she?"

"Oh, sure. There's nobody else like Bess," he agreed readily, then stared at his shoes again.

"She feels just the same way about you."

His eyes darted to her face, then over her shoulder. "You think so?"

"Oh, yes." Though she wanted badly to smile, Ryan kept her voice serious. "She told me how she first met you. I thought it was terribly romantic."

Link gave a nervous little laugh. "She was awful pretty. Lots of guys hang around her when we go on the road."

"I imagine so," Ryan agreed and gave him a mental shove. "But I think she has a taste for musicians. Piano players," she added when he looked back at her. "The kind who know how to write beautifully romantic songs. Time's wasting, don't you think?"

Link was staring at her as though trying to sort out her words. "Huh? Oh, yeah." He wrinkled his brow, then nodded. "Yeah, I guess so. I should go get her now."

"I think that's a very good idea." She did take his hand now, giving it a quick squeeze. "Have a good time."

"Okay." He smiled and turned for the door. With his hand on the knob, he stopped to look over his shoulder. "Ryan, does she really like piano players?"

"Yes, Link, she really does."

He grinned again and opened the door. "Bye."

"Goodbye, Link. Give Bess my love."

When the door shut, Ryan remained where she was a moment. What a sweet man, she thought, then crossed her fingers for Bess. They would be wonderful together if they could just get over the obstacle of his shyness. Well, Ryan thought with a pleased smile, she had certainly done all she could in her first attempt at matchmaking. The rest was up to the two of them.

Turning down the hall, she went to the library. The door was open, and she could hear Pierce's low-pitched voice as it carried to her. Even the sound of it had something stirring inside her. He was here with her, and they were alone. When she stood in the doorway, his eyes met hers.

Pierce smiled, and continued his conversation, gestured her inside. "I'll send you the exact specifications in writing," he said, watching Ryan enter and wander to a bookshelf. Why was it, he wondered, that the sight of her in one of those prim business suits never failed to excite him? "No, I'll need it completed in three weeks. I can't give you any more time than that," he continued with his eyes fixed on Ryan's back. "I need time to work with it before I can be sure I can use it."

Ryan turned around, then, perching on the arm of a chair, she watched him. He wore jeans with a short-sleeved sweatshirt, and his hair was disheveled, as though he had run his hands through it. She thought he had never looked more attractive, sunk back in an over-stuffed chair, more relaxed than usual. The energy was still there, the live-wire energy that seemed to spark from him onstage or off. But it was on hold, she mused. He was more at ease in this house than he was any-where else.

He continued to give instructions to whomever it was he spoke to, but Ryan watched his eyes skim her briefly. Something impish shot through her. Perhaps she could ruffle that calm of his.

Rising idly, she began to wander the room again, stepping out of her shoes as she did so. She took a book from the shelf, skimmed through it, then replaced it.

"I'll need the entire list delivered here," Pierce stated and watched Ryan slip out of her suit jacket. She draped it over the back of a chair. "Yes, that's exactly what I want. If you'll—" He broke off as she began to unbut-ton her blouse. She looked up when he stopped speak-ing and smiled at him. "If you'll contact me when you have…" The blouse slid to the floor before she casually unzipped her skirt. "When you have…" Pierce went on, struggling to remember what he had been saying, "the—ah—all the items, I'll arrange for the freight."

Bending over after she stepped out of her skirt, Ryan began to unhook her stockings. "No, that won't—it won't be necessary." She tossed her hair behind her shoulder and sent Pierce another smile. The look held for several pulsing seconds. "Yes," Pierce mumbled into the phone. "Yes, that's fine."

Leaving the pool of nylons on the discarded skirt, she straightened. Her chemise laced up the front. With one finger Ryan pulled at the small bow between her breasts until it loosened. She kept her eyes on his, smiling again when she watched them lower to where her fingers worked slowly with the laces.

"What?" Pierce shook his head. The man's voice had been nothing but an unintelligible buzz in his ear. "What?" he said again as the silk parted. Very slowly, Ryan drew it off. "I'll get back to you." Pierce dropped the receiver back on the hook.

"All finished?" she asked as she walked to him. "I wanted to talk to you about my wardrobe."

"I like what you have on." He pulled her into the chair with him and found her mouth. Tasting the wild need, she let herself go limp.

"Was that an important call?" she asked when his lips moved to her neck. "I didn't want to disturb you."

"The hell you didn't." He reached for her breast, groaning when he took possession. "God, you drive me crazy! Ryan…" His voice was rough with urgency as he slid her to the floor. "Now."

"Yes," she murmured even as he entered her.

He trembled as he lay on top of her. His breath was ragged. No one, he thought, no one had ever been able to destroy his control this way. It was terrifying. Part of him wanted to stand up and walk away—to prove he could still walk away. But he stayed where he was.

"Dangerous," he murmured in her ear just before he let the tip of his tongue trace it. He heard her sigh. "You're a dangerous woman."

"*Mmm,* how so?"

"You know my weaknesses, Ryan Swan. Maybe you are my weakness."

"Is that bad?" she murmured.

"I don't know." He lifted his head and stared down at her. "I don't know."

Ryan lifted a hand to tenderly brush the hair from his forehead. "It doesn't matter today. Today there's only the two of us."

The look he gave her was long and deep, as intense as the first time their eyes had met. "The more I'm with you, the more there are only the two of us."

She smiled, then pulled him back to cradle him in her arms. "The first time you kissed me, the whole world dropped away. I tried to tell myself you had hypnotized me."

Pierce laughed and reached up to fondle her breast. The nipple was still taut, and she quivered at his touch. "Do you have any idea how badly I wanted to take you to bed that night?" He ran his thumb lazily back and forth over the point of her breast, listening to her quickening breathing as he spoke. "I couldn't work, I couldn't sleep. I lay there thinking about how you'd looked in that little bit of silk and lace."

"I wanted you," Ryan said huskily as fresh passion kindled. "I was shocked that I'd only known you for a few hours and I wanted you."

"I would have made love to you like this that night." Pierce touched his mouth to hers. He kissed her, using his lips only until hers were hot and soft and hungry. Both of his hands were in her hair now, drawing it back from her face as his tongue gently plundered.

It seemed he would kiss her endlessly. There were soft, murmuring sounds as their lips parted and met again, then again. Hot, heady, unbearably sweet. He stroked her shoulders, lingering at the slope while the kiss went on and on. She knew the world centered on his lips.

No matter where else he touched, his mouth remained on hers. He might run his hands wherever he chose, but his kiss alone kept her prisoner. He seemed to crave her taste more than he craved breath. She gripped his shoulders, digging her nails into his flesh and totally unaware of it. Her only thought was that the kiss go on forever.

He knew her body was totally his and touched where it gave them both the most pleasure. At the slightest urging, her legs parted for him. He traced a fingertip up and down the inside of her thigh, delighting in its silken texture and in her trembling response. He passed over the center of her only briefly on the journey to her other thigh, all the while toying with her lips.

He used his teeth and his tongue, then his lips only. Her delirious murmuring of his name sent fresh thrills racing along his skin. There was the subtle sweep of her hips to trace, the curve of her waist. Her arms were satin smooth. He could find endless delight in touching only them. She was his—he thought it again and had to control an explosive urge to take her quickly. Instead, he let the kiss speak for him. It spoke of dark, driving needs and infinite tenderness.

Even when he slipped inside her, Pierce continued to savor the taste of her mouth. He took her slowly, waiting for her needs to build, forcing back his own passion until it was no longer possible to deny it.

His mouth was still crushed to hers when she cried out with the final flash of pleasure.

No one but her, he thought dizzily as he breathed in

the scent of her hair. No one but her. Ryan's arms came
around him to keep him close. He knew he was trapped.

Hours later Ryan slid two steaks under the broiler.
She was dressed now in a pair of Pierce's jeans, cinched
at the waist with a belt, with the legs rolled up several
times to adjust for their difference in height. The sweatshirt bagged over her hips. Ryan pushed the sleeves up
past the elbow while she helped him prepare dinner.

"Do you cook as well as Link?" she demanded, turning to watch him add croutons to the salad he was making.

"No. When you're kidnapped, Miss Swan, you can't
expect gourmet meals."

Ryan went to stand behind him, then slipped her arms
around his waist. "Are you going to demand a ransom?"
With a sigh she rested her cheek on his back. She had
never been happier in her life.

"Perhaps. When I'm through with you."

She pinched him hard, but he didn't even flinch.
"Louse," she said lovingly, then slipped her hands under
his shirt to trail her fingers up his chest. This time she
felt him quiver.

"You distract me, Ryan."

"I was hoping to. It isn't the simplest thing to do,
you know."

"You've been having a remarkable streak of success,"
he commented as she ran her hands over his shoulders.

"Can you really dislocate your shoulders to get out
of a straightjacket?" she wondered aloud as she felt the
strength of their solidity.

Amused, he continued to cube cheese for the salad.
"Where did you hear that?"

"Oh, somewhere," she said vaguely, not willing to admit she had devoured every write-up she could find on him. "I also heard you have complete control over your muscles." They rippled under her curious fingers. She pressed into his back, enjoying the faint forest scent that clung to him.

"Do you also hear that I only eat certain herbs and roots that I gather under a full moon?" He popped a morsel of cheese in his mouth before he turned to gather her into his arms. "Or that I studied the magic arts in Tibet when I was twelve?"

"I read that you were tutored by Houdini's ghost," she countered.

"Really? I must have missed that one. Very flattering."

"You really enjoy the ridiculous things they print about you, don't you?"

"Of course." He kissed her nose. "I'd have a sorry sense of humor if I didn't."

"And of course," she added, "if the fact and fantasy are so mixed, nobody ever knows which is which or who you are."

"There's that, too." He twined a lock of her hair around his finger. "The more they print about me, Ryan, the more actual privacy I have."

"And your privacy is important to you."

"When you grow up the way I did, you learn to value it."

Pressing her face to his chest, Ryan clung to him. Pierce put his hand under her chin and lifted it. Her eyes were already glistening with tears.

"Ryan," he said carefully, "there's no need for you to feel sorry for me."

"No." She shook her head, understanding his reluctance to accept sympathy. It had been the same with Bess. "I know that, but it's difficult not to feel sorry for a small boy."

He smiled, brushing a finger over her lips. "He was very resilient." He set her away from him. "You'd better turn those steaks."

Ryan busied herself with the steaks, knowing he wanted the subject dropped. How could she explain she was hungry for any detail of his life, anything that would bring him closer to her? And perhaps she was wrong, she thought, to touch on the past when she was afraid to touch on the future.

"How do you like them cooked?" she asked as she bent down to the broiler.

"*Mmm,* medium rare." He was more interested in the view she provided as she leaned over. "Link has his own dressing made up for the salad. It's quite good."

"Where did he learn to cook?" she asked as she turned the second steak.

"It was a matter of necessity," Pierce told her. "He likes to eat. Things were lean in the early days when we were on the road. It turned out he was a lot more handy with a can of soup than Bess or me."

Ryan turned and sent him a smile. "You know, they were going to San Francisco today."

"Yes." He quirked a brow. "So?"

"He's just as crazy about her as she is about him."

"I know that, too."

"You might have done something to move things along after all these years," she stated, gesturing with the kitchen fork. "After all, they're your friends."

"Which is exactly why I don't interfere," he said mildly. "What did you do?"

"Well, I didn't interfere," she said with a sniff. "I merely gave him a very gentle shove in the right direction. I mentioned that Bess has a preference for piano players."

"I see."

"He's so shy," she said in exasperation. "He'll be ready for social security before he works up the nerve to—to…"

"To what?" Pierce asked, grinning.

"To anything," Ryan stated. "And stop leering at me."

"Was I?"

"You know very well you were. And anyway—" She gasped and dropped the kitchen fork with a clatter when something brushed past her ankles.

"It's just Circe," Pierce pointed out, then grinned as Ryan sighed. "She smells the meat." He picked up the fork to rinse it off while the cat rubbed against Ryan's legs and purred lovingly. "She'll do her best to convince you she deserves some for herself."

"Your pets have a habit of catching me off guard."

"Sorry." But he smiled, not looking sorry at all.

Ryan put her hands on her hips. "You like to see me rattled, don't you?"

"I like to see you," he answered simply. He laughed and caught her up in his arms. "Though I have to admit, there's something appealing about seeing you wear my clothes while you putter around the kitchen in your bare feet."

"Oh," she said knowingly. "The caveman syndrome."

"Oh, no, Miss Swan." He nuzzled her neck. "I'm your slave."

"Really?" Ryan considered the interesting possibilities of the statement. "Then set the table," she told him. "I'm starving."

They ate by candlelight. Ryan never tasted a mouthful of the meal. She was too full of Pierce. There was wine—something smooth and mellow, but it might have been water, for all it mattered. In the baggy sweatshirt and jeans, she had never felt more like a woman. His eyes told her constantly that she was beautiful, interesting, desirable. It seemed as though they had never been lovers, never been intimate. He was wooing her.

He made her glow with a look, with a soft word or the touch of his hand on hers. It never ceased to please her, even overwhelm her, that he had so much romance in him. He had to know that she would be with him under any circumstances, yet he courted her. Flowers and candlelight and the words of a man captivated. Ryan fell in love again.

Long after both of them had lost any interest in the meal, they lingered. The wine grew warm, the candles low. He was content to watch her in the flickering light, to let her quiet voice flow over him. Whatever needs built inside him could be soothed by merely running his fingers over the back of her hand. He wanted nothing more than to be with her.

Passion would come later, he knew. In the night, in the dark when she lay beside him. But for now it was enough to see her smile.

"Will you wait for me in the parlor?" he murmured and kissed her fingers one at a time. Shivery delight shot up her arm.

"I'll help with the dishes." But her thoughts were far, far away from practical matters.

"No, I'll see to it." Pierce turned her hand over and pressed his lips to her palm. "Wait for me."

Her knees trembled, but she rose when he drew her to her feet. She couldn't take her eyes from his. "You won't be long?"

"No." He slid his hands down her arms. "I won't be long, love." Gently, he kissed her.

Ryan walked to the parlor in a daze. It hadn't been the kiss but the one simple word of endearment that had her heart pounding. It seemed impossible, after what they had been to each other, that a casual word would send her pulses racing. But Pierce was careful with words.

And it was a night for enchantment, she thought as she entered the parlor. A night made for love and romance. She walked to the window to look out at the sky. Even the moon was full, as if it knew it had to be. It was quiet enough that she could just hear the sound of waves against rock.

They were on an island, Ryan imagined. It was a small, windswept island in some dark sea. And the nights were long. There was no phone, no electricity. On impulse, she turned from the window and began to light the candles that were scattered around the room. The fire was laid, and she set a match to the kindling. The dry wood caught with a crackle.

Rising, she looked around the room. The light was just as she wanted it—insubstantial with shadows shifting. It added just a touch of mystery and seemed to reflect her own feelings toward Pierce.

Ryan glanced down at herself and brushed at the sweatshirt. If only she had something lovely to wear, something white and filmy. But perhaps Pierce's imagination would be as active as hers.

Music, she thought suddenly and looked around. Surely he had a stereo, but she wouldn't have any idea where to look for it. Inspired, she went to the piano.

Link's staff paper was waiting. Between the glow from the fire behind her and the candles on the piano, Ryan could see the notes clearly enough. Sitting down, she began to play. It took only moments for her to be caught up in the melody.

Pierce stood in the doorway and watched her. Although her eyes were fixed on the paper in front of her, they seemed to be dreaming. He'd never seen her quite like this—so caught up in her own thoughts. Unwilling to break her mood, he stood where he was. He could have watched her forever.

In the candlelight her hair was only a mist falling over her shoulders. Her skin was pale. Only her eyes were dark, moved by the music she played. He caught the faint whiff of wood smoke and melting wax. It was a moment he knew he would remember for the rest of his life. Years and years could pass, and he would be able to close his eyes and see her just like this, hear the music drifting, smell the candles burning.

"Ryan." He hadn't meant to speak aloud, indeed had only whispered her name, but her eyes lifted to his.

She smiled, but the flickering light caught the glistening tears. "It's so beautiful."

"Yes." Pierce could hardly trust himself to speak. A word, a wrong move might shatter the mood. What he saw, what he felt might be an illusion after all. "Please, play it again."

Even after she had begun, he came no closer. He wanted the picture to remain exactly as it was. Her lips were just parted. He could taste them as he stood there.

He knew how her cheek would feel if he laid his hand on it. She would look up at him and smile with that special warmth in her eyes. But he wouldn't touch her, only absorb all she was in this one special moment out of time.

The flames of the candles burned straight. A log shifted quietly in the grate. And then she was finished.

Her eyes lifted to his. Pierce went to her.

"I've never wanted you more," he said in a low, almost whispering voice. "Or been more afraid to touch you."

"Afraid?" Her fingers stayed lightly on the keys. "Why?"

"If I were to touch you, my hand might pass through you. You might only be a dream after all."

Ryan took his hand and pressed it to her cheek. "It's no dream," she murmured. "Not for either of us."

Her skin was warm and real under his fingers. He was struck by a wave of incredible tenderness. Pierce lifted her other hand, holding it as though it were made of porcelain. "If you had one wish, Ryan, only one, what would it be?"

"That tonight, just tonight, you'd think of nothing and no one but me."

Her eyes were brilliant in the dim, shifting light. Pierce drew her to her feet, then cupped her face in his hand. "You waste your wishes, Ryan, asking for something that already is." He kissed her temples, then her cheeks, leaving her mouth trembling for the taste of his.

"I want to fill your mind," she told him, her voice wavering, "so there's no room for anything else. Tonight I want there to be only me. And tomorrow—"

"Shh." He kissed her mouth to silence her, but so lightly she was left with only a promise of what was to come. "There's no one but you, Ryan." Her eyes were

closed, and he brushed his lips delicately over the lids. "Come to bed," he murmured. "Let me show you."

Taking her hand, he walked through the room, putting out the candles. He lifted one, letting its quivering light show them the way.

Chapter 14

They had to be separated again. Ryan knew it was necessary in the course of preparing the special. When she was lonely for him, she had only to remember that last magic night they had spent together. It would be enough to hold her until she could see him again.

Though she saw him off and on during the next weeks, it was only professionally. He came to her for meetings or to oversee certain points of his own business. He kept to himself on these. Ryan still knew nothing about the construction of the props and gags he would use. He would give her a detailed list of the illusions he would perform, their time sequence and only the barest explanation of their mechanics.

Ryan found this frustrating, but she had little else to complain about. The set was forming along the lines she, Bloomfield and Pierce had ultimately agreed on. Elaine

Fisher was signed for a guest appearance. Ryan had managed to hold her own through the series of tough, emotional meetings. And so, she recalled with amusement, had Pierce.

He could say more with his long silences and one or two calm words than a dozen frantic, bickering department heads. He sat through their demands and complaints with complete amiability and always came out on top.

He wouldn't agree to use a professional script for the show. It was as simple as that. He said no. And he had stuck to it—because he knew he was right. He had his own music, his own director, his own prop crew. Nothing would sway him from using his own people on key posts. He turned down six costume sketches with a careless shake of the head.

Pierce did things his own way and bent only when it suited him to bend. Yet Ryan saw that the creative staff, as temperamental as they came, offered little complaint about him. He charmed them, she noted. He had a way with people. He would warm you or freeze you—it only took a look.

Bess was to have the final say on her own wardrobe. Pierce simply stated that she knew best what suited her. He refused to rehearse unless the set was closed. Then he entertained the stagehands with sleight of hand and card tricks. He knew how to keep control without rippling the waters.

Ryan, however, found it difficult to function around the restrictions he put on her and her staff. She tried reasoning, arguing, pleading. She got nowhere.

"Pierce." Ryan cornered him on the set during a break in rehearsal. "I have to talk to you."

"Hmm?" He watched his crew set up the torches for the next segment. "Exactly eight inches apart," he told them.

"Pierce, this is important."

"Yes, I'm listening."

"You can't bar Ned from the set during rehearsal," she said and tugged on his arm to get his full attention.

"Yes, I can. I did. Didn't he tell you?"

"Yes, he told me." She let out a sigh of exasperation. "Pierce, as production coordinator, he has a perfectly legitimate reason to be here."

"He gets in the way. Make sure there's a foot between the rows, please."

"Pierce!"

"What?" he said pleasantly and turned back to her. "Have I told you that you look lovely today, Miss Swan?" He ran the lapel of her jacket between his thumb and forefinger. "That's a very nice suit."

"Listen, Pierce, you've got to give my people a little more room." She tried to ignore the smile in his eyes and continued. "Your crew is very efficient, but on a production of this size we need more hands. Your people know your work, but they don't know television."

"I can't have your people poking into my props, Ryan. Or wandering around when I'm setting up."

"Good grief, do you want them to sign a blood oath not to reveal your secrets?" she demanded, waving her clipboard. "We could set it up for the next full moon."

"A good idea, but I don't know how many of your people would go along with it. Not your production coordinator, at any rate," he added with a grin. "I don't think he'd care for the sight of his own blood."

Ryan lifted a brow. "Are you jealous?"

He laughed with such great enjoyment she wanted to hit him. "Don't be absurd. He's hardly a threat."

"That's not the point," she muttered, miffed. "He's very good at his job, but he can hardly do it if you won't be reasonable."

"Ryan," he said, looking convincingly surprised, "I'm always reasonable. What would you like me to do?"

"I'd like you to let Ned do what he has to do. And I'd like you to let my people in the studio."

"Certainly," he agreed. "But not when I'm rehearsing."

"Pierce," she said dangerously. "You're tying my hands. You have to make certain concessions for television."

"I'm aware of that, Ryan, and I will." He kissed her brow. "When I'm ready. No," he continued before she could speak again, "you have to let me work with my own crew until I'm sure it's smooth."

"And how long is that going to take?" She knew he was winning her over as he had everyone from Coogar down.

"A few more days." He took her free hand. "Your key people are here, in any case."

"All right," she said with a sigh. "But by the end of the week the lighting crew will have to be in on rehearsals. That's essential."

"Agreed." He gave her hand a solemn shake. "Anything else?"

"Yes." Ryan straightened her shoulders and shot him a level look. "The time for the first segment runs over by ten seconds. You're going to have to alter it to fit the scheduled run of the commercials."

"No, you'll have to alter the scheduled run of commercials." He gave her a light kiss before he walked away.

Before she could shout at him, Ryan found there was a rosebud pinned to her lapel. Pleasure mixed with fury until it was too late to act.

"He's something, isn't he?"

Ryan turned her head to see Elaine Fisher. "Something," she agreed. "I hope you're satisfied with everything, Miss Fisher," she continued, then smiled at the petite, kittenlike blonde. "Your dressing room's agreeable?"

"It's fine." Elaine flashed her winning, toothy smile. "There's a bulb burned out on my mirror, though."

"I'll see to it."

Elaine watched Pierce and gave her quick, bubbling laugh. "I've got to tell you, I wouldn't mind finding him in my dressing room."

"I don't think I can arrange that for you, Miss Fisher," Ryan returned primly.

"Oh, honey, I could arrange it for myself if it weren't for the way he looks at you." She sent Ryan a friendly wink. "Of course, if you're not interested, I could try to console him."

The actress's charm wasn't easy to resist. "That won't be necessary," Ryan told her with a smile. "It's a producer's job to keep the talent happy, you know."

"Why don't you see if you could come up with a clone for me?" Leaving Ryan, she walked to Pierce. "Ready for me?"

Watching them work together, Ryan saw that her instincts had been on the mark. They were perfectly suited. Elaine's frothy blond beauty and ingenue charm masked a sharp talent and flair for comedy. It was the exact balance Ryan had hoped for.

Ryan waited, holding her breath as the torches were

lit. It was the first time she had seen the illusion all the way through. The flames burned high for a moment, sending out an almost blinding light before Pierce spread his hands and calmed them. Then he turned to Elaine.

"Don't burn the dress," she cracked. "It's rented."

Ryan scribbled down a note to keep in the ad lib even as he began to levitate Elaine. In moments she was floating just above the flames.

"It's going well."

Glancing up, Ryan smiled at Bess. "Yes, for all the problems he causes, Pierce makes it impossible for it to go otherwise. He's relentless."

"Tell me about it." They watched him in silence a moment, then Bess squeezed Ryan's arm. "I can't stand it," she said in undertones to keep from disturbing the rehearsal. "I have to tell you."

"Tell me what?"

"I wanted to tell Pierce first, but…" She grinned from ear to ear. "Link and I—"

"Oh, congratulations!" Ryan interrupted and hugged her.

Bess laughed. "You didn't let me finish."

"You were going to tell me you're getting married."

"Well, yeah, but—"

"Congratulations," Ryan said again. "When did it happen?"

"Just now, practically." Looking a little dazed, Bess scratched her head. "I was in my dressing room getting ready when he knocked on the door. He wouldn't come in, he just stood there in the doorway sort of shuffling his feet, you know? Then all of a sudden he asked me if I wantcd to get married." Bess shook her head and laughed again. "I was so surprised, I asked him to whom."

"Oh, Bess, you didn't!"

"Yeah, I did. Well, you just don't expect that sort of question after twenty years."

"Poor Link," Ryan murmured with a smile. "What did he say?"

"He just stood there for a minute, staring at me and turning colors, then he said, 'Well, to me, I guess.'" She gave a low chuckle. "It was real romantic."

"I think it was lovely," Ryan told her. "I'm so happy for you."

"Thanks." After a breathy sigh, she looked over at Pierce again. "Don't say anything to Pierce, okay? I think I'll let Link tell him."

"I won't say anything," she promised. "Will you be married soon?"

Bess sent her a lopsided grin. "Sweetie, you better believe it. As far as I can see, we've already been engaged for twenty years, and that's long enough." She pleated the hem of her sweatshirt between her fingers. "I guess we'll just wait until after the special airs, then make the jump."

"Will you stay with Pierce?"

"Sure." She looked at Ryan quizzically. "We're a team. 'Course, Link and I will live at my place, but we wouldn't break up the act."

"Bess," Ryan began slowly. "There's something I've been wanting to ask you. It's about the final illusion." She sent Pierce a worried frown as he continued to work with Elaine. "He's so secretive about it. All he'll say so far is that it's an escape and he'll need four minutes and ten seconds from intro to finish. What do you know about it?"

Bess shrugged restlessly. "He's keeping that one close because he hasn't worked out all the bugs."

"What sort of bugs?" Ryan persisted.

"I don't know, really, except…" She hesitated, torn between her own doubts and her loyalty. "Except Link doesn't like it."

"Why?" Ryan put a hand on Bess's arm. "Is it dangerous? Really dangerous?"

"Look, Ryan, all the escapes can be dangerous, unless you're talking a straightjacket and handcuffs. But he's the best." She watched Pierce lower Elaine to the floor. "He's going to need me in a minute."

"Bess." She kept her hand firm on the redhead's arm. "Tell me what you know."

"Ryan." Bess sighed as she looked down at her. "I know how you feel about him, but I can't. Pierce's work is Pierce's work."

"I'm not asking you to break the magician's code of ethics," Ryan said impatiently. "He'll have to tell me what the illusion is, anyway."

"Then he'll tell you." Bess patted her hand but moved away.

The rehearsals ran over, as Pierce's rehearsals had a habit of doing. After attending a late-afternoon production meeting, Ryan decided to wait for him in his dressing room. The problem of the final illusion had nagged at her throughout the day. She hadn't liked the worried look in Bess's eyes.

Pierce's dressing room was spacious and plush. The carpeting was thick, the sofa plump and wide enough to double as a bed. There was a large-screen television, a complex stereo system and a fully stocked bar that she knew Pierce never used. On the wall were a pair of very good lithographs. It was the sort of dressing room Swan reserved for their special performers. Ryan doubted that Pierce spent more than thirty minutes a day within its walls when he was in L.A.

Ryan poked in the refrigerator, found a quart of orange juice and fixed herself a cold drink before sinking down on the sofa. Idly, she picked up a book from the table. It was one of Pierce's, she noted, another work on Houdini. With absent interest she thumbed through the pages.

When Pierce entered, he found her curled up on the sofa, halfway through the volume.

"Research?"

Ryan's head shot up. "Could he really do all these things?" she demanded. "I mean this business about swallowing needles and a ball of thread, then pulling them out threaded. He didn't really do that, did he?"

"Yes." He stripped out of his shirt.

Ryan gave him a narrowed look. "Can you?"

He only smiled. "I don't make a habit of copying illusions. How was your day?"

"Fine. It says in here that some people thought he had a pocket in his skin."

This time he laughed. "Don't you think you'd have found mine by now if I had one?"

Ryan set the book aside and rose. "I want to talk to you."

"All right." Pierce pulled her into his arms and began to roam her face with kisses. "In a few minutes. It's been a long three days without you."

"You were the one who went away," she reminded him, then halted his wandering mouth with her own.

"I had a few details to smooth out. I can't work seriously here."

"That's what your dungeon's for," she murmured and found his mouth again.

"Exactly. We'll go to dinner tonight. Some place with candles and dark corners."

"My apartment has candles and dark corners," she said against his lips. "We can be alone there."

"You'll try to seduce me again."

Ryan laughed and forgot what she had wanted to talk to him about. "I *will* seduce you again."

"You've gotten cocky, Miss Swan." He drew her away. "I'm not always so easy."

"I like challenges."

He rubbed his nose against hers. "Did you like your flower?"

"Yes, thank you." She circled his neck with her arms. "It kept me from harassing you."

"I know. You find me difficult to work with, don't you?"

"Extremely. And if you let anyone else produce your next special, I'll sabotage every one of your illusions."

"Well, then, I'll have to keep you and protect myself."

He touched his lips to hers gently, and the wave of love hit her with such force, such suddenness, Ryan clutched at him.

"Pierce." She wanted to speak quickly before the old fear prevented her. "Pierce, read my mind." With her eyes tightly shut, she buried her face against his shoulder. "Can you read my mind?"

Puzzled by the urgency in her tone, he drew her away to study her. She opened her eyes wide, and in them he saw that she was a little frightened, a little dazed. And he saw something else that had his heart taking an erratic beat.

"Ryan?" Pierce lifted a hand to her cheek, afraid he was seeing something only he needed to see. Afraid, too, that it was real.

"I'm terrified," she whispered. "The words won't come. Can you see them?" Her voice was jerky. She bit her lip to steady it. "If you can't, I'll understand. It doesn't have to change anything."

Yes, he saw them, but she was wrong. Once they were said, they changed everything. He hadn't wanted it to happen, yet he had known, somehow, they would come to this. He had known the moment he had seen her walk down the steps to his workroom. She was the woman who would change everything. Whatever power he had would become partially hers once he said three words. It was the only real incantation in a world of illusion.

"Ryan." He hesitated a moment but knew there was no stopping what already was. "I love you."

Her breath came out in a rush of relief. "Oh, Pierce, I was so afraid you wouldn't want to see." They drew together and clung. "I love you so much. So very much." Her sigh was shaky. "It's good, isn't it?"

"Yes." He felt her heartbeat match his own. "Yes, it's good."

"I didn't know I could be so happy. I wanted to tell you before," she murmured against his throat. "But I was so afraid. It seems silly now."

"We were both afraid." He drew her closer, but it still wasn't enough. "We've wasted time."

"But you love me," she whispered, only wanting to hear the words again.

"Yes, Ryan, I love you."

"Let's go home, Pierce." She ran her lips along his jaw. "Let's go home. I want you."

"Uh-uh. Now."

Ryan threw her head back and laughed. "Now? Here?"

"Here and now," he agreed, enjoying the flash of devilment in her eyes.

"Somebody might come in," she said and drew away from him.

Saying nothing, Pierce turned to the door and flicked the lock. "I don't think so."

"Oh." Ryan bit her lip, trying not to smile. "It looks like I'm going to be ravished."

"You could call for help," he suggested as he pushed the jacket from her shoulders.

"Help," she said quietly while he unbuttoned her blouse. "I don't think anyone heard me."

"Then it looks like you're going to be ravished."

"Oh, good," Ryan whispered. Her blouse slid to the floor.

They touched each other and laughed with the sheer joy of being in love. They kissed and clung as though there were no tomorrow. They murmured soft words and sighed with pleasure. Even when the lovemaking intensified and passion began to rule, there was an underlying joy that remained innocent.

He loves me, Ryan thought and ran her hands up his strong back. *He belongs to me.* She answered his kiss with fervor.

She loves me, Pierce thought and felt her skin heat under his fingers. *She belongs to me.* He sought her mouth and savored it.

They gave to each other, took from each other until

they were more one than two. There was rising passion, an infinite tenderness and a new freedom. When the loving was over, they could still laugh, dizzy with the knowledge that for them it was only the beginning.

"You know," Ryan murmured, "I thought it was the producer who lured the talent to the couch."

"Didn't you?" Pierce let her hair run through his fingers.

With a chuckle Ryan kissed him between the eyes. "You were supposed to think it was all your idea." Sitting up, she reached for her blouse.

Pierce sat up behind her and ran a fingertip up her spine. "Going somewhere?"

"Look, Atkins, you'll get your screen test." She squealed when he bit her shoulder. "Don't try to change my mind," she said before she slipped out of reach. "I'm finished with you."

"Oh?" Pierce leaned back on his elbow to watch her dress.

"Until we get home." Ryan wriggled into her teddy, then began to hook her stockings. She eyed his nakedness. "You'd better get dressed before I change my mind. We'll end up locked in the building for the night."

"I could get us out when we wanted to go."

"There are alarms."

He laughed. "Ryan, really."

She shot him a look. "I suppose it is a good thing you decided not to be a criminal."

"It's simpler to charge for picking locks. People will always find a fascination in paying to see if it can be done." He grinned as he sat up. "They don't appreciate it if you do it for free."

Curious, she tilted her head. "Have you ever come across a lock you can't beat?"

"Given enough time," Pierce said as he reached for his clothes, "any lock can be opened."

"Without tools?"

He lifted a brow. "There are tools, and there are tools."

Ryan frowned at him. "I'm going to have to check for that pocket in your skin again."

"Anytime," he agreed obligingly.

"You could be nice and teach me just one thing, like how to get out of those handcuffs."

"Uh-uh." He shook his head as he slipped into his jeans. "They might come in handy again."

Ryan shrugged as if she didn't care anyway and began to button her blouse. "Oh, I forgot. I wanted to talk to you about the finale."

Pierce pulled a fresh shirt out of the closet. "What about it?"

"That's precisely what I want to know," Ryan told him. "What exactly do you have planned?"

"It's an escape, I told you." He drew on the shirt.

"I need more than that, Pierce. The show goes on in ten days."

"I'm working it out."

Recognizing the tone, Ryan stepped to him. "No, this isn't a solo production. I'm the producer, Pierce; you wanted it that way. Now, I can go along with some of your oddities about the staff." She ignored his indignant expression. "But I have to know exactly what's going to be aired. You can't keep me in the dark with less than two weeks to go until taping."

"I'm going to break out of a safe," he said simply and handed Ryan her shoe.

"Break out of a safe." She took it, watching him. "There's more to it than that, Pierce. I'm not a fool."

"I'll have my hands and feet manacled first."

Ryan stooped to retrieve her other shoe. His continued reluctance to elaborate brought on a very real fear. Wanting her voice to be steady, she waited a moment. "What else, Pierce?"

He said nothing until he had buttoned his shirt. "It's a play on a box within a box within a box. An old gimmick."

The fear grew. "Three safes? One within the other?"

"That's right. Each one's larger than the last."

"Are the safes airtight?"

"Yes."

Ryan's skin grew cold. "I don't like it."

He gave her a calm measuring look. "You don't have to like it, Ryan, but you don't have to worry, either."

She swallowed, knowing it was important to keep her head. "There's more, too, isn't there? I know there is, tell me."

"The last safe has a time lock," he said flatly. "I've done it before."

"A time lock?" Ice ran down her back. "No, you can't. It's just foolish."

"Hardly foolish," Pierce returned. "It's taken me months to work out the mechanics and timing."

"Timing?"

"I have three minutes of air."

Three minutes! she thought and struggled not to lose control. "And how long does the escape take?"

"At the moment, just over three minutes."

"Just over," Ryan repeated numbly. "Just over. What if something goes wrong?"

"I don't intend for anything to go wrong. I've been over and over it, Ryan."

She spun away, then whirled back to him. "I'm not going to allow this. It's out of the question. Use the panther business for the finale, but not this."

"I'm using the escape, Ryan." His voice was very calm and very final.

"No!" Panicked, she grabbed his arms. "I'm cutting it. It's out, Pierce. You can use one of your other illusions or come up with a new one, but this is out."

"You can't cut it." His tone never altered as he looked down at her. "I have final say; read the contract."

She paled and stepped back from him. "Damn you, I don't care about the contract. I know what it says. I wrote it!"

"Then you know you can't cut the escape," he said quietly.

"I won't let you do this." Tears had sprung to her eyes, but she blinked them away. "You can't do it."

"I'm sorry, Ryan."

"I'll find a way to scrub the show." Her breath was heaving with anger and fear and hopelessness. "I can find a way to break the contract."

"Maybe." He laid his hands on her shoulders. "I'll still do the escape, Ryan, next month in New York."

"Pierce, God!" Desperately, she clung to his arms. "You could die in there. It's not worth it. Why do you have to try something like this?"

"Because I can do it. Ryan, understand that this is my work."

"I understand that I love you. Doesn't that matter?"

"You know that it does," he said roughly. "You know how much."

"No, I don't know how much." Frantically, she pushed away from him. "I only know that you're going to do this no matter how much I beg you not to. You'll expect me to stand by and watch you risk your life for some applause and a write-up."

"It has nothing to do with applause or write-ups." The first hint of anger shot into his eyes. "You should know me better than that."

"No, no, I don't know you," she said desperately. "How can I understand why you insist on doing something like this? It's not necessary to the show, to your career!"

He struggled to hold his temper in check and answered calmly. "It's necessary to me."

"Why?" she demanded furiously. "Why is it necessary to risk your life?"

"That's your viewpoint, Ryan, not mine. This is part of my work and part of what I am." He paused but didn't go to her. "You'll have to accept that if you accept me."

"That's not fair."

"Maybe not," he agreed. "I'm sorry."

Ryan swallowed, fighting back tears. "Where does that leave us?"

He kept his eyes on hers. "That's up to you."

"I won't watch." She backed to the door. "I won't! I won't spend my life waiting for the time you go too far. I can't." She fumbled for the lock with trembling fingers. "Damn your magic," she sobbed as she darted through the door.

Chapter 15

After leaving Pierce, Ryan went straight to her father's office. For the first time in her life she entered without knocking. Annoyed at the interruption, Swan bit off what he was saying into the phone and scowled up at her. For a moment he stared at her. He'd never seen Ryan like this: pale, trembling, her eyes wide and brilliant with suppressed tears.

"I'll get back to you," he muttered and hung up. She still stood by the door, and Swan found himself in the unusual position of not knowing what to say. "What is it?" he demanded, then cleared his throat.

Ryan supported herself against the door until she was sure her legs were steady enough to walk. Struggling for composure, she crossed to her father's desk. "I need—I want you to cancel the Atkins special."

"What!" He sprang to his feet and glared at her.

"What the hell is this? If you've decided to fall apart under the pressure, I'll get a replacement. Ross can take over. Damn it!" He slammed his hand on the desk. "I should have known better than to put you in charge in the first place." He was already reaching for the phone.

"Please." Ryan's quiet voice stopped him. "I'm asking you to pay off the contract and scrub the show."

Swan started to swear at her again, took another careful study of her face, then walked to the bar. Saying nothing, he poured a healthy dose of French brandy into a snifter. Blast the girl for making him feel like a clumsy ox. "Here," he said gruffly as he pushed the snifter into her hands. "Sit down and drink this." Not certain what to do with a daughter who looked shattered and helpless, he awkwardly patted her shoulder before he went back behind his desk.

"Now." Settled again, he felt more in control of the situation. "Tell me what this is all about. Trouble at rehearsals?" He gave her what he hoped was an understanding smile. "Now, you've been around the business long enough to know that's part of the game."

Ryan took a deep breath, then swallowed the brandy. She let it burn through the layers of fear and misery. Her next breath was steadier. She looked at her father again. "Pierce is planning an escape for the finale."

"I know that," he said impatiently. "I've seen the script."

"It's too dangerous."

"Dangerous?" Swan folded his hands on the desk. This he could handle, he decided. "Ryan, the man's a pro. He knows what he's doing." Swan tilted his wrist slightly so he could see his watch. He could give her about five minutes.

"This is different," she insisted. To keep from screaming, she gripped the bowl of the snifter tightly. Swan would never listen to hysterics. "Even his own people don't like it."

"All right, what's he planning?"

Unable to form the words, Ryan took another swallow of brandy. "Three safes," she began. "One within the other. The last one…" She paused for a moment to keep her voice even. "The last one has a time lock. He'll only have three minutes of air once he's closed inside the first safe. He's just—he's just told me that the routine takes more time than that."

"Three safes," Swan mused, pursing his lips. "A real show-stopper."

Ryan slammed down her glass. "Especially if he suffocates. Think what that will do for the ratings! They can give him his Emmy posthumously."

Swan lowered his brows dangerously. "Calm down, Ryan."

"I will not calm down." She sprang up from her chair. "He can't be allowed to do this. We have to cancel the contract."

"Can't do it." Swan lifted his shoulders to brush off the notion.

"Won't do it," Ryan corrected furiously.

"Won't do it," Swan agreed, matching her tone. "There's too much at stake."

"*Everything's* at stake!" Ryan shouted at him. "I'm in love with him."

He had started to stand and shout back at her, but her words took him by surprise. Swan stared at her. There were tears of desperation in her eyes now. Again he was at a loss. "Ryan." He sighed and reached for a cigar. "Sit down."

"No!" She snatched the cigar from his fingers and flung it across the room. "I will not sit down, I will not calm down. I'm asking for your help. Why won't you look at me?" she demanded in angry despair. "Really look at me!"

"I am looking at you!" he bellowed in defense. "And I can tell you I'm not pleased. Now you sit down and listen to me."

"No, I'm through listening to you, trying to please you. I've done everything you've ever wanted me to do, but it's never been enough. I can't be your son, I can't change that." She covered her face with her hands and broke down completely. "I'm only your daughter, and I need you to help me."

The words left him speechless. The tears unmanned him. He couldn't remember if he had ever seen her cry before; certainly she'd never done it this passionately. Getting awkwardly to his feet, he fumbled for his handkerchief. "Here, here now." He pushed the handkerchief into her hands and wondered what to do next. "I've always…" He cleared his throat and looked helplessly around the room. "I've always been proud of you, Ryan." When she responded by weeping more desperately, he stuck his hands in his pockets and lapsed into silence.

"It doesn't matter." Her voice was muffled behind the handkerchief. She felt a wave of shame for the words and the tears. "It doesn't matter anymore."

"I'd help you if I could," he muttered at length. "I can't stop him. Even if I could scrub the show and deal with the suits the network and Atkins would bring against Swan Productions, he'd do the damn thing anyway."

Faced with the bald truth, Ryan turned away from him. "There must be something…"

Swan shifted uncomfortably. "Is he in love with you?"

Ryan let out an unsteady breath and dashed the tears away. "It doesn't matter how he feels about me. I can't stop him."

"I'll talk to him."

Wearily, she shook her head. "No, it wouldn't do any good. I'm sorry." She turned back to her father. "I shouldn't have come here like this. I wasn't thinking straight." Looking down, she crumpled the handkerchief into a ball. "I'm sorry I made a scene."

"Ryan, I'm your father."

She looked up at him then, but her eyes were expressionless. "Yes."

He cleared his throat and found he didn't know what to do with his hands. "I don't want you to apologize for coming to see me." She only continued to look at him with eyes devoid of emotion. Tentatively, he reached out to touch her arm. "I'll do what I can to persuade Atkins to drop the routine, if that's what you want."

Ryan let out a long sigh before she sat down. "Thank you, but you were right. He'll do it another time, anyway. He told me so himself. I'm just not able to deal with it."

"Do you want Ross to take over?"

She pressed her fingers to her eyes. "No," she said with a shake of her head. "No, I'll finish what I started. Hiding won't change anything, either."

"Good girl," he said with a pleased nod. "Now, ah…" He hesitated while he sought the correct words. "About you and the magician." He coughed and fiddled with his tie. "Are you planning—that is, should I talk to him about his intentions?"

Ryan hadn't thought she could smile. "No, that won't be necessary." She saw relief in Swan's eyes and rose. "I'd appreciate some time off after the taping."

"Of course, you've earned it."

"I won't keep you any longer." She started to turn away, but he put a hand on her shoulder. Ryan glanced at him in surprise.

"Ryan…" He couldn't get a clear hold on what he wanted to say to her. Instead, he squeezed her shoulder. "Come on, I'll take you to dinner."

Ryan stared at him. When was the last time, she wondered, she had gone to dinner with her father? An awards banquet? A business party? "Dinner?" she said blankly.

"Yes." Swan's voice sharpened as his thoughts followed the same path Ryan's had. "A man can take his daughter to dinner, can't he?" He slipped his arm around her waist and led her to the door. How small she was! he realized with a jolt. "Go wash your face," he muttered. "I'll wait for you."

At ten o'clock the next morning Swan finished reading the Atkins contract a second time. A tricky business, he thought. It wouldn't be easy to break. But he had no intention of breaking it. That would not only be poor business sense but a useless gesture. He'd just have to deal with Atkins himself. When his buzzer sounded, he turned the contract facedown.

"Mr. Atkins is here, Mr. Swan."

"Send him in."

Swan rose as Pierce entered, and as he had done the first time, he walked across the room with his hand extended. "Pierce," he said jovially. "Thanks for coming up."

"Mr. Swan."

"Bennett, please," he said as he drew Pierce to a chair.

"Bennett," Pierce agreed, taking a seat.

Swan sat in the chair opposite him and leaned back. "Well, now, are you satisfied with how everything's going?"

Pierce lifted a brow. "Yes."

Swan took out a cigar. The man's too cool, he thought grudgingly. He doesn't give anything away. Swan decided to approach the subject from the side door. "Coogar tells me the rehearsals are smooth as silk. Worries him." Swan grinned. "He's a superstitious bastard, likes plenty of trouble before a taping. He tells me you could almost run the show yourself."

"He's a fine director," Pierce said easily, watching Swan light his cigar.

"The best," Swan agreed heartily. "We are a bit concerned about your plans for the finale."

"Oh?"

"This is television, you know," Swan reminded him with an expansive smile. "Four-ten is a bit long for one routine."

"It's necessary." Pierce let his hands rest on the arms of the chair. "I'm sure Ryan's told you."

Swan's eyes met the direct stare. "Yes, Ryan's told me. She came up here last night. She was frantic."

Pierce's fingers tensed slightly, but he kept his eyes level. "I know. I'm sorry."

"Look, Pierce, we're reasonable men." Swan leaned toward him, poking with his cigar. "This routine of yours sounds like a beauty. The time lock business is a real inspiration, but with a little modification—"

"I don't modify my illusions."

The cool dismissal had Swan blustering. "No contract's carved in stone," he said dangerously.

"You can try to break it," Pierce agreed. "It'll be a great deal more trouble for you than for me. And in the end it won't change anything."

"Damn it, man, the girl's beside herself!" Banging his thigh with his fist, Swan flopped back in the chair. "She says she's in love with you."

"She is in love with me," Pierce returned quietly and ignored the twist in his stomach.

"What the hell do you mean to do about it?"

"Are you asking me as her father or as Swan Productions?"

Swan drew his brows together and muttered for a moment. "As her father," he decided.

"I'm in love with Ryan." Pierce met Swan's stare calmly. "If she's willing to have me, I'll spend my life with her."

"And if she's not?" Swan retorted.

Pierce's eyes darkened, something flickered, but he said nothing. That was something he'd yet to deal with. In the brief passage of seconds Swan saw what he wanted to know. He pressed his advantage.

"A woman in love isn't always reasonable," he said with an avuncular smile. "A man has to make certain adjustments."

"There's very little I wouldn't do for Ryan," Pierce returned. "But it isn't possible for me to change what I am."

"We're talking about a routine," Swan tossed back, losing patience.

"No, we're talking about my way of life. I could drop this escape," he continued while Swan frowned at him, "but there'd be another one and still another. If Ryan can't accept this one now, how can she accept one later?"

"You'll lose her," Swan warned.

Pierce rose at that, unable to sit any longer. "Perhaps I've never had her." He could deal with the pain, he told himself. He knew how to deal with pain. His voice was even when he continued. "Ryan has to make her own choices. I have to accept them."

Swan rose to his feet and glared. "Damn if you sound like a man in love to me."

Pierce gave him a long, cold stare that had Swan swallowing. "In a lifetime of illusions," he said roughly, "she's the only thing that's real." Turning, he strode from the room.

Chapter 16

They would tape at six o'clock west coast time. By 4:00 p.m. Ryan had dealt with everything from an irate property manager to a frazzled hairstylist. There was nothing like a live broadcast to throw even the most seasoned veterans into a state of madness. As it was put to her by a fatalistic stagehand, "Whatever could go wrong, would." It wasn't what Ryan wanted to hear.

But the problems, the demands, the touch of insanity kept her from crawling into a convenient corner to weep. She was needed and had no choice but to be dependable. If her career was all she was going to have left, Ryan knew she had to give it her best shot.

She had avoided Pierce for ten days by keeping an emotional distance. They had no choice but to come together time and again, but only as producer and star. He made no attempt to close the gap between them.

Ryan hurt. At times it still amazed her how much. Still, she welcomed it. The hurt helped smother the fear. The three safes had been delivered. When she had forced herself to examine them, she had seen that the smallest was no more than three feet high and two feet across. The thought of Pierce folding himself into the small black box had her stomach rolling.

She had stood studying the largest safe with its thick door and complex time lock when she had sensed him behind her. When she had turned, they had looked at each other in silence. Ryan had felt the need, the love, the hopelessness before she had walked away from him. Neither by word nor gesture had he asked her to stay.

From then on Ryan had kept away from the safes, concentrating instead on the checking and rechecking of all the minute details of production.

Wardrobe had to be supervised. A broken spotlight needed repair at the eleventh hour. A sick technician had to be replaced. And timing, the most crucial element of all, had to be worked out to the last second.

There seemed to be no end to the last-minute problems, and she could only be grateful when each new one cropped up. There was no time for thinking, right up to the moment when the studio audience began to file in.

With her stomach in knots, her face composed, Ryan waited in the control booth as the floor director gave the final countdown.

It began.

Pierce was onstage, cool and competent. The set was perfect: clean, uncluttered and faintly mysterious with the understated lighting. In unrelieved black, he was a twentieth-century sorcerer with no need for magic wands or pointed hats.

Water flowed between his palms, fire shot from his fingertips. Ryan watched as he balanced Bess on the point of a saber, making her spin like a top, then drawing the sword out with a flourish until she spun on nothing at all.

Elaine floated on the torch flames while the audience held their breath. Pierce enclosed her in a clear glass bubble, covered it with red silk and sent it floating ten feet above the stage. It swayed gently to Link's music. When Pierce brought it down and whipped off the silk, Elaine was a white swan.

He varied his illusions—dashing, spectacular and simply beautiful. He controlled the elements, defied nature and baffled all.

"Going like a dream," Ryan heard someone say excitedly. "See if we don't cop a couple of Emmys for this one. Thirty seconds, camera two. God, is this guy good!"

Ryan left the control booth and went down to the wings. She told herself she was cold because the air-conditioning in the booth was turned up so high. It would be warmer near the stage. The lights there shone hotly, but her skin stayed chilled. She watched while he did a variation on the transportation illusion he had used in Vegas.

He never glanced in her direction, but Ryan sensed he knew she was there. He had to know, because her thoughts were so completely centered on him.

"It's going good, isn't it?"

Looking up, Ryan saw Link beside her. "Yes, perfect so far."

"I liked the swan. It's pretty."

"Yes."

"Maybe you should go into Bess's dressing room and

sit down," he suggested, wishing she didn't look so pale and cold. "You could watch on the TV in there."

"No. No, I'll stay."

Pierce had a tiger onstage, a lean, pacing cat in a gilt cage. He covered it with the same silk he had used on the bubble. When he removed it, Elaine was caged and the tiger had vanished. Knowing it was the last illusion before the final escape, Ryan took a deep breath.

"Link." She reached for his hand, needing something to hold on to.

"He'll be all right, Ryan." He gave her fingers a squeeze. "Pierce is the best."

The smallest safe was brought out, its door open wide as it was turned around and around to show its solidity. Ryan tasted the iron tang of fear. She didn't hear Pierce's explanation to the audience as he was manacled hand and foot by a captain of the Los Angeles Police Department. Her eyes were glued to his face. She knew the deepest part of his mind was already locked inside the vault. Already, he was working his way out. That's what she held on to as firmly as Link's hand.

He barely fit inside the first safe. His shoulders brushed the sides.

He won't be able to move in there, she thought on a stab of panic. As the door was shut, she took a step toward the stage. Link held her by the shoulders.

"You can't, Ryan."

"But, God, he can't move. He can't breathe!" She watched with mounting horror as the second safe was brought out.

"He's already out of the cuffs," Link said soothingly, though he didn't like watching the safe that held Pierce lifted and locked inside the second one. "He'll be opening the first door now," he said to comfort himself as much as Ryan. "He works fast. You know, you've seen him."

"Oh, no." The third safe had the fear rocketing almost beyond her control. She felt a bright dizziness and would have swayed if Link's hands hadn't held her upright. The largest safe swallowed the two others and the man inside. It was shut, bolted. The time lock was set for midnight. There was no way in from the outside now.

"How long?" she whispered. Her eyes were glued to the safe, on the shiny, complicated timer. "How long since he's been in?"

"Two and a half minutes." Link felt a bead of sweat run down his back. "He's got plenty of time."

He knew the safes fit together so snugly that the doors could only be pushed open far enough for a child to crawl through. He never understood how Pierce could twist and fold his body the way he did. But he'd seen him do it. Unlike Ryan, Link had watched Pierce rehearse the escape countless times. The sweat continued to roll down his back.

The air was thin, Ryan could barely draw it into her lungs. That was how it was inside the safe, she thought numbly. No air, no light. "Time, Link!" She was shaking like a leaf now. The big man stopped praying to answer.

"Two-fifty. It's almost over. He's working on the last one now."

Gripping her hands together, Ryan began to count off the seconds in her head. The roaring in her ears had her biting down hard on her lip. She had never fainted in her life, but she knew she was perilously close to doing so now. When her vision blurred, she squeezed her eyes tight to clear it. But she couldn't breathe. Pierce had no air now and neither did she. On a bubble of hysteria, she thought she would suffocate standing there as surely as Pierce would inside the trio of safes.

Then she saw the door opening, heard the unified gasp of relief from the audience before the burst of applause. He stood on the stage, damp with sweat and drawing in air.

Ryan swooned back against Link as darkness blocked out the spotlights. She lost consciousness for no more than seconds, coming back when she heard Link calling her.

"Ryan, Ryan, it's all right. He's out. He's okay."

Bracing herself against Link, she shook her head to clear it. "Yes, he's out." For one last second she watched him, then turning, she walked away.

The moment the cameras shut off, Pierce walked offstage. "Where's Ryan?" he demanded of Link.

"She left." He watched a trickle of sweat run down Pierce's face. "She was pretty upset." He offered Pierce the towel he'd been holding for him. "I think maybe she fainted for a minute."

Pierce didn't brush away the sweat, he didn't grin as he always did when an escape was completed. "Where did she go?"

"I don't know. She just left."

Without a word, Pierce went to look for her.

Ryan lay baking in the strong sun. There was an itch in the center of her back, but she didn't move to scratch it. She lay still and let the heat soak into her skin.

She had spent a week on board her father's yacht off the coast of St. Croix. Swan had let her go alone, as she requested, asking no questions when she had arrived at his house and asked for the favor. He'd made the arrangements for her and had taken her to the airport himself. Ryan was to think later that it was the first time he hadn't put her in a limo with a driver and sent her off to catch a plane by herself.

For days now she had lain in the sun, swam and kept her mind a blank. She hadn't even gone back to her apartment after the taping. She had arrived in St. Croix with the clothes on her back. Whatever she needed she bought on the island. She spoke to no one but the crew and sent no messages back to the States. For a week she simply slipped off the face of the earth.

Ryan rolled over on her back and dropped the sunglasses over her eyes. She knew that if she didn't force herself to think, the answer she needed would come to her in time. When it came, it would be right, and she would act on it. Until then, she waited.

In his workroom, Pierce shuffled and cut the Tarot cards. He needed to relax. The tension was eating at him.

After the taping he had searched the entire building for Ryan. When she was nowhere to be found, he had broken one of his own cardinal rules and had picked the lock on her apartment. He had waited for her through the next morning. She had never come home. It had driven him wild, furious. He'd let the rage take him, blocking out the pain. Anger, the undisciplined anger he never allowed himself, came in full force. Link had borne the brunt of his temper in silence.

It had taken Pierce days to regain his control. Ryan was gone, and he had to accept it. His own set of rules left him no choice. Even if he'd known where to find her, he couldn't bring her back.

In the week that had passed he had done no work. He had no power. Whenever he tried to focus his concentration, he saw only Ryan—felt her, tasted her. It was all he could conjure. He had to work his way back. Pierce knew if he didn't find his rhythm again soon he would be finished.

He was alone now, with Link and Bess honeymooning in the mountains. When he had regained some of his control, he had insisted they keep to their plans. He had sent them on their way, struggling to give them happiness while his own life loomed empty ahead of him.

It was time to go back to the only thing he had left. And even that brought a small trickle of fear. He was no longer sure he had any magic.

Setting the cards aside, Pierce rose to set up one of his more complicated illusions. He wouldn't test himself on anything simplistic. Even as he began to train his concentration, flex his hands, he looked up and saw her.

Pierce stared hard at the image. She had never come this clearly to him before. He could even hear her footsteps as she crossed the room to the stage. Her scent reached him first and had his blood humming. He wondered, almost dispassionately, if he were going mad.

"Hello, Pierce."

Ryan saw him jolt as if she had startled him out of a dream. "Ryan?" Her name on his lips was soft, questioning.

"Your front door wasn't locked, so I came in. I hope you don't mind."

He continued to stare at her and said nothing. She mounted the steps of the stage.

"I've interrupted your work."

Following her gaze, Pierce looked down at the glass vial in his hand and the colored cubes on the table.

"Work? It—no, it's all right." He set the vial down. He couldn't have managed the most basic illusion.

"This won't take long," Ryan told him with a smile. She had never seen him rattled and was all but certain she would never see him so again. "There's a new contract we need to discuss."

"Contract?" he repeated, unable to take his eyes from hers.

"Yes, that's why I've come."

"I see." He wanted to touch her but kept his hands on the table. He wouldn't touch what was no longer his. "You look well," he managed and started to offer her a chair. "Where have you been?" It was out before he could stop it; it was perilously close to an accusation. Ryan only smiled again.

"I've been away," she said simply, then took a step closer. "Have you thought of me?"

It was he who stepped back. "Yes, I've thought of you."

"Often?" The word was quiet as she moved toward him again.

"Don't, Ryan!" His voice was defensively sharp as he moved back.

"I've thought of you often," she continued as if he hadn't spoken. "Constantly, though I tried not to. Do you dabble in love potions, Pierce? Is that what you did to me?" She took another step toward him. "I tried very hard to hate you and harder still to forget you. Your magic's too strong."

Her scent whirled through his senses until they were all clouded with her. "Ryan, I'm only a man, and you're my weakness. Don't do this." Pierce shook his head and called on the last of his control. "I have work to do."

Ryan glanced at the table, then toyed with one of the colored cubes. "It'll have to wait. Do you know how many hours there are in a week?" she asked and smiled at him.

"No. Stop this, Ryan." The blood was pounding in his head. The need was growing unmanageable.

"A hundred and sixty-eight," she whispered. "A lot to make up for."

"If I touch you, I won't let you go again."

"And if I touch you?" She laid her hand on his chest.

"Don't," he warned quickly. "You should leave while you still can."

"You'll do that escape again, won't you?"

"Yes. Yes, damn it." His fingertips were tingling, demanding that he reach for her. "Ryan, for God's sake, go."

"You'll do it again," she went on. "And others, probably more dangerous, or at least more frightening, because that's who you are. Isn't that what you told me?"

"Ryan—"

"That's who I fell in love with," she said calmly. "I don't know why I thought I could or should try to change that. I told you once you were exactly what I wanted, that was the truth. But I suppose I had to learn what that meant. Do you still want me, Pierce?"

He didn't answer, but she saw his eyes darken, felt his heart speed under her hand. "I can leave and have a very calm, undemanding life." Ryan took the last step to him. "Is that what you want for me? Have I hurt you so much you wish me a life of unbearable boredom? Please, Pierce," she murmured, "won't you forgive me?"

"There's nothing to forgive." He was drowning in her eyes no matter how he struggled not to. "Ryan, for the love of God!" Desperate, he pushed her hand from his chest. "Can't you see what you're doing to me?"

"Yes, and I'm so glad. I was afraid you could really shut me out." She let out a quiet sigh of relief. "I'm staying, Pierce. There's nothing you can do about it." She had her arms around his neck and her mouth a breath away from his. "Tell me again that you want me to go."

"No." He dragged her against him. "I can't." His mouth was devouring hers. Power flowed into him again, hot and painful. He pressed her closer and felt her mouth respond to the savageness of his. "It's too late," he murmured. "Much too late." Excitement was burning through him. He couldn't hold her near enough. "I won't be able to leave the door open for you now, Ryan. Do you understand?"

"Yes. Yes, I understand." She drew her head back, wanting to see his eyes. "But it'll be closed for you, too. I'm going to see to it this is one lock you can't beat."

"No escape, Ryan. For either of us." And his mouth was on hers again, hot, desperate. He felt her give against him as he crushed her to him, but her hands were strong and sure on his body. "I love you, Ryan," he told her again as he roamed her face and neck with kisses. "I love you. I lost everything when you left me."

"I won't leave you again." She took his face in her hands to stop his wandering lips. "I was wrong to ask you what I did. I was wrong to run away. I didn't trust enough."

"And now?"

"I love you, Pierce, exactly as you are."

He pulled her close again and pressed his mouth to

her throat. "Beautiful Ryan, so small, so soft. God, how I want you. Come upstairs, come to bed. Let me love you properly."

Her pulses hammered at the quiet, rough words he spoke against her throat. Ryan took a deep breath, then, putting her hands on his shoulders, she pulled away. "There's the matter of a contract."

"The hell with contracts," he mumbled and tried to pull her back.

"Oh, no." Ryan stepped away from him. "I want this settled."

"I've already signed your contract," he reminded her impatiently. "Come here."

"This is a new one," she stated, ignoring him. "An exclusive life term."

He frowned. "Ryan, I'm not going to tie myself to Swan Productions for the rest of my life."

"Not Swan Productions," she countered. "Ryan Swan."

The annoyed retort on the tip of his tongue never materialized. She saw his eyes change, become intense. "What sort of contract?"

"A one-to-one, with an exclusivity clause and a life-time term." Ryan swallowed, losing some of the confidence that had carried her this far.

"Go on."

"It's to begin immediately, with the provision of a legally binding ceremony to follow at the first reasonable opportunity." She laced her fingers together. "With a proviso for the probability of offspring." She saw Pierce's brow lift, but he said nothing. "The number of which is negotiable."

"I see," he said after a moment. "Is there a penalty clause?"

"Yes. If you try to break the terms, I'm allowed to murder you."

"Very reasonable. Your contract's very tempting, Miss Swan. What are my benefits?"

"Me."

"Where do I sign?" he asked, taking her in his arms again.

"Right here." She let out a sigh as she lifted her mouth. The kiss was gentle, promising. With a moan, Ryan drew closer.

"This ceremony, Miss Swan." Pierce nibbled at her lip as his hands began to roam. "What do you consider the first reasonable opportunity?"

"Tomorrow afternoon." She laughed and again pulled out of his arms. "You don't think I'm going to give you time to find an escape hatch, do you?"

"I've met my match, I see."

"Absolutely," she agreed with a nod. "I have a few tricks up my sleeve." Lifting the Tarot cards, she surprised Pierce by fanning them with some success. She'd been practicing for months.

"Very good." He grinned and went to her. "I'm impressed."

"You haven't seen anything yet," she promised. "Pick a card," she told him, her eyes laughing. "Any card."

* * * * *

STORM WARNING

For Mom,
who wouldn't let my brothers clobber me—
even when I deserved it.

Chapter 1

The Pine View Inn was nestled comfortably in the Blue Ridge Mountains. After leaving the main road, the meandering driveway crossed a narrow ford just wide enough for one car. The inn was situated a short distance beyond the ford.

It was a lovely place, full of character, the lines so clean they disguised the building's rambling structure. It was three stories high, built of brick that had been weathered to a soft rose, the facade interspersed with narrow, white-shuttered windows. The hipped roof had faded long ago to a quiet green, and three straight chimneys rose from it. A wide wooden porch made a white skirt around the entire house and doors opened out to it from all four sides.

The surrounding lawn was smooth and well tended. There was less than an acre, house included, before the trees and outcroppings of rock staked their claim on the land. It was as if nature had decided that the house could have this much and no more. The effect was magnificent. The house and mountains stood in peaceful coexistence, neither detracting from the other's beauty.

As she pulled her car to the informal parking area at the side of the house, Autumn counted five cars, including her aunt's vintage Chevy. Though the season was still weeks off, it appeared that the inn already had several guests.

There was a light April chill in the air. The daffodils had yet to open, and the crocuses were just beginning to fade. A few azalea buds showed a trace of color. The day was poised and waiting for spring. The higher, surrounding mountains clung to their winter brown, but touches of green were creeping up them. It wouldn't be gloomy brown and gray for long.

Autumn swung her camera case over one shoulder and her purse over the other—the purse was of secondary importance. Two large suitcases also had to be dragged from the trunk. After a moment's struggle, she managed to arrange everything so that she could take it all in one load, then mounted the steps. The door, as always, was unlocked.

There was no one about. The sprawling living room which served as a lounge was empty, though a fire crackled in the grate. Setting down her cases, Autumn entered the room. Nothing had changed.

Rag rugs dotted the floor; hand-crocheted afghans were draped on the two patchworked sofas. At the windows were chintz priscillas and the Hummel collection was still on the mantel. Characteristically, the room was neat, but far from orderly. There were magazines here and there, an overflowing sewing basket, a group of pillows piled for comfort rather than style on the windowseat. The ambience was friendly with a faintly distracted charm. Autumn thought with a smile that the room suited her aunt perfectly.

She felt an odd pleasure. It was always reassuring to find that something loved hasn't changed. Taking a last quick glance around the room, she ran a hand through her hair. It hung past her waist and was tousled from the long drive with open windows. She gave idle consideration to digging out a brush, but promptly forgot when she heard footsteps down the hall.

"Oh, Autumn, there you are." Typically, her aunt greeted her as though Autumn had just spent an hour at the local supermarket rather than a year in New York. "I'm glad you got in before dinner. We're having pot roast, your favorite."

Not having the heart to remind her aunt that pot roast was her brother Paul's favorite, Autumn smiled. "Aunt Tabby, it's so good to see you!" Quickly she walked over and kissed her aunt's cheek. The familiar scent of lavender surrounded her.

Aunt Tabby in no way resembled the cat her name brought to mind. Cats are prone to snobbishness, disdainfully tolerating the rest of the world. They are known for speed, agility and cunning. Aunt Tabby was known for her vague meanderings, disjointed conversations and confused thinking. She had no guile. Autumn adored her.

Drawing her aunt away, Autumn studied her closely. "You look wonderful." It was invariably true. Aunt Tabby's hair was the same deep chestnut as her niece's, but it was liberally dashed with gray. It suited her. She wore it short, curling haphazardly around her small round face. Her features were all small-scaled—mouth, nose, ears, even her hands and feet. Her eyes were a mistily faded blue. Though she was halfway through her fifties, her skin refused to wrinkle; it was smooth as a girl's. She stood a half-foot shorter than Autumn and was pleasantly round and soft. Beside her, Autumn felt like a gangly toothpick. Autumn hugged her again, then kissed her other cheek. "Absolutely wonderful."

Aunt Tabby smiled up at her. "What a pretty girl you are. I always knew you would be. But so awfully thin." She patted Autumn's cheek and wondered how many calories were in pot roast.

With a shrug, Autumn thought of the ten pounds she had gained when she'd stopped smoking. She had lost them again almost as quickly.

"Nelson always was thin," Aunt Tabby added, thinking of her brother, Autumn's father.

"Still is," Autumn told her. She set her camera case on a table and grinned at her aunt. "Mom's always threatening to sue for divorce."

"Oh well." Aunt Tabby clucked her tongue and looked thoughtful. "I don't think that's wise after all the years they've been married." Knowing the jest had been lost, Autumn merely nodded in agreement. "I gave you the room you always liked, dear. You can still see the lake from the window. The leaves will be full soon though, but… Remember when you fell in when you were a little girl? Nelson had to fish you out."

"That was Will," Autumn reminded her, thinking back on the day her younger brother had toppled into the lake.

"Oh?" Aunt Tabby looked faintly confused a moment,

then smiled disarmingly. "He learned to swim quite well, didn't he? Such an enormous young man now. It always surprised me. There aren't any children with us at the moment," she added, flowing from sentence to sentence with her own brand of logic.

"I saw several cars. Are there many people here?" Autumn stretched her cramped muscles as she wandered the room. It smelled of sandalwood and lemon oil.

"One double and five singles," she told her. "One of the singles is French and quite fond of my apple pie. I must go check on my blueberry cobbler," she announced suddenly. "Nancy is a marvel with a pot roast, but helpless with baking. George is down with a virus."

She was already making for the door as Autumn tried to puzzle out the last snatch of information.

"I'm sorry to hear that," she replied with what she hoped was appropriate sympathy.

"I'm a bit shorthanded at the moment, dear, so perhaps you can manage your suitcases yourself. Or you can wait for one of the gentlemen to come in."

George, Autumn remembered. Gardener, bellboy and bartender.

"Don't worry, Aunt Tabby. I can manage."

"Oh, by the way, Autumn." She turned back, but Autumn knew her aunt's thoughts were centered on the fate of her cobbler. "I have a little surprise for you—oh, I see Miss Bond is coming in." Typically, she interrupted herself, then smiled. "She'll keep you company. Dinner's at the usual time. Don't be late."

Obviously relieved that both her cobbler and her niece were about to be taken care of, she bustled off, her heels tapping cheerfully on the hardwood floor.

Autumn turned to watch her designated companion enter through the side door. She found herself gaping.

Julia Bond. Of course, Autumn recognized her instantly. There could be no other woman who possessed such shimmering, golden beauty. How many times had she sat in a crowded theater and watched Julia's charm and talent transcend the movie screen? In person, in the flesh, her beauty didn't diminish. It sparkled, all the more alive in three dimensions.

Small, with exquisite curves just bordering on lush, Julia Bond was a magnificent example of womanhood at its best. Her cream-colored linen slacks and vivid blue cashmere sweater set off her coloring to perfection. Pale golden hair framed her face like sunlight. Her eyes were a deep summer blue. The full, shapely mouth lifted into a smile even as the famous brows arched. For a moment, Julia stood, fingering her silk scarf. Then she spoke, her voice smoky, exactly as Autumn had known it would be. "What fabulous hair."

It took Autumn a moment to register the comment. Her mind was blank at seeing Julia Bond step into her aunt's lounge as casually as she would have strolled into the New York Hilton. The smile, however, was full of charm and so completely unaffected that Autumn was able to form one in return.

"Thank you. I'm sure you're used to being stared at, Miss Bond, but I apologize anyway."

Julia sat, with a grace that was at once insolent and admirable, in a wingback chair. Drawing out a long, thin cigarette, she gave Autumn a full-power smile. "Actors adore being stared at. Sit down." She gestured. "I have a feeling I've at last found someone to talk to in this place."

Autumn's obedience was automatic, a tribute to the actress's charm.

"Of course," Julia continued, still studying Autumn's face, "you're entirely too young and too attractive." Settling back, she crossed her legs. Somehow, she managed to transform the wingback chair, with the small darning marks in the left arm, into a throne. "Then your coloring and mine offset each other nicely. How old are you, darling?"

"Twenty-five." Captivated, Autumn answered without thinking.

Julia laughed, a low bubbling sound that flowed and ebbed like a wave. "Oh, so am I. Perennially." She tossed her head in amusement, then left it cocked to the side. Autumn's fingers itched for her camera. "What's your name, darling, and what brings you to solitude and pine trees?"

"Autumn," she responded as she pushed her hair off her shoulders. "Autumn Gallegher. My aunt owns the inn."

"Your aunt?" Julia's face registered surprise and more amusement. "That dear fuzzy little lady is your aunt?"

"Yes." A grin escaped at the accuracy of the description. "My father's sister." Relaxed, Autumn leaned back. She was doing her own studying, thinking in angles and shadings.

"Incredible," Julia decided with a shake of her head. "You don't look like her. Oh, the hair," she corrected with an envious glance. "I imagine hers was once your color. Magnificent. I know women who would kill for that shade, and you seem to have about three feet of it." With a sigh, she drew delicately on her cigarette. "So, you've come to pay your aunt a visit."

There was nothing condescending in her attitude. Her eyes were interested and Autumn began to find her not only charming but likable. "For a few weeks. I haven't seen her in nearly a year. She wrote and asked me to come down, so I'm taking my vacation all at one time."

"What do you do?" Julia pursed her lips. "Model?"

"No." Autumn's laughter came quickly at the thought of it. "I'm a photographer."

"Photographer!" Julia exclaimed. She glowed with pleasure. "I'm very fond of photographers. Vanity, I suppose."

"I imagine photographers are fond of you for the same reason."

"Oh, my dear." When Julia smiled, Autumn recognized both pleasure and amusement. "How sweet."

"Are you alone, Miss Bond?" Her sense of curiosity was ingrained. Autumn had already forgotten to be overwhelmed.

"Julia, please, or you'll remind me of the half-decade that separates our ages. The color of that sweater suits you," she commented, eyeing Autumn's crewneck. "I never could wear gray. Sorry, darling," she apologized with a lightning-quick smile. "Clothes are a weakness of mine. Am I alone?" The smile deepened. "Actually, this little hiatus is a mixture of business and pleasure. I'm in between husbands at the moment—a glorious interlude." Julia tossed her head. "Men are delightful, but husbands can be dreadfully inhibiting. Have you ever had one?"

"No." The grin was irrepressible. From the tone, Julia might have asked if Autumn had ever owned a cocker spaniel.

"I've had three." Julia's eyes grew wicked and delighted. "In this case, the third was *not* the charm. Six months with an English baron was quite enough."

Autumn remembered the photos she had seen of Julia with a tall, aristocratic Englishman. She had worn tweed brilliantly.

"I've taken a vow of abstinence," Julia continued. "Not against men—against marriage."

"Until the next time?" Autumn ventured.

"Until the next time," Julia agreed with a laugh. "At the moment, I'm here for platonic purposes with Jacques LeFarre."

"The producer?"

"Of course." Again, Autumn felt the close scrutiny. "He'll take one look at you and decide he has a new star on the horizon. Still, that might be an interesting diversion." She frowned a moment, then shrugged it away. "The other residents of your aunt's cozy inn have offered little in the way of diversions thus far."

"Oh?" Automatically, Autumn shook her head as Julia offered her a cigarette.

"We have Dr. and Mrs. Spicer," Julia began. One perfectly shaped nail tapped against the arm of her chair. There was something different in her attitude now. Autumn was sensitive to moods, but this was too subtle a change for her to identify. "The doctor himself might be interesting," Julia continued. "He's very tall and nicely built, smoothly handsome with just the right amount of gray at the temples."

She smiled. Just then Autumn thought Julia resembled a very pretty, well-fed cat.

"The wife is short and unfortunately rather dumpy. She spoils whatever attractiveness she might have with a continually morose expression." Julia demonstrated it with terrifying skill. Autumn's laughter burst out before she could stop it.

"How unkind," Autumn chided, smiling still.

"Oh, I know." A graceful hand waved in dismissal. "I have no patience for women who let themselves go, then look daggers at those who don't. He's fond of fresh air and walking in the woods, and she grumbles and mopes along after him." Julia paused, giving Autumn a wary glance. "How do you feel about walking?"

"I like it." Hearing the apology in her voice, Autumn grinned.

"Oh well." Julia shrugged at eccentricities. "It takes all kinds. Next, we have Helen Easterman." The oval, tinted nails began to tap again. Her eyes drifted from Autumn's to the view out the window. Somehow, Autumn didn't think she was seeing mountains and pine trees. "She says she's an art teacher, taking time off to sketch nature. She's rather attractive, though a bit overripe, with sharp little eyes and an unpleasant smile. Then, there's Steve Anderson." Julia gave her slow, cat smile again. Describing men, Autumn mused, was more to her taste. "He's rather delicious. Wide shoulders, California blond hair. Nice blue eyes. And he's embarrassingly rich. His father owns, ah…"

"Anderson Manufacturing?" Autumn prompted and was rewarded with a beam of approval.

"How clever of you."

"I heard something about Steve Anderson aiming for a political career."

"Mmm, yes. It would suit him." Julia nodded. "He's very well-mannered and has a disarmingly boyish smile—that's always a political asset."

"It's a sobering thought that government officials are elected on their smiles."

"Oh, politics." Julia wrinkled her nose and shrugged away the entire profession. "I had an affair with a senator once. Nasty business, politics." She laughed at some private joke.

Not certain whether her comment had been a romantic observation or a general one, Autumn didn't pursue it. "So far," Autumn said, "it seems an unlikely menagerie for Julia Bond and Jacques LeFarre to join."

"Show business." With a smile, she lit another cigarette, then waved it at Autumn. "Stick with photography, Autumn, no matter what promises Jacques makes you. We're here due to a whim of the last and most interesting character in our little play. He's a genius of a writer. I did one of his screenplays a few years back. Jacques wants to produce another, and he wants me for the lead." She dragged deep on the cigarette. "I'm willing—really good scripts aren't that easy to come by—but our writer is in the middle of a novel. Jacques thinks the novel could be turned into a screenplay, but our genius resists. He told Jacques he was coming here to write in peace for a few weeks, and that he'd think it over. The charming LeFarre talked him into allowing us to join him for a few days."

Autumn was both fascinated and confused. Her question was characteristically blunt. "Do you usually chase writers around this way? I'd think it would be more the other way around."

"And you'd be right," Julia said flatly. With only the movement of her eyebrows, her expression turned haughty. "But Jacques is dead set on producing this man's work, and he caught me at a weak moment. I had just finished reading one of the most appalling scripts. Actually," she amended with a grimace, "three of the most appalling scripts. My work feeds me, but I won't do trash. So…" Julia smiled and moved her hands. "Here I am."

"Chasing a reluctant writer."

"It has its compensations."

I'd like to shoot her with the sun at her back. Low sun, just going down. The contrasts would be perfect. Autumn pulled herself back from her thoughts and caught up with Julia's conversation. "Compensations?" she repeated.

"The writer happens to be incredibly attractive, in that carelessly rugged sort of way that no one can pull off unless he's born with it. A marvelous change of pace," she added with a wicked gleam, "from English barons. He's tall and bronzed with black hair that's just a bit too long and always disheveled. It makes a woman itch to get her fingers into it. Best, he has those dark eyes that say 'go to hell' so eloquently. He's an arrogant devil." Her sigh was pure feminine approval. "Arrogant men are irresistible, don't you think?"

Autumn murmured something while she tried to block out the suspicions Julia's words were forming. It had to be someone else, she thought frantically. Anyone else.

"And, of course, Lucas McLean's talent deserves a bit of arrogance."

The color drained from Autumn's face and left it stiff. Waves of almost forgotten pain washed over her. *How could it hurt so much after all this time?* She had built the wall so carefully, so laboriously—how could it crumble into dust at the sound of a name? She wondered, dully, what sadistic quirk of fate had brought Lucas McLean back to torment her.

"Why, darling, what's the matter?"

Julia's voice, mixed with concern and curiosity, penetrated. As if coming up for air, Autumn shook her head. "Nothing." She shook her head again and swallowed. "It was just a surprise to hear that Lucas McLean is here." Drawing a deep breath, she met Julia's eyes. "I knew him…a long time ago."

"Oh, I see."

And she did see, Autumn noted, very well. Sympathy warred with speculation in both her face and voice. Autumn shrugged, determined to treat it lightly.

"I doubt he remembers me." Part of her prayed with fervor it was true, while another prayed at cross-purposes. Would he forget? she wondered. Could he?

"Autumn, darling, yours is a face no man is likely to forget." Through a mist of smoke, Julia studied her. "You were very young when you fell in love with him?"

"Yes." Autumn was trying, painfully, to rebuild her protective wall and wasn't surprised by the question. "Too young, too naive." She managed a brittle smile and for the first time in six months accepted a cigarette. "But I learn quickly."

"It seems the next few days might prove interesting, after all."

"Yes." Autumn's agreement lacked enthusiasm. "So it does." She needed time to be alone, to steady herself. "I have to take my bags up," she said as she rose.

While Autumn stretched her slender arms toward the ceiling, Julia smiled. "I'll see you at dinner."

Nodding, Autumn gathered up her camera case and purse and left the room.

In the hall, she struggled with her suitcases, camera and purse before beginning the task of transporting them up the stairs. Throughout the slow trek up the stairs, Autumn relieved tension by muttering and swearing. *Lucas McLean,* she thought and banged a suitcase against her shin. She nearly convinced herself that her ill humor was a result of the bruise she'd just given herself. Out of breath and patience, she reached the hallway outside her room and dumped everything on the floor with an angry thud.

"Hello, Cat. No bellboy?"

The voice—and the ridiculous nickname—knocked a few of her freshly mortared bricks loose. After a brief hesitation, Autumn turned to him. The pain wouldn't show on her face. She'd learned that much. But the pain was there, surprisingly real and physical. It reminded her of the day her brother had swung a baseball bat into her stomach when she had been twelve. *I'm not twelve now,* she reminded herself. She met Lucas's arrogant smile with one of her own.

"Hello, Lucas. I heard you were here. The Pine View Inn is bursting with celebrities."

He was the same, she noted. Dark and lean and male. There was a ruggedness about him, accented by rough black brows and craggy, demanding features that couldn't be called handsome. Oh, no, that was much too tame a word for Lucas McLean. Arousing, irresistible. Fatal. Those words suited him better.

His eyes were nearly as black as his hair. They kept secrets easily. He carried himself well, with a negligent grace that was natural rather than studied. His not-so-subtle masculine power drifted with him as he ambled closer and studied her.

It was then that Autumn noticed how hellishly tired he looked. There were shadows under his eyes. He needed a shave. The creases in his cheeks were deeper than she remembered—and she remembered very well.

"You look like yesterday." He grabbed a handful of her hair as he fastened his eyes on hers. She wondered how she could have ever thought herself over him. No woman ever got over Lucas. Sheer determination kept her eyes level.

"You," she countered as she opened her door, "look like hell. You need some sleep."

Lucas leaned on the doorjamb before she could drag her cases inside and slam the door. "Having trouble with one of my characters," he said smoothly. "She's a tall, willowy creature with chestnut hair that ripples down her back. Narrow hipped, with legs that go right up to her waist."

Bracing herself, Autumn turned back and stared at him. Carefully, she erased any expression from her face.

"She has a child's mouth," he continued, dropping his glance to hers a moment. "And a small nose, somewhat at odds with high, elegant cheekbones. Her skin is ivory with touches of warmth just under the surface. Her eyes are long lidded and ridiculously lashed—green that melts into amber, like a cat's."

Without comment, she listened to his description of herself. She gave him a bored, disinterested look he would never have seen on her face three years before. "Is she the murderer or the corpse?" It pleased Autumn to see his brows lift in surprise before they drew together in a frown.

"I'll send you a copy when it's done." He searched

her face, then a shutter came down, leaving his expression unreadable. That, too, she noted, hadn't changed.

"You do that." After giving her cases a superhuman tug, jettisoning them into her room, Autumn rested against the door. Her smile had no feeling. "You'll have to excuse me, Lucas, I've had a long drive and want a bath."

She closed the door firmly and with finality, in his face.

Autumn's movements then became brisk. There was unpacking to do and a bath to draw and a dress to choose for dinner. Those things would give her time to recover before she allowed herself to think, to feel. When she slipped into lingerie and stockings, her nerves were steadier. The worst of it had been weathered. Surely, she mused, the first meeting, the first exchange of words were the most difficult. She had seen him. She had spoken to him. She had survived. Success made her bold. For the first time in nearly two years, Autumn allowed herself to remember.

She had been so much in love. Her assignment had been an ordinary one—a picture layout of mystery novelist Lucas McLean. The result had been six months of incredible joy followed by unspeakable hurt.

He had overwhelmed her. She'd never met anyone like him. She knew now that there was no one else like him. He was a law unto himself. He had been brilliant, compelling, selfish and moody. After the first shock of learning he was interested in her, Autumn had floated along on a cloud of wonder and admiration. And love.

His arrogance, as Julia had said, was irresistible. His phone calls at three in the morning had been treasured. The last time she had been held in his arms, experiencing the wild demands of his mouth, had been as exciting as the first. She had tumbled into his bed like a ripe peach, giving up her innocence with the freedom that comes with blind, trusting love.

She remembered he'd never said the words she wanted to hear. She'd told herself she had no need for them—words weren't important. There were unexpected boxes of roses, surprise picnics on the beach with wine in paper cups and lovemaking that was both intense and all-consuming. What did she need with words? When the end had come it had been swift—but far from painless.

Autumn put his distraction, his moodiness down to trouble with the novel he was working on. It didn't occur to her that he'd been bored. It was her habit to fix dinner on Wednesdays at his home. It was a small, private evening, one she prized above all others. Her arrival was so natural to her, so routine, that when she entered his living room and found him dressed in dinner clothes, she only thought he had decided to add a more formal atmosphere to their quiet dinner.

"Why, Cat, what are you doing here?" The unexpected words were spoken so easily, she merely stared. "Ah, it's Wednesday, isn't it?" There was a slight annoyance in his tone, as though he had forgotten a dentist appointment. "I completely forgot. I'm afraid I've made other plans."

"Other plans?" she echoed. Comprehension was still a long way off.

"I should have phoned you and saved you the trip. Sorry, Cat, I'm just leaving."

"Leaving?"

"I'm going out." He moved across the room and stared at her. She shivered. No one's eyes could be as warm—or as cold—as Lucas McLean's. "Don't be difficult, Autumn, I don't want to hurt you any more than is necessary."

Feeling the tears of realization rush out, she shook her head and fought against acceptance. The tears sent him into a fury.

"Stop it! I haven't the time to deal with weeping. Just pack it in. Chalk it up to experience. God knows you need it."

Swearing, he stomped away to light a cigarette. She had stood there, weeping without sound.

"Don't make a fool of yourself, Autumn." The calm, rigid voice was more frightening to her than his anger. At least anger was an emotion. "When something's over, you forget it and move on." He turned back with a shrug. "That's life."

"You don't want me anymore?" She stood meekly, like a dog who waits to feel the lash again. Her vision was too clouded with tears to see his expression. For a moment, he was silent.

"Don't worry, Cat," he answered in a careless, brutal voice. "Others will."

She turned and fled. It had taken over a year before he had stopped being the first thing in her mind every morning.

But she had survived, she reminded herself. She slipped into a vivid green dress. And I'll keep right on surviving. She knew she was basically the same person who had fallen in love with Lucas, but now she had a more polished veneer. Innocence was gone, and it would take more than Lucas McLean to make a fool of her again. She tossed her head, satisfied with the memory of her reception to him. That had given him a bit of a surprise. No, Autumn Gallegher was no one's fool any longer.

Her thoughts drifted to her aunt's odd assortment of guests. She wondered briefly why the rich and famous were gathering here instead of at some exclusive resort. Dismissing the thought with a shrug, she reminded herself it was dinnertime. Aunt Tabby had told her not to be late.

Chapter 2

It was a strange assortment to find clustered in the lounge of a remote Virginia inn: an award-winning writer, an actress, a producer, a wealthy California businessman, a successful cardiovascular surgeon and his wife, an art teacher who wore St. Laurent. Before Autumn's bearings were complete, she found herself enveloped in them. Julia pounced on her possessively and began introductions. Obviously, Julia enjoyed her prior claim and the center-stage position it gave her. Whatever embarrassment Autumn might have felt at being thrust into the limelight was overridden by amusement at the accuracy of Julia's earlier descriptions.

Dr. Robert Spicer was indeed smoothly handsome. He was drifting toward fifty and bursting with health. He wore a casually expensive green cardigan with brown leather patches at the elbows. His wife, Jane, was also as Julia had described: unfortunately dumpy. The small smile she gave Autumn lasted about two seconds before her face slipped back into the dissatisfied grooves that were habitual. She cast dark, bad-tempered glances at her husband while he gave Julia the bulk of his attention.

Watching them, Autumn could find little sympathy for Jane and no disapproval for Julia—no one disapproves of a flower for drawing bees. Julia's attraction was just as natural, and just as potent.

Helen Easterman was attractive in a slick, practiced fashion. The scarlet of her dress suited her, but struck a jarring note in the simply furnished lounge. Her face was perfectly made-up and reminded Autumn of a mask. As a photographer, she knew the tricks and secrets of cosmetics. Instinctively, Autumn avoided her.

In contrast, Steve Anderson was all charm. Good looks, California style, as Julia had said. Autumn liked the crinkles at the corners of his eyes and his careless chic. He wore chinos easily. From his bearing, she knew he would wear black tie with equal aplomb. If he chose a political career, she mused, he should make his way very well.

Julia had offered no description of Jacques LeFarre. What Autumn knew of him came primarily from either the gossip magazines or his films. He was smaller than she had imagined, barely as tall as she, but with a wiry build. His features were strong and he wore his brown hair brushed back from his forehead where three worry lines had been etched. She liked the trim moustache over his mouth, and the way he lifted her hand to kiss it when they were introduced.

"Well, Autumn," Steve began with a smile. "I'm playing bartender in George's absence. What can I fix you?"

"Vodka Collins, easy on the vodka," Lucas answered. Autumn gave up the idea of ignoring him.

"Your memory's improved," she said coolly.

"So's your wardrobe." He ran a finger down the collar of her dress. "I remember when it ran to jeans and old sweaters."

"I grew up." Her eyes were as steady and as measuring as his.

"So I see."

"Ah, you have met before," Jacques put in. "But this is fascinating. You are old friends?"

"Old friends?" Lucas repeated before Autumn could speak. He studied her with infuriating amusement. "Would you say that was an accurate description, Cat?"

"Cat?" Jacques frowned a moment. "Ah, the eyes, *oui*." Pleased, he brushed his index finger over his moustache. "It suits. What do you think, *chérie*?" He turned to Julia, who seemed to be enjoying herself watching the unfolding scene. "She's enchanting, and her voice is quite good."

"I've already warned Autumn about you," Julia drawled, then gave Robert Spicer a glorious smile.

"Ah, Julia," Jacques said mildly, "how wicked of you."

"Autumn works the other side of the camera," Lucas stated. Knowing his eyes had been on her the entire time, Autumn was grateful when Steve returned with her drink. "She's a photographer."

"Again, I'm fascinated." Autumn's free hand was captured in Jacques's. "Tell me why you are behind the camera instead of in front of it? Your hair alone would cause poets to run for their pens."

No woman was immune to flattery with a French

accent, and Autumn smiled fully into his eyes. "I doubt I could stand still long enough to begin with."

"Photographers can be quite useful," Helen Easterman stated suddenly. Lifting a hand, she patted her dark, sleek cap of hair. "A good, clear photograph is an invaluable tool…to an artist."

An awkward pause followed the statement. Tension entered the room, so out of place in the comfortable lounge with its chintz curtains that Autumn thought it must be her imagination. Helen smiled into the silence and sipped her drink. Her eyes swept over the others, inclusively, never centering on one.

Autumn knew there was something here which isolated Helen and set her apart from the rest. Messages were being passed without words, though there was no way for Autumn to tell who was communicating what to whom. The mood changed swiftly as Julia engaged Robert Spicer in bright conversation. Jane Spicer's habitual frown became more pronounced.

The easy climate continued as they went in to dinner. Sitting between Jacques and Steve, Autumn was able to add to her education as she observed Julia flirting simultaneously with Lucas and Robert. She was, in Autumn's opinion, magnificent. Even through the discomfort of seeing Lucas casually return the flirtation, she had to admire Julia's talent. Her charm and beauty were insatiable. Jane ate in sullen silence.

Dreary woman, Autumn mused, then wondered what her own reaction would be if it were her husband so enchanted. Action, she decided, not silence. I'd simply claw her eyes out. The image of dumpy Jane wrestling with the elegant Julia made her smile. Even as she enjoyed the notion, she looked up to find Lucas's eyes on her.

His brows were lifted at an angle she knew meant amusement. Autumn turned her attention to Jacques.

"Do you find many differences in the movie industry here in America, Mr. LeFarre?"

"You must call me Jacques." His smile caused the tips of his moustache to rise. "There are differences, yes. I would say that Americans are more...adventurous than Europeans."

Autumn lifted her shoulders and smiled. "Maybe because we're a mixture of nationalities. Not watered down. Just Americanized."

"Americanized." Jacques tried out the word and approved it. His grin was younger than his smile, less urbane. "Yes, I would say I feel Americanized in California."

"Still, California's only one aspect of the country," Steve put in. "And I wouldn't call L.A. or southern California particularly typical." Autumn watched his eyes flick over her hair. His interest brought on a small flutter of response that pleased her. It proved that she was still a woman, open to a man—not just one man. "Have you ever been to California, Autumn?"

"I lived there...once." Her response to Steve, and the need to prove something to herself, urged her to turn her eyes to Lucas. Their gazes locked and held for one brief instant. "I relocated in New York three years ago."

"There was a family here from New York," Steve went on. If he'd noticed the look that had passed, he gave no sign. Yes, a good politician, Autumn thought again. "They just checked out this morning. The woman was one of those robust types with energy pouring out of every cell. She needed it," he added with a smile that was for Autumn alone. "She had three boys. Triplets. I think she said they were eleven."

"Oh, those beastly children!" Julia switched her attention from Robert and looked across the table. She rolled her summer blue eyes. "Running around like a pack of monkeys. Worse, you could never tell which one of them it was zooming by or leaping down. They did everything in triplicate." She shuddered and lifted her water glass. "They ate like elephants."

"Running and eating are part of childhood," Jacques commented with a shake of his head. "Julia," he told Autumn with a conspirator's wink, "was born twenty-one and beautiful."

"Anyone with manners is born twenty-one," Julia countered. "Being beautiful was simply a bonus." Her eyes were laughing now. "Jacques is crazy about kids," she informed Autumn. "He has three specimens of his own."

Interested, Autumn turned to him. She'd never thought of Jacques LeFarre in terms other than his work. "I'm crazy about them, too," she confessed and shot Julia a grin. "What sort of specimens do you have?"

"Boys," he answered. Autumn found the fondness in his eyes curiously touching. "They are like a ladder." With his hand, he formed imaginary steps. "Seven, eight and nine years. They live in France with my wife— my ex-wife." He frowned, then smoothed it away. Autumn realized how the worry lines in his brow had been formed.

"Jacques actually wants custody of the little monsters." Julia's look was more tolerant than her words. Here, Autumn saw, affection transcended flirtation. "Even though I hold your sanity suspect, Jacques, I'm forced to admit you make a better father than Claudette makes a mother."

"Custody suits are sensitive matters," Helen announced from the end of the table. She drank from her water glass, peering over the rim with small, sharp eyes. The look that she sent Jacques seemed to brush everyone else out of her line of vision. "It's so important that any…unsuitable information doesn't come to light."

Tension sprang back. Autumn felt the Frenchman stiffen beside her. But there was more. Undercurrents flowed up and down the long pine table. It was impossible not to feel them, though there was nothing tangible, nothing solid. Instinctively, Autumn's eyes sought Lucas's. There was nothing there but the hard, unfathomable mask she had seen too often in the past.

"Your aunt serves such marvelous meals, Miss Gallegher." With a puzzling, satisfied smirk, Helen shifted her attention to Autumn.

"Yes." She blundered into the awful silence. "Aunt Tabby gives food a high rating of importance."

"Aunt Tabby?" Julia's rich laugh warred with the tension, and won. The air was instantly lighter. "What a wonderful name. Did you know Autumn has an Aunt Tabby when you christened her Cat, Lucas?" She stared up at him, her eyes wide and guileless. Autumn was reminded of a movie Julia had been in, in which she played the innocent ingenue to perfection.

"Lucas and I didn't know each other well enough to discuss relatives." Autumn's voice was easy and careless and pleased her very much. So did Lucas's barely perceptible frown.

"Actually," he replied, recovering quickly, "we were too occupied to discuss family trees." He sent her a smile which sneaked through her defenses. Autumn's pulse hammered. "What did we talk about in those days, Cat?"

"I've forgotten," she murmured, knowing she had lost the edge before she'd really held it. "It was a long time ago."

Aunt Tabby bustled in with her prize cobbler.

There was music on the stereo and a muted fire in the hearth when they returned to the lounge. The scene, if Autumn could have captured it on film, was one of relaxed camaraderie. Steve and Robert huddled over a chessboard while Jane made her discontented way through a magazine. Even without a photographer's eye for color, Autumn knew the woman should never wear brown. She felt quite certain that Jane invariably would.

Lucas sprawled on the sofa. Somehow, he always managed to relax in a negligent fashion without seeming sloppy; there was always an alertness about him, energy simmering right under the surface. Autumn knew he watched people without being obvious—not because he cared if he made them uncomfortable, he didn't in the least—it was simply something he was able to do. And in watching them, he was able to learn their secrets. An obsessive writer, he drew his characters from flesh and blood. With no mercy, Autumn recalled.

At the moment, he seemed content with his conversation with Julia and Jacques. They flanked him on the sofa and spoke with the ease that came from familiarity; they shared the same world.

But it's not my world, Autumn reminded herself. I only pretended it was for a little while. I only pretended he was mine for a little while. She had been right when she told Lucas she had grown up. Pretend games were for children.

Yet, Autumn thought as she sat back and observed, there was a game of some sort going on here. There was a faint glistening of unease superimposed over the homey picture. Always attuned to contrasts, she could sense it, feel it. They're not letting me in on the rules, she mused, and found herself grateful. She didn't want to play. Making her excuses to no one in particular, Autumn slipped from the room to find her aunt.

Whatever tension she had felt evaporated the moment Autumn stepped into her aunt's room.

"Oh, Autumn." Aunt Tabby lifted her glasses from her nose and let them dangle from a chain around her neck. "I was just reading a letter from your mother. I'd forgotten it was here until this minute. She says by the time I read this, you'll be here. And here you are." Smiling, she patted Autumn's hand. "Debbie always was so clever. Did you enjoy your pot roast, dear?"

"It was lovely, Aunt Tabby, thank you."

"We'll have to have it once a week while you're with us." Autumn smiled and thought of how she liked spaghetti. Paul probably gets spaghetti on his visits, she mused. "I'll just make a note of that, else it'll slip right through my mind." Autumn recalled that Aunt Tabby's notes were famous for their ability to slip into another dimension, and felt more hopeful. "Where are my glasses?" Aunt Tabby murmured, puckering her impossibly smooth brow. Standing, she rummaged through her desk, lifting papers and peering under books. "They're never where you leave them."

Autumn lifted the dangling glasses from her aunt's

bosom, then perched them on her nose. After blinking a moment, Aunt Tabby smiled in her vague fashion.

"Isn't that strange?" she commented. "They were here all along. You're just as clever as your mother."

Autumn couldn't resist giving her a bone-crushing hug. "Aunt Tabby, I adore you!"

"You always were such a sweet child." She patted Autumn's cheek, then moved away, leaving the scent of lavender and talc hanging in the air. "I hope you like your surprise."

"I'm sure I will."

"You haven't seen it yet?" Her small mouth pouted in thought. "No, I'm quite sure I haven't shown you yet, so you can't know if you like it. Did you and Miss Bond have a nice chat? Such a lovely lady. I believe she's in show business."

Autumn's smile was wry. There was no one, she thought, absolutely no one like Aunt Tabby. "Yes, I believe she is. I've always admired her."

"Oh, have you met before?" Aunt Tabby asked absently as she shuffled the papers on her desk back into her own particular order. "I suppose I'd better show you now while I have it on my mind."

Autumn tried to keep up with her aunt's thought processes, but it had been a year since her last visit and she was rusty. "Show me what, Aunt Tabby?"

"Oh now, it wouldn't be a surprise if I told you, would it?" Playfully, she shook her finger under Autumn's nose. "You'll just have to be patient and come along with me." With this, she bustled from the room.

Autumn followed, deducing they were again discussing the surprise. She had to shorten her gait to match her aunt's. Autumn usually moved in a loose-limbed stride, a result of leanness and lengthy legs, while her aunt scuttled unrhythmically. Like a rabbit, Autumn thought, that dashes out in the road then can't make up its mind which way to run. As they walked, Aunt Tabby muttered about bed linen. Autumn's thoughts drifted irresistibly to Lucas.

"Now, here we are." Aunt Tabby stopped. She gave the door an expectant smile. The door itself, Autumn recalled, led to a sitting room long since abandoned and converted into a storage room. It was a convenient place for cleaning supplies, as it adjoined the kitchen. "Well," Aunt Tabby said, beaming, "what do you think?"

Searching for the right comment, Autumn realized the surprise must be inside. "Is my surprise in there, Aunt Tabby?"

"Yes, of course, how silly." She clucked her tongue. "You won't know what it is until I open the door."

With this indisputable logic, she did.

When the lights were switched on, Autumn stood stunned. Where she had expected to see mops, brooms and buckets was a fully equipped darkroom. Every detail, every piece of apparatus stood neat and orderly in front of her. Her voice had been left outside the door.

"Well, what do you think?" Aunt Tabby repeated. She moved around the room, stopping now and again to peer at bottles of developing fluid, tongs and trays. "It all looks so technical and scientific to me." The enlarger caused her to frown and tilt her head. "I'm sure I don't understand a thing about it."

"Oh, Aunt Tabby." Autumn's voice finally joined her body. "You shouldn't have."

"Oh dear, is something wrong with it? Nelson told me you developed your own film, and the company that brought in all these things assured me everything was proper. Of course…" Her voice wavered in doubt. "I really don't know a thing about it."

Her aunt looked so distressed, Autumn nearly wept with love. "No, Aunt Tabby, it's perfect. It's wonderful." She enveloped the small, soft body in her arms. "I meant that you shouldn't have done this for me. All the trouble and the expense."

"Oh, is that all?" Aunt Tabby interrupted. Her distress dissolved as she beamed around the room again. "Well, it was no trouble at all. These nice young men came in and did all the work. As for the expense, well…" She shrugged her rounded shoulders. "I'd rather see you enjoy my money now than after I'm dead."

Sometimes, Autumn thought, the fuzzy little brain shot straight through to sterling sense. "Aunt Tabby." She framed her aunt's face with her hands. "I've never had a more wonderful surprise. Thank you."

"You just have a good time with it." Aunt Tabby's cheeks grew rosy with pleasure when Autumn kissed them, and she eyed the chemicals and trays again. "I don't suppose you'll blow anything up."

Knowing this wasn't a pun, and that her aunt was concerned about explosions in her vague way, Autumn assured her she would not. Satisfied, Aunt Tabby then bustled off, leaving Autumn to explore on her own.

For more than an hour, Autumn lost herself in what she knew best. Photography, started as a hobby when she had been a child, had become both craft and profession. The chemicals and complicated equipment were no strangers to her. Here, in a darkroom, or with a camera in her hands, she knew exactly who she was and what she wanted. This was where she had learned control—

the same control she knew she had to employ over her thoughts of Lucas. She was no longer a dewy-eyed girl, ready to follow the crook of a finger. She was a professional woman with a growing reputation in her field. She had to hang on to that now, as she had for three years. There was no going back to yesterday.

Pleasantly weary after rearranging the darkroom to her own preference, Autumn wandered into the kitchen to fix herself a solitary cup of tea. The moon was round and white with a thin cloud drifting over it. Unexpectedly, a shudder ran through her, quick and chilling. The odd feeling she had sensed several times that evening came back. She frowned. Imagination? Autumn knew herself well enough to admit she had her share. It was part of her art. But this was different.

Discovering Lucas at the inn had jolted her system, and her emotions had been strained. That, she decided, was all that was wrong. The tension she had felt earlier was her own tension; the strain, her own strain. Dumping the remaining tea into the sink, she decided that what she needed was a good night's sleep. No dreams, she ordered herself firmly. She'd had her fill of dreams three years before.

The house was quiet now. Moonlight filtered in, leaving the corners shadowed. The lounge was dark, but as she passed, Autumn heard muted voices. She hesitated a moment, thinking to stop and say good-night, then she detected the subtle signs that told her this wasn't a conversation, but an argument. There was anger in the hushed, sexless voices. The undistinguishable words were quick, staccato and passionate. She walked by quickly, not wanting to overhear a private battle. A brief oath shot out, steeped in temper, elegant in French.

Climbing the stairs, Autumn smothered a grin. Jacques, she concluded, was probably losing patience with Lucas's artistic stubbornness. For entirely malicious reasons, she hoped the Frenchman gave him an earful.

It wasn't until she was halfway down the hall to her room that Autumn saw that she'd been wrong. Even Lucas McLean couldn't be two places at once. And he was definitely in this one. In the doorway of another room, Lucas was locked in a very involved embrace with Julia Bond.

Autumn knew how his arms would feel, how his mouth would taste. She remembered it all, completely, as if no years had come between to dull the sensations. She knew how his hand would trail up the back until he cupped around the neck. And that his fingers wouldn't be gentle. No, there were no gentle caresses from Lucas.

There was no need for her to worry about being seen. Both Lucas and Julia were totally focused on each other. Autumn was certain that the roof could have toppled over their heads, and they would have remained unmoving and entwined. The pain came back, hatefully, in full force.

Hurrying by, she gave vent to hideous and unwelcome jealousy by slamming her door.

Chapter 3

The forest was morning fresh. It held a tranquility that was full of tangy scents and bird song. To the east, the sky was filled with scuttling rags of white clouds. An optimist, Autumn put her hopes in them and ignored the dark, threatening sky in the west. Streaks of red still crowned the peaks of the mountains. Gently, the color faded to pink before it surrendered to blue.

The light was good, filtering through the white clouds and illuminating the forest. The leaves weren't full enough to interfere with the sun, only touching the limbs of trees with dots of green. Sometimes strong, the breeze bent branches and tugged at Autumn's hair. She could smell spring.

Wood violets popped out unexpectedly, the purple dramatic against the moss. She saw her first robin marching importantly on the ground, listening for worms. Squirrels scampered up trees, down trees and over the mulch of last year's leaves.

Autumn had intended to walk to the lake, hoping to catch a deer at early watering, but when her camera insisted on planting itself in front of her face again and again, she didn't resist. She ambled along, happy in the solitude and in tune with nature.

In New York, she never truly felt alone—lonely sometimes, but not solitary. The city intruded. Now, cocooned by mountains and trees, she realized how much she'd needed to feel alone. To recharge. Since leaving California and Lucas, Autumn hadn't permitted herself time alone. There had been a void that had to be filled, and she'd filled it with people, with work, with noise—anything that would keep her mind busy. She'd used the pace of the city. It had been necessary. Now, she wanted the pace of the mountains.

In the distance, the lake shimmered. Reflections of the surrounding mountains and trees were mirrored in the water, reversed and shadowy. There were no deer, but as she drew closer, Autumn noticed two figures circling the far side. The ridge where she stood was some fifty feet above the small valley which held the lake. The view was spectacular.

The lake itself stretched in a wide finger, about a hundred feet in length, forty in width. The breeze that caught at Autumn's hair where she strode didn't reach down to the water; its surface was clear and still. The opaque water gradually darkened towards the center, warning of dangerous depths.

Autumn forgot the people walking around the lake, her mind fully occupied with angles and depths of field and shutter speeds. The distance was too great for her to make them out even if she had been interested.

The sun continued its rise, and Autumn was content. She stopped only to change film. As she replaced the roll, she noted that the lake was now deserted. The light was wrong for the mood she wanted and, turning, she began her leisurely journey back to the inn.

This time, the stillness of the forest seemed different. The sun was brighter, but she felt an odd disquiet she hadn't experienced in the paler light of dawn. Foolishly, she looked back over her shoulder, then told herself she was an idiot. Who would be following her? And why? Yet the feeling persisted.

The serenity had vanished. Autumn forced herself to put aside an impulsive desire to run back to the inn where there would be people and coffee brewing. She wasn't a child to take flight at the thought of ogres or gnomes. To prove to herself that her fantasies hadn't affected her, she forced herself to stop and take the time to perfect a shot of a cooperative squirrel. A faint rustle of dead leaves came from behind her and terror brought her scrambling to her feet.

"Well, Cat, still attached to a camera?"

Blood pounding in her head, Autumn stared at Lucas. His hands were tucked comfortably into the pockets of his jeans as he stood directly in front of her. For a moment, she couldn't speak. The fear had been sharp and real.

"What do you mean by sneaking up behind me that way?" When it returned, her voice was furious. She was annoyed that she'd been foolish enough to be frightened, and angry that he'd been the one to frighten her. She pushed her hair back and glared at him.

"I see you've finally developed the temper to match your hair," he observed in a lazy voice. He crossed the slight distance between them and stood close. Autumn had also developed pride and refused to back away.

"It gets particularly nasty when someone spoils a shot." It was a simple matter to blame her reaction on his interference with her work. Not for a moment would she amuse him by confessing fear.

"You're a bit jumpy, Cat." The devil himself could take lessons on smiling from Lucas McLean, she thought bitterly. "Do I make you nervous?"

His dark hair curled in a confused tangle around his lean face, and his eyes were dark and confident. It was the confidence, she told herself, that she cursed him for. "Don't flatter yourself," she tossed back. "I don't recall you ever being one for morning hikes, Lucas. Have you developed a love of nature?"

"I've always had a fondness for nature." He was studying her with deep, powerful eyes while his mouth curved into a smile. "I've always had a penchant for picnics."

The pain started, a dull ache in her stomach. She could remember the gritty feel of sand under her legs, the tart taste of wine on her tongue and the scent of the ocean everywhere. She forced her gaze to stay level with his. "I lost my taste for them." She turned in dismissal, but he fell into step beside her. "I'm not going straight back," she informed him. The chill in her voice would have discouraged anyone else. Stopping, she took an off-center picture of a blue jay.

"I'm in no hurry," he returned easily. "I've always enjoyed watching you work. It's fascinating how absorbed you become." He watched her back, and let his eyes run down the length of her hair. "I believe you could be snapping a charging rhino and not give an inch until you'd perfected the shot." There was a slight pause as she remained turned away from him. "I saw that photo you took of a burned-out tenement in New York. It was remarkable. Hard, clean and desperate."

Wary of the compliment, Autumn faced him. She knew Lucas wasn't generous with praise. Hard, clean and desperate, she thought. He had chosen the words perfectly. She didn't like discovering that his opinion still mattered. "Thank you." She turned back to focus on a grouping of trees. "Still having trouble with your book?"

"More than I'd anticipated," he muttered. Suddenly, he swooped her hair up into his hands. "I never could resist it, could I?" She continued to give her attention to the trees. Her answer was an absent shrug, but she squeezed her eyes tightly shut a moment. "I've never seen another woman with hair like yours. I've looked, God knows, but the shade is always wrong, or the texture or the length." There was a seductive quality in his voice. Autumn stiffened against it. "It's unique. A fiery waterfall in the sun, deep and vibrant spilling over a pillowcase."

"You always had a gift for description." She adjusted her lens without the vaguest idea of what she was doing. Her voice was detached, faintly bored, while she prayed for him to go. Instead, his grip tightened on her hair. In a swift move, he whirled her around and tore the camera from her hands.

"Damn it, don't use that tone with me. Don't turn your back on me. Don't ever turn your back on me."

She remembered the dark expression and uncertain temper well. There'd been a time when she would have dissolved when faced with them. But not anymore, she thought fleetingly. Not this time.

"I don't cringe at being sworn at these days, Lucas." She tossed her head, lifting her chin. "Why don't you save your attention for Julia? I don't want it."

"So." His smile was light and amused in a rapid-fire change. "It was you. No need to be jealous, Cat. The lady made the move, not I."

"Yes, I noticed your mad struggle for release." Even as she spoke, she regretted the words. Annoyed, Autumn pushed away, but was only caught closer. His scent teased her senses and reminded her of things she'd rather forget. "Listen, Lucas," she ground out slowly as both anger and longing rose inside her. "It took me six months to realize what a bastard you are, and I've had three years to cement that realization. I'm a big girl now, and not susceptible to your abundant charms. Now, take your hands off me and get lost."

"Learned to sink your teeth in, have you, Cat?" To her mounting fury, his expression was more amused than insulted. His eyes lowered to her mouth for a moment, lingered then lifted. "Not malleable anymore, but just as fascinating."

Because his words hurt more than she had thought possible, she hurled a stream of abuse at him.

His laughter cut off her torrent like a slap. Abandoning verbal protest, Autumn began to struggle with a wild, furious rage. Abruptly, he molded her against him. Tasting of punishment and possession, his mouth found hers. The heat was blinding.

The old, churning need fought its way to the surface. For three years she had starved, and now all that hunger spilled out in response. There was no hesitation as her arms found their way around his neck. Eager for more, her lips parted. His mouth was urgent and bruising. The pain was like heaven, and she begged for more. Her blood was flowing again. Lucas let his mouth roam over her face, then come back to hers with new demands. Autumn met them and fretted for more. Time flew backward, then forward again before he lifted his face.

His eyes were incredibly dark, opaque with a passion she recognized. For the first time she felt the faint throbbing where his hands gripped her and his hold eased to a caress. The taste of him lingered on her lips.

"It's still there, Cat," Lucas murmured. With easy familiarity, he combed his fingers through her hair. "Still there."

All at once, pain and humiliation coursed through her. She pulled away fiercely and swung out a hand. He caught her wrist and, frustrated, she drew back with her other hand. His reflexes were too sharp, and she was denied any satisfaction. With both wrists captured, she could only stand struggling, her breath ragged. Tears burned at her throat, but she refused to acknowledge them. He won't make me cry, she vowed fiercely. He won't see me cry again.

In silence, Lucas watched her battle for control. There was no sound in the forest but Autumn's own jerking breaths. When she could speak, her voice was hard and cold. "There's a difference between love and lust, Lucas. Even you should know one from the other. What's there now may be the same for you, but not for me. I loved you. I *loved* you." The words were an accusation in their repetition. His brows drew together as his gaze grew intense. "You took it all once—my love, my innocence, my pride—then you tossed them back in my face. You can't have them back. The first is dead, the second's gone and the third belongs to me."

For a moment, they both were still. Slowly, without taking his eyes from hers, Lucas released her wrists. He didn't speak, and his expression told her nothing. Refusing to run from him a second time, Autumn turned and walked away. Only when she was certain he wasn't following did she allow her tears their freedom. Her statements about pride and innocence had been true. But her love was far from dead. It was alive, and it hurt.

As the red bricks of the inn came into view, Autumn dashed the drops away. There would be no wallowing in what was over. Loving Lucas changed nothing, any more than it had changed anything three years before. But she'd changed. He wouldn't find her weeping, helpless and—as he had said himself—malleable.

Disillusionment had given her strength. He could still hurt her. She'd learned that quickly. But he could no longer manipulate her as he had once. Still, the encounter with him had left her shaken, and she wasn't pleased when Helen approached from a path to the right.

It was impossible, without being pointedly rude, for Autumn to veer off and avoid her. Instead, she fixed a smile on her face. When Helen turned her head, the livid bruise under her eye became noticeable. Autumn's smile faded into quick concern.

"What happened?" The bruise looked painful and aroused Autumn's sympathy.

"I walked into a branch." Helen gave a careless shrug as she lifted her fingers to stroke the mark. "I'll have to be more careful in the future."

Perhaps it was her turmoil over Lucas that made Autumn detect some hidden shade of meaning in those words, but Helen seemed to mean more than she said. Certainly the eyes which met Autumn's were as hot and angry as the bruise. And the mark itself, Autumn mused, looked more like the result of contact with a violent hand than with any stray branch. She pushed the thought aside. Who would have struck Helen? she asked herself. And why would she cover up the abuse? Her own carelessness made more sense.

"It looks nasty," Autumn commented as they began to walk toward the inn. "You'll have to do something about it. Aunt Tabby should have something to ease the soreness."

"Oh, I intend to do something about it," Helen muttered, then gave Autumn her sharp-eyed smile. "I know just the thing. Out early taking pictures?" she asked while Autumn tried to ignore the unease her words brought. "I've always found people more interesting subjects than trees. I'm especially fond of candid shots." She began to laugh at some private joke. It was the first time Autumn had heard her laugh, and she thought how suited the sound was to Helen's smile. They were both unpleasant.

"Were you down at the lake earlier?" Autumn recalled the two figures she had spotted. To her surprise, Helen's laughter stopped abruptly. Her eyes grew sharper.

"Did you see someone?"

"No," she began, confused by the harshness of the question. "Not exactly. I saw two people by the lake, but I was too far away to see who they were. I was taking pictures from the ridge."

"Taking pictures," Helen repeated. Her mouth pursed as if she were considering something carefully. She began to laugh again with a harsh burst of sound.

"Well, well, such good humor for such early risers." Julia drifted down the porch steps. Her brow lifted as she studied Helen's cheek. Autumn wondered if the actress's shudder was real or affected. "Good heavens, what have you done to yourself?"

Helen's amusement seemed to have passed. She gave Julia a quick scowl, then fingered the bruise again. "Walked into a branch," she muttered before she stalked up the steps and disappeared inside.

"A fist more likely," Julia commented, and smiled. With a shrug, she dismissed Helen and turned to Autumn. "The call of the wild beckoned to you, too? It seems everyone but me was tramping through forests and over mountains at the cold light of dawn. It's so difficult being sane when one is surrounded by insanity."

Autumn had to smile. Julia looked like a sunbeam. In direct contrast to her own rough jeans and jacket, Julia wore delicate pink slacks and a thin silk blouse flocked with roses. The white sandals she wore wouldn't last fifty yards in the woods. Whatever resentment Autumn had felt for the actress attracting Lucas vanished under her open warmth.

"There are some," Autumn remarked mildly, "who might accuse you of laziness."

"Absolutely," Julia agreed with a nod and a smile. "When I'm not working, I wallow in sloth. If I don't get going again soon, my blood will stop flowing." She gave Autumn a shrewd glance. "Looks like you walked into a rather large branch yourself."

Bewilderment crossed Autumn's face briefly. Julia's eyes, she discovered, were very discerning. The traces of tears hadn't evaporated as completely as Autumn would have liked. Helplessly she moved her shoulders. "I heal quickly."

"Brave child. Come, tell mama all about it." Julia's eyes were sympathetic, balancing the stinging lightness of the words. Linking her arm through Autumn's, she began to walk across the lawn.

"Julia..." Autumn shook her head. Inner feelings were private. She'd broken the rule for Lucas, and wasn't certain she could do so again.

"Autumn." The refusal was firmly interrupted. "You do need to talk. You might not think that you look stricken, but you do." Julia sighed with perfect finesse. "I really don't know why I've become so fond of you; it's totally against my policy. Beautiful women tend to avoid or dislike other beautiful women, especially younger ones."

The statement completely robbed Autumn of speech. The idea of the exquisite, incomparable Julia Bond placing herself on a physical plane anywhere near Autumn's own seemed ludicrous to her. It was one matter to hear the actress speak casually of her own beauty, and quite another for her to speak of Autumn's. Julia's voice flowed over the gaping silence.

"Maybe it's the exposure to those two other females—one so dull and the other so nasty—but I've developed an affection for you." The breeze tugged at her hair, lifting it up so that the sunlight streamed through it. Absently, Julia tucked a strand behind her ear. On the lobe a diamond sparkled. Autumn thought it incongruous that they were walking arm in arm among her aunt's struggling daffodils.

"You're also a kind person," Julia went on. "I don't know a great many kind people." She turned to Autumn so that her exquisite profile became her exquisite full face. "Autumn, darling, I always pry, but I also know how to keep a confidence."

"I'm still in love with him," Autumn blurted out, then followed that rash statement with a deep sigh. Before she knew it, words were tumbling out. She left out nothing, from the beginning to the end, to the new beginning when he had come back into her life the day before. She told Julia everything. Once she'd begun, no effort was needed. She didn't have to think, only feel, and Julia listened. The quality of her listening was so perfect, Autumn all but forgot she was there.

"The monster," Julia said, but with no malice. "You'll find all men, those marvelous creatures, are basically monsters."

Who was Autumn to argue with an expert? As they walked on in silence, she realized that she did feel better. The rawness was gone.

"The main trouble is, of course, that you're still mad about him. Not that I blame you," Julia added when Autumn made a small sound of distress. "Lucas is quite a man. I had a tiny sample last night, and I was impressed." Julia spoke so casually of the passion Autumn had witnessed, it was impossible to be angry. "Lucas is a talented man," Julia went on. By her smile, Autumn knew that Julia was very much aware of the struggle that was going on within Autumn. "He's also arrogant, selfish and used to being obeyed. It's easy for me to see that, because I am, too. We're alike. I doubt very much if we could even enjoy a pleasant affair. We'd be clawing at each other before the bed was turned down."

Autumn found no response to make to the image this produced, and merely walked on.

"Jacques is more my type," Julia mused. "But his attentions are committed elsewhere." She frowned, and Autumn sensed that her thoughts had drifted to something quite different. "Anyway." Julia made an impatient gesture. "You just have to make up your mind what you want. Obviously, Lucas wants you back, at least for as long as it suits him."

Autumn tried to ignore the sting of honesty and just listened.

"Knowing that, you could enjoy a stimulating relationship with him, with your eyes open."

"I can't do that, Julia. The knowing won't stop the hurting. I'm not sure I can survive another...relationship with Lucas. And he'd know I was still in love with him." A flash frame of their parting scene three years before jumped into her mind. "I won't be humiliated again. Pride's the only thing I have left that isn't his already."

"Love and pride don't belong together." Julia patted Autumn's hand. "Well then, you'll have to barricade yourself against the assault. I'll run interference for you."

"How will you do that?"

"Darling!" She lifted her brow as the slow, cat smile drifted to her lips.

Autumn had to laugh. It all seemed so absurd. She lifted her face to the sky. The black clouds were winning after all. For a moment, they blotted out the sun and warmth. "Looks like rain."

Her gaze shifted back to the inn. The windows were black and empty. The struggling light fell gloomily over the bricks and turned the white porch and shutters gray. Behind the building, the sky was like slate. The mountains were colorless and oppressive. She felt a tickle at the back of her neck. To her puzzlement, Autumn found she didn't want to go back inside.

Just as quickly, the clouds shifted, letting the sun pour out through the opening. The windows blinked with light. The shadows vanished. Chiding herself for another flight of fancy, Autumn walked back to the inn with Julia.

Only Jacques joined them for breakfast. Helen was nowhere in sight, and Steve and the Spicers were apparently still hiking. Autumn trained her thoughts away from Lucas. Her appetite, as usual, was unimpaired and outrageous. She put away a healthy portion of bacon, eggs, coffee and muffins while Julia nibbled on a single piece of thin toast and sent her envious scowls.

Jacques seemed preoccupied. His charm was costing him visible effort. Memory of the muffled argument in the lounge came to Autumn's mind. Idly, she began to speculate on who he had been annoyed with. Thinking it over, the entire matter struck her as odd. Jacques LeFarre didn't seem to be the sort of man who would argue with a veritable stranger, yet, as Autumn knew, both Lucas and Julia had been preoccupied elsewhere.

Appearing totally at ease, Julia rambled on about a mutual friend in the industry. But she's an actress, Autumn reminded herself. A good one. She could easily know the cause of last night's animosity and never show a sign. Jacques, however, wasn't an actor. The distress was there; anger lay just beneath the polished charm. Autumn wondered at it throughout the meal, then dismissed it from her mind as she left to find her aunt. After all, she reflected, it wasn't any of her business.

Aunt Tabby was, as Autumn had known she would be, fussing with Nancy the cook over the day's menu.

Keeping silent, Autumn let the story unfold. It seemed that Nancy had planned on chicken while Aunt Tabby was certain they had decided on pork. While the argument raged, Autumn helped herself to another cup of coffee. Through the window, she could see the thick, roiling clouds continue their roll from the west.

"Oh, Autumn, did you have a nice walk?" When she turned, Autumn found her aunt smiling at her. "Such a nice morning, a shame it's going to rain. But that's good for the flowers, isn't it? Sweet little things. Did you sleep well?"

After a moment, Autumn decided to answer only the final question. There was no use confusing her aunt. "Wonderfully, Aunt Tabby. I always sleep well when I visit you."

"It's the air," the woman replied. Her round little face lit with pleasure. "I think I'll make my special chocolate cake for tonight. That should make up for the rain."

"Any hot coffee, Aunt Tabby?" Lucas swept into the kitchen as if he enjoyed the privilege daily. As always, when he came into a room, the air charged. This phenomenon Autumn could accept. The casual use of her aunt's nickname was more perplexing.

"Of course, dear, just help yourself." Aunt Tabby gestured vaguely toward the stove, her mind on chocolate cake. Autumn's confusion grew as Lucas strode directly to the proper cupboard, retrieved a cup and proceeded to fix himself a very homey cup of coffee.

He drank, leaning against the counter. The eyes that met Autumn's were very cool. All traces of anger and passion were gone, as if they had never existed. His rough black brows lifted as she continued to stare. The damnable devil smile tugged at his mouth.

"Oh, is that your camera, dear?" Aunt Tabby's voice broke into her thoughts. Autumn lowered her eyes.

The camera still hung around her neck, so much a part of her that she'd forgotten it was there.

"My, my, so many numbers. It looks complicated." Aunt Tabby peered at it through narrowed eyes, forgetting the glasses that dangled from her chain. "I have a very nice one, Autumn. You're welcome to use it whenever you like." After giving the Nikon another dubious glance, she beamed up with her misty smile. "You just push a little red button, and the picture pops right out. You can see if you've cut off someone's head or have your thumb in the corner right away, so you can take another picture. And you don't have to grope around in that darkroom either. I don't know how you see what you're doing in there." Her brows drew close, and she tapped a finger against her cheek. "I'm almost certain I can find it."

Autumn grinned. She was compelled to subject her aunt to yet another bear hug. Over the gray-streaked head, Autumn saw that Lucas was grinning as well. It was the warm, natural grin which came to his face so rarely. For a moment, she found she could smile back at him without pain.

Chapter 4

When the rain came, it didn't begin with the slow drip-drop of an April shower. As the sky grew hazy, the light in the lounge became dim. Everyone was back and the inn was again filled with its odd assortment of guests.

Steve, expanding on his role of bartender, had wandered to the kitchen to get coffee. Robert Spicer had trapped Jacques in what seemed to be a technical explanation of open-heart surgery. During the discussion, Julia sat beside him, hanging on every word—or seeming to. Autumn knew better. Occasionally, Julia sent messages across to her with her extraordinary eyes. She was enjoying herself immensely.

Jane sat sullen over a novel Autumn was certain was riddled with explicit sex. She wore dull brown again, slacks and a sweater. Helen, her bruise livid, smoked quietly in long, deep drags. She reminded Autumn eerily of Alice in Wonderland's caterpillar. Once or twice, Autumn found Helen's sharp eyes on her. The speculative smile left her confused and uncomfortable.

Lucas wasn't there. He was upstairs, Autumn knew, hammering away at his typewriter. She hoped it would keep him busy for hours. Perhaps he'd even take his meals in his room.

Abruptly, the dim light outdoors was snuffed out, and the room plunged into gloom. The warmth fled with it. Autumn shuddered with a sharp premonition of dread. The feeling surprised her, as storms had always held a primitive appeal for her. For a heartbeat, there was no sound, then the rain began with a gushing explosion. With instant force, instant fury, it battered against the windows, punctuated by wicked flashes of lightning.

"A spring shower in the mountains," Steve observed. He paused a moment in the doorway with a large tray balanced in his hands. The friendly scent of coffee entered with him.

"More like special effects," Julia returned. With a flutter of her lashes, she cuddled toward Robert. "Storms are so terrifying and moving. I find myself longing to be frightened."

It was straight out of *A Long Summer's Evening,* Autumn noted, amused. But the doctor seemed too overcome with Julia's ingenuous eyes to recognize the line. Autumn wanted to laugh badly. When Julia cuddled even closer and sent her a wink, Autumn's eyes retreated to the ceiling.

Jane wasn't amused. Autumn noticed she was no longer sullen but smoldering. Perhaps she had claws after all, Autumn thought, and felt she would like her better for it. It might be wise, she mused as Steve passed her a cup of coffee, if Julia concentrated on him rather than the doctor.

"Cream, no sugar, right?" Steve smiled down at her with his California blue eyes. Autumn's lips curved in response. He was a man with the rare ability to make a woman feel pampered without being patronizing. She admired him for it.

"Right. You've got a better memory than George." Her eyes smiled at him over the rim of her cup. "You serve with such style, too. Have you been in this line of work long?"

"I'm only here on a trial basis," he told her with a grin. "Please pass your comments on to the management."

Lightning speared through the gloom again. Jacques shifted in his seat as thunder rumbled and echoed through the room. "With such a storm, is it not possible to lose power?" he addressed Autumn.

"We often lose power." Her answer, accompanied by an absent shrug, brought on varying reactions.

Julia found the idea marvelous—candlelight was so wonderfully romantic. At the moment, Robert couldn't have agreed more. Jacques appeared not to care one way or the other. He lifted his hands in a Gallic gesture, indicating his acceptance of fate.

Steve and Helen seemed inordinately put out, though his comments were milder than hers. He mumbled once about inconveniences, then stalked over to the window to stare out at the torrent of wind and rain. Helen was livid.

"I didn't pay good money to grope around in the dark and eat cold meals." Lighting another cigarette with a swift, furious gesture, she glared at Autumn. "It's intolerable that we should have to put up with such inefficiency. Your aunt will certainly have to make the proper adjustments. I for one won't pay these ridiculous prices, then live like a pioneer." She waved her cigarette, preparing to continue, but Autumn cut her off. She aimed the cold, hard stare she had recently developed.

"I'm sure my aunt will give your complaints all the consideration they warrant." Turning pointedly away, she allowed Helen's sharp little darts to bounce off her. "Actually," she told Jacques, noting his smile of approval, "we have a generator. My uncle was as practical as Aunt Tabby is…"

"Charming," Steve supplied, and instantly became her friend.

After she'd finished beaming at him, Autumn continued. "If we lose main power, we switch over to the generator. With that, we can maintain essential power with little inconvenience."

"I believe I'll have candles in my room anyway," Julia decided. She gave Robert an under-the-lashes smile as he lit her cigarette.

"Julia should have been French," Jacques commented. His moustache tilted at the corner. "She's an incurable romantic."

"Too much…romance," Helen murmured, "can be unwise." Her eyes swept the room, then focused on Julia.

Before Autumn's astonished gaze, Julia transformed from mischievous angel to tough lady. "I've always found that only idiots think they're wise." Statement made, she melted back into a celestial being so quickly, Autumn blinked.

Seeing her perform on the screen was nothing compared to a live show. It occurred to Autumn that she had no inkling which woman was the real Julia Bond—if indeed she was either. The notion germinated that she really didn't know any of the people in that room. They were all strangers.

The air was still vibrating with the uncomfortable silence when Lucas entered. He seemed impervious to the swirling tension. Helplessly, Autumn's eyes locked on his. He came to her, ignoring the others in his cavalier fashion. The devil smile was on his face.

She felt a tremor when she couldn't stop the room from receding, leaving only him in her vision. Something of that fear must have been reflected in her face.

"I'm not going to eat you, Cat," Lucas murmured. Against the violent sounds of the storm, his voice was low, only for her. "Do you still like to walk in the rain?" The question was offhand, and didn't require an answer as he searched her face. "I remember when you did." He paused when she said nothing. "Your aunt sent you this." Lucas held out his hand, and Autumn's gaze dropped to it. Tension dissolved into laughter. "I haven't heard that in a long time," Lucas said softly.

She lifted her eyes to his again. He was studying her with a complete, singleminded intensity. "No?" As she accepted Aunt Tabby's famous red-button camera, her shoulders moved in a careless shrug. "Laughing's quite a habit of mine."

"Aunt Tabby says for you to have a good time with it." Dismissively, he turned his back on her and walked to the coffeepot.

"What have you got there, Autumn?" Julia demanded, her eyes following Lucas's progress.

Flourishing the camera, Autumn used a sober, didactic tone. "This, ladies and gentlemen, is the latest technological achievement in photography. At the mere touch of a button, friends and loved ones are beamed inside and spewed out onto a picture which develops before your astonished eyes. No focusing, no need to consult your light meter. The button is faster than the brain. Why, a child of five can operate it while riding his tricycle."

"It should be known," Lucas inserted in a dry voice, "that Autumn is a photographic snob." He stood by the window, carelessly drinking coffee while he spoke to the others. His eyes were on Autumn. "If it doesn't have interchangeable lenses and filters, multispeed shutters and impossibly complicated operations, it isn't a camera, but a toy."

"I've noticed her obsession," Julia agreed. She sent him a delicious look before she turned to Autumn. "She wears that black box like other women wear diamonds. She was actually tramping through the forest at the break of dawn, snapping pictures of chipmunks and bunnies."

With a good-natured grin, Autumn lifted the camera and snapped Julia's lovely face.

"Really, darling," Julia said with a professional toss of the head. "You might have given me the chance to turn my best side."

"You haven't got a best side," Autumn countered.

Julia smiled, obviously torn between amusement and insult while Jacques exploded with laughter. "And I thought she was such a sweet child," she murmured.

"In my profession, Miss Bond," Autumn returned gravely, "I've had occasion to photograph a fair number of women. This one you shoot from the left profile, that one from the right, another straight on. Still another from an upward angle, and so on." Pausing a moment, she gave Julia's matchless face a quick, critical survey.

"I could shoot you from any position, any angle, any light, and the result would be equally wonderful."

"Jacques." Julia placed a hand on his arm. "We really must adopt this girl. She's invaluable for my ego."

"Professional integrity," Autumn claimed before placing the quickly developing snapshot on the table. She aimed Aunt Tabby's prize at Steve.

"You should be warned that with a camera of any sort in her hands, Autumn becomes a dangerous weapon." Lucas moved closer. He lifted the snap of Julia and studied it.

Autumn frowned as she remembered the innumerable photographs she had taken of him. Under the pretext that they were art, she'd never disposed of them. She'd snapped and focused and crouched around him until, exasperated, he'd dislodged the camera from her hands and effectively driven photography from her mind.

Lucas saw the frown. With his eyes dark and unreadable, he reached down to tangle his fingers in her hair. "You never could teach me how to take a proper picture, could you, Cat?"

"No." The battle with the growing ache made her voice brittle. "I never taught you anything, Lucas. But I learned quite a bit."

"I've never been able to master anything but a one-button job myself." Steve ambled over. Autumn's camera sat on the table beside her. Picking it up, he examined it as if it were a strange contraption from the outer reaches of space. "How can you remember what all these numbers are for?"

When he perched on the arm of her chair, Autumn grasped at the diversion. She began a lesson in basic photography. Lucas wandered back to the coffeepot, obviously bored. From the corner of her eye, Autumn noticed Julia gliding to join him. Within moments, her hand was tucked into his arm, and he no longer appeared bored. Gritting her teeth, Autumn began to give Steve a more involved lesson.

Lucas and Julia left, arm in arm, ostensibly for Julia to nap and Lucas to work. Autumn's eyes betrayed her by following them.

When she dragged her attention back to Steve, she caught his sympathetic smile. That he understood her feelings was too obvious. Cursing herself, she resumed her explanations of f-stops, grateful that Steve picked up the conversation as if there had been no lull.

The afternoon wore on. It was a long, dreary day with rain beating against windows. Lightning and thunder came and went, but the wind built in force until it was one continuous moan. Robert tended the fire until flames crackled and spit. The cheery note this might have brought to the room was negated by Jane's sullenness and Helen's pacing. The air was tight.

Evading Steve's suggestion of cards, Autumn sought the peace and activity of her darkroom. As she closed and locked the door behind her, the headache which had started to build behind her temples eased.

This room was without tensions. Her senses picked up no nagging, intangible disturbances here, but were clear and ready to work. Step by step, she took her film through the first stages of development, preparing chemicals, checking temperatures, setting timers. Growing absorbed, she forgot the battering storm.

While it was necessary, Autumn worked in a total absence of light. Her fingers were her eyes at this stage and she worked quickly. Over the muffled sound of the storm, she heard a faint rattle. She ignored it, busy setting the timer for the next stage of developing. When the sound came again, it annoyed her.

Was it the doorknob? she wondered. Had she remembered to lock the door? All she needed at that point was for some layman to blunder in and bring damaging light with him.

"Leave the door alone," she called out just as the radio she had switched on for company went dead. There went the power, she concluded. Standing in the absolute darkness, Autumn sighed as the rattle came again.

Was it someone at the door, or just someone in the kitchen? Curious and annoyed, she walked in the direction of the door to make sure it was locked. Her steps were confident. She knew every inch of the room now. Suddenly, to her astonishment, pain exploded inside her head. Lights flashed and fractured before the darkness again became complete.

"Autumn, Autumn, open your eyes." Though the sound was far off and muffled, she heard the command in the tone. She resisted it. The nearer she came to consciousness, the more hideous grew the throbbing in her head. Oblivion was painless.

"Open your eyes." The voice was clearer now and more insistent. Autumn moaned.

Reluctantly, she opened her eyes as hands brushed the hair from her face. For a moment, she felt them linger against her cheek. Lucas came into focus gradually, dimming and receding until she forced him back, clear and sharp.

"Lucas?" Disoriented, Autumn could not think beyond his name. It seemed to satisfy him.

"That's better," he said with approval. Before any protest could be made, he kissed her hard, with a briefness that spoke of past intimacy. "You had me worried there a minute. What the hell did you do to yourself?"

The accusation was typical of him. She barely noticed it. "Do?" Autumn lifted a hand to touch the spot on her head where the pain was concentrated. "What happened?"

"That's my question, Cat. No, don't touch the lump." He caught her hand in his and held it. "It'll only hurt more if you do. I'm curious as to how you came by it, and why you were lying in a heap on the floor."

It was difficult to keep clear of the mists in her brain. Autumn tried to center in on the last thing she remembered. "How did you get in?" she demanded, remembering the rattling knob. "Hadn't I locked the door?" It came to her slowly that he was cradling her in his arms, holding her close against his chest. She struggled to sit up. "Were you rattling at the door?"

"Take it easy," he ordered as she groaned with the movement.

Autumn squeezed her eyes shut against the pounding in her head. "I must have walked into the door," she murmured, wondering at the quality of her clumsiness.

"You walked into the door and knocked yourself unconscious?" She couldn't tell if Lucas was angry or amused. The ache in her head kept her from caring one way or the other. "Strange, I don't recall you possessing that degree of uncoordination."

"It was dark," she grumbled, coherent enough to feel embarrassed. "If you hadn't been rattling around at the door…"

"I wasn't rattling around at your door," he began, but she cut him off with a startled gasp.

"The lights!" For a second time, she tried to struggle away from him. "You turned on the lights!"

"It was a mad impulse when I saw you crumpled on the floor," he returned dryly. Without any visible effort, he held her still. "I wanted to see the extent of the damage."

"My film!" Her glare was as accusing as her voice, but he responded with laughter.

"The woman's a maniac."

"Let go of me, will you?" Her anger made her less than gracious. Pushing away, she scrambled to her feet. At her movement, the pain grew to a crashing roar. She staggered under it.

"For God's sake, Autumn." Lucas rose and gripped her shoulders, steadying her. "Stop behaving like an imbecile over a few silly pictures."

This statement, under normal conditions, would have been unwise. In her present state of mind, it was a declaration of war. Pain was eclipsed by a pure silver streak of fury. She whirled on him.

"You never could see my work as anything but silly pictures, could you? You never saw me as anything but a silly child, diverting for a while, but eventually boring. You always hated being bored, didn't you, Lucas?" She made a violent swipe at the hair that fell over her eyes. "You sit with your novels and bask in the adulation you get and look down your nose at the rest of us. You're not the only person in the world with talent, Lucas. My abilities are just as creative as yours, and my pictures give me as much fulfillment as your silly little books."

For a moment, he stood in silence, studying her with a frown. When he did speak, his voice was oddly weary. "All right, Autumn, now that you've gotten that out, you'd better get yourself some aspirin."

"Just leave me alone!" She shook off the hand he put on her arm. Turning, she started to take her camera from the shelf she had placed it on before beginning her work. Glancing down at the table, she flared again. "What do you mean by messing around with my equipment? You've exposed an entire roll of film!" Seething with fury, she whirled on him. "It isn't enough to interrupt my work by fooling around at the door, then turn on the lights and ruin what I've started. You have to put your hands into something you know nothing about."

"I told you before, I wasn't fooling around at your door." His eyes were darkening dangerously. "I came back after the power went out and the generator switched on. The door was open, and you were lying in a heap in the middle of the floor. I never touched your damned film."

There was ice in his voice now to go with the heat in his eyes but Autumn was too infuriated to be touched by either. "Foolish as it may seem," he continued, "my concern and attention were on you." Moving toward her, he glanced down at the confusion on her work table. "I don't suppose it occurred to you that in the dark you disturbed the film yourself?"

"Don't be absurd." Her professional ability was again insulted, but he cut off her retort in a voice filled with strained patience. Autumn pondered on it. As she remembered, Lucas had no patience at all.

"Autumn, I don't know what happened to your film. I

didn't get any farther into the room than the spot where you were lying. I won't apologize for switching on the lights; I'd do precisely the same thing again." He circled her neck with his fingers and his words took on the old caressing note she remembered. "I happen to think your welfare is more important than your pictures."

Suddenly, her interest in the film waned. She wanted only to escape from him, and the feelings he aroused in her so effortlessly. Programmed response, she told herself. The soft voice and gentle hands tripped the release, and she went under.

"You're pale," Lucas muttered, abruptly dropping his hands and stuffing them into his pockets. "Dr. Spicer can take a look at you."

"No, I don't need—" She got no farther. He grabbed her arms with quicksilver fury.

"Damn it, Cat, must you argue with everything I say? Is there no getting past the hate you've built up for me?" He gave a quick shake. The pain rolled and spun in her head. For an instant, his face went out of focus as dizziness blurred her vision. Swearing with short, precise expertise, he pulled her close against him until the faintness passed. In a swift move, he lifted her into his arms. "You're pale as a ghost," he muttered. "Like it or not, you're going to see the doctor. You can vent your venom on him for a while."

By the time Autumn realized he was carrying her to her room, her temper had ebbed. There was only a dull, wicked ache and the weariness. Flagging, she rested her head against his shoulder and surrendered. This wasn't the time to think about the darkroom door or how it had come to be opened. It wasn't the time to think of how she had managed to walk into it like a perfect fool. This wasn't the time to think at all.

Accepting the fact that she had no choice, Autumn closed her eyes and allowed Lucas to take over. She kept them closed when she felt him lower her to the bed, but she knew he stood looking down at her a moment. She knew too that he was frowning.

The sound of his footsteps told her that he had walked into the adjoining bathroom. The faint splash of water in the sink sounded like a waterfall to her throbbing head. In a moment, there was a cool cloth over the ache in her forehead. Opening her eyes, Autumn looked into his.

"Lie still," he ordered curtly. Lucas brooded down at her with an odd, enigmatic expression. "I'll get Spicer," he muttered abruptly. Turning on his heel, he strode to the door.

"Lucas." Autumn stopped him because the cool cloth had brought back memories of all the gentle things he had ever done. He'd had his gentle moments, though she'd tried hard to pretend he hadn't. It had seemed easier.

When he turned back, impatience was evident in the very air around him. What a man of contradictions he was, she mused. Intemperate, with barely any middle ground at all.

"Thank you," she said, ignoring his obvious desire to be gone. "I'm sorry I shouted at you. You're being very kind."

Lucas leaned against the door and stared back at her. "I've never been kind." His voice was weary again.

Autumn found it necessary to force back the urge to go to him, wipe away his lines of fatigue. He sensed her thoughts, and his eyes softened briefly. On his mouth moved one of his rare, disarming smiles.

"My God, Cat, you always were so incredibly sweet. So terrifyingly warm."

With that, he left her.

Chapter 5

Autumn was staring at the ceiling when Robert entered. Shifting her eyes, she looked at his black bag dubiously. She'd never cared for what doctors carried inside those innocent-looking satchels.

"A house call," she said and managed a smile. "The eighth wonder of the world. I didn't think you'd have your bag with you on vacation."

He was quick enough to note her uneasy glance. "Do you travel without your camera?"

"Touché." She told herself to relax and not to be a baby.

"I don't think we'll need to operate." He sat on the bed and removed the cloth Lucas had placed there. "Mmm, that's going to be colorful. Is your vision blurred?"

"No."

His hands were surprisingly soft and gentle, reminding Autumn of her father's. She relaxed further and answered his questions on dizziness, nausea and so forth while watching his face. He was different, she noted. The competence was still there, but his dapper self-presentation had been replaced by a quiet compassion. His voice was kind, she thought, and so were his eyes. He was well suited to his profession.

"How'd you come by this, Autumn?" As he asked he reached in his bag and her attention switched to his hands. He removed cotton and a bottle, not the needle she'd worried about.

She wrinkled her nose ruefully. "I walked into a door."

He shook his head with a laugh, and began to bathe the bruise. "A likely story."

"And embarrassingly true. In the darkroom," she added. "I must have misjudged the distance."

His eyes shifted and studied hers a moment before they returned to her forehead. "You struck me as a woman who kept her eyes open," he said a bit grimly, Autumn thought, before he smiled again. "It's just a bump," he told her and held her hand. "Though my diagnosis won't make it hurt any less."

"It's only an agonizing ache now," Autumn returned, trying for lightness. "The cannons have stopped going off."

With a chuckle, he reached into his bag again. "We can do something about smaller artillery."

"Oh." She eyed the bottle of pills he held and frowned. "I was going to take some aspirin."

"You don't put a forest fire out with a water pistol." He smiled at her again and shook out two pills. "They're very mild, Autumn. Take these and rest for an hour or two. You can trust me," he added with exaggerated gravity as her brows stayed lowered. "Even though I am a surgeon."

"Okay." His eyes convinced her and she smiled back, accepting the glass of water and pills. "You're not going to take out my appendix or anything, are you?"

"Not on vacation." He waited until she had swallowed the medication, then pulled a light blanket over her. "Rest," he ordered and left her.

The next time Autumn opened her eyes, the room was in shadows. Rest? she thought and shifted under the blanket. I've been unconscious. How long? She listened. The storm was still raging, whipping against her windows with a fury she'd been oblivious to. Carefully, she pushed herself into a sitting position. Her head didn't pound, but a touch of her fingers assured her she hadn't dreamed up the entire incident. Her next thought was entirely physical—she discovered she was starving.

Rising, she took a quick glance in the mirror, decided she didn't like what she saw and went in search of food and company. She found them both in the dining room. Her timing was perfect.

"Autumn." It was Robert who spotted her first. "Feeling better?"

She hesitated a moment, embarrassed. Hunger was stronger, however, and the scent of Nancy's chicken was too tempting. "Much," she told him. She glanced at Lucas, but he said nothing, only watched her. The gentleness she had glimpsed so briefly before might have been an illusion. His eyes were dark and hard. "I'm starving," she confessed as she took her seat.

"Good sign. Any more pain?"

"Only in my pride." Forging ahead, she began to fill her plate. "Clumsiness isn't a talent I like to brag about, and walking into a door is such a tired cliché. I wish I'd come up with something more original."

"It's odd." Jacques twirled his fork by the stem as he studied her. "It doesn't seem to me that you would have the power enough to knock yourself unconscious."

"An amazon," Autumn explained and let the chicken rest for a delicious moment on her tongue.

"She eats like one," Julia commented. Autumn glanced over in time to catch the speculative look on her face before it vanished into a smile. "I gain weight watching her."

"Metabolism," Autumn claimed and took another forkful of chicken. "The real tragedy is that I lost the two rolls of film I shot on the trip from New York."

"Perhaps we're in for a series of accidents." Helen's voice was as hard as her eyes as they swept the table. "Things come in threes, don't they?" No one answered and she went on, fingering her own bruise. "It's hard to say what might happen next."

Autumn had come to detest the odd little silences that followed Helen's remarks, the fingers of tension that poked holes in the normalcy of the situation. On impulse, she broke her rule and started a conversation with Lucas.

"What would you do with this setting, Lucas?" She turned to him, but found no change in his expression. He's watching all of us, she thought. Just watching. Shaking off her unease, Autumn continued. "Nine people—ten really, counting the cook—isolated in a remote country inn, a storm raging. The main power's already snuffed out. The phone's likely to be next."

"The phone's already out," Steve told her. Autumn drew out a dramatic "Ah."

"And the ford, of course, is probably impassable." Robert winked at her, falling in with the theme.

"What more could you ask for?" Autumn demanded of Lucas. Lightning flashed, as if on cue.

"Murder." Lucas uttered the six-letter word casually, but it hung in the air as all eyes turned to him. Autumn shuddered involuntarily. It was the response she'd expected, yet she felt a chill on hearing it. "But, of course," he continued as the word still whispered in the air, "it's a rather overly obvious setting for my sort of work."

"Life is sometimes obvious, is it not?" Jacques stated. A small smile played on his mouth as he lifted his glass of golden-hued wine.

"I could be very effective," Julia mused. "Gliding down dark passageways in flowing white." She placed her elbows on the table, folded her hands and rested her chin on them. "The flame of my candle flickering into the shadows while the murderer waits with a silk scarf to cut off my life."

"You'd make a lovely corpse," Autumn told her.

"Thank you, darling." She turned to Lucas. "I'd much rather remain among the living, at least until the final scene."

"You die so well." Steve grinned across the table at her. "I was impressed by your Lisa in *Hope Springs*."

"What sort of murder do you see, Lucas?" Steve was eating little, Autumn noted; he preferred the wine. "A crime of passion or revenge? The impulsive act of a

discarded lover or the evil workings of a cool, calculating mind?"

"Aunt Tabby could sprinkle an exotic poison over the
food and eliminate us one by one," Autumn suggested
as she dipped into the mashed potatoes.

"Once someone's dead, they're no more use." Helen
brought the group's attention back to her. "Murder is a
waste. You gain more by keeping someone alive. Alive
and vulnerable." She shot Lucas a look. "Don't you
agree, Mr. McLean?"

Autumn didn't like the way she smiled at him. *Cool
and calculating.* Jacques's words repeated in her mind.
Yes, she mused, this was a cool and calculating woman.
In the silence, Autumn shifted her gaze to Lucas.

His face held the faintly bored go-to-hell look she
knew so well. "I don't think murder is always a waste."
Again, his voice was casual, but Autumn, in tune with
him, saw the change in his eyes. They weren't bored, but
cold as ice. "The world would gain much by the elimination of some." He smiled, and it was deadly.

They no longer seemed to be speaking hypotheti-
cally. Shifting her gaze to Helen, Autumn saw the quick
fear. *But it's just a game,* she told herself frantically
and looked at Julia. The actress was smiling, but there
was none of her summer warmth in it. She was enjoying watching Helen flutter like a moth on a pin. Noting
Autumn's expression of dismayed shock, Julia changed
the subject without a ripple.

After dinner, the group loitered in the lounge, but the
storm, which continued unabated, was wearing on the
nerves. Only Julia and Lucas seemed unaffected. Autumn noted how they huddled together in a corner, apparently enthralled with each other's company. Julia's

laughter was low and rich over the sound of rain. Once, she watched Lucas pinch a strand of the pale hair between his fingers. Autumn turned away. Julia ran interference expertly, and the knowledge depressed her.

The Spicers, without Julia as a distraction, sat together on the sofa nearest the fire. Though their voices were low, Autumn sensed the strain of a domestic quarrel. She moved farther out of earshot. A bad time, she decided, for Jane to confront Robert on his fascination with Julia when the actress was giving another man the benefit of her attentions. When they left, Jane's face was no longer sullen, but simply miserable. Julia never glanced in their direction, but leaned closer to Lucas and murmured something in his ear that made him laugh. Autumn found she, too, wanted out of the room.

It has nothing to do with Lucas, she told herself as she moved down the hall. I just want to say good-night to Aunt Tabby. Julia's doing precisely what I want her to—keeping Lucas entertained. He never even looked at me once Julia stepped in between. Shaking off the hurt, Autumn opened the door to her aunt's room.

"Autumn, dear! Lucas told me you bumped your head." Aunt Tabby stopped clucking over her laundry list and rose to peer at the bruise. "Oh, poor thing. Do you want some aspirin? I have some somewhere."

Though she appreciated Lucas's consideration in giving her aunt a watered-down version, Autumn wondered at the ease of their relationship. It didn't seem quite in character for Lucas McLean to bother overmuch with a vague old woman whose claim to fame was a small inn and a way with chocolate cake.

"No, Aunt Tabby, I'm fine. I've already taken something."

"That's good." She patted Autumn's hand and frowned briefly at the bruise. "You'll have to be more careful, dear."

"I will. Aunt Tabby…" Autumn poked idly at the papers on her aunt's desk. "How well do you know Lucas? I don't recall you ever calling a roomer by his first name." She knew there was no use in beating around the bush with her aunt. It would produce the same results as reading *War and Peace* in dim light—a headache and confusion.

"Oh, now that depends, Autumn. Yes, that really does depend." Aunt Tabby gently removed her papers from Autumn's reach before she focused on a spot in the ceiling. Autumn knew this meant she was thinking. "There's Mrs. Nollington. She has a corner room every September. I call her Frances and she calls me Tabitha. Such a nice woman. A widow from North Carolina."

"Lucas calls you Aunt Tabby," Autumn pointed out before her aunt could get going on Frances Nollington.

"Yes, dear, quite a number of people do. You do."

"Yes, but—"

"And Paul and Will," Aunt Tabby continued blithely. "And the little boy who brings the eggs. And…oh, several people. Yes, indeed, several people. Did you enjoy your dinner?"

"Yes, very much. Aunt Tabby," Autumn continued, determined that tenacity would prevail. "Lucas seems very much at home here."

"Oh, I am glad!" She beamed at her niece as she took Autumn's hand and patted it. "I do try so hard to make everyone feel at home. It always seems a shame to have to make them pay, but…" She glanced down at her laundry bills and began to mutter.

Give up, Autumn told herself. She kissed her aunt's cheek and left her to her towels and pillowcases.

It was growing late when Autumn finished putting her darkroom back in order. She left the door open this time and kept all the lights on. The echo of rain followed her inside as it beat on the kitchen windows. Other than its angry murmur, the house was silent.

No, Autumn thought, old houses are never silent. They creak and whisper, but the groaning boards and settling didn't disturb her. She liked the humming quality of the silence. Absorbed and content, she emptied trays and replaced bottles. She threw her ruined film into the wastecan with a sigh.

That hurts a bit, she thought, but there's nothing to be done about it. Tomorrow, she decided, she'd develop the film she'd taken that morning—the lake, the early sun, the mirrored trees. It would put her in a better frame of mind. Stretching her back, she lifted her hair from her neck, feeling pleasantly tired.

"I remember you doing that in the mornings."

Autumn whirled, her hair flying out from her shoulders as quick fear brought her heart to her throat. Pushing strands from her face, she stared at Lucas.

He leaned against the open doorway, a cup of coffee in his hand. His eyes locked on hers without effort.

"You'd pull up your hair, then let it fall, tumbling down your back until I ached to get my hands on it." His voice was deep and strangely raw. Autumn couldn't speak at all. "I often wondered if you did it on purpose, just to drive me mad." As he studied her face, he frowned, then lifted the coffee to his lips. "But, of course you didn't. I've never known anyone else who could arouse with such innocence."

"What are you doing here?" The trembling in her voice took some of the power out of the demand.

"Remembering."

Turning, she began to juggle bottles, jumbling them out of their carefully organized state. "You always were clever with words, Lucas." Cooler now that she wasn't facing him, she meticulously studied a bottle of bath soap. "I suppose you have to be in your profession."

"I'm not writing at the moment."

It was easier to deliberately misunderstand him. "Your book still giving trouble?" Turning, Autumn again noticed the signs of strain and fatigue on his face. Sympathy and love flared up, and she struggled to bank them down. His eyes were much too keen. "You might have more success if you'd get a good night's sleep." She gestured toward the cup in his hands. "Coffee's not going to help."

"Perhaps not." He drained the cup. "But it's wiser than bourbon."

"Sleep's better than both." She shrugged her shoulders carelessly. Lucas's habits were no longer her concern. "I'm going up." Autumn walked toward him, but he stayed where he was, barring the door. She pulled up sharply. They were alone. The ground floor was empty but for them and the sound of rain.

"Lucas." She sighed sharply, wanting him to think her impatient rather than vulnerable. "I'm tired. Don't be troublesome."

His eyes smoldered at her tone. Though Autumn remained calm, she could feel her knees turning to water. The dull, throbbing ache was back in her head. When he moved aside, she switched off the lights, then brushed past him. Swiftly, he took her arm, preventing what she had thought was going to be an easy exit.

"There'll come a time, Cat," he murmured, "when you won't walk away so easily."

"Don't threaten me with your overactive masculinity." Her temper rose and she forgot caution. "I'm immune now."

She was jerked against him. All she could see was his fury. "I've had enough of this."

His mouth took hers roughly; she could taste the infuriated desire. When she struggled, he pinned her back against the wall, holding her arms to her sides and battering at her will with his mouth alone. She could feel herself going under and hating herself for it as much, she told herself, as she hated him. His lips didn't soften, even when her struggles ceased. He took and took as the anger vibrated between them.

Her heart was thudding wildly, and she could feel the mad pace of his as they pressed together. Passion was all-encompassing, and her back was to the wall. There's no escape, she thought dimly. There's never been any escape from him. No place to run. No place to hide. She began to tremble with fear and desire.

Abruptly he pulled away. His eyes were so dark, she saw nothing but her own reflection. I'm lost in him, she thought. I've always been lost in him. Then he was shaking her, shocking a gasp out of her.

"Watch how far you push," he told her roughly. "Damn it, you'd better remember I haven't any scruples. I know how to deal with people who pick fights with me." He stopped, but his fingers still dug into her

skin. "I'll take you, Cat, take you kicking and screaming if you push me much further."

Too frightened by the rage she saw in his face to think
of pride, she twisted away. She flew down the hall and
up the stairs.

Chapter 6

Autumn reached her door, out of breath and fighting tears. He shouldn't be allowed to do this to her. She couldn't allow it. Why had he barged back into her life this way? Just when she was beginning to get over him. *Liar.* The voice was clear as crystal inside her head. You've never gotten over him. Never. But I will. She balled her hands into fists as she stood outside her door and caught her breath. I will get over him.

Hearing the sound of his footsteps on the stairs, she fumbled with the doorknob. She didn't want to deal with him again tonight. Tomorrow was soon enough.

Something was wrong. Autumn knew it the moment she opened her door and stumbled into the dark. The scent of perfume was so strong, her head whirled with it. She groped for the light and when it flashed on, she gave a small sound of despair.

The drawers and closet had been turned out and her clothes were tossed and scattered across the room. Some were ripped and torn, others merely lay in heaps. Her jewelry had been dumped from its box and tossed indiscriminately over the mounds of clothes. Bottles of cologne and powder had been emptied out and flung everywhere. Everything—every small object or personal possession—had been abused or destroyed.

She stood frozen in shock and disbelief. The wrong room, she told herself dumbly. This had to be the wrong room. But the lawn print blouse with its sleeve torn at the shoulder had been a Christmas gift from Will. The sandals, flung into a corner and slashed, she had bought herself in a small shop off Fifth Avenue the summer before.

"No." She shook her head as if that would make it all go away. "It's not possible."

"Good God!" Lucas's voice came from behind her. Autumn turned to see him staring into her room.

"I don't understand." The words were foolish, but they were all she had. Slowly, Lucas shifted his attention to her face. She made a helpless gesture. "Why?"

He came to her, and with his thumb brushed a tear from her cheek. "I don't know, Cat. First we have to find out who."

"But it's—it's so spiteful." She wandered through the rubble of her things, still thinking she must be dreaming. "No one here would have any reason to do this to me. You'd have to hate someone to do this, wouldn't you? No one here has any reason to hate me. No one even knew me before last night."

"Except me."

"This isn't your style." She pressed her fingers to her

temple and struggled to understand. "You'd find a more direct way of hurting me."

"Thanks."

Autumn looked over at him and frowned, hardly aware of what was being said. His expression was brooding as he studied her face. She turned away. She wasn't up to discussing Lucas McLean. Then she saw it.

"Oh, *no!*"

Scrambling on all fours, Autumn worked her way over the mangled clothes and began pushing at the tangled sheets of her bed. Her hands shook as she reached for her camera. The lens was shattered, with spiderweb cracks spreading over the surface. The back was broken, hanging drunkenly on one hinge. The film streamed out like the tail of a kite. Exposed. Ruined. The mirror was crushed. With a moan, she cradled it in her hands and began to weep.

Her clothes and trinkets meant nothing, but the Nikon was more to her than a single-reflex camera. It was as much a part of her as her hands. With it, she had taken her first professional picture. Its mutilation was rape.

Her face was suddenly buried against a hard chest. She made no protest as Lucas's arms came around her, but wept bitterly. He said nothing, offered no comforting words, but his hands were unexpectedly gentle, his arms strong.

"Oh, Lucas." She drew away from him with a sigh. "It's so senseless."

"There's sense to it somewhere, Cat. There always is."

She looked back up at him. "Is there?" His eyes were keeping their secrets so she dropped her own back to her mangled camera. "Well, if someone wanted to hurt me, this was the right way."

Her fingers clenched on the camera. She was suddenly, fiercely angry; it pushed despair and tears out of her mind. Her body flooded with it. She wasn't going to sit and weep any longer. She was going to do something. Pushing her camera into Lucas's hands, Autumn scrambled to her feet.

"Wait a minute." He grabbed her hand before she could rush from the room. "Where are you going?"

"To drag everyone out of bed," she snapped at him, jerking her hand. "And then I'm going to break someone's neck."

He didn't have an easy time subduing her. Ultimately, he pinned her by wrapping his arms around her and holding her against him. "You probably could." There was a touch of surprised admiration in his tone, but it brought her no pleasure.

"Watch me," she challenged.

"Calm down first." He tightened his grip as she squirmed against him.

"I want—"

"I know what you want, Cat, and I don't blame you. But you have to think before you rush in."

"I don't have anything to think about," she tossed back. "Someone's going to pay for this."

"All right, fair enough. Who?"

His logic annoyed her, but succeeded in taking her temper from boil to simmer. "I don't know yet." With an effort, she managed to take a deep breath.

"That's better." He smiled and kissed her lightly. "Though your eyes are still lethal enough." He loosened his grip, but kept a hold on her arm. "Just keep your claws sheathed, Cat, until we find out what's going on. Let's go knock on a few doors."

Julia's room adjoined hers, so Autumn steered there first. Her rage was now packed in ice. Systematic, she told herself, aware of Lucas's grip. All right, we'll be systematic until we find out who did it. And then...

She knocked sharply on Julia's door. After the second knock, Julia answered with a soft, husky slur.

"Get up, Julia," Autumn demanded. "I want to talk to you."

"Autumn, darling." Her voice evoked a picture of Julia snuggling into her pillows. "Even I require beauty sleep. Go away like a good girl."

"Up, Julia," Autumn repeated, barely restraining herself from shouting. "Now."

"Goodness, aren't we grumpy. I'm the one who's being dragged from my bed."

She opened the door, a vision in a white lace negligee, her hair a tousled halo around her face, her eyes dark and heavy with sleep.

"Well, I'm up." Julia gave Lucas a slow, sensual smile and ran a hand through her hair. "Are we going to have a party?"

"Someone tore my room apart," Autumn stated bluntly. She watched Julia's attention switch from the silent flirtation with Lucas to her.

"What?" The catlike expression had melted into a frown of concentration. An actress, Autumn reminded herself. She's an actress and don't forget it.

"My clothes were pulled out and ripped, tossed around the room. My camera's broken." She swallowed on this. It was the most difficult to accept.

"That's crazy." Julia was no longer leaning provocatively against the door, but standing straight. "Let me see." She brushed past them and hurried down the hall.

Stopping in the doorway of Autumn's room, she stared. Her eyes, when they turned back, were wide with shock. "Autumn, how awful!" She came back and slipped an arm around Autumn's waist. "How perfectly awful. I'm so sorry."

Sincerity, sympathy, shock. They were all there. Autumn wanted badly to believe them.

"Who would have done that?" she demanded of Lucas. Autumn saw that Julia's eyes were angry now. She was again the tough lady Autumn had glimpsed briefly that afternoon.

"We intend to find out. We're going to wake the others." Something passed between them. Autumn saw it flash briefly, then it was gone.

"All right," Julia said. "Then let's do it." She pushed her hair impatiently behind her ears. "I'll get the Spicers, you get Jacques and Steve. You," she continued to Autumn, "wake up Helen."

Her tone carried enough authority that Autumn found herself turning down the hall to Helen's room. She could hear the pounding, the answering stirs and murmurs from behind her. Reaching Helen's door, Autumn banged against it. This, at least, she thought, was progress. Lucas was right. We need a trial before we can hang someone.

Her knock went unanswered. Annoyed, Autumn rapped again. She wasn't in the mood to be ignored. Now there was more activity behind her as people came out of their rooms to stare at the disaster in hers.

"Helen!" She knocked again with fraying patience. "Come out here." She pushed the door open. It would give her some satisfaction to drag at least one person from bed. Ruthlessly, she switched on the light. "Helen, I—"

Helen wasn't in bed. Autumn stared at her, too

shocked to feel horror. She was on the floor, but she wasn't sleeping. She was done with sleeping. Was that blood? Autumn thought in dumb fascination. She took a step forward before the reality struck her.

Horror gripped her throat, denying her the release of screaming. Slowly, she backed away. It was a nightmare. Starting with her room, it was all a nightmare. None of it was real. Lucas's careless voice played back in her head. *Murder.* Autumn shook her head as she backed into a wall. No, that was only a game. She heard a voice shouting in terror for Lucas, not even aware it was her own. Then blessedly, her hands came up to cover her eyes.

"Get her out of here." Lucas's rough command floated through Autumn's brain. She was trapped in a fog of dizziness. Arms came round her and led her from the room.

"Oh, my God." Steve's voice was unsteady. When Autumn found the strength to look up at him, his face was ashen. She struggled against the faintness and buried her face in his chest. When was she going to wake up?

Confusion reigned around her. She heard disembodied voices as she drifted from horror to shock. There were Julia's smoky tones, Jane's gravelly voice and Jacques's rapid French-English mixture. Then Lucas's voice joined in—calm, cool, like a splash of cold water.

"She's dead. Stabbed. The phone's out so I'm going into the village to get the police."

"Murdered? She was murdered? Oh, God!" Jane's voice rose, then became muffled. Raising her head, Autumn saw Jane being held tightly against her husband.

"I think, as a precaution, Lucas, no one should leave the inn alone." Robert took a deep breath as he cradled his wife. "We have to face the implications."

"I'll go with him." Steve's voice was strained and uneven. "I could use the fresh air."

With a curt nod, Lucas focused on Autumn. His eyes never left hers as he spoke to Robert. "Have you got something to put her out? She can double up with Julia tonight."

"I'm fine." Autumn managed to speak as she drew back from Steve's chest. "I don't want anything." It wasn't a dream, but real, and she had to face it. "Don't worry about me, it's not me. I'm all right." Hysteria was bubbling, and she bit down on her lip to cut it off.

"Come on, darling." Julia's arm replaced Steve's. "We'll go downstairs and sit down for a while. She'll be all right."

"I want—"

"I said she'll be all right," Julia cut off Lucas's protest sharply. "I'll see to her. Do what you have to do." Before he could speak again, she led Autumn down the staircase.

"Sit down," she ordered, nudging Autumn onto the sofa. "You could use a drink."

Looking up, Autumn saw Julia's face hovering over hers. "You're pale," she said stupidly before the brandy burned her throat and brought the world into focus with a jolt.

"I'm not surprised," Julia murmured and sank down on the low table in front of Autumn. "Better?" she asked when Autumn lifted the snifter again.

"Yes, I think so." She took a deep breath and focused on Julia's eyes. "It's really happening, isn't it? She's really lying up there."

"It's happening." Julia drained her own brandy. Color

seeped gradually into her cheeks. "The bitch finally pushed someone too far."

Stunned by the hardness of Julia's voice, Autumn could only stare. Calmly, Julia set down her glass.

"Listen." Her tone softened, but her eyes were still cold. "You're a strong lady, Autumn. You've had a shock, a bad one, but you won't fall apart."

"No." Autumn tried to believe it, then said with more strength, "No, I won't fall apart."

"This is a mess, and you have to face it." Julia paused, then leaned closer. "One of us killed her."

Part of her had known it, but the rest had fought against the knowledge, blocking it out. Now that it had been said in cool, simple terms, there was no escape from it. Autumn nodded again and swallowed the remaining brandy in one gulp.

"She got what she deserved."

"Julia!" Jacques strode into the room. His face was covered with horror and disapproval.

"Oh, Jacques, thank God. Give me one of those horrible French cigarettes. Give one to Autumn, too. She could use it."

"Julia." He obeyed her automatically. "You musn't speak so now."

"I'm not a hypocrite." Julia drew deeply on the cigarette, shuddered, then drew again. "I detested her. The police will find out soon enough why we all detested her."

"*Nom de Dieu!* How can you speak so calmly of it?" Jacques exploded in a quick, passionate rage Autumn hadn't thought him capable of. "The woman is dead, murdered. You didn't see the cruelty of it. I wish to God I had not."

Autumn drew hard on her cigarette, trying to block out the picture that flashed back into her mind. She gasped and choked on the power of the smoke.

"Autumn, forgive me." Jacques's anger vanished as he sat down beside her and draped an arm over her shoulders. "I shouldn't have reminded you."

"No." She shook her head, then crushed out the cigarette. It wasn't going to help. "Julia's right. It has to be faced."

Robert entered, but his normally swinging stride was slow and dragging. "I gave Jane a sedative." With a sigh, he too made for the brandy. "It's going to be a long night."

The room grew silent. The rain, so much a part of the night, was no longer noticeable. Jacques paced the room, smoking continually while Robert kindled a fresh fire. The blaze, bright and crackling, brought no warmth. Autumn's skin remained chilled. In defense, she poured herself another brandy but found she couldn't drink it.

Julia remained seated. She smoked in long, slow puffs. The only outward sign of her agitation was the continual tapping of a pink-tipped nail against the arm of her chair. The tapping, the crackling, the hiss of rain, did nothing to diminish the overwhelming power of the silence.

When the front door opened with a click and a thud, all eyes flew toward the sound. Strings of tension tightened and threatened to snap. Autumn waited to see Lucas's face. It would be all right, somehow, as long as she could see his face.

"Couldn't get through the ford," he stated shortly as he came into the room. He peeled off a sopping jacket, then made for the community brandy.

"How bad is it?" Robert looked from Lucas to Steve, then back to Lucas. Already, the line of command had been formed.

"Bad enough to keep us here for a day or two," Lucas informed him. He swallowed a good dose of the brandy, then stared out the window. There was nothing to see but the reflection of the room behind him. "That's if the rain lets up by morning." Turning, he locked onto Autumn, making a long, thorough study. Again he had, in his way, pushed everyone from the room but the two of them.

"The phones," she blurted out, needing to say something, anything. "We could have phone service by tomorrow."

"Don't count on it." Lucas ran a hand through his dripping hair, showering the room with water. "According to the car radio, this little spring shower is the backlash of a tornado. The power's out all over this part of the state." He lit a cigarette with a shrug. "We'll just have to wait and see."

"Days." Steve flopped down beside Autumn, his face still gray. She gave him her unwanted brandy. "It could be days."

"Lovely." Rising, Julia went to Lucas. She plucked the cigarette from his fingers and drew on it. "Well." She stared at him. "What the hell do we do now?"

"First we lock and seal off Helen's room." Lucas lit another cigarette. His eyes stayed on Julia's. "Then we get some sleep."

Chapter 7

Sometime during the first murky light of dawn, Autumn did sleep. She'd passed the night lying wide-eyed, listening to the sound of Julia's gentle breathing beside her. Though she'd envied her ability to sleep, Autumn had fought off the drowsiness. If she closed her eyes, she might see what she'd seen when she opened Helen's door. When her eyes did close, however, the sleep was dreamless—the total oblivion of exhaustion.

It might have been the silence that woke her. Suddenly, she found herself awake and sitting straight up in bed. Confused, she stared around her.

Julia's disorder greeted her. Silk scarves and gold chains were draped here and there. Elegant bottles cluttered the bureau. Small, incredibly high Italian heels littered the floor. Memory returned.

With a sigh, Autumn rose, feeling a bit ridiculous

in Julia's black silk nightgown; it neither suited nor fit. After seeing herself in the mirror, Autumn was glad Julia had already awakened and gone. She didn't want to wear any of the clothes that might have survived the attack on her room, and prepared to change back into yesterday's shirt and jeans.

A note lay on them. The elegant, sloping print could only have been Julia's:

> Darling, help yourself to some undies and a blouse or sweater. I'm afraid my slacks won't fit you. You're built like a pencil. You don't wear a bra, and in any case, the idea of you filling one of mine is ridiculous.
>
> J.

Autumn laughed, as Julia had intended. It felt so good, so normal, that she laughed again. Julia had known exactly how I'd feel, Autumn realized, and a wave of gratitude swept through her for the simple gesture. She showered, letting the water beat hot against her.

Coming back to the bedroom, Autumn pulled out a pair of cobwebby panties. There was a stack of them in misted pastels that she estimated would cost as much as a wide-angle lens. She tugged on one of Julia's sweaters, then pushed it up to her elbows—it was almost there in any case. Leaving the room, she kept her eyes firmly away from Helen's door.

"Autumn, I was hoping you'd sleep longer."

She paused at the foot of the stairs and waited for Steve to reach her. His face was sleep shadowed and older than it had been the day before. A fragment of his boyish smile touched his lips for her, but his eyes didn't join in.

"You don't look as if you got much," he commented and lifted a finger to her cheek.

"I doubt any of us did."

He draped an arm over her shoulder. "At least the rain's slowed down."

"Oh." Realization slowly seeped in and Autumn gave a weak laugh. "I knew there was something different. The quiet woke me. Where is…" She hesitated as Lucas's name trembled on her tongue. "Everyone?" she amended.

"In the lounge," he told her, but steered her toward the dining room. "Breakfast first. I haven't eaten myself, and you can't afford to drop any weight."

"How charming of you to remind me." She managed a friendly grimace. If he could make the effort to be normal, so could she. "Let's eat in the kitchen, though."

Aunt Tabby was there, as usual, giving instructions to a much subdued Nancy. She turned as they entered, then enfolded Autumn in her soft, lavender-scented arms.

"Oh, Autumn, what a dreadful tragedy. I don't know what to make of it." Autumn squeezed her. Here was something solid to hold on to. "Lucas said someone killed the poor thing, but that doesn't seem possible, does it?" Drawing back, Aunt Tabby searched Autumn's face. "You didn't sleep well, dear. Only natural. Sit down and have your breakfast. It's the best thing to do."

Aunt Tabby could, Autumn mused, so surprisingly cut through to the quick when she needed to. She began to bustle around the room, murmuring to Nancy as Autumn and Steve sat at the small kitchen table.

There were simple, normal sounds and scents. Bacon,

coffee, the quick sizzle of eggs. It was, Autumn had to agree, the best thing to do. The food, the routine, would bring some sense of order. And with the order, she'd be able to think clearly again.

Steve sat across from her, sipping coffee while she toyed with her eggs. She simply couldn't summon her usual appetite, and turned to conversation instead. The questions she asked Steve about himself were general and inane, but he picked up the effort and went with it. She realized, as she nibbled without interest on a piece of toast, that they were supporting each other.

Autumn discovered he was quite well traveled. He'd crisscrossed all over the country performing various tasks in his role as troubleshooter for his father's con-glomerate. He treated wealth with the casual indifference of one who has always had it, but she sensed a knowl-edge and a dedication toward the company which had provided him with it. He spoke of his father with respect and admiration.

"He's sort of a symbol of success and ingenuity," Steve said, pushing his own half-eaten breakfast around his plate. "He worked his way up the proverbial ladder. He's tough." He grinned and shrugged. "He's earned it."

"How does he feel about you going into politics?"

"He's all for it." Steve glanced down at her plate and sent her a meaningful look. Autumn only smiled and shook her head. "Anyway, he's always encouraged me to 'go for what I want and I better be good at it.'" He grinned again. "He's tough, but since I am good at it and intend to keep it that way, we'll both be satisfied. I like paperwork." He gestured with both hands. "Organizing. Refining the system from within the system."

"That can't be as easy as it sounds," Autumn commented, encouraging his enthusiasm.

"No, but—" He shook his head. "Don't get me started. I'll make a speech." He finished off his second cup of coffee. "I'll be making enough of those when I get back to California and my campaign officially starts."

"It just occurs to me that you, Lucas, Julia and Jacques are all from California." Autumn pushed her hair behind her back and considered the oddity. "It's strange that so many people from the coast would be here at one time."

"The Spicers, too," Aunt Tabby added from across the room, deeply involved in positioning pies in the oven. "Yes, I'm almost sure Dr. Spicer told me they were from California. So warm and sunny there. Well—" she patted the range as if to give it the confidence it needed to handle her pies "—I must see to the rooms now. I moved you next door to Lucas, Autumn. Such a terrible thing about your clothes. I'll have them cleaned for you."

"I'll help you, Aunt Tabby." Pushing away her plate, Autumn rose.

"Oh no, dear, the cleaners will do it."

Smiling wasn't as difficult as Autumn had thought. "I meant with the rooms."

"Oh…" Aunt Tabby trailed off and clucked her tongue. "I do appreciate it, Autumn, I really do, but…" She looked up with a touch of distress in her eyes. "I have my own system, you see. You'd just confuse me. It's all done with numbers."

Leaving Autumn to digest this, she gave her an apologetic touch on the cheek and bustled out.

There seemed nothing to do but join the others in the lounge.

The rain, though it was little more than a mist now, seemed to Autumn like prison bars. Standing at the window in the lounge, she wished desperately for sun. Conversation did not sparkle. When anyone spoke, it was around or over or under Helen Easterman. Perhaps it would have been better if they'd closeted themselves in their rooms, but human nature had them bound together.

Julia and Lucas sat on the sofa, speaking occasionally in undertones. Autumn found his eyes on her too often. Her defenses were too low to deal with what one of his probing looks could do to her, so she kept her back to him and watched the rain.

"I really think it's time we talked about this," Julia announced suddenly.

"Julia." Jacques's voice was both strained and weary.

"We can't go on like this," Julia stated practically. "We'll all go crazy. Steve's wearing out the floor, Robert's running out of wood to fetch and if you smoke another cigarette, you'll keel over." Contrarily, she lit another herself. "Unless we want to pretend that Helen stabbed herself, we've got to deal with the fact that one of us killed her."

Into the penetrating silence, Lucas's voice flowed, calm and detached. "I think we can rule out suicide." He watched as Autumn pressed her forehead to the glass. "And conveniently, we all had the opportunity to do it. Ruling out Autumn and her aunt, that leaves the six of us."

Autumn turned from the window and found every eye in the room on her. "Why should I be ruled out?" She shuddered and lifted her arms to hug herself. "You said we all had the opportunity."

"Motive, Cat," he said simply. "You're the only one in the room without a motive."

"Motive?" It was becoming too much like one of his screenplays. She needed to cling to reality. "What possible motive could any of us have had?"

"Blackmail." Lucas lit a cigarette as she gaped at him. "Helen was a professional leech. She thought she had quite a little goldmine in the six of us." He glanced up and caught Autumn with one of his looks. "She miscalculated."

"Blackmail." Autumn could only mumble the word as she stared at him. "You're—you're making this up. This is just one of your scenarios."

He waited a beat, his eyes locked on hers. "No."

"How do you know so much?" Steve demanded. Slowly, Lucas's eyes swerved from Autumn. "If she were blackmailing you, it doesn't necessarily follow that she was blackmailing all of us."

"How clever of you, Lucas," Julia interjected, running a hand down his arm, then letting it rest on his. "I had no idea she was sticking her fangs in anyone other than the three of us." Glancing at Jacques, she gave him a careless shrug. "It seems we're in good company."

Autumn made a small sound, and Julia's attention drifted over to her. Her expression was both sympathetic and amused. "Don't look so shocked, darling. Most of us have things we don't particularly want made public. I might have paid her off if she'd threatened me with something more interesting." Leaning back, she pouted effectively. "An affair with a married senator…" She sent a lightning smile to Autumn. "I believe I mentioned him before. That hardly had me quaking in my shoes at the thought of exposure. I'm not squeamish about my indiscretions. I told her to go to hell. Of course," she added, smiling slowly, "there's only my word for that, isn't there?"

"Julia, don't make jokes." Jacques lifted a hand to rub his eyes.

"I'm sorry." Julia rose to perch on the arm of his chair. Her hand slipped to his shoulder.

"This is crazy." Unable to comprehend what was happening, Autumn searched the faces that surrounded her. They were strangers again, holding secrets. "What are you all doing here? Why did you come?"

"It's very simple." Lucas rose and crossed over to her, but unlike Julia, he didn't touch to comfort. "I made plans to come here for my own reasons. Helen found out. She was very good at finding things out—too good. She learned that Julia and Jacques were to join me." He turned, half blocking Autumn from the rest with his body. Was it protection, she wondered, or defense? "She must have contacted the rest of you, and made arrangements to have all her…clients here at once."

"You seem to know quite a bit," Robert muttered. He poked unnecessarily at the fire.

"It isn't difficult to figure out," Lucas returned. "I knew she was holding nasty little threats over three of us; we'd discussed it. When I noticed her attention to Anderson, and you and your wife, I knew she was sucking elsewhere, too."

Jane began to cry in dry, harsh sobs that racked her body. Instinctively, Autumn moved past Lucas to offer comfort. Before she was halfway across the room, Jane stopped her with a look that was like a fist to the jaw.

"You could have done it just as easily as anyone else. You've been spying on us, taking that camera everywhere." Jane's voice rose dramatically as Autumn froze. "You were working for her, you could have done it. You can't prove you didn't. I was with Robert." There was nothing bland or dull about her now. Her eyes were wild. "I was with Robert. He'll tell you."

Robert's arm came around her. His voice was quiet and soothing as she sobbed against his chest. Autumn didn't move. There seemed no place to go.

"She was going to tell you I was gambling again, tell you about all the money I'd lost." She clung to him, a sad sight in a dirt-brown dress. Robert continued to murmur and stroke her hair. "But I told you last night, I told you myself. I couldn't pay her anymore, and I told you. I didn't kill her, Robert. Tell them I didn't kill her."

"Of course you didn't, Jane. Everyone knows that. Come with me now, you're tired. We'll go upstairs."

He was leading her across the room as he spoke. His eyes met Autumn's half in apology, half in a plea for understanding. She saw, quite suddenly, that he loved his wife very much.

Autumn turned away, humiliated for Jane, sorry for Robert. The faint trembling in her hands indicated she'd been dealt one more shock. When Steve's arm came around her, she turned into it and drew the comfort offered.

"I think we could all use a drink," Julia announced. Moving to the bar, she poured a hefty glass of sherry, then took it to Autumn. "You first," she ordered, pressing the glass into her hand. "Autumn seems to be getting the worst of this. Hardly seems fair, does it, Lucas?" Her eyes lifted to his and held briefly before she turned back to the bar. He made no answer. "She's probably the only one of us here who's even remotely sorry that Helen's dead."

Autumn drank, wishing the liquor would soften the words.

"She was a vulture," Jacques murmured. Autumn saw the message pass between him and Julia. "But even a vulture doesn't deserve to be murdered." Leaning back, he accepted the glass Julia brought him. He clasped her hand as she once again sat on the arm of his chair.

"Perhaps my motive is the strongest," Jacques said and drank once, deeply. "When the police come, all will be opened and studied. Like something under a microscope." He looked at Autumn, as if to direct his explanation to her. "She threatened the happiness of the two things most important to me—the woman I love and my children." Autumn's eyes skipped quickly to Julia's. "The information she had on my relationship with this woman could have damaged my suit for custody. The beauty of that love meant nothing to Helen. She would turn it into something sordid and ugly."

Autumn cradled her drink in both hands. She wanted to tell Jacques to stop, that she didn't want to hear, didn't want to be involved. But it was too late. She was already involved.

"I was furious when she arrived here with her smug smile and evil eyes." He looked down into his glass. "There were times, many times, I wanted my hands around her throat, wanted to bruise her face as someone else had done."

"Yes, I wonder who." Julia caught her bottom lip between her teeth in thought. "Whoever did that was angry, perhaps angry enough to kill." Her eyes swept up, across Steve and Autumn and Lucas.

"You were at the inn that morning," Autumn stated. Her voice sounded odd, thready, and she swallowed.

"So I was." Julia smiled at her. "Or so I said. Being alone in bed is hardly an airtight alibi. No…" She leaned back on the wing of the chair. "I think the police will want to know who socked Helen. You came in with her, Autumn. Did you see anyone?"

"No." Her eyes flew instantly to Lucas. His were dark, already locked on her face. There were warning signals of anger and impatience she could read too easily. She dropped her gaze to her drink. "No, I…" How could she say it? How could she think it?

"Autumn's had enough for a while." Steve tightened his arm protectively around her. "Our problems don't concern her. She doesn't deserve to be in the middle."

"Poor child." Jacques studied her pale, strained face. "You've walked into a viper's nest, *oui*? Go sleep, forget us for a while."

"Come on, Autumn, I'll take you up." Steve slipped the glass from her hand and set it on the table. With one final glance at Lucas, Autumn went with him.

Chapter 8

They didn't speak as they mounted the steps. Autumn was too busy trying to force the numbness from her brain. She hadn't been able to fully absorb everything she'd been told. Steve hurried her by Helen's door before stopping at the one beside Lucas's.

"Is this the room your aunt meant?"

"Yes." She lifted both hands to her hair, pushing its weight away from her face. "Steve." She searched his face and found herself faltering. "Is all this true? Everything Lucas said? Was Helen really blackmailing all of you?" She noted the discomfort in his eyes and shook her head. "I don't mean to pry, but—"

"No," he cut her off, then let out a long breath. "No, it's hardly prying at this point. You're not involved, but you're caught, aren't you?"

The word was so apt, so close to her own thinking, that she nearly laughed. Caught. Yes, that was it exactly.

"It seems McLean is right on target. Helen had information concerning a deal I made for the company—perfectly within the circle of the law, but…" He gave a rueful smile and lifted his shoulders. "Maybe not quite as perfectly as it should have been. There was an ethical question, and it wouldn't look so good on paper. The technicalities are too complicated to explain, but the gist of it is I didn't want any shadows on my career. These days, when you're heading into politics, you have to cover all the angles."

"Angles," Autumn repeated and pressed her fingers to her temple. "Yes, I suppose you do."

"She threatened me, Autumn, and I didn't care for it—but it wasn't enough to provoke murder." He drew a quick breath and shook his head. "But that doesn't help much, does it? None of us are likely to admit it."

"I appreciate you telling me anyway," Autumn said. Steve's eyes were gentle on her face, but the lines and strain of tension still showed. "It can't be pleasant for you to have to explain."

"I'll have to explain to the police before long," he said grimly, then noted her expression. "I don't mind telling you, Autumn, if you feel better knowing. Julia's right." His fingers strayed absently to her hair. "It's much healthier to get it out in the open. But you've had enough for now." He smiled at her, then realized his hands were in her hair. "I suppose you're used to this. Your hair's not easy to resist. I've wanted to touch it since the first time I saw it. Do you mind?"

"No." She wasn't surprised to find herself in his arms, his mouth on hers. It was an easy kiss, one that comforted rather than stirred. Autumn relaxed with it, and gave back what she could.

"You'll get some rest?" Steve murmured, holding her to his chest a moment.

"Yes. Yes, I will. Thank you." She pulled back to look up at him, but her eyes were drawn past him. Lucas stood at the doorway of his room, watching them both. Without speaking, he disappeared inside.

When she was alone, Autumn lay down on the white heirloom bedspread, but sleep wouldn't come. Her mind ached with fatigue. Her body was numb from it, but sleep, like a spiteful lover, stayed away. Time drifted as her thoughts ran over each member of the group.

She could feel nothing but sympathy for Jacques and the Spicers. She remembered the Frenchman's eyes when he spoke of his children and could still see Robert protecting his wife as she sobbed. Julia, on the other hand, needed no sympathy. Autumn felt certain the actress could take care of herself; she'd need no supporting arm or soothing words. Steve had also seemed more annoyed than upset by Helen's threats. He, too, could handle himself, she felt. There was a streak of street sense under the California gloss; he didn't need Autumn to worry for him.

Lucas was a different matter. Though he had nudged admissions from the rest of them, whatever threat Helen had held over him was still his secret. He had seemed very cool, very composed when he'd spoken of blackmail—but Autumn knew him. He was fully capable of concealing his emotions when there was a purpose to it. He was a hard man. Who knew better than she?

Cruel? Yes, she mused. Lucas could be cruel. She still had the scars attesting to it. But murder? No. Autumn couldn't picture Lucas plunging something sharp into Helen Easterman. Scissors, she remembered, though she tried hard not to. The scissors that had lain on the floor beside Helen. No, she couldn't believe him capable of that. She wouldn't believe him capable of it.

Neither could she rationally believe it of any of the others. Could they all conceal such hate, such ugliness behind their shocked faces and shadowed eyes?

But, of course, one of them was the killer.

Autumn blanked it from her mind. She couldn't think of it anymore. Not just then. Steve's prescription was valid—she needed to rest. Yet she rose and walked to the window to stare out at the slow, hateful rain.

The knock at her door vibrated like an explosion. Whirling, she wrapped her arms protectively around her body. Her heart pounded while her throat dried up with fear. Stop it! she ordered herself. No one has any cause to hurt you.

"Yes, come in." The calmness of her own voice brought her relief. She was hanging on.

Robert entered. He looked so horribly weary and stricken, Autumn automatically reached out to him. She thought no more of fear. He clasped her hands and squeezed once, hard.

"You need food," he stated as he searched her face. "It shows in the face first."

"Yes, I know. My delicate hollows become craters very quickly." She made her own search. "You could use some yourself."

He sighed. "I believe you're one of those rare creatures who is inherently kind. I apologize for my wife."

"No, don't." His sigh had been long and broken. "She didn't mean it. We're all upset. This is a nightmare."

"She's been under a lot of strain. Before…" He broke off and shook his head. "She's sleeping now. Your head—" he brushed the hair from her forehead to examine the colorful bruise "—is it giving you any trouble?"

"No, none. I'm fine." The mishap seemed like some ridiculous comic relief in the midst of a melodrama now. "Can I help you, Robert?"

His eyes met hers, once, desperately, then moved away. "That woman put Jane through hell. If I'd just known, I would have put a stop to it long ago." Anger overpowered his weariness and he turned to prowl the room. "She tormented her, drained every drop of money Jane could raise. She played on a sickness, encouraging Jane to gamble to meet the payments. I knew nothing about it! I should have. Yesterday, Jane told me herself and I was going to enjoy dealing with the Easterman woman this morning." Autumn saw the soft, gentle hands clench into fists. "God help me, that's the only reason I'm sorry she's dead."

"Robert…" She wasn't certain what to say, how to deal with this side of his character. "Anyone would feel the same way," she said carefully. "She was an evil woman. She hurt someone you love." Autumn watched the fingers in his left hand relax, one at a time. "It isn't kind, but none of us will mourn her. Perhaps no one will. I think that's very sad."

He turned back and focused on her again. After a moment, he seemed to pull himself back under control. "I'm sorry you're caught up in this." With the anger gone from his eyes, they were vulnerable. "I'm going to go check on Jane. Will you be all right?"

"Yes."

She watched him go, then sank down into a chair. Each different crisis drained her. If possible, she was wearier now than before. When did the madness start?

Only a few days ago she'd been safe in her apartment in Manhattan. She'd never met any of these people who were tugging at her now. Except one.

Even as she thought of him, Lucas strode in through the door. He stalked over to her, stared down and frowned.

"You need to eat," he said abruptly. Autumn thought of how tired she was of hearing that diagnosis. "I've been watching the pounds drop off you all day. You're already too thin."

"I adore flattery." His arrogant entrance and words boosted her flagging energy. She didn't have to take abuse from Lucas McLean anymore. "Don't you know how to knock?"

"I've always appreciated the understatedness of your body, Cat. You remember." He pulled her to her feet, then molded her against him. Her eyes flashed with quick temper. "Anderson seems to have discovered the charm as well. Did it occur to you that you might have been kissing a murderer?"

He spoke softly while his hand caressed her back. His eyes were mocking her. Her temper snapped at the strain of fighting her need for him.

"One might be holding me now."

He tightened his fingers on her hair so that she cried out in surprise. The mockery was replaced by a burning, terrifying rage. "You'd like to believe that, wouldn't you? You'd like to see me languishing in prison or, better yet, dangling from the end of a rope." She would have shaken her head, but his grip on her hair made movement impossible. "Would that be suitable punishment for my rejecting you, Cat? How deep is the hate? Deep enough to pull the lever yourself?"

"No, Lucas. Please, I didn't mean—"

"The hell you didn't." He cut off her protest. "The thought of me with blood on my hands comes easily to you. You can cast me in the role of murderer, can't you? Standing over Helen with the scissors in my hand."

"No!" In defense, she closed her eyes. "Stop it! Please stop it." He was hurting her now, but not with his hands. The words cut deeper.

He lowered his voice in a swift change of mood. Ice ran down Autumn's back. "I could have used my hands and been more tidy." A strong, lean-fingered hand closed around her throat. Her eyes flew open.

"Lucas—"

"Very simple and no mess," he went on, watching her eyes widen. "Quick enough, too, if you know what to do. More my style. More—as you put it—direct. Isn't that right?"

"You're only doing this to frighten me." Her breath was trembling in and out of her lungs. It was as if he were forcing her to think the worst of him, wanting her to think him capable of something monstrous. She'd never seen him like this. His eyes were black with fury while his voice was cold, so cold. She shivered. "I want you to leave, Lucas. Leave right now."

"Leave?" He slid his hand from her throat to the back of her neck. "I don't think so, Cat." His face inched closer. "If I'm going to hang for murder, I'd best take what consolation I can while I have the chance."

His mouth closed fast over hers. She struggled against him, more frightened than she'd been when she'd turned on the light in Helen's room. She could only moan; movement was impossible when he held her this close. He slipped a hand under her sweater to claim her breast with the swift expertise of experience. Heart thudded madly against heart.

"How can anyone so skinny be so soft?" he murmured against her mouth. The words he'd spoken so often in the past brought more agony than she could bear. The hunger from him was thunderous; he was like a man who had finally broken free of his tether. "My God, how I want you." The words were torn from him as he ravaged her neck. "I'll be damned if I'll wait any longer."

They sank onto the bed. With all the strength that remained, she flailed out against him. Pinning her arms to her sides, Lucas stared down at her with a wild kind of fury. "Bite and scratch all you want, Cat. I've reached my limit."

"I'll scream, Lucas." The words shuddered out of her. "If you touch me again, I'll scream."

"No, you won't."

His mouth was on hers, proving him right and her wrong. His body molded to hers with bittersweet accuracy. She arched once in defense, in desperation, but his hands were roaming, finding all the secret places he'd discovered over three years before. There was no resisting him. The wild, reckless demand that had always flavored his lovemaking left her weak. He knew too much of her. Autumn knew, before his fingers reached the snap of her jeans, that she couldn't prevent her struggles from becoming demands. When his mouth left hers to roam her neck, she didn't scream, but moaned with the need he had always incited in her.

He was going to win again, and she would do nothing to stop him. Tears welled, then spilled from her eyes as she knew he'd soon discover her pitiful, abiding love. Even her pride, it seemed, again belonged to him.

Lucas stopped abruptly. All movement ceased when he drew back his head to stare down at her. She thought, through her blurred vision, that she saw some flash of pain cross his face before it became still and emotionless. Lifting a hand, he caught a teardrop on his fingertip. With a swift oath, he lifted his weight from her.

"No, I won't be responsible for this again." Turning, he stalked to the window and stared out.

Sitting up, Autumn lowered her face to her knees and fought against the tears. She'd promised herself he'd never see her cry again. Not over him. Never over him. The silence stretched on for what seemed an eternity.

"I won't touch you like this again," he said quietly. "You have my word, for what it's worth."

Autumn thought she heard him sigh, long and deep, before his footsteps crossed to her. She didn't look up, but only squeezed her eyes closed.

"Autumn, I...oh, sweet God." He touched her arm, but she only curled herself tighter into a ball in defense.

The room fell silent again. The dripping rain seemed to echo into it. When Lucas spoke again, his voice was harsh and strained. "When you've rested, get something to eat. I'll have your aunt send up a tray if you're not down for dinner. I'll see that no one disturbs you."

She heard him leave, heard the quiet click of her door. Alone, she kept curled in her ball as she lay down. Ultimately, the storm of tears induced sleep.

Chapter 9

It was dark when Autumn awoke, but she was not refreshed. The sleep had been only a temporary relief. Nothing had changed while she had slept. But no, she thought as she glanced around the room. She was wrong. Something had changed. It was quiet. Really quiet. Rising, she walked to the window. She could see the moon and a light scattering of stars. The rain had stopped.

In the dim light, she moved to the bathroom and washed her face. She wasn't certain she had the courage to look in the mirror. She let the cold cloth rest against her eyes for a long time, hoping the swelling wasn't as bad as it felt. She felt something else as well. Hunger. It was a healthy sign, she decided. A normal sign. The rain had stopped and the nightmare was going to end. And now she was going to eat.

Her bare feet didn't disturb the silence that hung over

the inn. She was glad of it. She wanted food now, not company. But when she passed the lounge, she heard the murmur of voices. She wasn't alone after all. Julia and Jacques were silhouetted by the window. Their conversation was low and urgent. Before she could melt back into the shadows, Julia turned and spotted her. The conversation ceased abruptly.

"Oh, Autumn, you've surfaced. We thought we'd seen the last of you until morning." She glided to her, then slipped a friendly arm around her waist. "Lucas wanted to send up a tray, but Robert outranked him. Doctor's orders were to let you sleep until you woke up. You must be famished. Let's see what your Aunt Tabby left for you."

Julia was doing all the talking, and quite purposefully leading Autumn away. A glance showed her that Jacques was still standing by the window, unmoving. Autumn let it go, too hungry to object.

"Sit down, darling," Julia ordered as she steered Autumn into the kitchen. "I'm going to fix you a feast."

"Julia, you don't have to fix me anything. I appreciate it, but—"

"Now let me play mother," Julia interrupted, pressing down on Autumn's shoulder until she sat. "You're past the sticky-finger stage, so I really quite enjoy it."

Sitting back, Autumn managed a smile. "You're not going to tell me you can cook."

Julia aimed an arched glance. "I don't suppose you should eat anything too heavy at this time of night," she said mildly. "There's some marvelous soup left from dinner, and I'll fix you my specialty. A cheese omelette."

Autumn decided that watching Julia Bond bustle around a kitchen was worth the market price of an ounce of gold. She seemed competent enough and kept up a bouncy conversation that took no brainpower to follow. With a flourish, she plopped a glass of milk in front of Autumn.

"I'm not really very fond of milk," Autumn began and glanced toward the coffeepot.

"Now, drink up," Julia instructed. "You need roses in your cheeks. You look terrible."

"Thanks."

Steaming chicken soup joined the milk, and Autumn attacked it with singleminded intensity. Some of the weakness drained from her limbs.

"Good girl," Julia approved as she dished up the omelette. "You look nearly human again."

Glancing over, Autumn smiled. "Julia, you're marvelous."

"Yes, I know. I was born that way." She sipped coffee and watched Autumn start on the eggs. "I'm glad you were able to rest. This day has been a century."

For the first time, Autumn noticed the mauve shadows under the blue eyes and felt a tug of guilt. "I'm sorry. You should be in bed, not waiting on me."

"Lord, but you're sweet." Julia pulled out a cigarette. "I haven't any desire to go up to my room until exhaustion takes over. I'm quite selfishly prepared to keep you with me until it does. Actually, Autumn," she added, watching through a mist of smoke, "I wonder if it's very wise for you to be wandering about on your own."

"What?" Autumn looked up again and frowned. "What do you mean?"

"It was your room that was broken into," Julia pointed out.

"Yes, but…" She was surprised to realize she'd almost overlooked the ransacking of her room with everything else that had happened. "It must have been Helen," she ventured.

"Oh, I doubt that," Julia returned and continued to sip contemplatively. "I very much doubt that. If Helen had broken into your room, it would have been to look for something she could use on you. She'd have been tidy. We've given this some thought."

"We?"

"Well, I've given it some thought," Julia amended smoothly. "I think whoever tore up your things was looking for something, then covered the search with overdone destruction."

"Looking for what?" Autumn demanded. "I don't have anything anyone here could be interested in."

"Don't you?" Julia ran the tip of her tongue over her teeth. "I've been thinking about what happened in your darkroom."

"You mean when the power went off?" Autumn shook her head and touched the bruise on her forehead. "I walked into the door."

"Did you?" Julia sat back and studied the harsh ceiling light. "I wonder. Lucas told me that you said you heard someone rattling at the knob and walked over. What if…" She brought her eyes back to Autumn's. "What if someone swung the door open and hit you with it?"

"It was locked," Autumn insisted, then remembered that it had been open when Lucas found her.

"There are keys, darling." She watched Autumn's face closely. "What are you thinking?"

"The door was open when Lucas—" She cut herself off and shook her head. "No, Julia, it's ridiculous. Why would anyone want to do that to me?"

Julia lifted a brow. "Interesting question. What about your ruined film?"

"The film?" Autumn felt herself being pulled in deeper. "It must have been an accident."

"You didn't spoil it, Autumn, you're too competent." She waited while Autumn spread her hands on the table and looked down at them. "I've watched you. Your movements are very fluid, very assured. And you're a professional. You wouldn't botch up a roll of film without being aware of it."

"No," Autumn agreed and looked back up. Her eyes were steady again. "What are you trying to tell me?"

"What if someone's worried that you took a picture they don't want developed? The film in your room was ruined, too."

"I can follow your logic that far, Julia." Autumn pushed aside the remaining omelette. "But then it's a dead end. I haven't taken any pictures anyone could worry about. I was shooting scenery. Trees, animals, the lake."

"Maybe someone isn't certain about that." She crushed out her cigarette in a quick motion and leaned forward. "Whoever is worried enough about a picture to risk destroying your room and knocking you unconscious is dangerous. Dangerous enough to murder. Dangerous enough to hurt you again if necessary."

Staring back, Autumn controlled a tremor. "Jane? Jane accused me of spying, but she couldn't—"

"Oh yes, she could." Julia's voice was hard again, and definite. "Face it, Autumn, anyone pushed hard enough is capable of murder. Anyone."

Autumn's thoughts flicked back to Lucas and the

look on his face when he had slipped his hand around her throat.

"Jane was desperate," Julia continued. "She claims to have made a full confession to Robert, but what proof is there? Or Robert, furious at what Helen had put his wife through, could have done it himself. He loves Jane quite a lot."

"Yes, I know." The sudden, sweeping anger in Robert's eyes flashed through her mind.

"Or there's Steve." Julia's finger began to tap on the table. "He tells me that Helen found out about some unwise deal he put through, something potentially damaging to his political career. He's very ambitious."

"But, Julia—"

"Then there's Lucas." Julia went on as if Autumn hadn't spoken. "There's a matter of a delicate divorce suit. Helen held information she claimed would interest a certain estranged husband." She lit another cigarette and let the smile float up and away. "Lucas is known for his temper. He's a very physical man."

Autumn met the look steadily. "Lucas is a lot of things, not all of them admirable, but he wouldn't kill."

Julia smiled and said nothing as she brought the cigarette to her lips. "Then there's me." The smile widened. "Of course, I claim I didn't care about Helen's threats, but I'm an actress. A good one. I've got an Oscar to prove it. Like Lucas, my temper is no secret. I could give you a list of directors who would tell you I'm capable of anything." Idly she tapped her cigarette in the ashtray. "But then, if I had killed her, I would have set the scene differently. I would have discovered the body myself, screamed, then fainted magnificently. As it was, you stole the show."

"That's not funny, Julia."

"No," she agreed and rubbed her temple. "It's not. But the fact remains that I could have killed Helen, and you're far too trusting."

"If you'd killed her," Autumn countered, "why would you warn me?"

"Bluff and double bluff," Julia answered with a new smile that made Autumn's skin crawl. "Don't trust anyone, not even me."

Autumn wasn't going to let Julia frighten her, though she seemed determined to do so. She kept her eyes level. "You haven't included Jacques."

To Autumn's surprise, Julia's eyes flickered, then dropped. The smooth, tapering fingers crushed out her cigarette with enough force to break the filter. "No, I haven't. I suppose he must be viewed through your eyes like the rest of us, but I know..." She looked up again, and Autumn saw the vulnerability. "I know he isn't capable of hurting anyone."

"You're in love with him."

Julia smiled, quite beautifully. "I love Jacques very much, but not the way you mean." She rose then and, getting another cup, poured them both coffee. "I've known Jacques for ten years. He's the only person in the world I care about more than myself. We're friends, real friends, probably because we've never been lovers."

Autumn drank the coffee black. She wanted the kick of it. *She'd protect him,* she thought. *She'd protect him any way she could.*

"I have a weakness for men," Julia continued, "and I indulge it. With Jacques, the time or place was never right. Ultimately, the friendship was too important to risk messing it up in the bedroom. He's a good, gentle man. The biggest mistake he ever made was in marrying Claudette."

Julia's voice hardened. Her nails began to tap on the table again, quicker than before. "She did her best to eat him alive. For a long time, he tried to keep the marriage together for the children. It simply wasn't possible. I won't go into details; they'd shock you." Tilting her head, Julia gave Autumn a smile that put her squarely into adolescence. "And, in any case, it's Jacques's miserable secret. He didn't divorce her, on the numerous grounds he could have, but allowed her to file."

"And Claudette got the children."

"That's right. It nearly killed him when she was awarded custody. He adores them. And, I must admit, they are rather sweet little monsters." The nails stopped tapping as she reached for her coffee. "Anyway, skipping over this and that, Jacques filed a custody suit about a year ago. He met someone shortly after. I can't tell you her name—you'd recognize it, and I have Jacques's confidence. But I can tell you she's perfect for him. Then Helen crawled her slimy way in."

Autumn shook her head. "Why don't they just get married?"

Julia leaned back with an amused sigh. "If life were only so simple. Jacques is free, but his lady won't be for another few months. They want nothing more than to marry, bring Jacques's little monsters to America and raise as many more as possible. They're crazy about each other."

Julia sipped her cooling coffee. "They can't live together openly until the custody thing is resolved so they rented this little place in the country. Helen found out. You can figure out the rest. Jacques paid her, for his children and because his lady's divorce isn't as cut-and-dried as it might be, but when Helen turned up here, he'd reached his limit. They argued about it one night in the lounge. He told her she wouldn't get another cent. I'm sure, no matter how much Jacques had already paid her, Helen would still have turned her information over to Claudette—for a price."

Autumn stared at her, unable to speak. She had never seen Julia look so cold. She saw the ruthlessness cover the exquisite face. Julia looked over, then laughed with genuine amusement.

"Oh, Autumn, you're like an open book!" The hard mask had melted away, leaving her warm and lovely again. "Now you're thinking I could have murdered Helen after all. Not for myself, but for Jacques."

Autumn fell into a fitful sleep sometime after dawn. This was no deep, empty sleep brought on by medication or exhaustion, but was confused and dream riddled.

At first, there were only vague shadows and murmured voices floating through her mind, taunting her to try to see and hear more clearly. She fought to focus on them. Shadows moved, shapes began to sharpen, then became fuzzy and disordered again. She pitted all her determination against them, wanting more than hints and whispers. Abruptly, the shadows evaporated. The voices grew to a roar in her ears.

Wild-eyed, Jane crushed Autumn's camera underfoot. She screamed, pointing a pair of scissors to keep Autumn at bay. "Spy!" she shouted as the cracking of the camera's glass echoed like gunfire. "Spy!"

Wanting to escape the madness and accusations,

Autumn turned. Colors whirled around her, then there was Robert.

"She tormented my wife." His arm held Autumn firmly, then slowly tightened, cutting off her breath. "You need some food," he said softly. "It shows in the face first." He was smiling, but the smile was a travesty. Breaking away, Autumn found herself in the corridor.

Jacques came toward her. There was blood on his hands. His eyes were sad and terrifying as he held them out to her. "My children." There was a tremor in his voice as he gestured to her. Turning, she fell into Steve.

"Politics," he said with a bright, boyish smile. "Nothing personal, just politics." Taking her hair, he wrapped it around her throat. "You got caught in the middle, Autumn." The smile turned into a leer as he tightened the noose. "Too bad."

Pushing away, she fell through a door. Julia's back was to her. She wore the lovely, white lace negligee. "Julia!" In the dream, the urgency in Autumn's voice came at a snail's pace. "Julia, help me."

When Julia turned, the slow, cat smile was on her face and the lace was splattered with scarlet. "Bluff and double bluff, darling." Throwing back her head, she laughed her smoky laugh. With the sound still spinning in her head, Autumn pressed her hands to her ears and ran.

"Come back to mother!" Julia called, still laughing as Autumn stumbled into the corridor.

There was a door blocking her path. Throwing it open, Autumn dashed inside. She knew only a desperate need for escape. But it was Helen's room. Terrified, Autumn turned, only to find the door closed behind her. She battered on it, but the sound was dull and flat. Fear was raw now, a primitive fear of the dead. She couldn't stay there. Wouldn't stay. She turned, thinking to escape through the window.

It wasn't Helen's room, but her own. There were bars at the windows, gray liquid bars of rain, but when she ran to them, they solidified, holding her in. She pulled and tugged, but they were cold and unyielding in her hands. Suddenly, Lucas was behind her, drawing her away. He laughed as he turned her into his arms.

"Bite and scratch all you want, Cat."

"Lucas, please!" There was hysteria in her voice that even the dream couldn't muffle. "I love you. I love you. Help me get out. Help me get away!"

"Too late, Cat." His eyes were dark and fierce and amused. "I warned you not to push me too far."

"No, Lucas, not you." She clung to him. He was kissing her hard, passionately. "I love you. I've always loved you." She surrendered to his arms, to his mouth. Here was her escape, her safety.

Then she saw the scissors in his hand.

Chapter 10

Autumn sat straight up in bed. The film of cold sweat had her shivering. During the nightmare, she had kicked off the sheets and blankets and lay now with only a damp nightgown for cover. Needing the warmth, she pulled the tangled blanket around her and huddled into it.

Only a dream, she told herself, waiting for the clarity of it to fade. It was only a dream. It was natural enough after the late-night conversation with Julia. Dreams couldn't hurt you. Autumn wanted to hang on to that.

It was morning. She trembled still as she watched the sunlight pour into her window. No bars. That was over now, just as the night was over. The phones would soon be repaired. The water in the ford would go down. The police would come. Autumn sat, cocooned by the blanket, and waited for her breathing to even.

By the end of the day, or tomorrow at the latest, ev-

erything would be organized and official. Questions
would be answered, notes would be taken, the wheels
of investigation would start to turn, settling everything
into facts and reality. Slowly her muscles began to relax
and she loosened her desperate grip on the blanket.

Julia's imagination had gotten out of hand, Autumn
decided. She was so used to the drama of her profession
that she had built up the scenario. Helen's death was a
hard, cold fact. None of them could avoid that. But Autumn was certain her two misfortunes had been uncon-
nected. If I'm going to stay sane until the police come,
she amended, I *have* to believe it.

Calmer now, she allowed herself to think. Yes, there
had been a murder. There was no glossing over that.
Murder was a violent act, and in this case, it had been a
personal one. She had no involvement in it. There wasn't
any correlation. What had happened in the darkroom
had been simple clumsiness. That was the cleanest and
the most reasonable explanation. As for the invasion of
her room... Autumn shrugged. It had been Helen. She'd
been a vicious, evil woman. The destruction of Autumn's
clothes and personal belongings had been a vicious, evil
act. For some reason of her own, Helen had taken a dislike to her. There was no one else at the inn who would
have any reason to feel hostility toward her.

Except Lucas. Autumn shook her head firmly, but
the thought remained. Except Lucas. She huddled the
blanket closer, cold again.

No, even that made no sense. Lucas had rejected her,
not the other way around. She had loved him. And he,
very simply, hadn't loved her. *Would that matter to him?*
The voice in her brain argued with the voice from her
heart. Ignoring the queaziness in her stomach, Autumn

forced herself to consider, dispassionately, Lucas in the role of murderer.

It had been obvious from the beginning that he was under strain. He hadn't been sleeping well and he'd been tense. Autumn had known him to struggle over a stage of a book for a week on little sleep and coffee, but he'd never shown the effects. All that stored energy he had was just waiting to take over whenever he needed it. No, in all her memory, she had never seen Lucas McLean tired. Until now.

Helen's blackmail must have disturbed him deeply. Autumn couldn't imagine Lucas concerning himself over publicity, adverse or otherwise. The woman involved in divorce must mean a great deal to him. She shut her eyes on a flash of pain and forced herself to continue.

Why had he come to the Pine View Inn? Why would he choose a remote place nearly a continent away from his home? To work? Autumn shook her head. It just didn't follow. She knew Lucas never traveled when he was writing. He'd do his research first, extensively if necessary, before he began. Once he had a plot between his teeth, he'd dig into his beachside home for the duration. Come to Virginia to write in peace? No. Lucas McLean could write on the 5:15 subway if he chose to. She knew no one else with a greater ability to block people out.

So, his reason for coming to the inn was quite different. Autumn began to wonder if Helen had been a pawn as well as a manipulator. Had Lucas lured her to this remote spot and surrounded her with people with reasons to hate her? He was clever enough to have done it, and calculating enough. How difficult was it going to be to prove which one of the six had killed her? Motive and opportunity he'd said—six people had both. Why should one be examined any closer than the others?

The setting would appeal to him, she thought as she looked out at mountains and pines. Obvious, Lucas had called it. An obvious setting for murder. But then, as Jacques had pointed out, life was often obvious.

She wouldn't dwell on it. It brought the nightmare too close again. Pushing herself from the bed, Autumn began to dress in her very tired jeans and a sweater Julia had given her the night before. She wasn't going to spend another day picking at her doubts and fears. It would be better to hang on to the knowledge that the police would be there soon. It wasn't up to her to decide who had killed Helen.

When she started down the stairs, she felt better. She'd take a long, solitary walk after breakfast and clear the cobwebs from her mind. The thought of getting out of the inn lifted her spirits.

But her confidence dropped away when she saw Lucas at the foot of the stairs. He was watching her closely, silently. Their eyes met for one brief, devastating moment before he turned to walk away.

"Lucas." She heard herself call out before she could stop herself. Stopping, he turned to face her again. Autumn gathered all her courage and hurried down the rest of the stairs. She had questions, and she had to ask them. He still mattered much too much to her. She stood on the bottom step so that their eyes would be level. His told her nothing. They seemed to look through her, bored and impatient.

"Why did you come here?" Autumn asked him

quickly. "Here, to the Pine View Inn?" She wanted him to give her any reason. She wanted to accept it.

Lucas focused on her intensely for a moment. There was something in his face for her to read, but it was gone before she could decipher it. "Let's just say I came to write, Autumn. Any other reason has been eliminated."

There was no expression in his voice, but the words chilled her. *Eliminated.* Would he choose such a clean word for murder? Something of her horror showed in her face. She watched his brows draw together in a frown.

"Cat—"

"No." Before he could speak again, she darted away from him. He'd given her an answer, but it wasn't one she wanted to accept.

The others were already at the table. The sun had superficially lightened the mood, and by unspoken agreement, the conversation was general, with no mention of Helen. They all needed an island of normalcy before the police came.

Julia, looking fresh and lovely, chattered away. Her attitude was so easy, even cheerful, that Autumn wondered if their conversation in the kitchen was as insubstantial as her nightmare. She was flirting again, with every man at the table. Two days of horror hadn't dulled her style.

"Your aunt," Jacques told Autumn, "has an amazing cuisine." He speared a fluffy, light pancake. "It surprises me at times because she has such a charming, drifting way about her. Yet, she remembers small details. This morning, she tells me she has saved me a piece of her apple pie to enjoy with my lunch. She doesn't forget I have a fondness for it. Then when I kiss her hand because I find her so enchanting, she smiled and wandered away, and I heard her say something about towels and chocolate pudding."

The laughter that followed was so normal, Autumn wanted to hug it to her. "She has a better memory about the guests' appetites than her family's," Autumn countered, smiling at him. "She's decided that pot roast is my favorite and has promised to provide it weekly, but it's actually my brother Paul's favorite. I haven't figured out how to move her toward spaghetti."

She gripped her fork tightly at a sudden flash of pain. Very clearly, Autumn could see herself stirring spaghetti sauce in Lucas's kitchen while he did his best to distract her. Would she never pry herself loose from the memories? Quickly, she plunged into conversation again.

"Aunt Tabby sort of floats around the rest of the world," she continued. "I remember once, when we were kids, Paul smuggled some formaldehyde frog legs out of his biology class. He brought them with him when we came on vacation and gave them to Aunt Tabby, hoping for a few screams. She took them, smiled and told him she'd eat them later."

"Oh, God." Julia lifted her hand to her throat. "She didn't actually eat them, did she?"

"No." Autumn grinned. "I distracted her, which of course is the easiest thing in the world to do, and Paul disposed of his biology project. She never missed them."

"I must remember to thank my parents for making me an only child," Julia murmured.

"I can't imagine growing up without Paul and Will." Autumn shook her head as old memories ran through her mind. "The three of us were always very close, even when we tormented each other."

Jacques chuckled, obviously thinking of his own children. "Does your family spend much time here?"

"Not as much as we used to." Autumn lifted her shoulders. "When I was a girl, we'd all come for a month during the summer."

"To tramp through the woods?" Julia asked with a wicked gleam in her eyes.

"That," Autumn returned mildly, and imitated the actress's arched-brow look, "and some camping." She went on, amused by Julia's rolling eyes. "Boating and swimming in the lake."

"Boating," Robert spoke up, cutting off a small, nagging memory. Autumn looked over at him, unable to hang on to it. "That's my one true vice. Nothing I like better than sailing. Right, Jane?" He patted her hand. "Jane's quite a sailor herself. Best first mate I've ever had." He glanced over at Steve. "I suppose you've done your share of sailing."

Steve answered with a rueful shake of his head. "I'm afraid I'm a miserable sailor. I can't even swim."

"You're joking!" This came from Julia. She stared at him in disbelief. Her eyes skimmed approvingly over his shoulders. "You look like you could handle the English Channel."

"I can't even handle a wading pool," he confessed, more amused than embarrassed. He grinned and gestured with his fork. "I make up for it in land sports. If we had a tennis court here, I'd redeem myself."

"Ah well." Jacques gave his French shrug. "You'll have to content yourself with hiking. The mountains here are beautiful. I hope to bring my children one day." He frowned, then stared into his coffee.

"Nature lovers!" Julia's smiling taunt kept the room

from sliding into gloom. "Give me smog-filled L.A. anytime. I'll look at your mountains and squirrels in Autumn's photographs."

"You'll have to wait until I add to my supply." She kept her voice light, trying not to be depressed over the loss of her film. She couldn't yet bring herself to think of the loss of her camera. "Losing that film is like losing a limb, but I'm trying to be brave about it." Taking a bite of pancake, she shrugged. "And I could have lost all four rolls instead of three. The shots I took of the lake were the best, so I can comfort myself with that. The light was perfect that morning, and the shadows…"

She trailed off as the memory seeped through. She could see herself, standing on the ridge looking down at the glistening water, the mirrored trees. And the two figures that walked the far side. That was the morning she had met Lucas in the woods, then Helen. Helen with an angry bruise under her eye.

"Autumn?"

Hearing Jacques's voice, she snapped herself back. "I'm sorry, what?"

"Is something wrong?"

"No, I…" She met his curious eyes. "No."

"I would think light and shadow are the very essence of photography," Julia commented, flowing over the awkward silence. "But I've always concerned myself with looking into the lens rather than through. Remember that horrible little man, Jacques, who used to pop up at the most extraordinary times and stick a camera in my face. What was his name? I really became quite fond of him."

Julia had centered the attention on herself so smoothly

that Autumn doubted anyone had noticed her own confusion. She stared down at the pancakes and syrup on her plate as if the solution to the mysteries of the universe were written there. But she could feel Lucas's eyes boring into her averted head. She could feel them, but she couldn't look at him.

She wanted to be alone, to think, to reason out what was whirling in her head. She forced down the rest of her breakfast and let the conversation buzz around her.

"I have to see Aunt Tabby," Autumn murmured, at last thinking she could leave without causing curiosity. "Excuse me." She had reached the kitchen door before Julia waylaid her.

"Autumn, I want to talk to you." The grip of the slender fingers was quite firm. "Come up to my room."

From the expression on the enviable face, Autumn could see arguing was useless. "All right, right after I see Aunt Tabby. She'll be worried because I didn't say good-night to her yesterday. I'll be up in a few minutes." She kept her voice reasonable and friendly, and managed a smile. Autumn decided she was becoming quite an actress herself.

For a small stretch of silence, Julia studied Autumn's face, then loosened her grip. "All right, come up as soon as you've finished."

"Yes, I will." Autumn slipped into the kitchen with the promise still on her lips. It wasn't difficult to go through the kitchen to the mud room without being noticed. Aunt Tabby and Nancy were deep in their morning argument. Taking down her jacket from the hook where she had placed it the morning of the storm, Autumn checked the pocket. Her fingers closed over the roll of film. For a moment, she simply held it in the palm of her hand.

Moving quickly, she changed from shoes to boots, transferred the film to the pocket of Julia's sweater, grabbed her jacket and went out the back door.

Chapter 11

The air was sharp. The rain had washed it clean. Budded leaves Autumn had photographed only days before were fuller, thicker, but still tenderly green. Her mind was no longer on the freedom she had longed for all the previous day. Now, Autumn was only intent on reaching the cover of the forest without being seen. She ran for the trees, not stopping until she was surrounded. Silence was deep and it cradled her.

The ground sucked and skidded under her feet, spongy with rain. There was some wind damage here and there that she noticed when she forced herself to move more carefully. Broken limbs littered the ground. The sun was warm, and she shed her jacket, tossing it over a branch. She made herself concentrate on the sights and sounds of the forest until her thoughts could calm.

The mountain laurel hinted at blooms. A bird circled overhead, then darted deeper into the trees with a sharp cry. A squirrel scurried up a tree trunk and peered down at her. Autumn reached in her pocket and closed her hand over the roll of film. The conversation in the kitchen with Julia now made horrible sense.

Helen must have been at the lake that morning. From the evidence of the bruise, she had argued violently with someone. And that someone had seen Autumn on the ridge. That someone wanted the pictures destroyed badly enough to risk breaking into both her darkroom and her bedroom. The film had to be potentially damaging for anyone to risk knocking her unconscious and ransacking her room. Who else but the killer would care enough to take such dangerous actions? Who else? At every turn, logic pointed its finger toward Lucas.

It had been his plans that brought the group together in the first place. Lucas was the person Autumn had met just before coming across Helen. Lucas had bent over her as she lay on the darkroom floor. Lucas had been up, fully dressed, the night of Helen's murder. Autumn shook her head, wanting to shatter the logic. But the film was solid in her hand.

He must have seen her as she stood on the ridge. She would have been in clear view. When he intercepted her, he had tried to rekindle their relationship. He would have known better than to have attempted to remove the film from her camera. She would have caused a commotion that would have been heard in two counties. Yes, he knew her well enough to use subtler means. But he wouldn't have known she had already switched to a fresh roll.

He had played on her old weakness for him. If she had submitted, he would have found ample time and opportunity to destroy the film. Autumn admitted, painfully, that she would have been too involved with him to have noticed the loss. But she hadn't submitted. This time, she had rejected him. He would have been forced to employ more extreme measures.

He only pretended to want me, she realized. That, more than anything else, hurt. He had held her, kissed her, while his mind had been busy calculating how best to protect himself. Autumn forced herself to face facts. Lucas had stopped wanting her a long time ago, and his needs had never been the same as hers. Two facts were very clear. She had never stopped loving him, and he had never begun to love her.

Still, she balked at the idea of Lucas as a cold-blooded killer. She could remember his sudden spurts of gentleness, his humor, the careless bouts of generosity. That was part of him, too—part of the reason she had been able to love him so easily. Part of the reason she had never stopped.

A hand gripped her shoulder. With a quick cry of alarm, she whirled and found herself face-to-face with Lucas. When she shrank from him, he dropped his hands and stuffed them into his pockets. His eyes were dark and his voice was icy.

"Where's the film, Autumn?"

Whatever color was left in her face drained. She hadn't wanted to believe it. Part of her had refused to believe it. Now, her heart shattered. He was leaving her no choice.

"Film?" She shook her head as she took another step back. "What film?"

"You know very well what film." Impatience pulled

at the words. He narrowed his eyes, watching her retreat. "I want the fourth roll. Don't back away from me!"

Autumn stopped at the curt command. "Why?"

"Don't play stupid." His impatience was quickly becoming fury. She recognized all the signs. "I want the
film. What I do with it is my business."

She ran, thinking only to escape from his words. It
had been easier to live with the doubt than the certainty.
He caught her arm before she had dashed three yards.
Spinning her around, he studied her face.

"You're terrified." He looked stunned, then angry.
"You're terrified of me." With his hands gripping hard
on her arms he brought her closer. "We've run the gamut,
haven't we, Cat? Yesterday's gone." There was a finality in his voice that brought more pain than his hands
or his temper.

"Lucas." Autumn was trembling, emotionally spent.
"Please don't hurt me anymore." The pain she spoke of
had nothing to do with the physical, but he released her
with a violent jerk. The struggle for control was visible
on his face.

"I won't lay a hand on you now, or ever again. Just
tell me where that film is. I'll get out of your life as
quickly as possible."

She had to reach him. She had to try one last time.
"Lucas, please, it's senseless. You must see that. Can't
you—"

"Don't push me!" The words exploded at her, rocking
her back on her heels. "You stupid fool, do you have any
idea how dangerous that film is? Do you think for one
minute I'm going to let you keep it?" He took a step toward her. "Tell me where it is. Tell me now, or by God,
I'll throttle it out of you."

"In the darkroom." The lie came quickly and without calculation. Perhaps that was why he accepted it so readily.

"All right. Where?" She watched his features relax slightly. His voice was calmer.

"On the bottom shelf. On the wet side."

"That's hardly illuminating to a layman, Cat." There was a touch of his old mockery as he reached for her arm. "Let's go get it."

"No!" She jerked away wildly. "I won't go with you. There's only one roll; you'll find it. You found the others. Leave me alone, Lucas. For God's sake, leave me alone!"

She ran again, skidding on the mud. This time he didn't stop her.

Autumn had no idea how far she ran or even the direction she took. Ultimately, her feet slowed to a walk. She stopped to stare up at a sky that had no clouds. What was she going to do?

She could go back. She could go back and try to get to the darkroom first, lock herself in. She could develop the film, blow up the two figures beside the lake and see the truth for herself. Her hand reached for the hated film again. She didn't want to see the truth. With absolute certainty, she knew she could never hand the film over to the police. No matter what Lucas had done or would do, she couldn't betray him. He'd been wrong, she thought. She could never pull the lever.

Withdrawing the film from her pocket, she stared down at it. It looked so innocent. She had felt so innocent that day, up on the ridge with the sun coming up. But when she had done what she had to do, she would never feel innocent again. She would expose the film herself.

Lucas, she thought and nearly laughed. Lucas

McLean was the only man on earth who could make
her turn her back on her own conscience. And when it
was done, only the two of them would know. She would
be as guilty as he.

Do it quickly, she told herself. Do it fast and think
about it later. Her palm was damp where the film was
cradled in it. You're going to have a whole lifetime to
think about it. Taking a deep breath, Autumn started to
uncap the plastic capsule she used to protect her unde-
veloped film. A movement on the path behind her had
her stuffing the roll back into her pocket and whirling
around.

Could Lucas have searched the darkroom so quickly?
What would he do now that he knew she had lied to
him? Foolishly, Autumn wanted to run again. Instead,
she straightened and waited. The final encounter would
have to come sooner or later.

Autumn's relief when she saw Steve approaching
quickly became irritation. She wanted to be alone, not
to make small talk and useless conversation while the
film burned in her pocket.

"Hi!" Steve's lightning smile did nothing to decrease
her annoyance, but Autumn pasted on one of her own. If
she were going to be playing a game for the rest of her
life, she might as well start now.

"Hello. Taking Jacques up on the hiking?" God, how
normal and shallow her voice sounded! Was she going
to be able to live like this?

"Yeah. I see you needed to get away from the inn,
too." Taking a deep breath of the freshened air, he flexed
his shoulders. "Lord, it feels good to be outside again."

"I know what you mean." Autumn eased the tension
from her own shoulders. This was a reprieve, she told

herself. Accept it. When it's over, nothing's ever going to be the same again.

"And Jacques is right," Steve went on, staring out through the thin leaves. "The mountains are beautiful. It reminds you that life goes on."

"I suppose we all need to remember that now." Unconsciously, Autumn dipped her hand in her pocket.

"Your hair glows in the sunlight." Steve caught at the ends and moved them between his fingertips. Autumn saw, with some alarm, that warmth had crept into his eyes. A romantic interlude was more than she could handle.

"People often seem to think more about my hair than me." She smiled and kept her voice light. "Sometimes I'm tempted to hack it off."

"Oh no." He took a more generous handful. "It's very special, very unique." His eyes lifted to hers. "And I've been thinking quite a lot about you the last few days. You're very special, too."

"Steve…" Autumn turned and would have walked on, but his hand was still in her hair.

"I want you, Autumn."

The words, so gentle, almost humble, nearly broke her heart. She turned back with apology in her eyes. "I'm sorry, Steve. I really am."

"Don't be sorry." He lowered his head to brush her lips. "If you let me, I could make you happy."

"Steve, please." Autumn lifted her hands to his chest. If only he were Lucas, she thought as she stared up at him. If only it were Lucas looking at me like this. "I can't."

He let out a long breath, but didn't release her.

"McLean? Autumn, he only makes you unhappy. Why won't you let go?"

"I can't tell you how many times I've asked myself the same question." She sighed, and he watched the sun shoot into her eyes. "I don't have the answer—except that I love him."

"Yes, it shows." Frowning, he brushed a strand of hair from her cheek. "I'd hoped you'd be able to get over him, but I don't suppose you will."

"No, I don't suppose I will. I've given up trying."

"Now I'm sorry, Autumn. It makes things difficult."

Autumn dropped her eyes to stare at the ground. She didn't want pity. "Steve, I appreciate it, but I really need to be alone."

"I want the film, Autumn."

Astonished, she jerked her head up. Without consciously making the step, she aligned herself with Lucas. "Film? I don't know what you mean."

"Oh yes, I'm afraid you do." He was still speaking gently, one hand stroking her hair. "The pictures you took of the lake the morning Helen and I were down there. I have to have them."

"You?" For a moment, the implication eluded her. "You and Helen?" Confusion turned into shock. She could only stare at him.

"We were having quite a row that morning. You see, she had decided she wanted a lump-sum payment from me. Her other sources were drying up fast. Julia wouldn't give her a penny, just laughed at her. Helen was furious about that." His face changed with a grim smile. "Jacques had finished with her, too. She never had anything worthwhile on Lucas in the first place. She counted on intimidating him. Instead, he told her to go to hell and threatened to press charges. That threw her off balance for a while. She must have realized Jane was on the edge. So...she concentrated on me."

He had been staring off into the distance as he spoke. Now, his attention came back to Autumn. The first hint of anger swept into his eyes. "She wanted two hundred and fifty thousand dollars in two weeks. A quarter of a million, or she'd hand over the information she had on me to my father."

"But you said what she knew wasn't important." Autumn let her eyes dart past his for a moment. The path behind them was empty. She was alone.

"She knew a bit more than I told you." Steve gave her an apologetic smile. "I could hardly tell you everything then. I've covered my tracks well enough now so that I don't think the police will ever know. It was actually a matter of extortion."

"Extortion?" The hand on her hair was becoming more terrifying with each passing moment. Keep him talking, she told herself frantically. Keep him talking and someone will come.

"Borrowing, really. The money will be mine sooner or later." He shrugged it off. "I just took some a little early. Unfortunately, my father wouldn't see it that way. I told you, remember? He's a tough man. He wouldn't think twice about booting me out the door and cutting off my income. I can't have that, Autumn." He flashed her a smile. "I have very expensive tastes."

"So you killed her." Autumn said it flatly. She was finished with horror.

"I didn't have a choice. I couldn't possibly get my hands on that much cash in two weeks." He said it so calmly, Autumn could almost see the rationale behind it. "I nearly killed her that morning down by the lake. She just wouldn't listen to me. I lost my temper and hit her. Knocked her cold. When I saw her lying there on the ground, I realized how much I wanted her dead."

Autumn didn't interrupt. She could see he was far from finished. Let him talk it out, she ordered herself, controlling the urge to break from him and run. Someone's going to come.

"I bent over her," he continued. "My hands were almost around her throat when I saw you standing up on the ridge. I knew it was you because the sun was shining on your hair. I didn't think you could recognize me from that distance, but I had to be sure. Of course, I found out later that you weren't paying attention to us at all."

"No, I barely noticed." Her knees were starting to shake. He was telling her too much. Far too much.

"I left Helen and circled around, thinking to intercept you. Lucas got to you first. Quite a touching little scene."

"You watched us?" She felt a stir of anger edge through the fear.

"You were too involved in each other to notice." He smiled again. "In any case, that's when I learned you'd been taking pictures. I had to get rid of that film; it was too chancy. I hated to hurt you, Autumn. I found you very attractive right from the first."

A rabbit darted down the path, veering off and bounding into the woods. She heard the call of a quail, faint with distance. The simple, natural texture of her surroundings gave his words a sense of unreality. "The darkroom."

"Yes. I was glad the blow with the door knocked you out. I didn't want to have to hit you with the flashlight. I didn't see your camera, but found a roll of film. I was so certain I had things taken care of. You can imagine how I felt when you said you'd lost two rolls, and that they were shots of your trip down from New York. I didn't know how the other roll had been ruined."

"Lucas. Lucas turned on the lights when he found me." Suddenly, through the horror came a bright flash of realization. *It hadn't been Lucas.* He'd done nothing but simply be who he was. She felt overwhelming relief at his innocence, then guilt at ever having believed what she had of him. "Lucas," she said again, almost giddy with the onslaught of sensations.

"Well, it hardly matters now," Steve said practically. Autumn snapped back. She had to keep alert, had to keep a step ahead of him. "I knew if I just took the film from your camera, you'd begin to wonder. You might start thinking too closely about the pictures you'd taken. I hated doing that to your things, breaking your camera. I know it was important to you."

"I have another at home." It was a weak attempt to sound unconcerned. Steve only smiled.

"I went to Helen's room right after I'd finished with yours. I knew I was going to have to kill her. She stood there pointing to the bruise and telling me it was going to cost me another hundred thousand. I didn't know what I was going to do... I thought I was going to strangle her. Then I saw the scissors. That was better—anyone could have used scissors. Even little Jane. I stopped thinking when I picked them up until it was over."

He shuddered, and Autumn thought, *Run! Run now!* But his hand tightened on her hair. "I've never been through anything like that. It was terrible. I almost folded. I knew I had to think, had to be careful, or I'd lose everything. Staying in that room was the hardest thing I've ever done. I wiped the handles of the scissors clean and tore up my shirt. Her blood was on it. I flushed the pieces down the toilet. When I got back to my room, I showered and went to bed. I remember being surprised that the whole thing took less than twenty minutes. It seemed like years."

"It must have been dreadful for you," Autumn murmured, but he was oblivious to the edge in her voice.

"Yes, but it was all working out. No one could prove where they were when Helen was killed. The storm— the phones, the power—that was all a bonus. Every one of us had a reason to want Helen out of the way. I really think Julia and I will be the least likely suspects when the time comes. The police should look to Jacques because he had more cause, and Lucas because he has the temper."

"Lucas couldn't kill anyone," Autumn said evenly. "The police will know that."

"I wouldn't bank on it." He gave her a crooked smile. "You haven't been so sure of that yourself."

She could say nothing when struck with the truth. *Why wasn't someone coming?*

"This morning, you started talking about four rolls of film, and the pictures you took of the lake. I could tell the moment when you remembered."

So much for my talent at acting, she thought grimly. "I only remembered there'd been people down by the lake that morning."

"You were putting it all together quickly." He traced a finger down her cheek and Autumn forced herself not to jerk away. "I had hoped to distract you, gain your affection. It was obvious you were hurting over McLean.

If I could have moved in, I might have gotten my hands on that film without having to hurt you."

Autumn kept her eyes and voice steady. He'd finished talking now; she could sense it. "What are you going to do?"

"Damn it, Autumn. I'm going to have to kill you."

He said it in much the same way her father had said, *"Damn it, Autumn, I'm going to have to spank you."* She nearly broke into hysterical giggles.

"They'll know this time, Steve." Her body was beginning to shake, but she spoke calmly. If she could reason with him...

"No, I don't think so." He spoke practically, as if he considered she might have a viable point. "I was careful to get out without being seen. Everyone's spread out again. I doubt anyone even knows you went outside. I wouldn't have known myself if I hadn't found your jacket and boots missing. Then again, if I hadn't found the jacket hanging on a branch and been able to follow your tracks from there, I wouldn't have found you so easily."

He shrugged, as if showing her why his reasoning was better than hers. "When you're found missing, I'll make certain I come this way when we look for you. I can do a lot of damage to the tracks and no one will know any better. Now, Autumn, I need the film. Tell me where you've put it."

"I'm not going to tell you." She tossed back her head. As long as she had the film, he had to keep her alive. "They'll find it. When they do, they'll know it was you."

He made a quick sound of impatience. "You'll tell me Autumn, eventually. It would be easier for you if you told me now. I don't want to hurt you any more than I have to. I can make it quick, or I can make it painful."

His hand shot out so swiftly, Autumn had no time to dodge the blow. The force of it knocked her back into a tree. The pain welled inside her head and rolled through, leaving dizziness. She clutched at the rough bark to keep her balance as she saw him coming toward her.

Oh no, she wasn't going to stand and be hit again. He'd gotten away with it twice, and twice was enough. With as much force as she could muster, she kicked, aiming well below the waist. He went down on his knees like a shot. Autumn turned and fled.

Chapter 12

She ran blindly. *Escape!* It was the only coherent thought in her brain. It wasn't until the first wave of panic had ebbed that Autumn realized she had run not only away from Steve, but away from the inn. It was too late to double back. She could only concentrate as much effort as possible into putting distance between them. She veered off the path and into thicker undergrowth.

When she heard him coming after her, Autumn didn't look back, but increased her pace. His breathing was labored, but close. Too close. She swerved again and plunged on. The ground sucked and pulled at her boots, but she told herself she wouldn't slip. If she slipped, he would be on top of her in a moment. His hands would be at her throat. *She would not slip.*

Her heart was pounding and her lungs were screaming in agony for more air. A branch whipped back, stinging her cheek. But she told herself she wouldn't stop. She would run and run and run until she no longer heard him coming after her.

A tree had fallen and lay drunkenly in her path. Without breaking stride, Autumn vaulted it, sliding for a moment when her boots hit the mud, then pounding on. He slipped. She heard the slick sound of his boots as they lost traction, then his muffled curse. She kept up her wild pace, nearly giddy at the few seconds his fall had given her.

Time and direction ceased to exist. For her, the pursuit had no beginning, no end. It was only the race. Her thoughts were no longer rational. She knew only that she had to keep running though she'd almost forgotten why. Her breath was coming in harsh gasps, her legs were like rubber. She knew only the mindless flight of the hunted—the naked fear of the hunter.

Suddenly, she saw the lake. It glistened as the sun hit its surface. With some last vestige of lucidity, Autumn remembered Steve's admission that morning. He couldn't swim. The race had a goal now, and she dashed for it.

Her crazed approach through the woods had taken her away from the ridge where the incline graduated for easy descent. Instead, she came to the edge of a cliff that fell forty feet in a sheer drop. Without hesitation, Autumn plunged down at full speed. She scrambled and slid, her fingers clawing to keep herself from overbalancing. Like a lizard, she clung to the mountain. Her body scraped on jagged rocks and slid on mud. Julia's designer sweater shredded. Autumn realized, as the pain grew hot, that her skin suffered equally. Fear pushed her beyond the pain. The lake beckoned below. Safety. Victory.

Still, he came after her. She could hear his boots clatter on the rocks above her head, jarring pebbles that rained down on her. Autumn leaped the last ten feet. The force of the fall shot up her legs, folding them under her until she rolled into a heap. Then she was scrambling and streaking for the lake.

She heard him cry out for her. With a final mad impetus, she flung herself into the water, slicing through its surface. Its sharp frigidity shocked her system and gave her strength. Clawing through it, she headed for depth. She was going to win.

Like a light switched off, the momentum which had driven her so wildly, sapped. The weight of her boots pulled her down. The water closed over her head. Thrashing and choking, Autumn fought for the surface. Her lungs burned as she tried to pull in air. Her arms were heavy, and her feeble strokes had her bobbing up and down. Mists gathered in front of her eyes. Still, she resisted, fighting as the water sucked at her. It was now as deadly an enemy as the one she had sought to escape.

She heard someone sobbing, and realized dimly it was her own voice calling for help. But she knew there would be none. The fight was gone out of her. Was it music she heard? She thought it came from below her, deep, beckoning. Slowly, surrendering, she let the water take her like a lover.

Someone was hurting her. Autumn didn't protest. Darkness blanketed her mind and numbed the pain. The pushing and prodding were no more irritating to her than a faint itch. Air forced its way into her lungs, and she moaned gently in annoyance.

Lucas's voice touched the edges of her mind. He was calling her back in a strange, unnatural voice. Panic? Yes, even through the darkness she could detect a note of panic. What an odd thing to hear in Lucas's voice. Her eyelids were heavy, and the darkness was so tempting. The need to tell him was stronger. Autumn forced her eyes open. Blackness receded to a verge of mist.

His face loomed over her, water streaming from it and his hair. It splattered cold on her cheeks. Yet her mouth felt warm, as if his had just left it. Autumn stared at him, groping for the power of speech.

"Oh, God, Autumn." Lucas brushed the water from her cheeks even as it fell on them again from his own hair. "Oh, God. Listen to me. It's all right, you're going to be all right, do you hear? You're going to be all right. I'm going to take you back to the inn. Can you understand me?"

His voice was desperate, as were his eyes. She'd never heard that tone or seen that expression. Not from Lucas. Autumn wanted to say something that would comfort him, but lacked the strength. The mists were closing in again, and she welcomed them. For a moment, she held them off and dug deep for her voice.

"I thought you killed her, Lucas. I'm sorry."

"Oh, Cat." His voice was intolerably weary. She felt his mouth touch hers. Then she felt nothing.

Voices, vague and without texture, floated down a long tunnel. Autumn didn't welcome them. She wanted her peace. She tried to plunge deeper into the darkness again, but Lucas had no respect for what anyone else wanted. His voice broke into her solitude, suddenly clear and, as always, demanding.

"I'm staying with her until she wakes up. I'm not leaving her."

"Lucas, you're dead on your feet." Robert's voice was low and soothing, in direct contrast to Lucas's. "I'll stay with Autumn. It's part of my job. She's probably going to be floating in and out all night. You wouldn't know what to do for her."

"Then you'll tell me what to do. I'm staying with her."

"Of course you are, dear." Aunt Tabby's voice surprised Autumn even in the dim, drifting darkness. It was so firm and strong. "Lucas will stay, Dr. Spicer. You've already said it's mainly a matter of rest, and waiting until she wakes naturally. Lucas can take care of her."

"I'll sit with you, Lucas, if you'd like…all right, but you've only to call me." Julia's voice rolled over Autumn, as smoky as the mists.

Suddenly, she wanted to ask them what was happening. What they were doing in her own private world. She struggled for words and formed a moan. A cool hand fell on her brow.

"Is she in pain?" Was that Lucas's voice? Autumn thought. Trembling? "Damn it, give her something for the pain!"

The darkness was whirling again, jumbling the sounds. Autumn let it swallow her.

She dreamed. The deep black curtain took on a velvet, moonlight texture. Lucas stared down at her. His face seemed oddly vivid for a dream. His hand felt real and cool on her cheek. "Cat, can you hear me?"

Autumn stared at him, then drew together all her

scraps and rags of concentration. "Yes." She closed her eyes and let the darkness swirl.

When her eyes reopened, he was still there. Autumn swallowed. Her throat was burning dry. "Am I dead?"

"No. No, Cat, you're not dead." Lucas poured something cool down her throat. Her eyes drooped again as she tried to patch together her memory. It was too hard, and she let it go.

Pain shot through her. Unexpected and sharp, it rocketed down her arms and legs. Autumn heard someone moan pitifully. Lucas loomed over her again, his face pale in a shaft of moonlight. "It hurts," she complained.

"I know." He sat beside her and brought a cup to her lips. "Try to drink."

Floating, like a bright red balloon, Autumn felt herself drift through space. The pain had eased as she stumbled back into consciousness. "Julia's sweater," she murmured as she opened her eyes again. "It's torn. I think I tore it. I'll have to buy her another."

"Don't worry about it, Cat. Rest." Lucas's hand was on her hair and she turned her face to it, seeking reassurance. She floated again.

"I'm sure it was valuable," she murmured, nearly an hour later. "But I don't really need that new tripod. Julia lent me that sweater. I should have been more careful."

"Julia has dozens of sweaters, Cat. Don't worry."

Autumn closed her eyes, comforted. But she knew her tripod would have to wait.

"Lucas." She pulled herself back, but now the moonlight was the gray light of dawn.

"Yes, I'm here."

"Why?"

"Why what, Cat?"

"Why are you here?"

But he moved out of focus again. She never heard his answer.

Chapter 13

The sunlight was strong. Used to darkness, Autumn blinked in protest.

"Ah, are you with us to stay this time, Autumn, or is this another quick visit?" Julia bent over her and patted her cheek. "There's a bit of color coming back, and you're cool. How do you feel?"

Autumn lay still for a moment and tried to find out. "Hollow," she decided, and Julia laughed.

"Trust you to think of your stomach."

"Hollow all over," Autumn countered. "Especially my head." She glanced confusedly around the room. "Have I been sick?"

"You gave us quite a scare." Julia eased down on the bed and studied her. "Don't you remember?"

"I was…dreaming?" Autumn's search for her memory found only bits and pieces. "Lucas was here. I was talking to him."

"Yes, he said you were drifting in and out through the night. Managed to say a word or two now and again. Did you really think I'd let you sacrifice your new tripod?" She kissed Autumn's cheek, then held her a moment. "God, when Lucas carried you in, we thought…" Shaking her head briskly, she sat up. Autumn saw that her eyes were damp.

"Julia." Autumn squeezed her eyes a moment, but nothing came clear. "I was supposed to come to your room, but I didn't."

"No, you didn't. I should have dragged you with me then and there. None of this would have happened." She stood up again. "It appears Lucas and I were both taken in by those big green eyes. I don't know how much time we wasted searching for that damn film before he went back to find you."

"I don't understand. Why…" As she reached up to brush at her hair, Autumn noticed the bandages on her hands. "What are these for? Did I hurt myself?"

"It's all right now." Julia brushed away the question. "I'd better let Lucas explain. He'll be furious that I chased him downstairs for some coffee, and you woke up."

"Julia—"

"No more questions now." She cut Autumn off as she plucked a robe from a chair. "Why don't you slip this on. You'll feel better." She eased the silk over Autumn's arms and covered more bandages. The sight of them brought added confusion, more juggled memories. "Just lie still and relax," Julia ordered. "Aunt Tabby already has some soup simmering, just waiting for you. I'll tell her to pour it into an enormous bowl."

She kissed Autumn again, then glided to the door.

"Listen, Autumn." Julia turned back with a slow, cat smile. "He's been through hell these past twenty-four hours, but don't make it too easy for him."

Autumn frowned at the door when Julia had gone and wondered what the devil she was talking about.

Deciding she wouldn't find any answers lying in bed, Autumn dragged herself out. Every joint, every muscle revolted. She nearly succumbed to the desire to crawl back in, but curiosity was stronger. Her legs wobbled as she went to the mirror.

"Good God!" She looked, Autumn decided, even worse than she felt. The bruise on her temple had company. There was a light discoloration along her cheekbone and a few odd scratches. There was a sudden, clear memory of rough bark scraping against her hands. Lifting them, Autumn stared at the bandages. "What have I done to myself?" she asked aloud, then belted the robe to disguise the worst of the damage.

The door opened, and in the reflection she watched Lucas enter the room. He looked as though he hadn't slept in days. The lines of strain were deeper now and his chin was shadowed and unshaven. Only his eyes were the same. Dark and intense.

"You look like hell," she told him without turning. "You need some sleep."

He laughed. In a gesture of weariness she had never seen in him, he lifted his hands to run them down his face. "I might have expected it," he murmured. He sighed, then gave her a smile from the past. "You shouldn't be out of bed, Cat. You're liable to topple over any minute."

"I'm all right. At least I was before I looked in the

mirror." Turning, she faced him directly. "I nearly fainted from shock."

"You are," he began in quiet, serious tones, "the most beautiful thing I've ever seen."

"Kindness to the invalid," she said, looking away. That had hurt, and she wasn't certain she could deal with any more pain. "I could use some explanations. My mind's a little fuddled."

"Robert said that was to be expected after…" He trailed off and jammed clenched fists into his pockets. "After everything that's happened."

Autumn looked again at her bandaged hands. "What did happen? I can't quite remember. I was running…" She lifted her eyes to his and searched. "In the woods, down the cliff. I…" She shook her head. There were only bits and pieces. "I tore Julia's sweater."

"God! You would latch on to a damn sweater!" His explosion had Autumn's eyes widening. "You almost drowned, and all you think about is Julia's sweater."

Her mouth trembled open. "The lake." Memory flooded back in a tidal wave. She leaned back against the dresser. "Steve. It was Steve. He killed Helen. He was chasing me. The film, I wouldn't give it to him." She swallowed, trying to keep calm. "I lied to you. I had it in my pocket. I kept running, but he was right behind me."

"Cat." She backed away, but he wrapped his arms around her. "Don't. Don't think about it. Damn it, I shouldn't have told you that way." He pressed his cheek against her hair. "I can't seem to do anything properly with you."

"No. No, let me think it through." Autumn pushed away. She wanted the details. Once she had them all, the fear would ease. "He found me in the woods after you'd gone in. He'd been with Helen down by the lake the morning I was taking pictures. He told me he had killed her. He told me everything."

"We know all of it," Lucas cut her off sharply. "He let out with everything once we got him back here. We got through to the police this morning." He whipped out a cigarette and lit it swiftly. "He's already in custody. They've got your film, too, for whatever it's worth. Jacques found it on the path."

"It must have fallen out of my pocket. Lucas, it was so strange." Her brow knitted as she remembered the timeless incident with Steve. "He apologized for having to kill me. Then when I told him I wouldn't give him the film, he slugged me so hard I saw stars."

Face thunderous, Lucas spun around and stalked to the window. He stared out without speaking.

"When he came at me again, I kicked him, hard, where I knew it would do the most damage."

She heard Lucas mutter something so uncharacteristically vulgar she thought she misunderstood. For a time she rambled about her flight through the woods, talking more to herself than to him.

"I saw you when you started your suicidal plunge down the cliff." His back was still to her, his voice still rough. "How in God's name you managed to get to the bottom without cracking your skull…" Lucas turned when Autumn remained silent. "I'd been tracking you through the woods. When I saw you were making for the lake, I veered off and started for the ridge. I hoped to cut Anderson off." He pulled on his cigarette, then took a long, shuddering breath. "I saw you flying down those rocks. You never should have made it down alive.

I called you, but you just kept tearing for the lake. I was on him before you hit the water."

"I heard someone call. I thought it was Steve." She pushed a bandaged hand against her temple. "All I could think about was getting into the water before he caught me. I remembered he couldn't swim. Then when I had trouble keeping myself up, I panicked and forgot all those nifty rules you learn in lifeguard class."

Very slowly, very deliberately, Lucas crushed out his cigarette. "By the time I finished kicking his head in, you were already floundering. How you got out so far after the run you'd had, and with boots that must weigh twenty pounds, I'll never know. I was a good ten yards from you when you went under the last time. You sank like a stone."

He turned away again to stare out the window. "I thought..." He shook his head a moment, then continued. "I thought you were dead when I dragged you out. You were dead white and you weren't breathing. At least not enough that I could tell." He took out another cigarette and this time had to fight with his lighter to get flame. He cursed and drew deeply.

"I remember you dripping on me," Autumn murmured into the silence. "Then I thought I died."

"You damn near did." The smoke came out of his lungs in a violent stream. "I must have pumped two gallons of water out of you. You came around just long enough to apologize for thinking I killed Helen."

"I'm sorry, Lucas."

"Don't!" His tone was curt as he swung around again. "But I should never have—"

"No?" He cut her off with one angry word. "Why?

It's easy enough to see how you reached your conclusions, culminating with my last attack about the film."

After a moment, Autumn trusted herself to speak. "There were so many things you said that made me think...and you were so angry. When you asked me for the film, I wanted you to tell me anything."

"But instead of explanations, I bullied you. Typical of me, though, isn't it?" He drew a breath, but his body remained tense. "That's another apology I owe you. I seem to have chalked up quite a few. Would you like them in a group, Cat, or one at a time?"

Autumn turned away from that. It wasn't an apology she wanted, but an explanation. "Why did you want it, Lucas? How did you know?"

"It might be difficult for you to believe at this point, but I'm not completely inhuman. I wanted the film because I hoped, if I had it and made it known that I did, that you'd be safe. And..." She turned back as a shadow crossed his face. "I thought you knew, or had remembered what was on the film, and that you were protecting Anderson."

"Protecting him?" Astonishment reflected in her voice. "Why would I do that?"

He moved his shoulders in a shrug. "You seemed fond of him."

"I thought he was nice," Autumn said slowly. "I imagine we all did. But I hardly knew him. As it turns out, I didn't know him at all."

"I misinterpreted your natural friendliness for something else. Then compounded the mistake by overreacting. I was furious that you gave him what you wouldn't give me. Trust, companionship. Affection."

"Dog in the manger, Lucas?" The words shot out icily.

A muscle twitched at the corner of his mouth in contrast to another negligent shrug. "If you like."

"I'm sorry." With a sigh, Autumn pushed wearily at her hair. "That was uncalled for."

"Was it?" he countered and crushed out his cigarette. "I doubt that. You're entitled to launch a few shafts, Cat. You've taken enough of them from me."

"We're getting off the point." She moved away. Julia's silk robe whispered around her. "You thought I was protecting Steve. I'll accept that. But how did you know he needed protecting?"

"Julia and I had already pieced together a number of things. We were almost certain he was the one who had killed Helen."

"You and Julia." Now she turned to him, curious. Autumn gestured with her hands, then stopped as the pain throbbed in them. "You're going to have to clear things up, Lucas. I might still be a little dim."

"Julia and I had discussed Helen's blackmail thoroughly. Until her murder, we centered on Jacques's problem. Neither Julia nor I were concerned with the petty threats Helen held over us. After she was killed and your room broken into, we tossed around the idea that they were connected. Autumn, why don't you get back in bed. You're so pale."

"No." She shook her head, warding off the creeping warmth the concern in his voice brought her. "I'm fine. Please, don't stop now."

He seemed about to argue, then changed his mind. "I'd never believed you'd ruin your own film, or knock yourself senseless. So, Julia and I began a process of elimination. I hadn't killed Helen, and I knew that Julia hadn't. I'd been in her room that night receiving a heated lecture on my technique with women until I came down to see you. And I'd passed Helen in the hall right before I'd gone into Julia's room, so even if Julia'd had the inclination to kill Helen, it's doubtful that she would have had two identical white negligees. There'd have been blood." He shrugged again. "In any case, if Julia had killed her, she probably would have admitted it."

"Yes." Autumn gave a murmured agreement and wondered what Julia's lace-clad lecture had included.

"I've known Jacques for years," Lucas continued. "He's simply not capable of killing. Julia and I all but eliminated the Spicers. Robert is entirely too dedicated to life to take one, and Jane would dissolve into tears."

Lucas began to pace. "Anderson fit the bill. And, for reasons of my own, I wanted it to be him. Our intrepid Julia copped the spare key from Aunt Tabby and searched his room for the shirt he had worn the night of the murder. I nearly strangled her when she told me she'd done it. She's quite a woman."

"Yes." Jealousy warred with affection. Affection won. "She's wonderful."

"The shirt wasn't there. Julia claims to have an unerring eye for wardrobe, and I wanted to believe her. We decided you should be put on guard without going into specifics. I thought it best if you were wary of everyone. We decided that Julia would talk to you because you'd trust her more quickly than you'd trust me. I hadn't done anything to warrant your trust."

"She frightened me pretty successfully," Autumn recalled. "I had nightmares."

"I'm sorry. It seemed the best way at the time. We thought the film had been destroyed, but we didn't want to take any chances."

"She was telling Jacques that night, wasn't she?"

"Yeah." Lucas noted the faint annoyance in her tone. "That way there would have been three of us to look out for you."

"I might have looked out for myself if I'd been told."

"No, I don't think so. Your face is a dead giveaway. That morning at breakfast when you started rambling about a fourth roll and remembered, everything showed in your eyes."

"If I'd been prepared—"

"If you hadn't been a damn fool and had gone with Julia, we could have kept you safe."

"I wanted to think," she began, angry at being kept in the dark.

"It was my fault." Lucas held up a hand to stop her. "The whole thing's been my doing. I should have handled things differently. You'd never have been hurt if I had."

"No, Lucas." Guilt swamped her when she remembered the look on his face after he had dragged her from the lake. "I'd be dead if it weren't for you."

"Good God, Cat, don't look at me like that. I can't cope with it." He turned away. "I'm doing my best to keep my word. I'll get Robert; he'll want to examine you."

"Lucas." She wasn't going to let him walk out that door until he told her everything. "Why did you come here? And don't tell me you came to Virginia to write. I know—I remember your habits."

Lucas turned, but kept his hand on the knob. "I told you before, the other reason no longer exists. Leave it."

He had retreated behind the cool, detached manner he used so well, but Autumn wasn't going to be shoved aside. "This is my aunt's inn, Lucas. Your coming here, however indirectly, started this chain of events. I have a right to know why you came."

For several seconds, he stared at her, then his hands sought his pockets again. "All right," he agreed. "I don't suppose I have any right to pride after this, and you deserve to get in a few licks after the way I've treated you." He came no closer, but his eyes locked hard on hers. "I came here because of you. Because I had to get you back or go crazy."

"Me?" The pain was so sharp, Autumn laughed. She would not cry again. "Oh Lucas, please, do better." She saw him flinch before he walked again to the window. "You tossed me out, remember? You didn't want me then. You don't want me now."

"Didn't want you!" He whirled, knocking over a vase and sending it crashing. The anger surrounding him was fierce and vivid. "You can't even comprehend how much I wanted you, have wanted you all these years. I thought I'd lose my mind from wanting you."

"No, I won't listen to this." Autumn turned away to lean against the bedpost. "I won't listen."

"You asked for it. Now you'll listen."

"You told me you didn't want me," she flung at him. "I never meant anything to you. You told me it was finished and shrugged your shoulders like it had been nothing all along. Nothing, *nothing's* ever hurt me like the way you brushed me aside."

"I know what I did." The anger was gone from his voice to be replaced by strain. "I know the things I said to you while you stood there staring at me. I hated myself. I wanted you to scream, to rage, to make it easy for me to push you out. But you just stood there with tears falling down your face. I've never forgotten how you looked."

Autumn pulled herself together and faced him again. "You said you didn't want me. Why would you have said it if it weren't true?"

"Because you terrified me."

He said it so simply, she slumped down on the bed to stare at him. "Terrified you? *I* terrified *you*?"

"You don't know what you did to me—all that sweetness, all that generosity. You never asked anything of me, and yet you asked everything." He began to pace again. Autumn watched him in bewilderment. "You were an obsession, that's what I told myself. If I sent you away, hurt you badly enough to make you go, I'd be cured. The more I had of you, the more I needed. I'd wake up in the middle of the night and curse you for not being there. Then I'd curse myself for needing you there. I had to get away from you. I couldn't admit, not even to myself, that I loved you."

"Loved me?" Autumn repeated the words dumbly. "You loved me?"

"Loved then, love now and for the rest of my life." Lucas drew in a deep breath as if the words had left him shaken. "I wasn't able to tell you. I wasn't able to believe it." He stopped pacing and looked at her. "I've kept close tabs on you these past three years. I found all sorts of excuses to do so. When I found out about the inn, and your connection with it, I began to fly out here off and on. Finally, I admitted to myself that I wasn't going to make it without you. I mapped out a plan. I had it all worked out." He gave her an ironic smile.

"Plan?" Autumn repeated. Her mind was still whirling.

"It was easy to plant the idea in Aunt Tabby's head to

write you and ask you to visit. Knowing you, I was sure you'd come without question. That was all I needed. I was so sure of myself. I thought all I'd have to do would be to issue the invitation, and you'd fall right back into my arms. Just like old times. I'd have you back, marry you before you sorted things out and pat myself on the back for being so damn clever."

"Marry me?" Autumn's brows flew up in astonishment.

"Once we were married," Lucas went on as if she hadn't interrupted, "I'd never have to worry about losing you again. I'd simply never give you a divorce no matter how you struggled. I deserved a good kick in the teeth, Cat, and you gave it to me. Instead of falling into my arms, you turned up your nose and told me to get lost. But that didn't throw me off for long. No, you'd loved me once, and I'd make you love me again. I could deal with the anger, but the ice…

"I didn't know I could be hurt that way. It was quite a shock. Seeing you again…" He paused and seemed to struggle for words. "It was torture, pure and simple, to be so close and not be able to have you. I wanted to tell you what you meant to me, then every time I got near you I'd behave like a maniac. The way you cringed from me yesterday, telling me not to hurt you again, I can't tell you what that did to me."

"Lucas—"

"You'd better let me finish," he told her. "I'll never be able to manage this again." He reached for a cigarette, changed his mind, then continued. "Julia roasted me, but I couldn't seem to stop myself. The more you resisted, the worse I treated you. Every time I approached you, I ended up doing the wrong thing. That day, up in your room…" He stopped and Autumn watched the struggle on his face. "I nearly raped you. I was crazy with jealousy after seeing you and Anderson. When I saw you cry—I swore I'd never be responsible for putting that look on your face again.

"I'd come up that day, ready to beg, crawl, plead, whatever it took. When I saw you kissing him, something snapped. I started thinking about the men you'd been with these past three years. The men who'd have you again when I couldn't."

"I've never been with any man but you," Autumn interrupted quietly.

Lucas's expression changed from barely suppressed fury to confusion before he studied her face with his familiar intensity. "Why?"

"Because every time I started to, I remembered he wasn't you."

As if in pain, Lucas shut his eyes, then turned from her. "Cat, I've never done anything in my life to deserve you."

"No, you probably haven't." She rose from the bed to stand behind him. "Lucas, if you want me, tell me so, and tell me why. Ask me, Lucas. I want it spelled out."

"All right." He moved his shoulders as he turned back, but his eyes weren't casual. "Cat…" He reached up to touch her cheek, then thrust the hand in his pocket. "I want you, desperately, because life isn't even tolerable without you. I need you because you are, and always were, the best part of my life. I love you for reasons it would take hours to tell you. Take me back, please. Marry me."

She wanted to throw herself into his arms, but held back. *Don't make it too easy on him.* Julia's words played back in her head. No, Lucas had had too much come too easily to him. Autumn smiled at him, but didn't reach out.

"All right," she said simply.

"All right?" He frowned, uncertain. "All right what?"

"I'll marry you. That's what you want, isn't it?"

"Yes, damn it, but—"

"The least you could do is kiss me, Lucas. It's traditional."

Lightly, he rested his hands on her shoulders. "Cat, I want you to be sure, because I'll never be able to let go. If it's gratitude, I'm desperate enough to take it. But I want you to think about what you're doing."

She tilted her head. "You did know I thought it was you with Helen on that film?"

"Cat, for God's sake—"

"I went into the woods," she continued mildly. "I was just about to expose that film when Steve found me. Lucas." She inched closer. "Do you know how I feel about the sanctity of film?"

His breath came out in a small huff of relief as he lifted a hand to either side of her face. He grinned. "Yes. Yes, I do. Something about the eleventh commandment."

"Thou shalt not expose unprocessed film. Now—" she slid her arms up his back "—are you going to kiss me, or do I have to make you?"

* * * * *